THE DAVID WRIGHT O'BRIEN MEGAPACK®

THE DAVID WRIGHT O'BRIEN MEGAPACK®

DAVID WRIGHT O'BRIEN

Edited by
Von Rothenberger

WILDSIDE PRESS

THE DAVID WRIGHT O'BRIEN MEGAPACK®

Photograph on page 7 (David Wright O'Brien) taken from an original print from the November 1940 issue of *Amazing Stories*. Photograph on page 14 courtesy of American Battle Monuments Commission and used by permission.

"Meet the Authors: David Wright O'Brien" originally appeared in *Amazing Stories*, November 1940. "Truth Is a Plague!" originally appeared in *Amazing Stories*, February 1940. "The Man the World Forgot" originally appeared in *Fantastic Adventures*, April 1940 under the pseudonym John York Cabot. "Trapped on Titan" originally appeared in *Amazing Stories*, June 1940. "John Brown's Body" originally appeared in *Amazing Stories*, May 1940 (written with William P. McGivern.) "Suicide Squadrons of Space" originally appeared in *Amazing Stories*, August 1940. "The Strange Voyage of Hector Squinch" originally appeared in *Fantastic Adventures*, August 1940. "Bill of Rights, 5,000 A.D." originally appeared in *Fantastic Adventures*, June 1941, under the pseudonym John York Cabot. "Beyond the Time Door" originally appeared in *Fantastic Adventures*, March 1941. "Sharbeau's Startling Statue" originally appeared in *Fantastic Adventures*, November 1942, under the pseudonym Clee Garson. "The Softly Silken Wallet" originally appeared in *Fantastic Adventures*, July 1946. "The Place is Familiar" originally appeared in *Fantastic Adventures*, February 1944.

Contents

INTRODUCTION

VON ROTHENBERGER

DAVID WRIGHT O'BRIEN:
WARRIOR WRITER

David Wright O'Brien (January 1, 1918—December 11, 1944) was an American fantasy and science fiction (f&sf) writer who in just a few short years wrote over one hundred f&sf stories—under his own name and under the pseudonyms John York Cabot, Duncan Farnsworth, Bruce Dennis, and Clee Garson—as well as numerous stories in other literary genres. O'Brien was killed in action during a bombing raid over Germany in World War II at the age of 26.

David was the youngest of two children born to Chicago lawyer Edward and Paula (Wright) O'Brien. Literary prowess ran in the family as his uncle was Farnsworth Wright, the legendary editor of *Weird Tales* Magazine. Early in life he became fast friends with William P. McGivern, later himself a noted author.

Tragedy struck the O'Brien family when the father, Edward, died suddenly at the age of 48. Only 13 years old, young David worked at odd jobs to support the family. He managed to graduate from high school in 1936 and spent the next three years in college, supporting himself by working as the police reporter for a Chicago newspaper.

In 1939 David decided to embark on a writing career and approached Ziff-Davis Productions, a Chicago-based company who published several "pulp magazines," and its managing editor, Raymond A. Palmer. That year saw David's first three stories appear in the short-lived magazine *South Seas Stories* and a fourth published in the December issue of *Air Adventures* Magazine, both Ziff-Davis titles. At age 22 his first f&sf story, "Truth Is a Plague!" appeared in the February 1940 issue of *Amazing Stories* magazine. That May the story "John Brown's Body" was published in *Amazing*, marking both the first appearance of an O'Brien and McGivern collaboration as well as being William P. McGivern's first-ever published f&sf story. The two writing partners opened an office together in Chicago that soon became a hangout for fellow Ziff-Davis writers such as Don Wilcox. In his July 1989 essay *"Some Echoes of the Windy City"* (*Pulp Vault* magazine, July 1989, Issue #5) Don recalled meeting the pair:

> Another Chicago writer, possibly quite new at fiction spinning, was Dave O'Brien, who set a mood of laughter wherever he went. I would soon make the acquaintance of his friend and partner, Bill McGivern, another sharp-witted Irish boy. They were both on their way to popularity, making their typewriters sing, and I'm not sure how they knew which one of them was the author of some of their fluffy, witty humor yarns. Such titles as "The Little Man Who Wasn't All There" could pop up like popcorn in the midst of an evening's banter.
>
> There was always anxiety over whether a story would be accepted or rejected, but Dave and Bill had their imaginary gadgets to carry them through. They would spin their invisible prayer wheels. Acceptance! Acceptance! Oops! Reject? Get a bigger wheel with a faster spin. They rarely missed.... Dave O'Brien and Bill McGivern, who were now renting a small midtown studio for daytime work, asked me if I would care to share their space. Dave and Bill! Those geniuses of wit and humor. I could foresee that every break from our typewriters would be sparked with original repartee. But no, it wouldn't have worked for me.

In these early years of his editorial reign, Palmer came to rely on O'Brien, McGivern, and Wilcox as the three young writers who could produce tens of thousands of words on a monthly basis of solid, story-driven fiction for several different types of pulp magazines that Ziff-Davis launched in the early 1940s. These included not only *Amazing Stories* and *Fantastic Adventures* but also *Mammoth Detective, Mammoth Mystery, Mammoth Western*, and others.

David's career thus started out pretty well and his tales proved popular with the reading public. O'Brien was a sharp and creative writer who showed improvement with each new story. David often displayed a strain of humor in his stories of madcap invention as well as a taste for science fiction adventure. In his later stories, O'Brien concentrated on creating more fully-developed characters, especially in the ones he wrote while cooped up in the belly of a B-17 bomber, such as "The Place is Familiar," considered by many to be his finest work.

* * * *

Two major events in 1941 marked a turning point in David's life. On June 21st he married Eileen O'Connor in a ceremony attended by nearly the entire Ziff-Davis company, with his best man being William McGivern. Then on October 7, 1941, just four months later, the five foot-nine, 166-pound O'Brien enlisted in the U.S. Army, where he was assigned to the U.S. Army Air Corps for training. Interestingly, on his enlistment papers he listed his civilian vocation at the time as being a "musician and teacher of music." David continued writing the entire time he was in the armed forces, adding "corporal" before all his pseudonyms.

In 1943 the now Sergeant O'Brien was sent to England, where he was assigned to the Eighth Air Force, 944th Bomb Group, 332nd Bomb Squadron. The B-17-G bomber he served aboard was nicknamed "Sally." In the crew of nine, O'Brien served in the *togglier* position, the person responsible for hitting the toggle switch at the precise moment that released the payload of bombs over the intended target. O'Brien participated in bombing raids over Germany throughout the latter half of 1943 and all of 1944.

In December 1944, American B-17 bombers including "Sally" left their base in England on a raid that targeted the railroad marshaling yard in the city of Giessen, Germany, located just to the north of Frankfurt. During World War II, Giessen offered many industrial targets as well as a German air force base and was an important link in the German transportation system.

The following paragraph is the Eyewitness Statement taken from the official Army Air Corps Missing Air Crew Report (MACR) on "Sally" that was prepared on December 18, 1944 by 2nd Lieutenant Thomas G. S. Houser, Air Corps, Operations Administration Office:

"#2 engine started to throw oil just before reaching the target. Feathered #2 engine after bombs away. Then #1 engine ran away and after some difficulty with it, it was finally feathered. Also not drawing full power on #3 engine. Losing about 500 feet per minute at this time. Jettisoned all equipment. Trying to make Liege [Belgium], but realized that they couldn't; so they bailed out on Pilot's orders at 50°15'N—06°20'E at approximately 1410 hours. A/C [aircraft] flying on about 20 degrees right bank at 2,000 feet. Visibility about 200 yards, ceiling 200 feet. Flying on W-NW heading of approximately 290 degrees. The Top Turret Engineer, Navigator, Radio Operator, Tail Gunner and Ball Turret Gunner got out and are now back. The Left Waist Gunner was seen to get out but no definite information is known pertaining to his present status. The returned crew members do not know what happened to the Pilot, Co-pilot, and Togglier. However, they think that these three should have had time to bail out. The returned crew members landed within a mile of each other and right in our front lines. 1st Army troops picked them up immediately and they were flown back to Aldermaston, England in a C-47 from an A/D 3 or 4 miles NW of Liege on 13 December 1944."

Raymond A. Palmer, in the editor's column "The Observatory," *Amazing Stories*, June 1945, wrote:

"News has come to us that David Wright O'Brien, bombardier on a B-17, has been missing in action over Germany since December 11, 1944. We're sitting here now, holding thumbs for the best damn writer we've got, and we'll let you know when word comes out of Germany—which ought to be soon, if the Russians have their way. Added bad news is the information that Dave's lifelong buddy, and our own writer pal, William P. McGivern, has been wounded in the fighting in Italy. We're waiting to hear from Bill, who, it is reported, is perfectly able to write his own letters."

(Each magazine issue was compiled several months prior to the actual date of the issue, hence the long delay in the editor relating relevant news, as seen here in informing the magazine readers of O'Brien's disappearance.)

Palmer, in "The Editor's Notebook," *Fantastic Adventures*, July 1945, wrote:

"The readers of this magazine will be saddened by the news that one of their best liked authors has been killed in action. David Wright O'Brien, bombardier on a flying fortress, was killed over Germany on December 11, 1944. He was one of two men in the plane who were unable to parachute to safety. The loss of O'Brien means a great deal more to us than this news implies, for now it can be revealed that he made several other names popular in this and other magazines. He was also John York Cabot, Duncan Farnsworth, Clee Garson, Bruce Dennis, Richard Vardon, and others. This in itself will astound our readers, because it is a well-known fact that each of these names appeared as the byline on enough fiction to represent the output of any ordinary writer.

"But Dave was no ordinary writer. He wrote and sold as much as 50,000 words monthly, all of a very high caliber. He was the only writer for the Ziff-Davis magazines who was able to continue writing after his entry into the Air Force and wrote 350,000 words in little over a year, most of it under the most trying circumstances. Several manuscripts were actually written in the air!

"Your editor misses him personally, most of all because for many years we, together with William P. McGivern, were pals in every way, including escapades that make us blush to remember. It was the hardest job of our career to notify McGivern, lying in a hospital in Italy from wounds suffered in the terrific mountain action in that country, of the death of the one man he loved most. Your editor can testify to a friendship between the two that he has never seen equaled. They were raised together, went to school together, and later wrote together in the same Chicago downtown office.

"Dave's last letter to us warned us very solemnly that the war was far from over, and he spoke of the hell he was in with such emphasis as we have never known him to use. He knew something we do not and he gave his life because he knew. Perhaps we'll never realize just how much we owe to him and to all those others of his buddies who have made the supreme sacrifice."

Sgt. David Wright O'Brien's body was found with the wreckage of the bomber "Sally." He was laid to rest in the Henri-Chapelle American Cemetery near Hombourg, Belgium, not far from the site of the plane crash. David was posthumously awarded both the Air Medal and the Purple Heart for service to his country.

* * * *

"We present this tribute by one of David Wright O'Brien's fellow writers as one of the most fitting of all, from one of his buddies who is carrying on where he left off—to final victory."

—Raymond A. Palmer in the Readers Page, Fantastic Adventures Magazine, July 1945.

IN MEMORIAM

"Confirmation has been received of the death in action of David Wright O'Brien on a B-17 mission over Germany last December 11th. To the Chicago writers who knew Dave O'Brien, and to the thousands who read his stories in Ziff-Davis fiction magazines, Dave's passing comes as another harsh reminder that war takes the best from among us, for reasons which few of us are so naive as to explain away.

"Dave O'Brien practically grew up with *Amazing Stories*, and *Fantastic Adventures*. One of his very first yarns, 'Truth Is a Plague,' was so good that Phil Stong included it in his [1939] anthology *The Other Worlds*.

"Dave, in fact, was himself somewhat out of this world. Spiritual depression, frustration, doubts as to his place in the world never assailed him. To many of us he seemed uncommonly good-natured, with a grin and a wisecrack for any and all occasions.... They say that the spirit of elves inhabits the soul of an Irishman. Dave was as Irish as they come, not in brogue or in affectation but in his general outlook. Minor disappointments did not get him down. If the prophet of doom had come around to his door? Dave would have conked him over the noggin with a bottle of Scotch.

"Dave grew up to wreck his first car, become a favorite with Ziff-Davis readers, get married and find himself involved in the four freedoms and the Atlantic charter. He chose to implement his place in the war as an aerial gunner. The last stories he did for *Fantastic*, in fact, were partially plunked out on a portable typewriter in England while Dave was on a training flight.

"With Dave gone, an empty seat will speak poignantly at the festive table when, after the war, his friends get together in Chicago to chew the fat and exchange wartime experiences, some bitter, some cynical, none of them easy to forget.

"'You guys are a bunch of creeps,' Dave would say disgustedly, if he were present. 'It was a great war, and you know it. For the first time in your lives, Uncle Sam supported you instead of Editor Ray Palmer, and you're still kicking!'

"Yes, that would be just like Dave. Like, Dave, and, in a sense, like the thousands of other young fellows who went off to war with a grin and a joke, never to return in this world.

"In another world? Well, when Dave got to heaven, St. Peter didn't ask to see his army dog tags.... 'Come in, son, come in,' said the keeper of the gate. 'We need somebody around, to brighten up the place. Glad to have you aboard.'

"'Glad to be aboard, sir,' said David Wright O'Brien. 'I'll do the best I can.'"

—Arthur T. Harris, Military Secret, U. S. A.

* * * *

David Wright O'Brien's death cut short story a literary career that held great promise. No one can say whether O'Brien's career would have been as successful as that of his buddy William P. McGivern, who went on to author more than twenty novels. Raymond Palmer treasured O'Brien's last few stories and published them sparingly over the next few years.

"David Wright O'Brien's last manuscripts will soon be published, and 'Room With a View' is one of them. When we look under 'O' in our files, we feel a terrific sense of loss to note that there are so few of his manuscripts remaining. We can't help clutching to every memory we have of the lad. To say that we loved him would scarcely describe our feelings. With this issue we dole out another of his always top notch stories, savoring every word as we do so."

—Raymond A. Palmer in "The Observatory," *Amazing Stories*, May 1946.

* * * *

Eight O'Brien f&sf stories were posthumously published. The last story, and 108th of David's 13-year writing career, was "The Martian Cross". It appeared in the December 1952 issue of *Amazing Stories* magazine under the pseudonym "Cleer Garson."

The 12 stories for this volume were selected to represent David Wright O'Brien's brief yet prolific fantasy and science fiction career and the distinct writing style he was known and respected for by his peers. I hope that you read them with great enjoyment and take away a greater appreciation—as I have—for a writer from the Golden Age who was taken from us far too soon.

The grave of David Wright O'Brien, Plot G, Row 11, Grave 65, in Henri-Chapelle American Cemetery near Hombourg, Belgium. Photograph taken January 12, 2016 courtesy of the American Battle Monuments Commission and used by permission.

MEET THE AUTHORS: DAVID WRIGHT O'BRIEN

I was born on the back of a racing camel in the middle of the Gobi Desert, and by the time I was four years old I was peddling papers in the streets of Port Said and had taken to drink. My friends said I had no future.

On my sixth birthday I met my first dancing girl. Her name was Lola and she worked in the notorious Cafe Roue, a joint run by my great-uncle, Ben Abu. I wanted Lola to run away with me and every night we'd munch opium krispies and discuss means of escape. She's still there.

My friends said I was all washed up.

Taking the bulrushes by the roots, I faced the facts. Here I was, seven years old and a failure. Of course I held the rough-'n'-tumble, catch-as-catch-can championship of Middle-Arabia. But what does untrained muscle amount to, anyway? I couldn't go on like that forever.

I put in my application with a troupe of whirling dervishes, and one month later, having passed my examination, entered a monastery.

But once again Fate kicked me in the stomach. It seems that the monk factory was one of those cloistered joints. Everything done behind high wall. What fun was there to whirling if no one could watch? Dizzy and disillusioned, I resigned.

My friends were now openly pointing the finger of scorn. The world flew 'round the opium parlors, *"O'Brien has gone phffffft!"*

At ten years of age I couldn't stand it any longer. I came to the United States to seek my fortune. After working the Union Pacific Line as a candy butcher and inventing the electric light—oops, sorry, that was Edison....

As I was saying, I came to America, and subsisted for weeks on nothing but the crumbs I was able to scrape out of the bottoms of New York's automats. It was ghastly, and there were times when I was almost desperate enough to look for a job.

But enough of the sordidness of my early childhood! Enough of the stark truth and grim reality! Let us continue in a lighter vein. Let us, just for the sheer hell of it, skip a few years.

I found myself in Chicago, entering Loyola Academy in search of education. Under the tutelage of the football mentors, I spent four years learning how to clip the legs out from under a defensive half-back and whistle at pretty young things on street corners.

Having a firm grip on culture, and practically none at all on myself, I got a job as a police reporter. This led, quite naturally, to a position digging ditches.

Deciding to take a whack at "higher" education, I left my shovel and entered a local institution celebrated as being the only kindergarten in the nation awarding college degrees.

The "college" dropped football, throwing me and a number of other subsidized slap-happies off the payroll. After a merry interchange of insults with the Dean, who hated every itsy-bitsy intestine in my anatomical structure, I bid adieu to the dump.

Next to the University of Chicago, where I spent a year as a cinder in the educational eye of Prexy Hutchins. Inasmuch as I was hacking out fiction and holding down a news feature job on the side, I decided to leave the Midway to Compton and other show-offs.

Been pounding out stories with wild enthusiasm ever since in order to assure an exceptionally lovely little red-headed colleen that we will live happily ever after. As a sort of sideline I accumulate utterly staggering debts and play a little game I have called, "Dodge The Creditor."

I detest people who, when informed that I write, ask me: "What do you do for a living?"

If I were asked (and it isn't likely I will be) to name America's most promising young fiction writer, I'd pick William P. McGivern.

The fact that I owe him ten bucks has nothing to do with the choice. I owe Jack West money, but I'm not saying a word.

I have a child-like faith in the Constitution, the Bill of Rights, and in my ability to say "slipshod" after seven drinks.

Editor's Note: Mr. O'Brien has adopted a rather facetious tone in this bit about himself, but in reality, he is a very serious-minded young man, and his work to date in science fiction and in general adventure fiction has made good the prediction we made a year ago when we said he was a lad to watch.

The latest news we have on his progress, is of the inclusion of one of his stories in an anthology of imaginative fiction. The story which has been mentioned is "Truth is a Plague!," which was his first story for Amazing Stories.

Recently, his "Suicide Squadrons of Space" received first place in reader reaction for August. We have on hand three more yarns by O'Brien, excluding the story presented in this issue. Coming soon is a time-travel story with a new twist.

Mr. O'Brien is the nephew of the late Farnsworth Wright, famous weird story editor.

—Raymond Palmer, Editor,
Amazing Stories, November 1940.

TRUTH IS A PLAGUE!

"We won't say any more about the stories in this issue, beyond mentioning that Nelson S. Bond winds up his Deluge novel in fine style. And Harl Vincent does an undersea yarn in an excellent manner, with David Wright O'Brien bringing a story rather unusual to the pages of Amazing Stories."

—Raymond A. Palmer in the editor's column
"The Observatory," *Amazing Stories*, February 1940

Almost everyone in Weston saw the planes that morning. Crowds pouring from the subways and elevators on their way to work stopped in the middle of the business district to crane their necks heavenward in gaping astonishment. Traffic became horribly snarled, and the policemen let it stay that way while they, too, watched the writing in the sky.

Ordinary commercial smokewriting would not have merited more than a passing glance from the citizenry of Weston. But this was certainly different. To begin with there were ten planes printing the sky message. Secondly, they were flying so low that it appeared as if they would inevitably crash into the office buildings of the district. And last but not least, there was the message itself.

"HONESTY," it read, "IS THE BEST POLICY!"

The skywriting continued for another half hour, during which time the message must have been spelled out fifty times in all. Then the smoke planes departed, and Weston was shrouded by the cloak of blue vapor left in their wake.

* * * *

In the twenty-first floor of the Radio Building, located in the heart of Weston, Jack Train, staff announcer for Station W-E-S-T, left the window where he had been watching the skywriting. It was two minutes to nine, and he was due in Studio F at nine o'clock.

"Whew!" snorted Train, "those ships were flying so low you could even smell the smoke." He sniffed deeply as if to prove it to himself.

"Funny smoke at that," he said as he entered Studio F. "It's sort of sweet and fresh smelling."

He cleared his throat and looked at the glass partition behind which the engineer was sitting. The engineer signaled the "on-the-air."

"Goooood morning, ladies and gentlemen. This is Jack Train, your Pobo Toothpaste announcer, greeting you. Have you brushed your teeth today? Don't forget, Pobo is the Toothpaste Supreme. It gives your molars that brilliant lustre so necessary to movie stars. It removes dirty, dingy stains."

As if in a dream, Train heard his voice continuing gaily on past the point where the commercial ended.

"Yes indeed. It removes stains. It removes enamel. Give it a little time and it removes your teeth, too!"

* * * *

The business man was coughing slightly. Smoke always made his throat harsh, and those blankety-blank skywriters spread enough smoke around the city to gag a man. He turned into his office building and was standing in front of the elevator when someone slapped him on the back. It was Jones, another business associate whom he hadn't seen in several weeks.

"Good old J. T.," boomed Jones. "Glad to see you, old boy. How have you been? Where've you been keeping yourself? Really great to see you, great!"

A mechanical smile came to the business man's face as he opened his mouth to reply. Something, at that moment, seized control of his tongue.

"You're a damned liar," he heard himself saying. "We hate one another's guts and you know it."

* * * *

Linda Meade, salesgirl in Weston's most exclusive millinery shop, brought forth another hat for Mrs. Blythe. It was the fourteenth hat that Linda had tried on the society matron in the last half hour. Mrs. Blythe coughed disapprovingly as Linda adjusted the hat. "Terribly smoky in here, m'dear."

"It's from those skywriters, madam," Linda explained patiently. "They flew so low that the entire city seems to be filled with it."

Mrs. Blythe, hat on head, began peering this way and that into the mirror before her. She turned to Linda, smiling sweetly. "What do you think of this one, m'dear?"

"It makes you look," said Linda, horrified at what she knew was coming, "like a rather pretty mountain goat!"

* * * *

Lance Randell placed the telephone back in its cradle and turned to face Professor Merlo. "It's a call from the airport," he stated. "The planes are all in. They've covered the city with our smokewriting."

Professor Merlo, a sparse, bird-like little man, ran a nervous hand through his white hair. "Fine," he said, "splendid. In another hour we should be getting reports on the effect of our experiment."

Randell grinned. "You mean your experiment, Professor. Your experiment, not mine."

"Without your financial backing," the Professor reminded him, "it would still be a dream. It is yours as much as mine." He beamed fondly on the rugged young man.

"It's still hard to believe," said Randell reflectively. "A gas made from Truth Serum. If it has effect, Professor, are you still sure it will make everyone tell the truth?"

"Yes, my boy. Dishonesty will be an impossibility, providing the gas works."

"Utopia?"

"Maybe. We must first see what effect it has on one city. If it works on Weston we can change the world. At the end of this hour, every citizen in Weston should be affected by it."

Lance Randell lit a cigarette as the Professor fell silent. For the first time in his life, Randell told himself, he was putting his wealth to a good use. A world of Truth! Little shivers of excitement ran through him at the thought of how near they were to changing the course of destiny. He drummed his fingers impatiently on the arm of his chair. This waiting was nerve-racking.

Restlessly he went to the window and gazed for a moment at the serenity of the countryside. "Nice out here," he observed. "So quiet. But right this minute, this peace is killing me."

He turned back from the window. "If you don't mind, I'm going into the city."

Professor Merlo smiled. "Go ahead. I'm a little old to be impatient. I'll stay here to get the reports, and then you might drive back to give me a first hand account."

Randell grabbed his hat. "Swell. Soon as I take a look at our Utopia, I'll call you."

A few minutes later, behind the wheel of his roadster, Randell said to himself, "Somehow this is like—like playing God!"

It sent a shudder through him.

* * * *

It was only a fifteen minute drive from Professor Merlo's suburban laboratories to the city limits of Weston, but Randall tried to make it in ten. Halfway there, two sirens began to scream behind him.

"Pull over," snarled the motorcycle copper on his right. Randell brought his car to an abrupt stop. His pursuers walked over to his car. They looked grim and determined and were pulling little black books from their hip pockets.

"Thought you'd shake us at the city limits, eh?"

"I suppose you're gonna tell us you didn't know how fast you was going?" said the second, a tall, morose fellow, the sarcasm dripping from him. "A lousy seventy-five per."

Randell would have sworn that it wasn't his own voice replying with such cheerful unconcern. "Yes," he heard himself saying, "I had been hoping to shake you fellows at the city limits. You wouldn't have been able to pinch me in Weston, y'know. I was not, however, doing seventy-five. Last time I looked, I was inching up close to ninety."

During the ominous silence that followed this announcement, Randell collected the pieces. He sniffed the air suspiciously. Yes, there it was, that faint, sweet freshness! No wonder: the Truth Gas extended all the way to the city limits!

Suddenly the realization hit him. The officers, themselves, must be affected by the gas, too!

Randell kept his face straight during his next question. "Haven't you policemen ever broken the speeding laws?"

The policemen started to speak and stopped. They looked at each other queerly. "Of course," they declared in stupefied unison. "Lots of times!"

"Fun, ain't it?"

"Great sport," said the flabbergasted motorcycle cops.

"Now," said Randell severely, "after admitting that you break the speed laws yourselves, adding that it's great fun, do you still think you ought to give me a ticket?"

"No," said the morose cop, with an oddly bright glance. "It wouldn't be fair!"

"Well," said Randell, putting his car into gear, "so long, then!"

In his rear vision mirror Lance Randell could see the bewildered motor cops standing at the city limits, scratching their heads. He couldn't hold back any longer. He broke into peals of laughter. But he wasn't laughing by the time he arrived in Weston's business district.

CHAPTER II

The Unexpected Truth

Doris Martin sat at her neat little desk in the ornate offices of Lance Randell Enterprises, Inc., sorting the batch of morning mail. The clock on her desk told her that it was almost ten o'clock. She sighed. The Boss could be expected about noon, if he came in at all that day.

At the thought of Lance Randell, Doris permitted herself another sigh, and still sighing she stared for a moment into the mirror. An oval face, framed by auburn hair and presenting a pert, freckled nose, level gray eyes and mischievous mouth, stared back at her.

The mouth smiled, revealing an even row of dazzlingly white teeth. "You," declared the mouth, "might as well be an office fixture." Doris snapped the compact shut. She coughed slightly. The office seemed terribly smoky this morning. Probably due to those planes that had been skywriting over the city.

She got up to close the window next to her desk when she saw the familiar blue roadster roll up in front of the building. She watched the rugged figure of her boss get quickly out of the car and walk swiftly to the entrance.

She walked back to her desk and sat down, making a conscious effort to assemble the mail. It wasn't any use. There were little thoughts spinning around in her mind....

Doris heard the doorknob turning, and her heart did a more than its usual routine flip-flop. Randell came into the room.

"How's the staff?"

He always said that to her. It was his standard form of greeting, rain or shine, day in and day out. And he seldom waited for an answer. He just kept walking into his office. Doris followed him.

"Here's your mail, Mr. Randell," she said, keeping her voice carefully impersonal.

She watched him while he sorted swiftly through the letters, noticing the way he hunched his wide shoulders in preoccupation. Then fearing that he might glance up, she turned back to some trivial matter.

"Ahhh." She knew from the sound of his sigh that he'd come to the letter he was looking for. The perfumed message from the bubble dancer.

"Darling," Randell read to himself, "even a day away from you seems like simply years." As he read on, all thoughts of the past twenty-four hours vanished. From time to time he repeated his sigh. Finally there was the signature, "Your darling Edie."

He looked up from the letter, entranced. "She's wonderful," he said rhetorically to his secretary, "isn't she?"

"Do you mean Miss Dalmar?" Doris heard herself reply.

Randell seemed startled back to reality. He wasn't expecting an answer to his statement. "Why, yes," he said "who else would I mean?"

Doris was flustered. Something had happened. She never meant to say that. It just popped out, and to her astonishment a torrent of words was following her first unintended sentence. She heard her voice continue.

"If you mean she's wonderful," Doris was saying, "I don't think she is. As a matter of fact I think she's nothing but a cheap, gold-digging little vixen. If you'd remove her warpaint, keep her away from the beauty parlor, and eliminate the dubious glamour of her profession, you'd see nothing but a washed-out, frizzled haired little know-nothing!"

* * * *

Randell's jaw was hanging foolishly agape at the outburst.

"You are just sap enough," Doris went on, "to think that she loves you. She hasn't room enough in that shallow heart of hers for love of anything but money and herself. You have plenty of money, and that's what she's after. Everyone in town knows it but you." Her voice was shaking now, and she knew that she would be crying in another minute.

Automatically Doris was picking up her things, moving toward the door. "It probably never entered your skull that there might be someone in the world who'd care for you even if you didn't have a—"

She was at the door, now, her hand on the knob, speaking again. "It probably never occurred to you that someone could love you so much that nothing else mattered except to see you do something with your utterly pleasant and equally worthless life besides waste it on a bubble dancer!"

For five full minutes Lance sat on the edge of his desk, staring at the door. "Well, I'll be damned," he kept repeating to himself. "Well, I'll be damned!"

His brain was going through the futile thought mechanisms that confront any man when trying to arrive at a logical reason for the actions of a woman. Suddenly the explanation flashed before him. He had forgotten all about the experiment, all about the gas! Doris was affected by the Truth Gas, that explained it all!

But if she—no, it couldn't be. Lance tried to eliminate the logical conclusion to his deductions. With a sinking feeling he was realizing that if the Truth Gas was the cause of her outburst, what she said must have been true, even about Edie!

Lance dashed for the door. There was only one answer to the agony of doubt that filled his mind. Edie was the only person who could supply that answer!

CHAPTER III

The Plague Grows

The ash tray next to the radio in Professor Merlo's study was heaped with cigarette stubs. Slumped in an armchair before the radio ever since Randell's departure, Professor Merlo had been listening to news flashes from the scene of his Truth Gas experiment.

To be precise about it, the first bulletin was read at 9:45.

"The Weston Board of Health," said the announcer, "is investigating the rumor that an odd epidemic of insanity has broken forth in the heart of the city's business district. Victims of this strange malady are reported to be possessed with the desire to make preposterous and often insulting statements. As yet, however, these rumors have not been authenticated." Professor Merlo smiled. The announcer concluded with, "This bulletin has come to you through the courtesy of the Weston Daily Herald, the World's Worst Newspaper!"

Professor Merlo had guffawed. Now several hours after that, however, his laughter was changed to shocked amazement.

"It can't be so," the white haired little man was telling himself. "All this is but the first spasm. When it has spent itself, everything will settle into our expected pattern. Out of it will grow perfect order and Utopia. It is only natural that confusion should be the first result of such an experiment. By noon everything should be well again!"

But even as he spoke, the Professor had a feeling of uneasiness. He'd been saying the same thing for the last hour and a half. The Professor gulped, his Adam's apple bobbing along his scrawny neck like an egg in a hose. He wished fervently that Randell would return.

The radio news announcer was jabbering excitedly once more. Dully, like a man expecting an unavoidable blow, Merlo turned his head to listen.

"As the strange epidemic of mass insanity grows in Weston, today, it has been learned that three more suicides have occurred in the business district. These happened when the owners of Weston's three largest department stores leaped to their deaths rather than meet the financial ruin facing their establishments."

The Professor shuddered. He was expecting something like that ever since the bulletin of an hour ago which stated that the clerks in the downtown department stores were selling all goods at less than cost price. Fifteen minutes after that particular bulletin it was announced that delighted shoppers were buying up every bit of stock in the stores—at a net loss of several million dollars to the owners of the stores.

The announcer was babbling on, "This brings today's death rate to the staggering total of one hundred persons. Many of these, as you probably learned in previous flashes, were victims of murder."

* * * *

Professor Merlo cringed, remembering the thirty-or-so husbands whose wives dispatched them to their Maker over blood-stained breakfast tables, the fifty-odd revenge slayings perpetrated by persons who learned of long-concealed treacheries by friends or partners, the suicides whose doctors were forced to admit that they were victims of incurable diseases.

"God," Professor Merlo muttered, covering his face with his hands, "God!"

"Police have stated," continued the announcer, "that they are as yet unable to control the army of a thousand men and women who have formed a marching brigade through the streets of the city. These marchers, victims of the strange malady, were all thrown out of work early this morning when they told insulted employers what they thought of them. At present they are fairly orderly, but it is feared that, once they realize their power, looting and bloodshed will result."

Professor Merlo winced, thinking of the hundreds more who would join the marchers the moment the department stores were shut down.

The telephone was jangling insistently, and Merlo crossed the room slowly to where it stood. He knew what the call would probably be. He'd had nine of them already. He picked the receiver off the hook. "Yes?"

"Hello, Professor Merlo?" a voice on the other end inquired. In an almost toneless whisper the Professor admitted it was.

"This is J. Weems Sharp," said the voice. The Professor was sure of the call now. "Yes," said Merlo, "I think I understand what you're calling for. You want to tell me that you're withdrawing your endowment from my Civic Scientific Foundation."

The voice was amazed. "Yes, that's right. How did you know?"

Merlo ignored the question. "You want to withdraw your endowment from the Foundation because you are quite willing to admit that you don't give a damn for the betterment of your fellows."

"That's right," agreed the voice. "I never cared what happened to the masses. No sense in my wasting money on other people when I can keep it all for myself. I was a chump to let you talk me into it for the past ten years. Now it can go to the devil, I—" Professor Merle put his thumb down on the hook, breaking the connection.

"That makes the tenth one," he told himself bitterly, beginning to pace the floor. "They can all tell the truth, now. They'll admit that they're miserly monsters, and refuse to give any more to scientific charity. It's just about the end of my Foundation. Oh Lord," he thought, "for ten years I've been able to play on the hypocrisy of those money-bags, making them shell out money for the good of their fellowman, pleasing their egos by giving their charity a lot of publicity. But now," he shuddered, "they admit that they don't give a damn for charity!"

* * * *

The Civic Scientific Foundation had been the pride and joy of Merlo's existence, and seeing it crumble was one of the hardest blows of the day. Ten years of progress was being wiped out in the space of several hours.

It was clear to the Professor, now, what he and Lance failed to take into consideration before the experiment. People affected by the Truth Gas would not only tell what they knew to be true, but would also admit to things which had been lying under the hypocritical cloak of their subconscious thoughts for years. In other words, the gas was exposing ideas which people never even previously suspected they cherished!

"Something," muttered the tightlipped scientist, "has to be done, and done fast." He paused before the window. And as he looked out across the country-side, it seemed as though nature itself had fallen under the mood of gloomy foreboding. The sun was hidden behind ominous formations of black rain-laden clouds.

CHAPTER IV

Lance Makes a Test

If Lance Randell hadn't been so preoccupied with the doubts that clouded his romance he might have noticed the growing confusion in Weston. As it was, however, he looked neither left nor right as he put his high-powered roadster into gear and shot out for the Weston Tower Hotel where the blonde Edie had an apartment.

The crowds that were beginning to surge through the streets escaped his notice, the clang of speeding ambulances and police wagons failed to enter his brain, so one-tracked was his determination.

In a little less than three minutes after he'd left the office Randall drew up in front of the elaborate canopy marking the entrance to the skyscraping Weston Tower Hotel. Edie's apartment was on the fortieth floor, and Randell didn't bother to telephone from the lobby. He crossed the room swiftly and stepped into an elevator.

Edie Dalmar, when she opened the door, was astonished to see a breathless and strangely intense Lance Randell standing there with his hat in his hand. For a moment her oval, doll-like features registered amazement, then

Weston's Loveliest Bubble Dancer regained her composure. She arched delicately penciled eyebrows in a smile.

"Daahhling, what a surprise! What are you doing heah at this hour?"

Lance entered the room and put his hat on the mantel. He turned and spoke.

"Edie, there are some things I have to ask you. It's very important, and I don't want you to be angry with me."

Edie moved sinuously across the room, smoothing her blonde hair with scarlet nailed fingers. She sat down on the couch and turned violet eyes on Lance. "Why, deah, ah don't know jes' what it's all about, but go right ahead and ask me anything you want to."

Lance removed an enormous, floppy Cupid doll from the cushion next to her and sat down. For a moment he was silent. This wasn't going to be easy. He knew that any question he'd ask would bring a starkly truthful answer. But he had to know. He forced himself to speak.

"Edie, do you really love me?"

The bubble dancer opened her slightly petulant lips to protest, but Lance went on. "I mean, do you love me for myself? Is it, is it me that you love, or is it my money?"

There, Lance told himself, it was done. He felt his heart hammering wildly as Edie started to speak. He felt as though the answer would mean the difference between life and death.

"Why, daahhling, of course I love you! Honey, whatevah made you fancy that I cared a speck about your money? I'd marry you even if you were a pauper!"

Randell was ecstatic in his relief. They were all wrong! Doris had been a spiteful, jealous wench. Edie was true! He knew it all along, Edie was true! She didn't give a damn for his money. She loved him for himself alone.

By now, however, Edie was pouting. Two enormous tears began to trickle down her cheeks. She was sobbing silently, dabbing at her eyes with a scrap of lace.

* * * *

"Honey," said Randell, sensing that he had wounded her feelings, "I never meant to doubt you, honestly. I'm sorry I ever asked you, but I was desperately unsure. I had to know. Please forgive me."

Edie, however, was not so easily consoled. She increased her snuffling. "You thought I, I, I was cheap!" she wailed.

Lance Randell had a sudden inspiration. "Edie!"

No reply, merely more snuffling.

"Edie," he repeated. This time she looked up.

"What?" she asked between sobs.

"You know that coat you admired so much the other day?"

Edie's snuffling lessened perceptibly. "Yes?"

"I'd like you to have it as a present, dear."

Gone were the tears, silenced was the sobbing. Edie's doll face was wreathed in smiles. She was in his arms.

"Daahhling," breathed Edie.

"My dear," said Randell.

The floppy Cupid doll looked up from the floor where it had been dropped, its button eyes shining cynically.

* * * *

With singing heart Lance left Edie's apartment. The world was once more righted, and now he had time to think of the second most important thing in his life, the experiment. Then, too, he'd almost forgotten that Merlo was waiting for a call from him back in the laboratories.

He glanced at his watch. 10:30. Plenty should be happening by now. The gas had had more than an hour and a half to take effect on the populace. There should be some interesting developments. There were.

As he stepped from the elevator into the lobby, Randell was immediately aware that things were popping in the Weston Tower Hotel. There had been a scant twenty people sitting about in the spacious room when Randell had first arrived there. Now, not more than a half hour later, the place was literally jammed with people. Everyone seemed to be talking at once, and in the voices there was a growing undercurrent of hysteria.

The fever spot seemed to be located around the Room Desk, and Randell began elbowing through the mob, moving in that direction.

"Stand back, buddy!"

Lance Randell was in the front of the circle around the Desk, when a blue-clad arm shot out to stop his progress. He noticed, then, that a cordon of eight policemen had blocked off a space around the Desk, and were holding the crowd back.

In the middle of the space, face downward, lay a gray haired man dressed in morning coat and striped trousers. His head was pillowed in a pool of his own blood, and his right hand held a death-like clutch on an automatic pistol.

Horrified, Randell addressed the policeman who barred his way.

"What happened, Officer?"

"Suicide," was the terse reply. "Shot himself while we were on the way to get him."

A pop-eyed little man on his right supplied Lance with the rest of the information.

"It's Gordon Carver," the little man blurted. "He's killed himself, rather than go to jail."

Gordon Carver! Randell was stunned. Gordon Carver was Weston's greatest philanthropist, most charitable millionaire, a leading citizen! He looked at the millionaire's body, so queerly sprawled out across the cold marble floor. The pop-eyed champ was still talking.

"Yeah," said Pop-Eyes, "he called the Police about a half an hour ago, confessed that he had committed some crime years ago, and was an escaped convict. He told them to come to the Weston Tower Hotel, that he'd be waiting in the lobby to surrender to 'em." Pop-Eyes paused to shudder. "I guess he couldn't stand the thought of going back to prison, so he plugged hisself just as the cops walked in the lobby."

* * * *

Suddenly Lance Randell knew that he had to get away from that circle. He fought his way back through the crowd, feeling that he might succumb to nausea at any moment. The voices all around him were still floating to his consciousness. "What's happened to this town?" "It's the end of the world." "Terrible, out in the streets, rioting." "I saw a little child… killed.…"

Randell found a telephone booth, managed to push inside. With a hand that trembled slightly, he fished through his pockets until he found a nickel. Then he was dialing Professor Merlo's number. After what seemed like an eternity he heard the old scientist's voice.

"Professor, it's me—Lance. I—" he was cut off by the sharp voice on the other end of the wire.

"Yes," he heard Merlo saying, "I know all about it. Got it all through news flashes. We haven't any time to lose. Have to act quickly. Where are you?"

"At the Weston Towers, but—" Kendall began.

"Stay there," Merlo continued, "I'll meet you as quickly as possible. Every moment that this gas stays over the city means more lives. I think I've hit on a solution."

"How? What?" Randell began. Then he cursed. Merlo had hung up.

What did the old man mean? What possible solution could there be? They had no anti-toxin to the gas. They knew that it would wear off in twenty-four hours, of course, but in twenty-four hours—. He shuddered at the thought of what was in store for Weston if the gas held that long!

A feeling of utter hopelessness, complete futility came over Randell as he stepped back into the lobby of the Weston Towers. Another twenty-four hours before the gas would drift from the city. Twenty-four hours in which hell would rage unchecked! The thought was staggering. Foolishly, it occurred to him that he was suffering the same emotions that Dr. Frankenstein had known upon creating his monster.

Then and there his heart went into a sickening tailspin. He had forgotten about Edie! If this bedlam was going to continue throughout Weston, no one would be safe. He had to get her out of the city, had to get her to safety while there was still time. Desperately, Randell began to push back through the crowded lobby toward the elevators.

CHAPTER V

Lance Gets a Shock

Professor Merlo waited a moment after hanging up on Lance Randell. Then he picked up the telephone again and dialed a number. As the receiver buzzed in his ear he drummed his fingers impatiently on the table, staring out the window at the darkening skies.

"It should work," the old man muttered to himself. "It has to work." Then he heard a voice on the other end of the wire.

"Weston Contractors," said the voice.

Merlo began speaking excitedly, emphatically, allowing his listener no time for interruptions. After several minutes he concluded, "Is everything straight? It's a question of time. I want them there as quickly as possible."

"Certainly, Professor," was the reply. "I understand. We'll get them there as fast as is humanly possible. But such an enormous load of sand, I can't imagine what you intend—"

"Damn you," shouted Merlo, his face purpling, "you don't have to imagine. All you have to do is get them there, and get them there in a hurry!"

"Yes, Professor," the voice was startled, "never fear. They'll be there on time."

Merlo slammed the instrument back on its cradle and stood up. He seized his hat from the top of a bookcase and stamped out of the room. A few moments later he was turning his black sedan out of his garage and onto the highway leading to Weston. Then he pushed the accelerator down to the floorboards....

Less than a mile from the Weston Tower Hotel, a pretty, red-headed young girl was being swept along by the semi-frantic crowds thronging the business district. For the first time since she dashed tearfully from the offices of Lance Randell Enterprises, over an hour ago, Doris Martin was becoming aware of the frenzied hysteria gripping the city.

Despair at what she said to the man she loved had driven her into the streets, made her wander about aimlessly, until finally, Doris Martin knew what she had to do. And she was going to do it. No one on earth could stop her.

People were passing her, crowds elbowed by, the ordinary hum of the city increased to a tone approaching an angry howl, but Doris walked on, scarcely conscious of anything but the pavement beneath her feet. Where she was going, how long she'd been walking, nothing made any difference.

"Watch where ye're goin', sister!"

Doris had a confused vision of a fat red face peering angrily at her. A sweaty, shirt-sleeved fellow in a sailor straw had wrapped his pudgy hand around her arm and jerked her backward. Her first instinct was one of anger, and she started to speak.

"Ya wanna get kilt?" The fat man was pointing to the cars rushing by in the street, and then Doris realized that they were standing on the curbing, that the fat fellow had pulled her out of the path of the automobiles hurtling past them.

Her ears were torn by the screech of hastily applied automobile brakes. Out of the corner of her eye she saw a black sedan jolting to an abrupt stop. Terrified, she stood rooted in the center of the street.

"Good God, girl," someone shouted. "I might have killed you!" Doris saw that it was the driver of the sedan, and that he was climbing out of his car. The driver was walking over to her now, his face white, jaws shut.

"Doris!" The driver stopped short in shocked amazement.

* * * *

It was then that she recognized Professor Merlo. He had her by the arm, was propelling her to his car and talking rapidly. "What are you doing here? Life isn't safe anywhere in Weston. You must be mad to be roaming the streets while this turmoil is raging. Don't you know, haven't you seen it?"

They were in Merlo's sedan now, once more moving along in the stream of traffic. Doris found her voice at last. "Where are you going, Professor? What, what has happened to the city?"

"Plenty," Merlo snapped. "We're going to the Weston Towers. Lance is there, waiting for me. There's a lot to be done. Can't explain it all now."

At the mention of Lance, Doris paled. "Good!" she said firmly. "I was on my way there. I've a little business of my own there."

"Not with Lance, I suspect?" said Merlo, looking at her with less surprise than he might have.

"No," Doris' voice was amazingly different. "I'll tend to that—"

Suddenly the little black sedan shot across an intersection at the same moment that a lumber truck came hurtling through from the side street. It was too late for Merlo to swing the sedan out of its path. The sickening, futile squealing of brakes preceded the rending crash of a side-on collision. In the blackness that was closing around him, Merlo heard a woman scream....

* * * *

It had only been his dogged determination that enabled Lance Randell to get Edie Dalmar to leave her apartment. At first she was coyly amused at his insistence that she dress and leave with him immediately. Then, as she began to notice the unsmiling set to his mouth, the feverish gleam in his eyes, she became a little frightened and decided to humor him.

They stepped out of the elevator into the lobby and Randell looked swiftly through the crowd in an effort to see if Merlo had arrived yet. Edie tugged at his sleeve.

"Jus' what is this heah all about, daahling?" she demanded. Randell tore his eyes from the crowd. Wordlessly he took her arm, piloting her across the room to a quiet corner. They found a lounge.

"What's this all about?" repeated Edie, her voice oddly different in accent. She jerked her arm out of his grasp.

"Look, Honey," he began in a rush of words. "As I said before. Something terrible has happened to the city. I can't tell you any more than that for the present. You'll have to trust me. It isn't safe in Weston any more, and I'm going to get you out of here as soon as Merlo comes!"

Edie's starry eyes narrowed perceptibly. "Have you gone daffy?"

Lance Randell groaned. Then, remembering Edie had seen nothing of the effects of the gas, hadn't even heard of it yet, he made another effort to explain.

"Listen, Darling. Weston is a city suddenly gone mad. Something has happened. It's no longer safe to go out into the streets. Business is being ruined. Financial houses are collapsing. Lives are being taken recklessly. You must understand me, you have to believe me. If this keeps up, dear, everything will be ruined. It begins to look like you'll have to keep your promise about marrying me even if I were a pauper." Lance stopped abruptly. Edie was staring at him strangely.

"What's that you just said?" she demanded frigidly.

"I said that all business is being ruined. It means that all my investments will be wiped out if this continues, that I'll be a pauper," said Lance in confusion.

"Are you sure of that?" Her tone was like an Arctic breeze.

"I'm afraid so." Randell had pushed his hat back on his forehead and was staring in amazement at the expression that crossed Edie's face.

"Then," said Edie deliberately, "you might as well get out of my sight, you boob. Do you think for a minute that I have any time for a pauper. Why, you sap, all I ever wanted was your dough. This little gal looks out for herself. If you haven't got the bankroll I can get a guy that has." She was standing up now, looking scornfully at him. "Excuse me, chump. I'm leaving. Don't bother to come again!"

Feeling as if he had just been thoroughly gone over by a steam roller, Randell sat gazing in aching astonishment at Edie's retreating back.

CHAPTER VI

Sand—And Rain

For a time Lance Randell was unable to do anything more than stare dumbly into space. Edie Dalmar's sudden change had affected him just as forcibly as a left hook to the jaw, leaving him dazed, uncomprehending, paralyzed. His first reactions were those of hurt and bewilderment, bitterness and heartbreak. Then reason began to return, and with it the demand for an explanation of her actions.

She undoubtedly was acting under the effects of the gas, he was certain of that much. But why hadn't she spoken the truth when he talked to her in her apartment? Why didn't the gas influence her until they were down in the lobby?

Suddenly Randell looked at his watch. He remembered at that moment that Merlo should be somewhere in the lobby. The Professor had had more than enough time to get there. His personal troubles vanished as he realized once more that as every moment passed Weston was coming closer and closer to the brink of utter madness. And then, as he glanced in the direction of the revolving doors at the hotel entrance, he gasped.

A grotesque caricature of a man was entering. On his head was a battered fedora, mashed down over wild white hair and a blood-caked brow. His suit was literally ripped to shreds, the left pants leg torn off at the knee, and the coat sticky with oil and blood. He looked wildly about for an instant—

Randell gasped again, "Professor Merlo!"

In several swift strides Randell was at the old man's side. He threw an arm around his waist and half-carried him over to a couch. "Wasn't sure I'd make it," Merlo said faintly. "There was an accident. Truck. Hit me from the side. Doris, Doris Martin was in the car with me. I must have been out cold for five minutes. When I came around, she was gone. Couldn't look for her. Came the rest of the way by cab. Had to tell you. We must work fast!"

"Where is Doris—" But Randell stopped, fighting to drive all other thoughts from his mind. One thing alone was more important than any others. "Remember you said you'd found a solution?"

"Yes," Merlo said quietly. "It's in the weather."

Lance Randell felt suddenly sick inside. The old man was out of his head, delirious from the accident. His mouth felt dry, and all at once he knew it was all over.

They were beaten. There would be no solution. The one chance of saving the city was in the Professor's plan. And that plan had evidently been jarred from the old man's mind in the collision. Automatically he listened, while the Professor went on:

"Did you notice the weather?"

"No," Randell said, trying to keep the bitterness from his voice.

"Rainclouds," said Merlo, "huge formations of them above Weston. I called the weather bureau. But the rain isn't expected until evening. Then it will be too late. We can't wait for evening, Lance. We must have rain, now. Evening will be too late." The Professor stopped, and looked at Lance strangely. "My God, Lance, don't you see what I'm getting at? Do you think I'm out of my head? Rain! Rain! It'll save us, man. Remember your elementary chemistry! The rain will destroy our Truth Gas, will disintegrate its molecular formation! Water can do that to gas, don't you see?"

There was life once more in Randell's expression, hope in his eyes as he spoke. Gone was his conviction that Merlo was babbling. "Good Lord, I see what you mean, Professor! But you said that rain isn't expected until evening—"

"That's what I said," agreed Merlo, "but we're going to *make rain*, Lance. Now!"

Randell was visibly perplexed, but he waited while Merlo continued.

"I've ordered sand," said the Professor, "twelve trucks of it. They should be at the Weston Airport this minute. I've hired airplanes. They're the type used in spraying vegetation and smoking orchards. Those planes are going to fly above the raincloud formations.

They're going to *bomb* the clouds, with sand!"[1]

"But—"

"With sand!" repeated Merlo. "The sand will shatter the cloud formations and release the rain on the city immediately!"

* * * *

Lance Randell was on his feet. "You say the planes and the sand are waiting at the Airport?"

1   Nothing is so tantalizing to drought sufferers as rainclouds which, because of some peculiar quirk in atmospheric conditions, refuse to precipitate rain. In the Southwestern section of the country, considerable success in the past was achieved by airplanes which sprayed or "bombed" with sand stubborn rainclouds above drought-stricken crops or sun-baked city streets. Action of the sand on the clouds released the rain.—Editor.

Merlo nodded. "I'd planned that we both go to the field. It will make it easier if there are two of us to direct the operations."

The youth helped the old scientist to his feet. "Think you'll be okay, Professor?"

"I think so," said Merlo. But his face was a sickening white.

Randell looked quickly at the Professor, indecision crossing his face. At that instant confusion broke forth in the lobby of Weston Towers, signaled by a hoarse shout of terror from the direction of the elevators. Then a woman screamed and every voice in the place became raised in bedlam.

The Professor and Randell wheeled in the direction of this fresh outburst. People were rushing back and forth in front of a corner elevator like so many frightened chickens. They seemed desperately eager to get away from that particular spot.

Then they saw the cause of the terror, a mousey little man who was standing alone in the elevator, shouting hysterically. The fellow had one hand on the controls and the other was clutching a small, vial-like object.

"Going up, going up, going up," his voice carried to where Randell and Professor Merlo were standing.

"Good Lord," someone cried, "Stop him before it's too late."

"Get the Manager," a woman was screaming. "He wants to kill himself."

Lance cursed in anguish. Another one. He struggled through the retreating crowds until he stood behind a cordon of the more courageous spectators, some twenty feet from the elevator row. Merlo had followed directly behind him.

"Get back," the bespectacled little fellow in the elevator was shouting. "Get away from here, all of you, unless you want to come with me!"

The man peered owlishly at the crowd through the thick lenses of his glasses, raising the object in his hand aloft. "This is nitroglycerine! It can blow us all to eternity! Stand back!"

Instinctively, the row in front of Lance and Merlo surged back. Lance turned to Merlo. "It's another suicide attempt!"

The little man was shouting at the crowd again. "I'm going up through this roof. Up in a blaze of glory. Glory, for the first time in my miserable life! I've been kidding myself too long. My worthless hide doesn't mean a thing in the scheme of things, and all the time I've been a miserable failure, a fraud. But this morning I stopped lying to myself. Now I'm going out—out and up—with this nitro in my hand! Who wants to come along, eh? Who wants to come along?"

The Professor put a hand to his head, wiping away beads of perspiration. He looked at Randell. "There's nothing we can do about it."

"Good God," Randell cried, "we can't let him kill himself. It's our fault if he dies!" His voice had become anguished, impassioned, and Merlo placed a quieting hand on his arm.

"Steady, Lance. We couldn't foresee all this. There's nothing we can do about it. Every minute we stand here means at least ten such similar deaths throughout the city. Our duty is at the Airport. Let's get out of here, immediately."

Suddenly Lance Randell trembled. Then he quieted.

"You're right. Sorry. Let's get going!" He turned, pushing back through the crowd, when he noticed that Merlo was not moving. The Professor stood frozen motionless, staring in astonishment at the elevator.

"Going up! Going up!" Randell heard the demonical little man chanting. He also heard a gasp from the crowd, heard Merlo mutter a familiar name incredulously. Randell spun around to face the elevator.

"Doris!" the name tumbled from his lips in horror, for from a side entrance to the lobby Doris Martin was walking in a direct line toward the madman's elevator!

In the brief agonized glimpse Lance Randell had of the girl he could see instantly that something was wrong. She walked with the measured step of a sleepwalker, her face blank, eyes unseeing. And in the shocked hush that fell over the lobby he heard her muttering almost inaudibly.

"Lance Randell, you're a fool. A fool." She seemed to be sobbing. "I love you, Lance. She'll never take you...."

* * * *

"GOING up! Going up!" The wild cry of the maniac rang out through the sudden silence like an unclean cackle. He swung the grilled doors of the elevator open momentarily, and in that instant Doris Martin, unseeingly, stepped inside the cage.

"Ha—ha! Going up, sister! Glad you're coming along!"

As the elevator door clanged shut Lance Randell's mind became a crimson blot. With an animal snarl he lashed out at the bodies that had blocked his way to the elevator, beating a path before him, hurling himself through the opening. He didn't notice Merlo barging along behind him. He didn't notice anything but the cage with the little suicide and the dazed young girl.

A wild laugh came from the tiny cage, and Randell shouted as he saw it start upward. The light above the door flickered white. Merlo was beside Randall by this time, grabbing him by the arm. He wheeled as he felt the old man's fingers digging into his sleeve.

"What in the hell are we standing here for?" Randell yelled. "Doris is in that elevator, and by God I'm going after her!"

"Get a grip on yourself, Lance," Merlo's fingers dug deeper into his arm and his voice was low, fierce. "Remember what I told you, man. For every moment that we're delayed from the Airport, something like this happens somewhere else in Weston. We've wasted too much time already!"

The Professor's voice brought calm back to Randell—calm and agony at the full import of the situation. "Professor," he muttered shakily, "Doris will be blown to eternity. I have to follow!"

"You'll be sacrificing a hundred lives for one."

Randell looked at the small puddle of blood forming beneath Merlo's leg. "Can you make it alone, Professor?"

"You love the girl?" The Professor's voice was soft.

"Yes...I never realized...." said Randell, and he realized with bitter irony that the Truth Gas was at work once more.

Merlo held out his hand. "I'll make it, Lance, somehow. God give you luck, lad, and speed!" Then the Professor was gone, moving unsteadily off through the crowds. The open door of an adjoining elevator caught Randell's eye and he stepped toward it without hesitation.

"Don't be a fool," snapped a voice directly behind him.

Lance Randell wheeled to see a tall, broad shouldered fellow standing behind him. "Keep out of that elevator. Get back into the crowd. There's a lunatic loose in an elevator with a vial of nitroglycerine. We're clearing the lobby."

"Thanks," Randell grated, "for the information!" As he spoke his fist swung simultaneously. The efficient-looking young gentleman went down heavily. The elevator doors closed with a wild clang.

Lance Randell grabbed the controls of the car, throwing them forward instantly. In his heart was the horrible fear that he'd wasted too much time, that he would be too late. The car lurched forward from the quick start, then shot upward. From the moment when he first spied the insane operator in the elevator, something had been hammering at the back of his consciousness. It seemed to hinge, somehow with Edie Dalmar. And now, with every second holding the answer between life and death, he racked his brain in an effort to hit upon a plan.

HE knew that his only hope of stopping the suicide, saving Doris, lay in that elusive subconscious discovery. He glanced swiftly about the narrow confines of the cage, mentally thanking God that it was not one of the modern, room-type elevators enclosed on all sides. Instead, the upper-half of the walls were merely spaced iron grillwork, making it possible to see across the shaft from one elevator to another.

He peered out through the grill. With a silent prayer of thanks he saw that the cables in the adjoining shaft were moving slowly.

"He's taking his time," he muttered. "If I can catch the car before he drives it through the roof I—" Suddenly the elusive plan that had been hiding in his subconscious was crystallized for Randell. He had it.

Of course! The Truth Gas didn't carry to the upper floors of the hotel. It was a heavier than air substance. That accounted for Edie being unaffected by it when she was in her apartment!

His plan was clear in his mind, now. He knew that his one chance of saving Doris lay in forcing the lunatic to the upper floors of the Hotel without discharging the nitro. Once above the gas, the little man would return to normality, would listen to reason.

The little car shot past the twenty-fifth floor. Five floors more and Randell caught a glimpse of the understructure of his quarry's elevator.

Face taut, Randell began to slow his own cage. Three seconds, and he was adjoining the death car. He threw his controls back to stop.

"Ha!" He could see the crazed little man turn from where he stood at the controls of the car. He peered through the grillwork at Randell.

Suddenly the suicide's voice cackled, "So you want to come along, too?"

His eyes sweeping desperately across the car in an effort to see Doris, Randell called, "Where's the girl?"

The little man glanced downward in devilish amusement. "She's lying on the floor. Passed out a moment after we started up."

Randell was talking rapidly, "You can't take that girl to her death. For the love of heaven, man, she has nothing to do with you or your life. Let her out!"

Another hysterical burst of laughter from the demented little fellow was the only answer. Randell opened his mouth to speak, when the other car began to ascend once more. Cursing, he threw the controls forward again.

"32" flashed by.

"33" dropped past. "36" faded by, and cold sweat trickled off Randell's forehead, smarting into his eyes. He forced himself to look upward, catching a glimpse of the car above. Suddenly he cursed. Something was wrong.

The other car had come, to a stop, and was bobbing between floors. "He's going to drop the nitro," Randell thought desperately. He slowed his tiny cage down until he was beside the other.

Looking across the shaft, he was startled. Neither Doris nor the nitro-man was visible!

Instinctively he called out, "Doris!"

The silent elevator shafts echoed and re-echoed his cry.

He set his controls, rushing to the grillwork wall, trying to get a better view of the cage in the opposite shaft. Then he saw them. In one corner of the elevator Doris was laying face downward. In the front, next to the controls, the madman was stretched out flat on his back. Next to his open hand was the vial of nitroglycerine—rolling gently back and forth on the floor of the car!

With a numbing sensation of horror, Randell saw that the controls of the car were not set correctly, that they might slip any moment!

Steeling himself, he swept his eyes across the cage in the opposite shaft, looking frantically for some solution to the dilemma. The car was stuck between floors, making it impossible to get to it from a ball door.

Randell realized as much instantly. There was only one other solution, and breathing a silent supplication for time, he set to work on the wall grill-work of his cage.

Precious moments rushed by as he began the laborious effort required to unscrew the thick screen fastenings. It would have been a difficult enough job with tools, but Randell had only his hands, and inside of two minutes they were torn and bleeding.

* * * *

Sobbing under his breath, knowing that the controls might loosen in the opposite car at any instant, Lance Randell paused only to wipe away the sweat that clouded his eyes. Then at last one side of the screen was loosened.

It was enough. Calling on every last ounce of strength, he pulled backward on the grilling, bending it enough to push his head and shoulders through the scant opening. Hoisting himself up to the ledge where the screening began, he stood teetering, looking down thirty-seven floors of elevator shaft.

He closed his eyes for a moment, grating his teeth against the pain he knew was coming, then seized one of the black, greasy cables with his lacerated hands. It was an almost superhuman act of will that let him swing his feet from the comparatively safe ledge of his own car out into space.

For an agonized second, Randell was sure that his grip on the cable was loosening, that he was going to pitch headlong down the shaft. He wrapped his legs around the huge black coil, hoping to God that the grease wouldn't make such a grip impossible. It was now or never.

One hand lost the cable. The motion made him slide several sickening feet. His hand caught the grilling on the death car, held him there.

With his free hand Randell went to work on the screen fastenings of the cage in which Doris was lying. Time was a blur now, and every frantic second spent in tearing at the bolt fastenings seemed like a section of eternity. He knew he wasn't going to make it, felt his legs growing weak in their grip around the cable, felt the flesh tearing open wider and wider on the hand clutching the coil. But he continued feverishly.

The grilled siding was almost opened, one more bolt, it was loose....

Through the daze of sweat, exhaustion and pain Randell knew that he had to throw all his weight over the half-side of the death car, and as he realized the fact, he caught a split-second vision of the vial of nitroglycerine on the floor, of the control lever that might slip with the slightest jarring of the cage.

He grabbed, releasing all but his legs from the cable, got his elbows over the side of the car. Now his legs were free, and he was clambering into the tiny elevator, making for the controls....

DORIS stood close against Lance Randell, and his arms were around her. They stood in the street outside the Weston Towers. The angry howl of the city had subsided to a tranquil hum, above which could be heard the drone of many airplanes, growing softer, fainter.

Tiny grains of sand were falling in many places over the city, but they were unfelt, locked in droplets of rain. And the rain kept falling gently, steadily, washing away the madness and sorrow and death that a plague of truth had given freedom.

Lance Randell looked down at the girl.

"Why, darling," he said softly, "you're crying!"

She turned her face upward. "No," she murmured, "it's just the rain on my cheeks."

He drew her tighter. "Liar," he whispered....

THE MAN THE WORLD FORGOT

"If you've glanced at the contents page of this issue, you've seen a lot of new names. James Norman, John Broome, and John York Cabot. These three are first-timers in Fantastic Adventures. And we think you'll agree that each one has given us a pretty good yam for their debut in our magazine. Personally, your editor likes 'The Man the World Forgot' by John York Cabot, which is a delightful bit of real fantasy. It has the sort of idea we kick ourselves over when we see how simple and how good it is, and wonder why we never get ideas like it."

—Raymond A. Palmer, "The Editor's Notebook,"
Fantastic Adventures, April 1940.

POSITIVELY PHOTOGRAPHIC

"Sirs: The May issue was quite good, but it did not compare with the excellence of your April issue—the best of them all. 'The Man the World Forgot' was splendidly thought-provoking and the illustration by [Julian] Krupa was positively photographic. He did one other in this style and they both are revolutionary in magazine art. More like this, by all means."

—Charles Hidley, New York, New York,
Letter to the Editor, *Fantastic Adventures*, August 1940.

* * * *

None of the passengers on the eight-twenty paid the slightest attention to Lucius Beem when he climbed aboard the city-bound express. However, Mr. Beem, clad in his usual unassuming gray suit, hat, and topcoat, didn't deem it unusual. Few people ever paid any attention to him.

"It is," remarked the drab Mr. Beem as he took a seat, "a fine morning. A very fine morning, indeed."

The occupant of the seat in which Mr. Beem had deposited himself gazed vaguely at the little man.

"Oh, ah, yes, it's a nice morning, Mr.—er—Mr.—"

Mr. Beem sighed resignedly. So few people remembered his name. "Mr. Beem," he told his fellow passenger. "My name is Mr. Beem." He decided regretfully it would be no good to remind the man that this was the sixteenth time in the past month that he had forgotten his name; that for ten years they both had been riding to the city on the same train almost always seated together.

"Ah, yes, of course," commented the passenger. "Mr. Dream. How silly of me to forget."

Mr. Beem buried his plain face in his newspaper and gave himself up to a summary of the day's news. Fifteen minutes later he looked up from his paper and once more spoke to the passenger sitting beside him.

"Isn't it strange," commented Mr. Beem, pointing to a column in the newspaper, "that the famous Professor Snell is unable to get anyone to offer himself for radium tests? You'd think there would be someone who was interested enough in the betterment of the world to offer his body to science."

"Uh?" The passenger gave Mr. Beem a vacuous glance. "Did you say something?"

"I said…" Mr. Beem sighed and gave it up. The man had already turned away.

MR. BEEM stepped off the train at his station and wended his drab way through the milling crowds of people to the tiny coffee shop in the corner of the depot. It was a ten year habit of his to breakfast here daily on rolls and coffee before going to the office.

Mr. Beem slid into a stool at the counter. When Cleo, the waitress, came over to take his order Mr. Beem's plain face broke into what he intended to be an engaging smile. There was something solid about seeing Cleo every morning. As long as he could remember, the girl had been a waitress at that counter.

"Good morning, Cleo," said Mr. Beem warmly. "A fine morning, isn't it?"

The girl's face was blank. "Yeah," she nodded noncommittally. Then: "What'll it be?"

Mr. Beem's voice carried a reprimanding note. "The usual, if you please."

"And what," she inquired sharply, "is the usual?"

Mr. Beem sighed heavily. "Coffee and rolls." He suddenly felt a little lonely. People never noticed him particularly. Things like this had happened many times in his simple, unadorned existence. But this particular morning was worse than any other Mr. Beem had ever experienced. With a doleful eye on the wall clock, Mr. Beem sipped his coffee.

STEPPING into the elevator of his office building, Mr. Beem nodded soberly to the operator. "Mornin', Tad," he muttered. After cheerfully greeting the other office arrivals by name, Tad favored his drab little passenger with a flat uninterested glance.

It was Tad's boast that he knew the floors, offices, and names of all the building regulars whom he carried throughout the day. Consequently, Mr. Beem eyed him dourly when, once the elevator was shooting upward, Tad turned toward him. "Floor, please?"

But when he stepped into the office of Sharpe and Sholt, where he'd held a small position for the past fifteen years, Mr. Beem completely forgot the other incidents of the morning.

For Lola, the switchboard operator, stopped him at the gate. "Is there someone you wish to see?"

Mr. Beem was not the type of person to be actually aghast. But for the first time in his life he came pretty close to the real emotion.

"Someone I want to see?" Mr. Beem was dazed.

"Are you joking, Lola?"

Lola's face was apologetic. "I'm sorry, sir. Evidently you've been here before. But have you an appointment with anyone?"

"I, that is, why, uh, I work here," stammered Mr. Beem.

"Work *here*?" The girl's voice was suddenly a mixture of suspicion and incredulity. "Work here?"

Suddenly she began shooting plugs in and out of the board. Lights flickered across its face. "Mr. Sharpe," she was speaking, "there's a man out here whom I've never seen in all my life. He claims he's an employee; wants to get into the office…What did you say?"

Lola turned to the stricken Mr. Beem. "Mr. Sharpe wants to know your name, sir. He says if it's work you want, please leave your name and we'll call you if anything turns up."

"Tell him," Mr. Beem was growing frantic, "my name is Beem. I don't know what's happened to you, Lola, but surely Mr. Sharpe will know.…"

"He says his name is Team," Lola spoke into the phone, "or something like that…What?…Yes, sir, I'll tell him." She faced Mr. Beem again.

"Mr. Sharpe said he's never heard of you, but if you'll list your qualifications on this· application blank," she held out a sheet of paper, "he'll be glad to get in touch with you if anything turns up.…"

She stopped suddenly, jaw agape, for the gray, mousy little man was dashing out of the office, running pell-mell down the corridor as if a million devils pursued him.…

* * * *

For almost an hour after Mr. Beem left his office, he wandered bewilderedly through the streets, his mind a jumbled haze of half-formed questions, suspicions, answers. During the first part of this aimless wandering, the suspicion was gradually growing on Mr. Beem—the world had gone mad!

But at length he had been forced to discard that explanation, remembering that it is the trait of a lunatic to think everyone but himself insane. Then his mind turned to stories he had read, stories in which men wandered about unrecognized by anyone. Those stories invariably ended by the disclosure that the wanderer was really dead. Was he, Mr. Beem, dead? The thought was horrifying, and Mr. Beem drove it from his mind. No! He was certainly not dead.

Mr. Beem eventually found his footsteps leading him to the depot. Almost without realizing it, he bought his ticket on the suburban train, and sat down to wait for its arrival. His mind was now clear on one point. He was going back to his house. Martha, his wife, would be surprised to see him, since he hadn't come home so early from work since that time when his appendix burst.

It would take a great deal of explaining to Martha to make her realize what had happened, but she was his only chance of comfort, his only remaining stability. Maybe, when she got the doctor for him, it would be decided that all Mr. Beem needed was a long rest from the office. That was it, nerve strain.

Turning up the street to his little suburban nest was a comforting feeling to Mr. Beem. The familiar line of poplar trees and white picket fences gave him a vague sense of assurance. As he opened his own white picket gate, and went up the walk, he actually whistled in relief. It was a tuneless whistle, dreary, flat, off-key.

Martha had never given him his own key, so Mr. Beem was forced to use the door knocker.

Mr. Beem strove to register a reassuring smile as his wife came to the door. He didn't want her to be shocked or frightened, thinking he was sick.

He could hear her heels clicking across the floor inside the house. The door swung open. Mr. Beem stepped forward.

"Hello, honey," said Mr. Beem, "don't be frightened. I just felt I'd like to come home today."

But he only progressed a few feet, for Mrs. Beem was looking at him with mingled astonishment and indignation on her face. Before he could step through the door she slammed it against his foot.

"Why, Martha, what's the matter? I'm all right. What's wrong?" Mr. Beem's voice almost lost its drabness and swift, sickening terror assailed his knees.

His wife's voice was high, shrill, carrying almost out into the street. "Whoever you are, salesman or masher, you have a nerve calling me honey and trying to force your way into this house. Get away from here immediately, or I'll call the police!"

Then she delivered a nasty kick on the shin of the leg Mr. Beem still had wedged in the doorway. He withdrew it swiftly, and Instantly the door slammed shut. He heard his wife slide a safety bolt home, then her heels were clicking over the floor again.

For several dazed minutes Mr. Beem stood on the doorstoop of his home, rubbing painfully at his injured shin. Panic was clutching with icy fingers at his brain.

Rubbing the back of his hand across his eyes, the bewildered Mr. Beem staggered down the steps of his home and once more wandered idly through the streets. Moment by moment desperation bubbled to a near explosive pitch beneath the drab exterior of the anguished little man.

Deep in a hidden corner of his brain a voice was persisting maddeningly, mockingly, "You're going crazy, Mr. Beem. That's what's wrong, Mr. Beem. You're going crazy."

Mr. Beem stood stock still in the middle of the sidewalk, bracing himself against the thought. "I'm not," he declared. "I'm not going crazy." He looked up and down the sidewalk but there was no one to contradict this statement. Brushing away a sudden tear, Mr. Beem set off in the direction of the train station....

* * * *

Two hours later a distraught Mr. Beem, dressed drably in gray, stood nervously before a frosted door on the twelfth floor of a downtown office building. The inscription on the frosted glass read, "Dr. Clarence Q. Zale, Psychiatrist."

The plain-faced little fellow coughed nervously, threw back his sloping shoulders, took a deep breath, and entered the office.

He found himself standing in a sort of tiny reception room. Beyond it was another frosted glass door, bearing the simple inscription, "Dr. Zale."

The second frosted door opened and a tall, bearded, impressive looking man of about fifty stepped into the reception room to face Mr. Beem. He smoothed the lapels of his Prince Albert coat professionally, gave his ordinary visitor a casual glance, and spoke.

"I am Dr. Zale. Did you wish to see me?"

"Yes," said Mr. Beem, "I wanted to see you. I think I am losing my mind!"

"Tsk!" said Dr. Zale abstractedly, "how unfortunate. Step into my office, please."

It was perhaps fifteen minutes later when Mr. Beem concluded the story of his life, the record of the happenings of the morning.

Dr. Zale rose from his desk. "This," he pronounced, "is incredible."

Mr. Beem merely looked at the psychiatrist with a sort of dog-like trust and hope.

"If everything you tell me is true," Dr. Zale continued, "you are the most unique psychological case I have ever encountered. You, Mr. Leem, are the perfect example of the *Negative Personality!*"

Mr. Beem was frightened. "*The Negative Personality?*"

"Exactly. Personality, Mr. Weem, is in reality a sort of vibrant electric aura[2] that surrounds the individual. If the vibrancy of the aura is strong, then the individual has what is known as a *Positive Personality*. If the vibrancy is weak, then the individual has a *Negative Personality*."

The psychiatrist paused to give Mr. Beem time to absorb this, then continued. "From what you have told me of your life, Mr. Deem, you have always had an unusually weak personality wave. People have always had a difficult time remembering you, because of this. Lately, your positive vibrancy charge has been growing weaker and weaker."

Dr. Zale's pause, this time, was for the sake of drama. "Today, Mr. Ream, you stopped emanating your positive personality aura entirely, and instead began exuding negative personality currents!"

The horror stricken Mr. Beem was not too clear on the meaning of the psychiatrist's statement, but, the tone of the man's voice was enough to turn him deathly pale. "No," gasped the unoriginal Mr. Beem.

"Yes," declared Dr. Zale. "With the result that the world has completely forgotten you. As far as people who have met you before are concerned, you've never existed! You make an instant negative impression of great force!"

Mr. Beem sat limply on his straight chair, clasping and unclasping his hands in an agony of despair. There was mute appeal in his drab watery eyes as he fixed them on the psychiatrist.

"But don't fear for your identity, Mr. Jeem," Dr. Zale was saying. "From this moment on you will go down in history. You are the greatest medical phenomenon of all time!" The doctor's voice was working up to a fever pitch of excitement. His eyes gleamed.

"Stay right where you are," said Dr. Zale. "Don't move an inch. I'm going down the hall to call in four other psychiatrists in the building. They must see you, Mr. Queem." He dashed to the door, stopped, then returned to Mr. Beem's chair. "Stay right where you are," he directed again, patting

---

2   Many psychologists hold that personality powers of otherwise unprepossessing people are due to some indefinable magnetism, but there is no actual proof as yet that this is a fact. However there is no proof against it either.—Editor]

the little man on the shoulder. "Don't move out of this office. I'll be back with the others in an instant!"

Mr. Beem sank obediently into the chair.

Dr. Zale practically flew out of his office and into the long corridor. His steps rang along the marble floor for perhaps ten yards. Then they faltered, stopped abruptly.

They sounded again, returning slowly. The psychiatrist walked slowly into the office, crossed to the coat rack and took his hat and coat down. He donned them, muttering to himself, paid no attention to Mr. Beem, and walked out once more.

Puzzled, Mr. Beem stared after him, then sank back in his chair to wait. He waited a long time, fidgeting nervously. Once or twice he rose to his feet and began to walk up and down, then timidly returned to his chair.

But Dr. Zale did not return.

At length Mr. Beem realized the truth. He had been forgotten once more!

* * * *

As Mr. Beem sorrowfully departed from the psychiatrist's office, he choked back the lump that rose in his scrawny throat. Why, he wondered with a sort of anguished longing, couldn't he have been an amnesia victim instead of a *Negative Personality*—and a *Perfect* one at that? Then, instead of the world forgetting him, he could have forgotten the world.

But as the little man stepped out into the street once more he knew in his very ordinary heart that this would be slight consolation.

It was dinnertime and looking wistfully into the windows of the houses he passed, Mr. Beem thought poignantly of his own little green shuttered abode, and of the supper that Martha was eating. The thought of his wife, who no longer realized she had a husband, was more than Mr. Beem could stand. So he pushed it aside with desperate concentration on more bitter matters. There was the river, for example. It was only a scant few blocks away. It would be a short walk. The bridge rail wasn't high—

Mr. Beem shuddered at the thought. He wasn't a coward. But deliberate suicide was too much like the last resort of a quitter, a beaten man.

"I'm not a quitter. I'm not beaten," Mr. Beem told himself savagely. But even as he did so, the pathetic futility of his situation flooded back on him. What was there to do? Where was there to go?

The world had no place for a man it had forgotten.

Mr. Beem dug his hands into his gray coat pockets and trudged onward. There was suddenly something determined, something fiercely combative in his chest. It was something he couldn't quite put into words. He merely knew that somehow, some way, he was going to make the world conscious of his identity. And not just as a man, but as a great man, an everlasting figure in the eyes of posterity.

Living or dying, both were unimportant in the face of this new determination that burned in the breast of the negative Mr. Beem. It no longer mattered to him what happened to the physical Mr. Beem, just so long as the immortal Lucius Beem, Hero, carried on in his wake.

"And there will be an immortal Beem!" the drab little man said aloud. Even as he spoke, a thought which had been hammering at the door of his subconscious for the past few minutes suddenly became crystal clear.

The news item of the morning. The one he had read to the passenger beside him. The piece about the scientist who sought a human guinea pig for his radium experiments! Surely this was Fortune smiling on Mr. Beem. Here was the chance he wanted, the opportunity to impress Lucius Beem upon the world in such a fashion that he would be remembered as long as time existed.

He would be the man of the hour. His name would forever be imprinted on the ledgers of science and progress! Then he would have identity. Being!

Tiny icicles of excitement ran up and down the little man's spine as he stood there under a streetlight, contemplating on the magnitude of such an act. Then a swift unpleasant thought jarred him from the rosy world he'd entered. Supposing the scientist had already gotten a subject?

No, it couldn't be. Fate couldn't play such a monstrous trick on Mr. Beem! But time was essential. One never could tell when someone else might decide to offer himself for the experiment.

* * * *

There was a newsstand at the corner, and Mr. Beem drew up panting before it a moment later. Then, stepping under a street lamp, the little man paged frantically through the newspaper, searching for the item concerning the scientist's radium experiment. At last, he found it on the second page, buried in a small column on the bottom. It was a condensation of the morning item, merely stating that Professor Snell was still unable to find a volunteer for his experiment.

Clutching the newspaper in one hand, Mr. Beem wildly signaled a cab with the other. As the taxi drew up before him, Mr. Beem glanced hastily at the address of Professor Snell as the paper gave it.

"Forty-nine, sixty-six Vine Street," he blurted to the driver, "and hurry!"

The cabby slammed the door behind his passenger and threw the hack into gear. Then they were shooting down the illuminated boulevards. It was fifteen minutes later when, with a screech of brakes, the taxi drew up before the address Mr. Beem had given the driver. The cabby didn't have a chance to open the door for his passenger, for Mr. Beem was out of the car like a shot, digging in his pocket for his wallet.

"What do I owe you?" he said breathlessly.

A frown of perplexity creased the cabby's brow. Swiftly he wheeled about to glance in the back seat. Then, jaw hanging open, he looked at Mr. Beem.

"Well," snapped the little man impatiently, "what do I owe you?"

"Look," the cabby blurted hoarsely, "is this a joke or sump'in?" Mr. Beem started to reply, but the driver continued. "Are youse the guy I picked up, or am I gain' nuts? I never seen youse before in all my life. Don't remember what the guy I picked up looked like, but I coltenly ain't never seen' youse before!"

Mr. Beem could waste no more precious moments. He shoved a bill into the bewildered driver's paw, and ran up the steps of the home of Professor Snell.

A short, plump, energetic little man admitted Mr. Beem to the house. His bright, button eyes swept in every drab feature of the breathless visitor, then he spoke. "I am Professor Snell. Is there something I can do for you?"

"Professor," panted Mr. Beem, "I read about your need in the papers."

"Ah, yes," the plump scientist agreed sadly. "At the climax of my investigations into radium possibilities, I can find no volunteer to serve as final proof of my conclusions."

Mr. Beem took a deep breath. "Professor Snell! I am your man!"

A light flashed into the scientist's eyes. But as he spoke his voice was careful, calm. "Do you understand what it implies, this experiment in radium?" He went on before Mr. Beem could interrupt. "You might come out of it all unscathed. Then again—" he shrugged expressively—" you might never come out of it."

Mr. Beem heard his own voice answering hoarsely. "I understand that part of it. But it makes no difference to me. All I care for is my duty to posterity, and the fact that my slight contribution shall be remembered."

The Professor crossed to Mr. Beem, took his hand. "You are a brave man. No matter what comes of this, your part will always be remembered, never fear. I shall see to that."

There was mistiness in the drab little chap's eyes as he gripped the scientist's hand in his own. At last. Here was positive assurance that Mr. Beem would return to the minds of the world never to leave again!

"We might as well start immediately," he said huskily.

Professor Snell was suddenly the man of science. "Good. I'm glad you prefer it that way." He reached for a tablet of paper on the table beside them. "Please," he said, handing the tablet to Mr. Beem, "write your name there. And the names of people whom I can notify…" He broke off significantly.

"There are no other names besides my own," said Mr. Beem. Then, glowing with a deep, burning pride, he scrawled his signature on the pad....

* * * *

They were in the laboratory of Professor Snell. Everything surrounding Mr. Beem was white and efficiently scientific. The plump little professor was busily arranging various instruments about a large, coffin-like box. Mr. Beem was gazing at the box when Snell explained. "You will be sealed into that radium cask," he declared. "Your stay inside the cask depends on split-second timing. That clock," he pointed to a delicate instrument beside the box, "Is set going the moment the cask is sealed. From it I can tell when the precise number of hours and seconds has arrived for you to be taken forth again."

Minutes later Mr. Beem, lying on his back in the radium casket, heard the terse "Luck" spoken by the professor, the lid sliding across the top of the casket. Then darkness surrounded him...

"Three hours and thirty-seven seconds should be correct," muttered Professor Snell, setting the time gadget on the side of the cask. There was a vibrant excitement in his voice. He looked for a moment at the cask, then turned and stepped swiftly out of the room. There were some telephone calls to be made to his associates.

* * * *

Early the following morning, as Professor Snell tinkered with his radium cask, vaguely wishing that he could find a volunteer for his experiment, his sharp eyes noted the thin film of dust that lay inside the casket. "Hmmm," murmured the scientist. "I wonder how that got there?"

Mr. Beem had been forgotten again.

TRAPPED ON TITAN

David Wright O'Brien's 'Trapped on Titan' first appeared the June 1940 issue of Amazing Stories Magazine. This action adventure takes place on the largest moon in the Saturn planetary system, Titan, deserted by Earthmen for the past five centuries and declared off-limits. Yet two pilots are forced to land there in their crippled spaceship and encounter a lovely woman, both fascinating and terrifying. Where did she come from? How has she survived the extremely hostile natives? A straight-forward space yarn in which O'Brien can be seen honing his craft of storytelling, albeit within the narrow constraints set out by the magazine editor that he is writing for.

"Hello...Hello, Earth...Hello...Calling wave nine, Space Ship Corporation...Wave nine...Calling Space Ship Corporation. Standing by for radiophone from Space Ship Corporation...Wave nine...Come in, Earth."

Chet Chadwick pushed a lank strand of black hair from his forehead and snapped on the radiophone receptor button beside his seat in the control room of the gigantic space liner. For a moment he shifted his lanky frame to face his co-pilot, chubby Monk Sands. "Wonder what in hell they want?"

Sands' round pleasant features were noncommittal, and he shrugged his wide plump shoulders in bewilderment. "Dunno. Mebbe the Chief wants to check on us, huh?"

In the next instant the radiophone receptor crackled faintly, and after a blurred vibration hum a voice flooded into the control room. At the sound of the first several words, both pilots sat bolt upright. The voice was low, sweet, and feminine.

"Hello, Chet," said the feminine voice. "How are you darling? And how is dear Monk?"

Chet Chadwick sucked in his breath sharply, ignoring the sharp glance that Monk Sands suddenly turned on him. The voice went on.

"I'll bet you two big Test Pilots are surprised to hear from me, darlings," the voice cooed. "But I just couldn't wait three more days until you returned to Earth, Chet—and you too, Monk. I just couldn't wait to see you both, so I asked your boss to let me talk to you from the company control rooms.

"Just in case you haven't guessed who this is, Chet—and Monk, I won't make you worry. It's Olga, darlings. Do hurry back from your nasty test trials in that nasty old space liner, Chet darling. And you, too, Monk. See you in three days, dears."

Crackling came back to the radiophone receptor, the hum grew once more, and the light above the board indicated that the conversation was concluded. Chet Chadwick leaned over and snapped off the button, still keeping his eyes averted from those of his copilot.

"So!" Monk Sands' voice broke the ominous silence. "So!"

"Now, Monk," Chadwick began, repressing a smile.

"Don't now-Monk me," his companion bellowed as his usually bland face took on a slow tinge of purple. "So it's Chet and Monk, eh? Since when have you been beating my time with Olga, you louse?"

Chadwick struggled to assume an air of injured innocence. He raised his hands from the controls of the space liner in an expressive gesture. "Monk," his voice was reproachful, "do you think I'd double-cross a pal?"

The rotund little Test Pilot's voice shook with rage and sarcasm as he replied. "Oh no, you skunk, you'd never double-cross a pal. You've never kept your paws off my women in all the time I've had the misfortune to know you. There was Winnie in Singapore, Carol on Venus, Marge on Ceres, Helen on Jupiter—," his voice broke off disgustedly. Then: "So many more that I can't remember them all. And now, damn your long hide, I find out you've been trying to make a name for yourself with Olga!"

Chadwick kept his face straight, but his gray eyes twinkled as he spoke. "Now Monk, you know that there isn't anything between Olga and I. The only reason she pays any attention to me is because I'm your buddy. It's purely platonic, I swear!"

"Platonic! Yah, just like Romeo and Juliet were platonic!"

"Now Monk. This isn't any time for a misunderstanding. We can't argue about women. We've got to put this baby into a power drop in another moment. Hell, if we don't finish these tests, we'll never get this liner back to Earth in three days."

"You're changing the subject," Sands said suspiciously.

"We can talk it over when we get our tests done," Chadwick replied. Then, as if the matter were closed until future notice, he began to check his instrument panel. Sands watched him wordlessly, seething in rage and indignation.

"Check the percussion panel," Chadwick instructed his infuriated companion. Sands, muttering sullenly to himself, began to make a systematic check of the gauges before him. After a moment he looked up. "All set!"

Chadwick finished his own readings, nodding as he lifted his head. "Good enough, dearie. Hang on tight. We're going to give this ship plenty of hell in a minute."

* * * *

Cutting the rockets to half-percussion drive, Chadwick gave the huge space liner its head, and in the space of several swift seconds the nose of the ship dropped with sickening suddenness. At that moment, as the enormous experimental liner slid into a power drop through space, Chadwick spoke one taunting sentence to his copilot.

"Olga's a good kid," he said, "but I never could stand her lipstick!" Then he threw open the percussion throttle, driving the liner into a steep dive.

As the rockets banged to an explosive crescendo, so did Monk Sands.

His mouth fell open and his hands, letting free of the dual controls, worked convulsively. He was literally sputtering with outraged indignation. Chet Chadwick had only time to shout, "Dammit, you goof, get your paws back on those controls!"

But even as the words left Chadwick's mouth, he knew it was too late. The pull of the dive on the controls was too much for one pilot to guide. He felt the force of the recoil tear them from his hands. Even above the noise of the rockets, both pilots heard the sound of the magnetic direction gear snapping, whipping off into space, leaving the liner rudderless.

Instantly Chadwick cut off the percussion throttle and, with the aid of his co-pilot, pulled the nose of the gigantic liner to an even keel once more. Out of control, the liner was drifting listlessly in space.

"Now you've done it!" Chadwick's voice was a bark.

"Me?" Sands' tone was almost squeaky in its rising ire. "Me?"

"Who in hell but you?" Chadwick demanded. "Couldn't even keep your paws on the controls long enough to complete a test. I oughta—" he broke off significantly.

Sands was on his feet instantly, fists balled, advancing toward his co-pilot. "Go ahead. Finish your sentence. You oughta what?"

Chadwick uncoiled his lanky frame from his seat and faced Sands.

"Oughta bust you on the button!" Chadwick said.

"Why, you elongated, woman-stealing skunk! Just try it, that's all I'd like. Just try it!"

Suddenly Chadwick relaxed. "This is a fine howdoyuhdo. Here we are fighting over a woman while we drift about in a crippled ship!"

Sands, frowning, turned and walked to the porthole at the left of the control room. "Cripes," he said looking out at the blackness surrounding the liner. "I'd forgotten. What in hell are we gonna do?"

"We'll have to make repairs. That much is certain. We can't maneuver this baby back to Earth without a magnetic direction gear. It's also certain that we can't fix it while we're dangling here in space," Chadwick answered.

"Mebbe we ought to find out where we are?" Sands decided.

"Check on the radio compass," his companion instructed. "We're only a day out of Saturn's range. We must be somewhere above one of her moons."

Monk Sands grunted reply as he bent above the compass chart. His curly blond head moved up and down several times as he took "shootings" of their position. At last he raised his head and faced Chadwick.

"We're lucky," he said tersely, "and then again we're not."

"What do you mean?"

"Since we can only move up or down, it's a damned lucky thing that we're over a planet. But since that planet happened to be one of the zoned areas, we're not so lucky."

Chadwick whistled. The "zoned areas" were those planets marked off by Earth Council as uninhabitable and worthless for any one of a number of reasons. They lay outside the interplanetary transportation lanes and were never troubled by interplanetary contact. It was a cinch that it would be next to impossible to make any repairs on a zoned planet.

"What's the name of this blob in the cosmos that we're hanging over?" Chadwick asked.

"Titan," Sands replied. Then he picked up an interplanetary pilot guide, thumbing through it. "To give it the way the book does," he announced. "Titan zoned area, one of the satellites of Saturn. Climatically uninhabitable, this world was deserted in 2021 when its radium deposits were exhausted."

The chubby pilot closed the book and looked at his companion.

"Hell," Chadwick replied sourly. "Titan hasn't seen a human being in five hundred years. How the devil are we ever going to make our repairs in a place like that?"

"We can't be choosy," Sands replied. "So down we go."

Chadwick took his place before the controls once more. As he did so, he spoke. "Mebbe we'd better notify Earth and have them send someone out to pick us up."

Monk Sands looked at him quizzically. "And have those boobs back at the plant find out what happened?" There was reproach in his voice.

"Yeah," Chadwick agreed. "I didn't think of that. I guess we'd better not. We can make the repairs ourselves." He paused, as though searching for a reason stronger than mere pride. "Besides," he added. "It would take them damn near three days to get here."

As the pair concentrated their silent attention on getting the huge space liner safely down to the planet that lay somewhere below them, both were thinking one thing, the team of Chadwick and

Sands had a long reputation to live up to—and they'd be damned if they'd fold up on this job....

* * * *

Twelve almost wordless hours later—during which time there had been no mention of Olgas in particular and women in general—Chet Chadwick looked up from his control panel.

"There she is," he said briefly. "Titan!"

Monk Sands was silent as he looked down at the rapidly approaching satellite, but he nodded his head in reply.

Twenty minutes later, both pilots watched the rough terrain rushing up at them, and braced themselves for the necessarily bumpy landing that was to come. Handling the controls was delicate for some moments, but five minutes later Chet Chadwick rose from his seat and stepped to the side portholes of the space liner.

The huge craft had been eased down in the middle of what seemed to be a vast pampas, broken only by jutting crags of lunar rock formation. To every side seemed to stretch waste and desolation.

"No wonder they abandoned the place, once the radium sources had been sapped," Sands remarked.

Silently, then, the pair walked over to the lockers in the compartment behind the control room. There they began to laboriously clothe themselves in space suits. They were dressed and standing before the compression door when Chadwick signalled Sands to tune in his receptor box for conversation.

"One of us better wait inside here, while the other takes a look around," Chadwick said from inside his glass helmet.

Sands nodded, stepping toward the door, but Chadwick's tall form blocked his way. "You wait. I'll go outside," he commanded. Sands shrugged and watched his companion press the compression door release and disappear out onto the plains of Titan. Then he walked over to the control panels and sat down to wait Chadwick's return.

Twenty minutes later, Monk Sands was growing impatient. Sweat was rolling down his face from the heat of the cabin and he rose to peer out of the porthole in an effort to see Chadwick.

But the other was not in sight.

Ten minutes more passed, and Monk Sands was feeling a bit of worry as well as impatience. He rose, cursing, and walked over to the compression door, pressing the release button. An instant later he stepped out onto the rocky terrain.

* * * *

About him stretched the same dull gray reaches of crags and pampas that he had glimpsed from inside the ship. But as he looked to left and right, he was still unable to catch sight of Chadwick. He looked back at the long, bullet-like hulk of the space liner. Perhaps Chet was over on the other side. Laboriously, Sands began to trudge around the nose of the ship. He had rounded the front and was able to glimpse the territory on the other side of the large liner when he gasped in astonishment, stopping dead in his tracks. At the tail of the liner, coming toward him, was Chadwick's lanky form. But that wasn't what made Monk Sands gape unbelievingly. Chet was walking beside another space clad figure—and through the glass helmet of the other's suit, Monk recognized the features of an astonishingly pretty young woman!

"Well I'll be a blank-blink-blank," Monk muttered. "That roving Casanova can find a woman even on an uninhabited planet!" Then his eyes widened in appreciation. "And what a looker! How in hell did that doll ever get on this godforsaken spot?"

Sands had forgotten that Chet was now within range of his receptor-transmitter apparatus, and was startled to hear his fellow pilot's reply. "What do you think of this baby?" Chadwick's excited voice came to him.

Chadwick and the strange girl were within ten yards of Sands, now. "Where did you find her?" the chubby co-pilot asked.

"Lord knows," Chadwick replied. "She came out from behind one of those crags after I left the ship." He pointed to the garb of the girl. "What do you think of that space suit?"

Sands frowned. He hadn't noticed it until now, but the girl was wearing a space suit that had been outmoded for centuries. No wonder the girl was silent. She didn't even have communication gear.

Then the two men and the girl were together, and Monk took a swift appraisal of the strange young lady. His first guess, as to her prettiness, had been wrong. She wasn't pretty. She was beautiful, excruciatingly beautiful!

Red half-parted lips above a delicately molded chin, tilted nose, level gray eyes, and a tumbled halo of lustrous raven hair gave ample testimony that the body within the cumbersome space suit was also lovely.

For fully a minute, Monk gaped stupidly at the incredible beauty of the girl, then he turned to Chadwick.

"What, that is, how—I thought—"

"That Titan was uninhabited," Chadwick finished for him. "Yeah, so did I. But this cutie here seems to disprove it."

The girl was watching both Sands and Chadwick closely, as if in an effort to follow their conversation by the movements of their lips. Then Chadwick had a possessive arm around her waist and began to move toward the nose of the space liner. Sands was at the side of his co-pilot and the girl instantly.

"What's the pitch, Chet?" the rotund little pilot asked.

"Want to get her inside the cabin of the ship," Chadwick explained. "Then she can remove her space helmet and we can communicate with her."

"If," Sands interposed, "she speaks a language we can understand."

"That won't make a great deal of difference," Chadwick answered, and Sands saw him grin beneath his glass helmet.

"Oh," the little pilot put a fine edge of sarcasm into his tone, "so it's going to be Chet Chadwick, Interplanetary Romeo all over again, eh?"

"Stick to Olga," his companion snapped. "You were all hot and hiccuppy about her a little while ago."

* * * *

The trio was just rounding the nose of the ship when it happened. Sands heard Chadwick curse in wild surprise, and at the same instant felt a whip-like tentacle wrap around his waist, lifting him high into the air. He threshed his arms wildly about in a desperate effort to free himself.

The tentacle tightened, yet held him gently. Sands stopped kicking and turned his head—to meet the wild stare of Chadwick who was held in exactly the same position by another tentacle.

Then his eyes met the vapid gaze of two flat, enormously large eyes, peering out from the round blue skull of an incredible monster!

Sands tried to shout, and suddenly realized the uselessness of such an action. He heard Chadwick spluttering helplessly from his dangling perch in the other tentacle of the creature. Something prompted him to look down at the ground, and to his amazement he saw the girl, unmolested and unperturbed, staring calmly at the scene!

Then, gently, Sands felt the tentacle lowering him to the ground once more, saw Chadwick also being deposited back on his feet. Both of them wheeled instantly, the moment they felt their feet touching ground, and faced the towering creature.

"Leaping meteorites!" Sands blurted. "And we thought Titan was uninhabited. What sort of a thing is this?"

"Not a very lovely looking specimen, whatever he is," Chadwick said hoarsely. "Where did he come from so fast?" I didn't see him around when I ran into the girl."

At mention of the girl, Sands wheeled to face her. Her face still wore the same look of solemn appraisal.

Bewilderedly, he turned again to face the tentacled monster. The creature, Sands could see more clearly now, was fully thirteen feet tall, with grotesque, spindly legs that accounted for three-fourths of its incredible height. Its thin torso was wasp-waisted, and of a mottled blue-green coloring. The tentacles, he saw, emerged from elbows on either arm, and were purple colored and the length of a man's body. Each arm, if they could be called arms, possessed two of these tentacles.

Instinctively, Monk Sands and Chet Chadwick moved closer together, as though their nearness might ward off any further designs of the towering monster. Sweat was rolling profusely down Monk's round face, and looking at Chadwick he saw that the other was swallowing slowly.

Then the girl stepped before them, placing her hands on the arm of each, moving them forward toward the Titanian. Chadwick and Sands tore free from her grasp at the same moment.

"Lovely girl friends, you pick," Sands grated, "she wants to feed us to her pet."

Suddenly the huge monster bent slightly, and in a swift motion threw his tentacles around the pair once more. The girl was gazing at them solemnly still, but was pointing toward a crag of lunar formation in the distance.

"She likes our company," Chadwick said unsmilingly, "and seems to think that we'd better go in that direction if we know what's good for little boys."

Sands looked swiftly upward again, met the flat emotionless eyes of the Titanian. "I think we'd better get moving, then. Before Oscar, here, gets any more ideas."

Then, with the girl leading the way, and the Titanian bringing up the rear, the strange procession began to move off across the rocky terrain.

They were within a hundred yards of the lunar rock formation that the girl had indicated when she turned, beckoning them to move ahead of her. Sands wasn't certain, but he thought, as they drew closer to the gigantic crag, that he could see a stirring behind it.

"There seems to be something moving around behind that knoll," he said to Chadwick.

"Probably pixies," his companion replied sardonically.

A split-second later, Monk's suspicions were confirmed, for moving with awkward swiftness, three Titanians, identical to their captor in the rear, stepped forth from behind the crag and advanced toward them!

"A welcoming committee from the Chamber of Commerce," Monk heard Chadwick mutter, without a trace of humor in his voice. And as his companion spoke, Sands realized that the lanky pilot was just as apprehensive as himself, but was trying to keep his own and Monk's courage alive.

The Titanians were on them in the next moment, forming a sort of guard around the pair as they approached the huge crag. "Mebbe," Sands said hoarsely, "we can make a break for it?"

Chadwick's voice was sharp, but calming. "Take it easy, Monk. There's nothing we can do until we get the wind of this thing."

As they rounded the crag the little party stopped abruptly, Sands and Chadwick gasping in astonishment at the same moment. The crag was nothing more than a hollowed shaft, stone on one side, and structural chrome on the other. It was the worked-out pit of a very old radium mine.

* * * *

For a moment the grotesque Titanians milled about uncertainly. The two earthmen took advantage of this to survey their surroundings. The shaft was bored into the rock formation of the crag on a steadily declining angle, but the most astonishing feature of it was its proportions. One of the Titanians happened to be standing at the entrance to the pit, and comparative measurements showed that it was wide and high enough to enable the creature to move about comfortably at its mouth.

"These are the ancient radium mines of 2000," Chadwick almost whispered, "but they've been enlarged all out of proportion to fit the bodies of these tower creatures."

"But—," Sands words were cut off sharply, for in that instant he felt the tentacles of one of the Titanians wrap about his waist, saw another seize Chadwick—and then the two earthmen were carried bodily down the steep incline, into the darkness of the shaft!

Everything was blackness in another moment. "Chet," Sands heard himself shouting, "are you all right?" He could still hear the heavy breathing of his companion coming through his receptor.

"Yeah, fella. I'm okay," Chadwick's reply was reassuring. "How about you? What kind of a ride are you getting?"

Under any other circumstances the chubby little pilot would have laughed aloud at the bland unconcern in his lanky pal's voice. As it was, however, he gained relief and a sense of strengthened courage from the other's reply.

"I'm still in circulation," he said, trying to keep his voice as unconcerned as Chadwick's. Then further conversation became impossible as the journey grew rougher. It seemed as though every step taken by the Titanian who held him was getting more and more awkward. Evidently the footing on the shaft was becoming increasingly difficult.

The tentacles still held him with firm but unyielding gentleness, but as the creature lurched awkwardly along through the darkness, the rocking motion smashed Monk's head against the thick glass of his space helmet several times.

He could hear a muttered curse from Chadwick, and guessed that the other was finding the same difficulty. Then another jarring step sent his head smashing into the side of the helmet for the third time. It was a harder blow than any of the others, and left him dizzy, sick, nauseated. Blood trickled from the corner of his mouth and he licked it back with his tongue.

There wasn't the faintest glimmer of light anywhere in the shaft, and Sands wondered about the large circular eyes of the monsters, wondered if perhaps they could see in the blackness of the old mine.

Suddenly, out of his receptor apparatus, he heard the sound of a sharp cry from Chadwick, followed by a noise like a long sigh.

"Chet," Monk shouted quickly. "Chet, are you okay?"

There was no answer, merely the faint sound of subdued breathing. "Chet," Sands shouted again. "What's happened? Can't you hear me?"

Monk Sand's head smashed against the glass plate of his helmet for the fourth time....

* * * *

"Monk," a voice was crying, "Monk! Snap out of it!"

Sands opened his eyes slowly, shut them again for an instant to accustom himself to the blinding glare of his surroundings. He moved his hand to shield his eyes and became aware that he was no longer clad in his space suit. Monk opened his eyes once more to become fully cognizant of his surroundings for the first time.

Chadwick was bending over him, had been the one who shook him into consciousness. He noticed that Chet, too, was no longer wearing space gear.

A second glance told him that he was lying on damp stone m the center of an incredibly large cavern of some sort. The ceiling of the place, far above them, was marked by jagged icicle-like formations of rock that hung pendant-fashion downward.

The cavern itself was almost a mile in circumference, entirely clear of any obstructions. At one end of it, much to Monk's astonishment, was a long elevated rock platform on which were assembled some fifty human beings, laboriously swinging large sledge hammers on a huge sheet of metal that moved along before them!

Chadwick noticed Sand's expression.

"Yeah, Monk," he said softly, "it's not a dream. Those are earthmen. Don't ask me how they got here!" Chadwick pointed his finger at the opposite end of the cavern. "Those human beings are slaves to the Titanians!"

Monk saw some twenty of the grotesque, tentacled creatures moving about a raised dais at the other end of the enormous natural room. On the dais, squatting ludicrously and Buddha-like on an elevated throne, was another of the Titanians—his feelers holding a sort of double-knobbed sceptre!

"The King, or Boss, or High-Mucky-Muck, ruler of this joint!" Chadwick said.

And then, while his rotund companion listened with growing incredulity, Chet Chadwick related the events that occurred after he regained consciousness. He had, Chadwick said, been jolted into insensibility when his head smashed into the side of the turret-like space helmet. That was just before Monk received a similar blow and was knocked out. Later, Chadwick woke in in the cavern, beside Sands. The girl that they had first encountered was standing above him, no longer dressed in the cumbersome and antiquated space suit in which they had first seen her.

"My Lord, Monk," Chet went on explosively, "you've never seen such a woman! Glorious!"

"She was a knockout, even in the space suit," Sands observed dryly. Chadwick resumed his narration. The girl had been able to speak English, had told him that she and the other earth people in the cave were enslaved by the spindle-legged Titanians.

"But where are they from, the girl and the earth people?" Sands demanded excitedly. "Why did they come to Titan when they know it's been sectored off by Earth Council for the last five centuries?"

"Don't know," Chadwick replied. "She didn't get a chance to tell me that. They—the Titanians took her off before she had a chance to explain. She did say, however, that she was forced to remain calm, placid, when we were seized by the strange creatures."

"Yah," said Sands accusingly, "I was coming to that. Why did she seem to act like she was watching nothing at all when Oscar sneaked upon us?"

"She says she had to; that we'd have been snuffed out if we'd been warned and tried to resist!"

Sands' cherubic features wrinkled in perplexity. "What does it all add up to? Where'd they take the girl?"

"I didn't see that," Chadwick continued, "because one of them stalked over to me, whipped me up in his tentacles and carried me over to the Big Shot—the lad over there on the dais, with the sceptre in his hand." Chadwick paused for breath, wiping perspiration from his stubbled jaw.

"Get on with it," Sands snapped impatiently.

"Well, the Big-Shot held that damned sceptre over me—I was still dangling in the air, held by those tentacles—and moved it back and forth across my head. I couldn't get a good glance at it, for I'd slipped my helmet back on after they'd taken the girl away, but it seemed to be a phosphorous sort of wand, made out of some blue metal.

"The thing crackled with electrical vibrations, and I felt the damndest buzzing sensation in my head. Then, after about two minutes of this, the Big-Shot seemed satisfied, and ordered me to be taken back. I watched while they did the same thing to you. You were still unconscious at the time. Then they brought you back."

"Which—?" said Monk.

"—Brings us up to date. They took our space suits away and I brought you around less than five minutes after that happened." Chadwick concluded.

"It sounds like something out of a twentieth century nursery rhyme," said Sands. "Now what are we going to do about it?"

* * * *

Chadwick turned his lean profile toward the other end of the huge cavern. His eyes narrowed as he gazed at the rock formation on which the earthmen were working ceaselessly with their great sledges. It was difficult, from where the two pilots were, to make out anything but general appearances of the toiling earthmen. The distance was too great for facial characteristics to be visible.

"Did the girl tell you how many earthmen the Titanians had in captivity?" Sands asked, noticing the object of his pal's attention.

"I'm not sure, but I think that those lads swinging the hammers up there, and the girl herself, are the only people of our race, besides ourselves, on this miserable planet."

Suddenly Chadwick's face tensed. He grabbed his co-pilot by the arm. "Listen, it just occurred to me. One girl and close to fifty men! Doesn't that sound odd?"

Monk frowned. "You don't know that she's the only earth woman held captive here."

Chadwick became impatient. "Do you think those people up there, swinging those big hammers, are women?" he replied sarcastically.

Monk whistled. "Mebbe you're right. It does seem damned odd!"

"And another thing," Chadwick was continuing with tense excitement, "I'm trying to remember a remark she made just before the Titanians took her away." He paused, knitting his brows in fierce concentration. "I was still groggy for the better part of the few moments speech I had with her.

But I think—mind you I'm not sure—she made some remark about brains. Something about watching the 'sapper'!"

"'Sapper'," Monk replied, "What in the name of everything unholy is a 'sapper'?"

Chadwick never had a chance to reply, for at that moment, apparently at a command from the grotesque Titanian on the dais, two of the spindle-legged creatures advanced stolidly across the cavern floor toward them.

"Here they come. Hang on to your hat!" Monk shouted, rising to his feet. Chadwick was instantly beside him, and the two watched the Titanians moving swiftly down on them.

"Take it easy, Monk," Chadwick said, hitching his belt in a gesture characteristic of the lanky test pilot when in trouble. "They haven't actually harmed us as yet, and maybe they don't intend to."

"Yah," Monk said from the side of his mouth, eyes fixed on the advancing monsters. "Yah, mebbe they don't. But I don't think that's love gleaming out of their popeyes!"

Then the nightmarish creatures were towering above them, their tentacle arms weaving back and forth, wide flat eyes expressionless.

"What I wouldn't do for a ray gun at this minute!" grated Sands.

"I told you to take it easy," Chadwick warned. "Any protection we could use is back in the spaceship. Don't forget it!"

The tentacles were whipping menacingly about the pair, as if in an effort to herd them in a certain direction.

The pair turned and began a rapid march across the damp stone floor of the cavern, drawing closer and closer to the sledge-swinging toilers. The Titanians kept an insistent pressure behind them.

Fifty yards from the long stone platform on which the earthmen were toiling, Chadwick halted abruptly, grabbing his companion's arm.

"Monk!" His voice was hoarse. "Monk, for God's sake, look!"

Chadwick pointed at the group on the stone platform.

The bodily contours of the men on the platform were human, but their actual appearance was ape-like, hairy, almost aboriginal! They paused now in their labor. It was clear that they had seen the two new arrivals, for eyes gleamed sharply from beneath incredibly shaggy eyebrows, and thick lips drew back from fang-like teeth as they conversed among one another excitedly.

Their gibberish, which carried across the intervening distance to the horrified pair, was a weird combination of snarls and mangled English!

Bands of iron, linked by a long chain, were fastened around the necks and legs of each of the half-humans on the platform!

* * * *

At that moment the Titanians, evidently enraged at the delay, swept their whip-like arms around the two, and carried them the remaining distance.

Bedlam broke loose among the toilers as Sands and Chadwick sprawled on the stone ledge at their feet. For an instant the huge cavern was ominously silent. Then the ape-like men broke forth in a frenzied commotion of half-howls and shouts.

There was a sudden flurry at the other end of the vast cave. Eight or ten Titanians moved with incredible speed across the damp floor. In what seemed less than seconds, they were grouped along the platform, their tentacles lashing out on the backs of the shackled workers.

Gentleness was gone from the touch of those odd appendages. They flailed mercilessly down upon the unprotected hides of the slaves. A pungent acrid odor filled the air.

Monk and Chet were lying face downward on the ledge between the two groups—Titanians and half-humans.

"That smell!" Chet gasped. "It's burning flesh!"

Monk was staring in fascination at the spindle-legged monsters. "Their tentacles are red-hot whips," he said hoarsely. "Those damned monsters have some electrical force in their bodies. Look at the sparks flying from them!"

Chadwick, who had been giving his attention to the plight of the sledge slaves, turned his head for an instant to see their tormentors.

What Sands had shouted was true. Electrical sparks were literally flashing and crackling from the incredibly grotesque bodies of the Titanians!

Then, as suddenly as they had started the commotion, the shackled workers dropped to their knees, moaning piteously, their heads lowered under the cruel beatings.

Minutes later, the whip-like arms of the Titanians ceased. Methodically, then, the number who had come to the platform with the first outbreak moved back across the cavern to the dais of their leader on the opposite side. The two creatures who had herded Monk and Chet across the cavern still hovered over them, as if waiting a command.

It came.

The Titanians lifted Chet and Monk once more, and carried them to a passage that led off from the center of the cavern into a darkened alcove. Then down the passageway, finally pausing before an enormous metal door.

One of the spindle creatures pushed this inward, revealing a brightly lighted, but small and stone-hewn prison cell. Chet and Monk were dropped to the floor of the place. The Titanians retreated, clanging the door shut behind them.

"I must say," Monk said bitterly when he and Chet were alone a few seconds later, "that we can't complain about not being taken on a tour of the joint. They've moved us around more than a pair of checkers."

Chadwick didn't reply. His brows were wrinkled in concentration, and his lips were a thin tight line across his face.

"Monk," he said after a moment. "Remember what I told you about the girl, about those slaves on the platform being her people?"

Sands climbed to his feet, scratching his head in confusion. "Damn! I almost forgot about that. Why," he paused, trying to phrase what he wanted to say, "those poor devils couldn't be of the same genus as her. It's impossible, Chet. Impossible!"

"That's just what I mean," Chadwick groaned desperately, placing his head wearily in his hands. "It's impossibly confusing. Aside from the small fact that we might not be alive in any succeeding minute, there's this snarled mystery to worry about."

"Let's worry about us, and the 'small matter' of our lives, first," Sands said dryly. "Then, if we have the time or inclination, we can look up anything we don't know about the joint in a nice encyclopedia!" He walked over to the tall metal door, and after gazing at it and rubbing his hand along its surface, kicked it experimentally with his foot.

"If we can figure this out," Chadwick said half to himself, "we might be able to find the key to get us out of this mess."

"It's all very logical," his companion agreed dryly, "but doesn't make a hell of a lot of sense!" Before turning back to Chadwick, Monk gave the door a parting kick. The kick was answered from the other side of the door!

The confinements of the small cell were deathly silent as Monk and Chadwick, heads cocked breathlessly to one side, listened for a repetition of the noise.

Seconds passed.

Then it came again, this time a little louder. The sound of a foot tapping twice on the metal door. Both men looked questioningly at one another.

"It's a cinch it isn't our long legged buddies," Chadwick whispered.

"Yah," Monk replied with heavy sarcasm. "Go to the door and let 'em in, whoever it is."

Chadwick withered his plump little companion with a glance, then stepped swiftly over to the metal door. After listening with his ear to the metal sheeting, he rapped twice on it with his fist.

Two more raps answered.

"Earthmen?" The words were faint, coming from the other side of the door, and the pair opened their mouths to reply simultaneously.

Monk let Chet take over.

"Yes," the lanky pilot agreed. "Who is it?"

"It is the girl who met you above the ground, when you landed on Titan," came the soft reply.

Chadwick steadied his hammering pulses, saying, "Can you help us out of here?"

"There is a loose stone beside the door," the voice answered. "It is as high as a man's chin." Monk was already groping along the wall in search of the stone.

"She said a *man's* chin, runt!" Chadwick snorted, pushing him aside to search for the stone himself. In a moment he grunted in satisfaction, his fingers tugging at a loose stone the dimensions of a large baseball. Then it was in his hand, and while they gazed in popeyed astonishment, the door opened noiselessly!

The girl with the red lips and raven hair stood at the threshold. Her face wore the same expression of calm detachment as when Chadwick had last seen her.

"Come," she said speaking swiftly, "follow me. There is a place we can hide until it is over!"

The girl was dressed in a tight tunic which, Chadwick noted, was as outmoded as her space suit had been. Once more his brows kinked in concentration. There was something strange that he couldn't quite place, about her.

At another side passage the girl turned.

"Wait," she said breathlessly. Then she moved her hand along the damp stone walls of the passage, searching for something. She found it and in an instant an electrical whine filled the air. A moment later a portion of the wall moved slowly outward, revealing the brightly lighted interior of another stone chamber

They were inside, the girl, Chet, and Monk, and the wall was swinging back into place. Chadwick faced the girl. "Come, now. What's all this about? Tell us what's happened, how you got here, who those poor devils shackled to the steel-hammering line are!"

The girl looked at them for a moment, her red lips half parted, her gray eyes misted. When she spoke her voice was low and liquid, like bubbling music.

"My name," she began simply, "is Naomi Brand. For what has seemed to be many years, I have been held captive on Titan—one woman with fifty men of our race. We are, all of us, earth dwellers. The monstrous creatures you have seen are the inhabitants of Titan—spindle-legged beings who have lived for centuries in the depth of Titan's darkened sub-areas."

Naomi Brand seemed to shudder for a moment, then, mechanically, as if she had told the story to herself repeatedly, she continued. "When we first fell into the hands of the creatures of Titan we were on our way back to Earth. We had no suspicion that such danger lurked on this planet. But swiftly, and without warning, the Titans captured our party, killed my father, and all the women save myself."

Chadwick was swallowing hard, his brow furrowed with a frown.

The girl went on. "They took the men, shackling them to stone—as you saw—and made them slaves. Myself, when they found I was unfit for work, they permitted me to survive somehow."

Naomi Brand broke, her voice choking. "You are the first earthmen to arrive here since our capture. I have waited, prayed, for aid—and now that you've come, you, too, are victims of the spindled monsters."

Naomi Brand broke into sobs, and Monk Sands moved instinctively to her, put his arms comfortingly about her.

"Okay, Romeo," Chadwick snapped. "Break it up. We've got a lot to get done, and a lot more to find out!"

Monk Sands glared at his fellow pilot savagely. "Listen, Chet, this poor kid has gone through a million hells. Don't you have any heart in you?"

Chadwick's lean features were grim and uncompromising as he replied with a fierce patience. "Look, Monk. This is no time to get full of tears and flapdoodle. We're in one helluva jam, and unless we can figure this thing out pretty quick— we're never going to have to!"

Naomi's tears stopped as suddenly as they started, and she turned her lovely face to Chadwick questioningly. "What will we be able to do?"

Chet started a furious pacing back and forth across the damp floor of the stone chamber. Desperately, he tugged at a wild lock of his lank black hair, as if in an effort to drag ideas from his skull by the violence of the gesture.

"Have to know more," he said, stopping suddenly. "What were you telling me before—about 'sappers', I mean?"

Naomi's eyes were wide. "The brain sappers?"

Both Monk and Chadwick showed their amazement in the glances they turned on Naomi. "Brain sappers?" they chorused bewilderedly.

"Yes," Naomi answered. "The sceptre held in the hand of the King Titanian. It is charged with electrical vibrations from his body, I believe. When waved above the head of an earthman, the voltage set up produces a state similar to hypnosis."

"How do you know this?" Chet demanded.

"Why," Naomi answered in perplexity. "It was done to the men on the long stone platform, when all of us were first captured. It is the reason why they have never been able to plan, plot to free themselves from the domination of the Titanians."

Sands' face was pale as he turned to Chadwick. "Chet, good Lord, did you hear what she said? That electrical hocus-pocus was done to both of us, too!"

Chadwick bit his underlip. "Yeah, it was. But, so far, there hasn't been any effect on either of us. And the girl—," he broke off, turning to Naomi. "What about it? Was the 'sapper', or whatever you call it, used on you?"

Naomi shook her head in negative reply. "Just on the men," she said.

Suddenly Chadwick took a fresh attack on the problem. "You haven't seen the men who were captured in your party—except from a distance—since they were shackled to the work line, have you?"

Naomi shuddered. "No. I have only seen them from a distance."

Chadwick sighed inwardly. Then the girl didn't know the change that had come over her friends since their capture. It was just as well. If she were to see them now, half-human, gibbering—

"There's only one thing we can do, Chet," Sands' voice brought Chadwick out of his speculations. "We must get back to the spaceship. We've got weapons aboard that can burn these monsters to an elongated crisp."

Chadwick looked at Naomi. "How well do you know these underground passages?"

"Perfectly," the girl answered. "I have been allowed to roam."

"Good," the lanky pilot broke in. "You'll have to lead us out of here, and up to our ship."

The trio was moving toward the wall exit of the chamber, and Naomi was tugging at the stone that would set the door in motion, when Sands spoke.

"Wait," he said. "Our space gear has been taken from us. We won't even be able to step out into that atmosphere without it."

Chadwick cursed. For a moment he hesitated. Then Naomi broke in. "It is all right. I know where there are other space suits. The ones that were taken from my party when we were seized!"

Both men looked at the girl with relief. "That's all I want to know," Sands declared. "Let's get going!"

* * * *

Through the darkened passages and along the damp corridors, Monk and Chet followed Naomi. After what seemed to be miles of groping progress, the girl halted.

"In here," she whispered into the darkness. They followed her through a low opening in a dimly-lit alcove off the passage.

"We are just below the main chamber," Naomi whispered. The sound of sledges, ringing faintly in the distance verified her remark.

Naomi crossed the tiny cave and bent over a mound in one of the corners. When Chadwick and Sands joined her, they saw that she was rummaging through a pile of dusty, antiquated, space suits. "Here they are," she breathed. "Select suits to fit you."

"Must have gotten these at an antique sale," Sands muttered as the three began to dress themselves in the outmoded space gear.

"These belonged to your party?" Chadwick said curiously.

"Yes," Naomi replied. "But they have not been used for some time."

Chadwick was directly under the ceiling opening, and as he climbed into the clumsy suit, the glow struck directly on lettering that was stamped inside his space jacket. For a moment he looked at it in stark disbelief. That date—he opened his mouth, as though to speak, then abruptly clamped his jaws tight.

In order to facilitate conversation, the trio carried their antiquated space helmets under their arms as they moved along the passageway. Although Sands and Chadwick were forced to hold fast to each other's belts, Naomi moved swiftly along through the utter blackness without faltering for an instant. Chadwick's eyes narrowed as he noticed this, but he said nothing. After what seemed an eternity of pushing along through the darkened tunnels of Titan, Naomi paused, pointing to a faint glow far down the corridor.

"That opening," she said, "is one I discovered some time ago. It is too small for the Titans and was made when—" she stopped abruptly. "It is too small for the Titanians," she repeated quickly, "and consequently is unobserved and unused by them."

For a second, Chadwick felt an unexplainable chill run down his spine. Then Monk was talking excitedly. "There's no sense in all three of us trying to make it to the space liner. It merely triples our chances of being discovered. One of us will have a better chance alone, Chet. And the other can stay with Naomi." As Monk spoke his arm was once again around Naomi's waist.

"You wait with me, here—Monk," Naomi said softly. "It is so dark, and I fear the horrible creat—"

Chadwick broke in. "Okay," he snapped, "it looks like I'm elected. You two remain here. I'll be back—with enough ray juice to fry this joint." He looked at Sands for an instant, trying to flash him a message, but his companion was gazing, cow-eyed, into the girl's lovely gray eyes.

Moments later, Chadwick made his way cautiously forth from the tunnel opening and out onto the barren wastes of Titan, He moved swiftly, taking shelter behind occasional lunar rock formations. He saw no sign of the Titanians, but remembering their swift approach, took no chances. In the distance, he could see the gigantic space liner, apparently unmolested as yet.

Working his way along slowly but steadily, Chadwick gave thought to Monk, back in the cave with Naomi. There was something fishy, something very fishy, about that girl—about this whole damned mess. Those half-human slaves in the enormous cavern—Naomi's party—could they have degenerated so, merely through hypnosis administered by the King Titanian.

Suddenly two spindle-legged Titanians moved across his line of vision. Chadwick dropped flat on his face behind a rock. They disappeared, finally, behind a series of crags some five hundred yards away. Chadwick moved once more.

And these suits—antiquated, impossibly outmoded, Naomi had said they belonged to her party. Chadwick's lean face, beneath the turret of his space helmet, was worried, perplexed. What was all this adding up to?

Chadwick was a hundred yards from the space liner when his jaw dropped open in amazement. It wasn't the spaceship which he and Monk had arrived in—but instead, was a weatherbeaten, smaller, odd-looking craft!

He cursed, fluently, roundly, savagely. Precious moments wasted because he had mistaken this for the space liner in the murk! An unbidden thought brought an odd feeling creeping up the base of his spine. Was this the space ship used by Naomi and her people when they arrived on, or were leaving, Titan!

"I've a hunch," the lean pilot muttered to himself, "that this is going to fill in a lot of answers!" He advanced to the weatherbeaten space craft.

Fifteen yards short of the ship, he stopped. "My God," he said hoarsely, "it can't be!" His lips moved mechanically as he read the inscription on the side of the ship.

"PLANETARY MINING CORPORATION," it said. "TITAN RADIUM BASE". Then, underneath the huge lettering: "Final Expedition, 2000 A.D."

* * * *

Everything was swimming before Chadwick's eyes. 2000 A.D.! Mechanically, he approached the ship. Five hundred years old! *Five hundred years old!*

The gnawing suspicion that had been preying on him for the past hours was now a ghastly certainty. Naomi and the slave-men of the Titanians were the surviving members of the last mining expedition on Titan—an expedition that had been concluded five centuries ago. *Somehow, in some incredible fashion, Naomi and the men on the work platform in the cavern had remained alive on Titan for five hundred years!*

He pictured Naomi, probably in the arms of his pal at that moment. Unexplainably he shuddered. *Five hundred years old!*

Then he was inside the ancient spaceship. Everything, as he moved about the cabin, confirmed his suspicions. Every gadget, instrument, and weapon in the ship was an antique in space travel. But everything seemed miraculously preserved—preserved like Naomi.

Chadwick strapped several old-fashioned rocket guns to his waist and clambered out of the ancient space ship.

He paused for an instant, to test the antiquated weapons on a jutting rock formation just outside the ship. They performed admirably, burning blue holes in the rock. Chadwick stuffed them back in his waistband and proceeded on.

Chadwick was not interrupted on his way back to the tunnel entrance. As a result, he was back at the entrance in less than ten minutes. He looked back over his shoulder before entering the shaft. All clear. He hadn't been seen.

"Monk," Chadwick took his helmet off, and shouted down the darkened passage. "Monk! Where are you?"

There was no answer. A moment later, when he came to the place he'd left his pal and Naomi, they were nowhere to be seen!

Then he was moving, almost running, down the long passageway of the deserted radium pits. His breath was hot in his lungs, and fear burned in his brain—fear that he was late, too late, to do anything for Monk.

"That damned little fool," Chadwick gasped. "I should have seen that he'd gone daffy over the girl. He was ready to do any fool stunt she asked of him."

Chadwick lost track of time. As he groped, half-running, half-stumbling, along the damp darkness of the tunnel, everything but his one determination became a blur to him. It might have been hours, or merely minutes, before he stumbled upon a side shaft leading to a white glare of light in the distance.

"The cavern," Chadwick muttered. "That must be the main cavern to the joint!"

He burst into the enormous high-ceiling room. The sight that met his eyes stunned him momentarily. Monk was playing hero to a packed house!

Perhaps forty Titanians stood stoically herded in a corner, their tentacled arms hanging limply at their sides, their flat, expressionless faces fixed unwaveringly at a small space-suited figure before them—Monk Sands.

Chadwick's flickering glance took in the dais where the King Titanian had held court, and gasped. The spindle-legged creature was sprawled grotesquely forward on his face, feelers outstretched and twitching spasmodically. There was a flaming red hole in the center of the monster's body!

Monk Sands was holding an ancient rocket pistol, pointing it on the emotionless Titanians.

At the far corner of the room, moving along the stone platform and unshackling the hairy, aboriginal men, was Naomi! Chadwick shouted.

Monk wheeled, to look swiftly in his direction. At that instant the first of the Titanians lunged awkwardly but swiftly forward. Chadwick brought one of his rocket guns up level, prayed for accuracy at that distance, and squeezed the trigger.

The gun flashed flame. The Titanian fell to the cavern floor—a hole burned through the center of his strange head. Then the others were moving—heedless of the pistols of the two earthmen, their flailing tentacles snapping through the air with the speed of whips.

Monk dashed toward Chadwick, and the two stood side by side. In the next confusing moments Monk and Chet pumped their ancient weapons for all they were worth, sending one after another of the onrushing Titanians crashing to the stone floor.

Chadwick had felled one of the creatures, burning through the monster's spindle legs and didn't notice the creature moving along on its stumps toward him. He heard Monk's hoarse shout, stepped back in time to avoid the stinging blow directed at his head. His gun flashed again, and the creature sank to the stone for good.

"Come on," Chadwick shouted. "They're too much for us. Let's get the hell out of here!"

Monk gave him an astonished look. "Leave Naomi? Don't be a sap. Do what you want to do, Chadwick, I'm staying by her!" Their exchange was cut off once more by the necessity of rapid rocket work on more advancing Titanians.

Sweat ran down Chadwick's angular face. He cursed loudly. From the corner of his eye, he could see Naomi freeing the last of the half-humans.

* * * *

The shrieks and yowls of the horde of hairy Earthmen dashing heedlessly across the stone floor toward the spindle-legs was a horrifying din. The ape-like men were fifty yards from the creatures of Titan before they were noticed. Then they were in the midst of the spindle-legs, clawing, tearing!

Chadwick saw one vicious ape-man spring almost six feet from the floor to clutch at the waist of a Titanian. In the next moment the flailing arms of the monster beat down on the unprotected back of the half-human. But the aboriginal sank his long fangs into the Titanians chest, and the creature rolled to the floor—blue liquid oozing from the gaping wound.

Chadwick was looking for Naomi. Finally he saw her. Monk did too, and shouted in terror. "Naomi!"

But the Titanian was swifter than the guns of Monk or Chadwick, swifter than the death that was coming over him. The creature's tentacles flashed out, winding python-like about Naomi's waist, crushing in mercilessly.

When Chet and Monk got to Naomi's side, the Titanian was dead—his tentacles still wrapped around the waist of the crushed slim body. A crushed body from which no blood ran!

But Monk hadn't noticed this in his grief. He dropped to his knees, weeping hysterically, pillowing Naomi's raven-haloed head in his lap.

Chet had no time to think. He stood above Monk and the dying girl, pumping his rocket pistol with a fury born of blind rage. "Five hundred years...five hundred of them...centuries..." the words flashed over and over again in his brain.

Most of the Titanians were battling desperately with their former slaves. Chet grabbed Monk by the arm.

"Quick," he shouted. "To the passage. Get out while we can!"

"No," Monk snarled. "I'm staying. Naomi's gone. I'm gonna stay here until every one of those—are gone, too!"

There was nothing else for Chadwick to do. With a grunt, he brought his pistol butt down on his pal's head. He caught Monk's limp body as the little fellow sagged forward. Throwing him over his shoulder, Chadwick ran....

Once above ground, staggering under the weight of the limp body, Chadwick looked wildly about. There was no sign of Titanians. Those above ground were probably hastening below to aid their fellow-monsters in the battle against the half-humans. There would be no time for them to repair their own space liner. Chadwick struck out without hesitation for the ancient rocket ship he'd left less than an hour ago.

If it was preserved like everything else it'd still be in running order.

Some hours later, Chet Chadwick, at the controls of a spluttering antiquated rocket ship—a mere five hundred years old—looked down at the stirring form of his rotund companion. The bump he'd laid on Monk Sands' head was as big as an egg. Chadwick grinned.

"He's going to have a hard time forgetting Naomi," he said half-aloud. "Poor devil." But it'd be much better than knowing that Naomi had been worse than dead for five hundred years, only this screwy radium tainted world kept her in a false life. What would have happened if we'd gotten her away in space, away from the radiations....? Chadwick shuddered and turned pale.

For a moment he was silent, his angular features bathed in reflection. "I know what I'll do," Chadwick said softly. "I'll let him have Olga back again! That'll make him forget, and what he don't know will never bust him!"

JOHN BROWN'S BODY

(WITH WILLIAM P. MCGIVERN)

"The other day David Wright O'Brien dropped into your editor's office and sat down for a little discussion. He advanced several very unusual ideas, and we immediately set him to work finishing them up. His present story in this issue is a sample of what we mean by unusual ideas. Certainly your editor would never have believed a mere wash machine could produce such an amazing and delightful tale as 'John Brown's Body', but O'Brien did it (with the help, incidentally, of William P. McGivern, whom we certainly don't want to slight—a couple of Irishmen are positively not to be slighted) and we rushed the story into print."

—Raymond A. Palmer in "The Observatory,"
Amazing Stories, May 1940.

* * * *

"Throckmorton making an inspection—this morning!"

John Brown uttered the words in a horrified tone. His hands fluttered nervously. He looked helplessly around the washing machine department of Throckmorton's Department Store, then back at his fellow salesman, suddenly trembling.

"Oh, dear," he gasped, "I just know something will go wrong. I never was lucky on Mondays."

Thaddeus Throckmorton, owner and president of the store, would make one of his surprise tours of inspection this morning, and when Thaddeus Throckmorton "toured" there wasn't a department, section, or counter that was safe from his pompous, if none too nimble-witted, speeches and suggestions.

Mr. Brown had reason to tremble. For he had worries. Overdue payments to the Acme Loan Company, the interdepartment sales contest, and now, to top it all off, the visit from President Throckmorton himself. John Brown prayed fervently that the collector from the loan company wouldn't come barging into the store while the Boss was around.

As he heard Mr. Throckmorton's booming voice coming down the aisle, he even thought of running madly from the store. But instead his watery blue eyes darted nervously over the familiar shining line of washers, swung to the middle of the floor, and rested on the giant model washing machine that had just been installed for advertising purposes.

A huge affair—six feet high and six feet wide—it had been the result of a brainstorm by Thaddeus Throckmorton himself. On his last visit to John Brown's department, Mr. Throckmorton, after "tsking" at the lamentable lack of sales, hit upon the idea of a colossal, glorified washer to lure customers closer to John Brown's wares.

Even John Brown was forced to admit the idea was a honey. And as the sounds of Mr. Throckmorton's voice grew closer, the little washing machine salesman stepped closer to the gigantic display machine and with his handkerchief flicked a microscopic atom of dust from one of the steel braces.

Exactly three seconds later John Brown's heart plummeted to his heels, then promptly shot upward to catch somewhere in the region of his throat. Mr. Throckmorton had arrived!

The president and owner of Throckmorton's Department Store did not enter the washing machine sector—he invaded it. A general at the head of his legions could not have impressed John Brown more than the portly Mr. Throckmorton, followed by subalterns, did at that moment.

John Brown coughed, almost strangling, then blurted a squeaky "Good morning." Then, hastily in afterthought: "—sir!"

Mr. Throckmorton's large, expensively clad body turned to face the stooped, drab little salesman. The president was dignified, pompous, and impressive. But no one could say he was not democratic. He said, "Good morning, Brown."

Then, with a firm, searching, uncompromising eye, Mr. Throckmorton surveyed the section in which he stood. An almost paternal gleam shot into his eye as he spied the colossal display machine.

"Sales improved any since this has been installed, Brown?" inquired Mr. Throckmorton in a tone of voice which implied that sales damned well should have improved.

"Yes," said the breathless Mr. Brown. "Yes, sir."

"Harrumph," the owner made a pleasurable noise in his throat. "Harrumph, quite naturally." He strode to where the machine stood in the center of the section and, raising himself on tip-toe, peered into its depths.

"Pardon me, sir," ventured Mr. Brown. "Pardon me, but you can obtain a much more satisfactory view of the inner workings from the special platform on the other side."

"Capital," said Mr. Throckmorton. "Very interesting exhibit. My own idea, I might add."

Mr. Brown led his employer to the other side of the machine where they ascended a series of wooden steps leading to an elevated platform from which they could gaze comfortably down into the bowels of the machine.

"Big, isn't it?" said John Brown, peering over his employer's shoulder.

"Quite," said Mr. Throckmorton proudly. "Biggest of its kind. Turn it on, please."

John Brown bent over and his hand found the switch that started the huge machine revolving. As the noise of the motor picked up momentum he stared in rapt fascination at the giddying whirl of paddles and discs inside the spacious stomach of the washer. By the time he straightened up the humming had grown to a smooth roar. He stepped forward to gaze downward. Then, like a bursting bomb insofar as results were concerned, the terrible thing happened.

His feet tangled with the electric cord that ran along the platform, and in the next instant he lost his balance and lunged forward. His bony shoulder drove into Mr. Throckmorton's wide back, and for an awful minute they staggered on the brink of the machine.

And the next instant, with a hoarse bass bellow from Mr. Throckmorton and a shrill soprano scream from John Brown, they tumbled into the whirring machine.

* * * *

The screaming whistle of the revolving demonstrator, the roar of the motor, the wild shrieks and shouts that issued from the washer all blended together in a weird crescendo, instantly creating a commotion in the store.

Salesmen and clerks, floorwalkers and customers, all raced to the spot. Mr. Darnell, of neckties and ribbons, arrived first. He ran up the steps in back of the machine and yelled over his shoulder, "Get a stretcher. Somebody fell into the big washer." He threw off the switch and stared with anticipatory horror as the huge disc began to slow down, expecting to find a tangled mass of arms and legs. But instead, as the revolutions decreased, he was amazed to see both occupants unscathed and unharmed.

It was a further shock when he recognized the portly frock-coated figure of the store's president. Mr. Throckmorton seemed to be all right and was making a ludicrous attempt to rise to his feet in spite of the rotating machine. The other figure in the machine was sitting up with his hand pressed tightly over his eyes.

The frock-coated figure of Mr. Throckmorton staggered a little and then collapsed in a very undignified heap. He stared wildly about, then threw an arm about his face.

"Please," he wailed, "it was an accident. I couldn't help it. I stumbled. Please forgive me," Mr. Throckmorton said. "Please, don't fire me!"

The small figure in the sack-like brown suit sat up with a jerk, shaking his head. "You stupid clumsy fool," he bellowed. "You damned near killed me. I'll have you fired so fast it'll take your breath away!"

Mr. Darnell, of neckties and ribbons, opened and closed his mouth like a gaping fish. Was he crazy, or was Brown really giving Throckmorton hell? And was Throckmorton begging Brown not to fire him? It was incredible.

The large impressive figure in the frock-coat was on his knees almost crying over the rumpled little man in the baggy brown suit.

"Oh please," Mr. Throckmorton begged, "give me another chance." He fumbled in his pocket for a handkerchief, wiping a tear from his eye. "I couldn't help it," he wailed again. "It was an accid—" His voice broke, faltered and stopped in his throat.

He stared incredulously at the large diamond cuff links that were attached to his shirt. Like a man in a dream his eyes traveled up his fat arms and down his expansive front. Diamond stickpin, figured cravat, silk shirt, expensive English suit. Horror-stricken, he felt his face. Soft smooth skin, double chin, fat bulging jowls. Panic-stricken he climbed to his feet.

"What's happened to me? My body...!" cried the frock-coated figure wildly.

"Everything's all right, Mr. Throckmorton," Mr. Darnell said, his face pale with anxiety. "I've sent for a ladder. It's coming directly."

"But I'm not Mr. Throckmorton," he protested wildly. "I'm John Brown."

Mr. Darnell tried to smile understandingly, but only succeeded in looking very bewildered. "Of course, Mr. Throckmorton. You're a little shocked. Terrible experience to go through."

"Stop calling me Throckmorton," John Brown said hysterically. "I just look like him. This is his body, but I'm really me."

"Of course," said Mr. Darnell, "you're you. You're Mr. Throckmorton." He pointed to the machine. "There's Mr. Brown."

* * * *

John Brown looked and found himself looking at himself. Not as he was now, but as he should be. Baggy brown suit. Thin brown hair. Weak blue eyes. John Brown closed his eyes and counted to ten. It didn't help. And John Brown abruptly realized the truth.

"We've changed bodies—somehow!" he said to himself in an amazed, hoarse whisper.

The figure on the floor was still rubbing his eyes and shaking his head.

"Help me up," he shouted. "Try and kill a man and then refuse to help him, eh? I tell you, Brown, you'll regret this day as long as you live. You can't trifle with a Throckmorton and get away scot free."

John Brown stooped over and helped him to his feet. "I'm sorry," he began, breathless with unaccustomed effort, but the other cut him off.

"Sorry!" he exploded. "A fine thing to tell a man after you've nearly killed him. I...." His mouth fell open. His eyes bulged out until they looked like huge marbles. He opened and closed his mouth soundlessly once— twice—then fainted quietly away.

Someone was sliding a ladder into the machine and in a few seconds Mr. Darnell and two of the uniformed maintenance men were descending into the washer.

"Terrible experience," said Mr. Darnell. "But everything's all right now."

John Brown stared at his strange fat body and heaved a terrified sigh. As the brisk men in uniform picked up his limp and sagging body, he felt like crying.

"Everything is all wrong," he said unhappily.

"Terrible experience," said Mr. Darnell for the third time. "Mr. Brown will be all right I'm sure. They're taking him to the employees' washroom for first aid."

"They can't do that," John Brown cried, suddenly horrified.

"It's a pleasant enough washroom," Mr. Darnell said timidly. "Couch, first aid—"

"You'd better take him to his office."

"But, Mr. Throckmorton, Mr. Brown has no office."

John Brown stared strangely at his new body again, then made a sudden decision.

"But of course," he amended. "For a moment I didn't think. Have Mr. Brown brought to my office."

"Yes, sir. Anything else?"

In all of John Brown's drab, colorless forty-three years of existence no one had ever called him "sir" and waited expectantly and diffidently for another order. It was a heady intoxicating feeling. Like strong wine. John Brown took a deep breath, fingered his heavy gold watch chain.

"One more thing."

"Yes."

"Be quick about it."

"Oh yes, sir." Mr. Darnell bobbed his head and ducked off down the aisle.

* * * *

John Brown watched him hurry off and there was a strange speculative light in his eye. It was the first time in his life that he had ever known the thrill of power.

In spite of the delightful feeling of importance that his new presence gave him, John Brown was glad to see his old body being carried into Mr. Throckmorton's office. He turned to the curious crowd in the doorway and fixed them with a cold stare.

They melted away.

He instructed the attendants to stretch their burden on a comfortable daybed that was placed against the wall and then dismissed them.

He surveyed the luxurious surroundings with satisfaction. Not half bad. He seated himself at Mr. Throckmorton's gleaming mahogany desk and waited for the president to come around.

It was a very odd situation. It was more than odd. It was unbelievable, incredible, amazing and unimaginable. Still it had happened.

He, John Brown, was J. Thaddeus Throckmorton and the pompous department store head was now an ordinary wash machine salesman. Poetic justice, that's what it was!

John Brown opened a teakwood humidor and selected a fat perfecto cigar. He was just touching the flame from the silver desk lighter to it, when the figure on the couch groaned, and struggled to a sitting position. Throckmorton, in John Brown's body, stared blankly about the room for an instant, then leaped to his feet. He looked down at himself, felt his face and then rushed to the desk.

"It's some kind of a trick," he shouted. "Get away from my desk, you impostor."

"It's no trick," John Brown said. "Something happened to us in the washer. We switched bodies."

"That doesn't give you any right to sit there smoking my dollar cigars. I am J. Thaddeus Throckmorton. Nothing can change that."

"Sure," John Brown admitted. "You're Throckmorton. I'm Brown. But only two people in the world know that. If I wanted to I could call the building police and have you thrown out of my office. If you kept insisting that you were me they'd lock you up in the booby hatch. I don't like this any better than you do, but we'll have to make the best of it until something straightens us out."

Throckmorton collapsed in a chair as if his legs were suddenly filled with water. "But what am I going to do?"

John Brown blew a cloud of smoke toward the ceiling before answering. "There's a job in the washing machine department that needs a good man. You can have that. You see, I don't need it any more." He leaned back in the cushioned swivel chair and smiled complacently. "I seem to have been *promoted* a little."

Mr. Throckmorton was gazing at John Brown with a sort of dawning apprehension. When at last he found his voice he spoke in a husky whisper. "You, you mean you're going to let this continue?" he gasped.

* * * *

John Brown folded his thick hands over his new stomach and gazed benignly at the figure he used to be. "Why not?" he inquired with cold matter-of-factness. "What is there that we can possibly do about it?" Then he smiled thoughtfully. "Besides, with the exception of my rather absurd new body, I think I rather like what has happened. I'm a lot wealthier, have a lot more power at this minute than I had fifteen minutes ago."

Mr. Throckmorton, from his new but very drab body, could only sputter in futile rage. "What," he managed to blurt after a moment, "is wrong with my body?"

"Which," asked John Brown with devilish amusement, "your new body, or the one I'm wearing at present?"

"My own, my honest-to-goodness, genuine body!" spat Mr. Throckmorton. "What's wrong with it, I say?"

Mr. John Brown looked thoughtfully at his portly new figure. "Well," he said after a moment, "it's horribly fat to begin with. Then, you're not the handsomest devil in the world, y'know." He held up a warning hand as Mr. Throckmorton began to protest. "And your taste in clothes is much too loud, too pretentious. You dress, if you'll pardon my candor, in a more or less hideous fashion."

"Damn you, Brown," snarled the store owner, "I resent your remarks. I ought to fire you!"

"Tsk," admonished John Brown. "Remember your new station, Mr. Throckmorton. You are now a washing machine salesman. If there's any firing to be done, I'll take care of it. I'm president, remember."

Thaddeus Throckmorton, speechless with rage, could only glare helplessly at John Brown as he continued.

"Yes," said Brown reflectively. "I am going to outfit you—that is, myself, in some decent raiment. Something less ridiculous than what I'm wearing at present."

"Leave my body alone," shrieked Thaddeus Throckmorton. "It's dressed in the best of taste, and I won't have it looking foolish! Leave those clothes exactly as they are, do you understand me?"

"It's my body, now," declared John Brown. "At least my personality is inhabiting it at the moment. I refuse to have my personality dashing about in such ludicrous garments. The body is bad enough, Lord knows, but I don't have to look like a circus clown on top of it."

Mr. Throckmorton turned the matter over to the gods, and once his choice selection of epithets was concluded he buried his face—or rather, John Brown's face—in his hands. "Ohhhhh," moaned the president of Throckmorton's Department Store, "oooooohhh!"

"Come, come," demanded John Brown after several minutes of this, "stop all that carrying on. You don't hear me complaining, do you? After all, I haven't got the best bargain in the world from this. There isn't any sense in crying over spilled personalities."

Mr. Throckmorton gave him the benefit of an anguished glance. "It's easy for you to talk," he sobbed. "But I'm the one to get the worst of this deal!"

"Tush," cried John Brown. "I think you'll do well selling washing machines, once you get the knack of it. They're a lot of fun. Besides, think of the twenty percent commission you're working on. A man can do a lot on twenty percent commission. In no time at all you ought to be department head."

"Yes?" said Mr. Throckmorton dubiously.

"Absolutely," John Brown assured him. "There is plenty of room for promotion in Throckmorton's. It's a sort of a slogan, y'know. So you shouldn't feel amiss starting as a washing machine salesman. There's plenty of room for promotion."

"Fluuumph," said Mr. Throckmorton. "I'd almost forgotten that slogan."

"I've never forgotten it," said John Brown casually. "I remember hearing it eighteen years ago when I started selling washing machines here."

Mr. Throckmorton broke out in a new series of groans, and John Brown, smiling quietly to himself, exhaled expensive blue clouds of smoke thoughtfully at the ceiling.

Quite suddenly, Mr. Throckmorton seemed to calm down. Noticing the swift transition of manner, John Brown looked at him in perplexity. Something was wrong somewhere. Throckmorton, in Brown's body of course, was almost looking pleased. He was whistling a half-tune through his teeth, an old habit of John Brown's when secretly happy about something.

"Remind me," John Brown told Mr. Throckmorton, "to discard that irritating whistle when I get my own body back. It's extremely annoying."

"I'm very pleased," smirked Mr. Throckmorton. "Very, very pleased at what I have just remembered."

"So I gather," John Brown acknowledged dryly. "I seem to remember my own face well enough to know when it is registering signs of pleasure. Might I ask what it is that makes you look like a cat at a banquet of canaries?"

Mr. Throckmorton rose swiftly. "Nothing," he lied easily. "I was just thinking, that's all. Just thinking."

With that, Mr. Throckmorton crossed to the door and turned momentarily to face John Brown. "Have to be getting downstairs, I suppose. Washing machines to sell, and all that," he smirked. "Toodle-oo!"

* * * *

For three minutes John Brown, in his new body, sat staring thoughtfully at the door. Mr. Throckmorton's exit had left him rather bewildered and vaguely uneasy. What was the ex-president so damned pleased about? Why had the sudden change come over him? John Brown was not long in finding out.

There was a precise tapping on the door, startling Mr. Brown out of his mental misgivings. "Come in," he snapped. "Come in and stop that damned rat-tat-tat."

A short, thin, bespectacled young man whom Mr. Brown remembered as being secretary and aide-de-camp to Mr. Throckmorton, stepped into the room. John Brown remembered that his name was Quaggle and that he was a sort of junior executive in the store.

"Well, Quaggle?" Mr. Brown forced his voice to carry the coolness commonly associated with authority.

Quaggle cleared his throat noisily, inserting a thin finger beneath his stiff collar. "Frankly, sir, I'm worried," he declared throatily. "The situation is serious."

"What situation?" Brown asked blankly.

Quaggle choked back his amazement, and with reproach dripping from his every word, replied, "Why, THE situation, sir, concerning the bank's refusal to extend your loan."

If John Brown had been sitting in an electric chair, he couldn't have been more shocked. Loans, Debts, Trouble, the Three Musketeers of Mr. Brown's past life, were once more cropping up to plague him in his new existence!

Quaggle continued, apparently unaware of the hunted look that had suddenly crept into the other's eyes. "What do you plan to do about it, Mr. Throckmorton?"

John Brown realized that a reply was expected—swift, sure, and decisive. John Brown could think of nothing swift, sure, or decisive to say. But he tried.

"It's an ill wind that hasn't got a silver lining, Quaggle," he said reassuringly. "Remember that!"

"Why?" Quaggle asked logically enough.

Brown had a sudden inspiration, remembering a poem from his high school days. "Yours is not to reason why, yours is but to do and die!" he blurted triumphantly.

Quaggle backed toward the door visibly impressed. "Yes, sir. Quite right. It is a pleasure to realize that you are ready to face them!"

John Brown paled. "Face who?" he heard his voice saying weakly.

"Why, the gentlemen from the bank. At the board of directors' meeting, at two o'clock this afternoon." He stopped to stare apprehensively at his employer. "What's wrong? Do you feel ill, sir?"

John Brown was clutching miserably at Throckmorton's overstuffed midriff. "*I* have a headache," he wailed, "and he has to pick this moment to get indigestion. Between the two of us we're driving me mad!"

This was too much for Quaggle. He flew from the room....

* * * *

When J. Thaddeus Throckmorton, vested in the person of John Brown, arrived on the floor of the washing machine section he was humming happily. It was almost with a sort of fondness that he gazed at the gigantic display washer which had been the cause of his present state. There were worse fates than being a washing machine salesman. Washing machine salesmen had small worries and smaller salaries. But they were better off, far better off, than department store executives about to be thrown into bankruptcy.

Mr. Throckmorton threw John Brown's thin shoulders back and inflated John Brown's chest. For the first time in many moons there was a swagger in John Brown's manner.

"Jesta minute, fella!"

Mr. Throckmorton felt a hand jab him forcefully between the shoulder blades, and he turned to face a thin, sharp-nosed, moustached individual wearing a belligerent smile.

"Yuh're John Brown, ain't yuh?"

Mr. Throckmorton hesitated only a moment. "Yes," he acknowledged.

"Well, Brown," the thin man's beady eyes gleamed triumphantly and he pulled a notebook from his pocket, "I'm from the Acme Loan Company."

"So," said Mr. Throckmorton icily, "so?"

The false smile faded from the crooked mouth. "Don't git uppity, Brown. I ain't no vassal. I'm here to see that you make yer payment fer last month, or else."

It occurred to Mr. Throckmorton that he had been stupid to imagine John Brown had no debts. Oh, well, probably some piddling thing. Write out a check for the fellow and clear it up. In the next instant Mr. Throckmorton recalled that he could no longer write out checks.

"Or else what?" said Mr. Throckmorton. He rather liked that. He had heard the phrase once in a gangster movie, but had never been able to use it inasmuch as no one ever said "or else" to Thaddeus Throckmorton. He almost had a warm feeling toward the collector for giving him the opportunity. "Or else what?" he repeated.

"Or else—" The irritating collector moved in closer and pushed his forefinger against his debtor's chest "—we'll have to garnishee yer wages! It might mean yer job, Brown."

Mr. Throckmorton wrinkled John Brown's forehead in perplexity. He would have to find out more about this.

"How much do I owe?" he asked.

"Two hunnert bucks is the principal. Yer interest fer this month and last month is fifteen bucks." The collector had opened the pages in his notebook and was running a grimy thumb down a column of figures.

"Here." Mr. Throckmorton grabbed the book from the fellow's paws. "Let me see that." In the next moment his jaw fell open in sheer astonishment. "Why," he blurted, "this debt is over four years old!"

"No foolin'," said the leering collector.

"And I've paid, that is, *he's* paid—"

"*You've* paid, Brown. Don't give me none of that *he* business," the collector corrected.

"I've paid the Acme Loan Company well over four hundred dollars in that time!" finished the astounded Mr. Throckmorton.

"So what?" said the collector, scratching his scraggly moustache nonchalantly.

"That's twice the amount originally borrowed! Which amounts to nothing more or less than sheer banditry!" stormed Mr. Throckmorton.

"Look," said the collector with feigned boredom, "are yuh gonna pay up yer installment, or aren't yuh? Make up yer mind, Brown. If yuh don't pay, we'll take the matter up wit yer boss!"

John Brown would have trembled under such circumstances. But Thaddeus Throckmorton was not used to trembling under any circumstances. Mr. Throckmorton's personality directed. John Brown's body acted. In the next several minutes the patrons of Throckmorton's Department Store were amazed to see a drab, somewhat moth-eaten little salesman ushering a terrified and bewildered collector out of the premises by the scruff of the neck.

"And if I see you around here again," bellowed Throckmorton with a well directed kick at the collector's nether extremities, "I'll have you put in jail!" Having concluded an unpleasant matter, Mr. Throckmorton rubbed John Brown's hands together with some degree of satisfaction, turned and retraced his steps to the washing machine section.

"Now to get down to work," he muttered, striding onto the display floor....

* * * *

"Now to get down to work," said the small, white-haired, sour little man at the head of the gleaming conference table. John Brown, seated at the opposite end of the table, shivered apprehensively. The rasping voice of the white-haired gentleman had jerked him back to reality. For the past hour he had wandered aimlessly about the spacious offices of Thaddeus Throckmorton in a sort of semi-stupor, half-dazedly, half-frantically trying to figure out a solution to his dilemma. But only two solutions had offered themselves—one to confess the incredible body-swapping of the past hours, the other to commit suicide. The first was out of the question, and he lacked the courage for the second.

And now, somehow, he found himself sitting at the ringside of his own Waterloo. The sour little gentleman, Pearson, president of the bank, was looking balefully at John Brown, letting the silence of the room weave into a cold blanket around him. At length he spoke.

"Throckmorton, I, for one, have had about enough of your eternal twaddle. Your bullying, blustering stupidity, your confounded unreasonable egotism, have just about bankrupted this store."

"But—" protested Mr. Brown.

"Never mind the 'buts,'" Pearson continued acidly. "You're not bullying us any longer. Your high-handed methods and your refusal to take advice are the reasons why we won't trust you with another cent of our money."

In all of John Brown's forty-three years of existence he had never bullied anyone. In fact it had never even occurred to him to bully anyone. He felt he was being unfairly treated. Instinct brought him to his feet, opened his mouth in protest.

Mr. Pearson sensed the beginning of another Throckmorton tantrum. He was determined to nip it in the bud.

"Sit down," he bellowed. "I have the floor!"

Everyone in the room, including Mr. Pearson, was amazed to see the portly, frock-coated figure slump meekly into his chair. Mr. Pearson was surprised and gratified by the easy victory. In a kindlier tone he continued:

"After all, Thaddeus, you've no one to blame but yourself. If you had taken our advice, as well as our loans, the last two times, you wouldn't find yourself with your back against the wall now. Under the circumstances, we can't renew the loan." Mr. Pearson sat down with an air of finality.

Everyone in the room regarded the frock-coated figure of the department store owner half-fearfully, half-expectantly. It had never been the nature of Thaddeus Throckmorton to take a blow sitting down. Seconds ticked into a minute, and still there was silence.

Mr. Pearson cleared his throat. "Well?"

Every eye in the room was fixed on John Brown as he rose to reply. "You are quite right," he said simply, resuming his seat.

* * * *

If he had ridden into the room naked on a tricycle, John Brown could not have created a greater furor. Out of the sudden tumult and babble of voices, Mr. Pearson's thin cry for order was heard. When the room had at last quieted, the white-haired little banker spoke.

"Did I—did I hear you rightly, Thaddeus?" There was shocked astonishment in Pearson's voice. "Do you actually agree with us?"

The portly figure rose again. "I not only agree with you, I might add to your statements. Thaddeus Throckmorton—that is to say the old Thaddeus Throckmorton—was also an overbearing, asinine know-nothing." John Brown then resumed his seat, feeling a certain vicious satisfaction in having so humbled the body of the man who had been his overlord for eighteen years. Come what may, he had gotten even with Thaddeus Throckmorton.

Mr. Pearson's voice was unsteady as he spoke. "This is incredible. If you can stand before us, Thaddeus, and openly admit your shortcomings, you're a better man than any of us had imagined." There were murmurs of assent throughout the group. "It's obvious that you've changed, how or why is unimportant. The fact that you have, is all that counts."

There was a general murmuring of assent, with only a few protesting voices breaking through. When Pearson resumed, Mr. Brown was stunned by the drastic reversal of fortune. It was so unexpected—so impossible—he couldn't believe his ears. "We had made up our minds not to advance a nickel to the old Thaddeus Throckmorton, but the situation is drastically reversed. We'll give you your loan!"

There was a brief, dramatic silence, immediately followed by a wild burst of applause. Then the directors were surrounding John Brown, slapping him on the back, pumping his hand. He struggled to his feet, dazed. Out of the sea of beaming faces swimming in front of him, he saw Mr. Pearson. "Congratulations, Thaddeus. Whatever made you change so?" the banker smiled.

"I wish I knew," said John Brown mournfully. "I only wish I knew!"

Thaddeus Throckmorton, in the person of John Brown, stood on the floor of the washing machine department. He raked his eyes over the circle of curious customers drifting about.

"By thunder," he shouted, "you need washing machines and I'm going to sell 'em to you. You need washing machines more than any crowd I have ever seen." He paused to let this sink in and then suddenly pointed dramatically to a large florid-faced gentleman who blushed painfully as Throckmorton glared at him.

"You," Throckmorton said bitterly, "look as if you haven't laundered that shirt you're wearing for two weeks. It's a disgrace. I doubt very much if the management would allow me to sell you a machine. After all," he said frigidly, "a Throckmorton washer has a certain position to maintain."

"Is that so?" the florid-faced gentleman said belligerently. "If you think I'm not good enough for your machines you're nuts. I'll buy a machine— I'll buy two machines and you won't stop me. If you try it I'll sue you and the company for plenty."

"If you're small enough to take advantage of a legal technicality," Throckmorton said icily, "there's nothing I can do about it. Take the machines. Both of them," he added with a peculiar gleam in his eye.

In a minute the florid-faced gentleman was signing the order blank which Throckmorton had thrust contemptuously into his hands.

"I know my rights," he said loudly. "These big stores can't make a monkey out of me." Holding his receipt aloft like a victory banner he struggled through the growing crowd and disappeared.

Throckmorton paused only long enough to insert a fresh order blank in his book before singling out the next victim. His greedy eye fastened on a pale, thin young man in the front row.

The intended victim began to cast about for an avenue of escape as Throckmorton bore down on him.

"Young man," Throckmorton began pleasantly enough, "you need a washing machine."

The prospect retreated a step. "No," he said feebly, "I don't."

"Don't contradict me," Throckmorton said sharply. He extended the order blank inexorably. "Right on the bottom line."

"We send our laundry out," the thin young man protested.

"Stop changing the subject," Throckmorton said irritably. "You're trying my patience. I warn you, don't push me too far. No more nonsense. Sign right here."

"But," the young man repeated wildly, "we send our laundry out."

"Oh for the Lord's sake," Throckmorton exploded, "will you stop drooling about what you do with your laundry? You've just about exhausted the possibilities of that subject."

"But what'll I do with a washing machine?"

"This is not the information desk," Throckmorton said witheringly. "But since you are apparently incapable of thinking for yourself, I'll tell you. You can wash the dishes in it."

The young man looked dubious. He also looked desperate.

"Won't they break?" he asked hopefully.

"Not if you use cardboard dishes," Throckmorton said in the tone one uses with a backward child. "Now," he continued ominously, "any more objections?"

The young man shook his head weakly. He signed falteringly and scuttled away shaking his head foolishly.

Customers, attracted by the crowd, were hurrying to the scene, jostling one another and overflowing into the aisles and adjoining sections.

Throckmorton was in his element. He was always at his best before a large audience. And now he proceeded to go to town.

"Take your time," he said in a voice that would have done justice to a circus barker. "There's one for everybody. No one will be disappointed." He ran an eye over the crowd and at that minute a happy inspiration occurred to him. It was so simple that he wondered why he had not thought of it at once.

"To save time," he announced pompously, "I shall have to ask you to form a line, starting at this counter and extending back as far as necessary. In that way I won't be bothered running about from person to person." He clapped his hands together smartly. "Quickly now, double file. A little snap to it, please."

A lieutenant, perhaps even a general, would have envied the authority Mr. Throckmorton put into these last commands.

Those on the fringes of the crowd began to melt away, but the majority, hypnotized by Mr. Throckmorton's Napoleonic manner, filed meekly into line.

Like a bossy traffic cop, he harangued them until an orderly procession wound snake-like out of the washing machine department and into the rest of the store. Then, pompously and importantly, Mr. Throckmorton strode to the head of the line. Rubbing his hands gloatingly he went to work.

It was mass production for the masses. Assembly line selling. As the line filed past Mr. Throckmorton the stack of signed order blanks grew higher and higher. The few who demurred were contemptuously dismissed and subjected to a violent storm of abuse as they departed.

Mr. Throckmorton was enjoying himself immensely. He was enjoying himself to such an extent that he didn't feel the tap on his shoulder until it was repeated for the third time.

He swung around, rather annoyed, to meet the stern and disapproving presence of Mr. Codger. Mr. Codger was floor manager. Mr. Codger stared at the crowd, at the apparent confusion and finally at what he thought to be Mr. Brown. He tweaked his sharp nose, a habit of his when he was not pleased.

"We are not," he said coldly, "conducting a rummage sale. Your sales tactics are definitely out of line with our policy. If it happens again, Brown, you're through."

"To blazes with our policy," Mr. Throckmorton bellowed. "I'm selling washing machines." He picked up the thick pile of orders and shoved them into Mr. Codger's hands. "Take these down to the stock room. Be back in an hour for more."

Mr. Codger leafed through the blanks with widening eyes. Then he jerked a long form blank out of his pocket and ran a finger down a column. He grabbed Mr. Throckmorton by the arm, spinning him around.

"Don't sell any more machines," he hissed. "You've already sold more than we have in stock. It'll be two weeks before we can get another supply. Now get these people out of here."

"All out, eh?" observed Mr. Throckmorton with no little regret. "And just when it was getting to be such fun." He was turning away from Mr. Codger when a gleam leaped into his eye, caused by the sight of the huge display washer.

"How about that one?" demanded Mr. Throckmorton. "Is it sold yet?"

"Don't be absurd, Brown." Codger's voice was scornful. "That is merely for advertising purposes."

"Is that so?" said Mr. Throckmorton in the tone of one who has accepted challenge. His eyes darted over the remaining line of curious customers. Then he rubbed his hands, moving off in the direction of a new victim....

It took John Brown a little while to get down to the washing machine section, and on arriving there he found bedlam.

John Brown managed to push his way through the jamming aisles. By the time he had reached the group crowded in front of the washing machine department, he was perspiring and out of breath.

Mr. Darnell, of neckties and ribbons, was futilely wringing his hands and fluttering around the fringes of the scene. Mr. Brown grabbed the fellow's arm, drawing him aside from the commotion.

"What's going on here?" he demanded.

Mr. Darnell was decidedly agitated. "It's Brown," he almost squealed. "The little fool, oh the little fool, it's the second time today!"

John Brown had to shake the trembling Mr. Darnell to make him continue. "Come, come," he shouted. "What happened?"

"Brown was trying to sell a customer the gigantic washer. He had sold out all the others—guess it went to his head—and he tripped, just like he did this morning. Now Brown and the customer are whirling around inside the machine!"

Time hung motionless as the full import of Darnell's words came crashing in on John Brown—Throckmorton—in his body—was whipping about in the washing machine with a strange customer. Supposing—supposing—Mr. Brown hated to think of it—SUPPOSING IT HAPPENED ONCE MORE!

From a distance, Mr. Darnell's terrified voice came to him. "It's awful, sir. The poor customer and that crazy little salesman. The poor customer, she's—"

"She," bellowed John Brown. "Did you say 'she'?"

"Yes, sir," bleated Darnell. "It's a lady customer."

But John Brown hadn't waited to hear the last of Darnell's statement. With a hoarse yell he was up the steps to the platform around the huge washer. His mind was made up. There was only one thing to do.

Mr. Darnell, standing stricken and helpless in front of the excited crowd, caught a glimpse of the expansive bottom and flying coat-tails of his employer as they disappeared into the whirring machine. And as he vanished into the thick of things, Mr. Darnell thought he heard him say:

"Everything comes out in the wash—it always does!"

SUICIDE SQUADRONS OF SPACE

"Sirs: In the current issue of *Amazing Stories* I liked 'Suicide Squadrons of Space' by David Wright O'Brien best. Second was 'Lost Treasure of Mars' by Edmond Hamilton. Interplanetary stuff is the most interesting material of all, I think—so let's have plenty of it."

—Phil McDanhls, Burbank, California,
in a <u>Letter to the Editor</u>, Amazing Stories, October 1940.

Editor's Response: You selected the two leading stories in the August [1940] issue, judging from our survey of letters received. The stories in the August issue rated as follows:

1. Suicide Squadrons of Space
2. Lost Treasure of Mars
3. The Living Mist
4. Mystery of the Mind Machine
5. Murder in the Time World
6. The Incredible Theory of Dr. Penwing
7. The Man Who Knew All the Answers

We will certainly continue our interplanetary stories.—Editor.

* * * *

"Sirs: Having read your August issue of *Amazing Stories*, I am forced to admit that it was wonderful, swell, a knockout, etcetera. However, I think 'The Man Who Knew All the Answers' is exactly where it belongs—at the bottom! A dud. Your best story was 'Suicide Squadrons of Space.' Boy-oh-boy! Hot dawg!...."

—Jack Townsend, Wilson, North Carolina,
Letter to the Editor, *Amazing Stories*, October 1940.

* * * *

"I suppose," said the flight commander, "that you officers are the replacements I asked for."

Then he thought to himself: "Why in hell does War College insist on sending these punks up to the front? The poor kids are just babies. Fresh and eager, with no idea in the world of what they're getting in for. They probably think war in space is a glorious adventure."

For a moment the tall, lean-muscled flight commander stood silently behind his desk, his tired gray eves moving in restless appraisal over the four uniformed young men standing at rigid attention before him. With a gesture of infinite weariness, he rubbed a strong brown band across the bronzed and hardened lines of his youthful features.

"I suppose, too, that your instructors at War College recommended you all very highly."

Noticing the flush of embarrassment that crossed the faces of the young officers, the flight commander softened his tone.

"There was no contempt intended in my statement, gentlemen. I was merely thinking of my own days in War College. That wasn't so long ago, y'know."

Again the flight commander thought to himself:

"No, that wasn't so long ago. Just ten years. I was a punk then, too. The Fourth World War[3] was in its fortieth year, then. Now it's been going on for fifty years. I'm only thirty years old, and I feel like a hundred."

Suddenly the flight commander broke off his thoughts abruptly. For the first time, he noticed that there were only four of the young replacement officers standing before him.

"Where is your other fellow officer?" he asked a blond, smooth-cheeked lad standing nearest to him. "There were supposed to be five replacements, not four."

The pink-skinned youth spoke promptly.

"Commander Walters detained him, sir. He is to join us shortly."

The flight commander nodded. "I see. Well, let's get down to introductions, gentlemen. As you all know, my name is Starke, Flight Commander Craig Starke. I'll be in charge while we're all together." He paused. "Sound off your own names, gentlemen."

"Chanes, sir," said the young officer who had spoken a moment before. Then, in succession, the other three junior officers gave their names, eagerly and with pride.

Flight Commander Starke smiled for the first time since the replacements stepped into his office.

3   The Fourth World War started in the year 2500—the 26th century—with the United States against the Mongol hordes, who had conquered all of Earth except this country. In their onward sweep of conquest, the yellow legions had seized the interplanetary colonies of all nations except Space Base 10, a U.S. possession, where the action in this story takes place. The Asiatic hordes are being led by Kama Khan, a direct descendant of his famous forerunner, Genghis Khan.—Editor.

"Very well, gentlemen. I'm more than certain we'll get along splendidly. Return to your quarters. I'll expect you all out at assembly in the morning. Never forget, we're fighting a war!"

The replacements were pushing out through the door when Craig Starke spoke again.

"By the way, Chanes, what the name of the fifth officer?"

Chanes appeared slightly embarrassed.

"Lieutenant Dick Starke, sir. Your brother!" Then he was gone.

Craig Starke sank slowly back in his swivel-chair, an expression of mingled anger, amazement and shock crossing his features. He ran his hand through his lank black hair, and the line of his jaw slowly hardened, set.

For fully five minutes he remained as he was, staring at the door. His brother, Dick. He hadn't seen Dick in ten years; no, twelve. Dick was a young, blond, smiling kid, gray-eyed and stocky—almost the opposite of his elder brother—when he'd seen him last. Dick was going to be a doctor. Had said so, dedicated his youth to it.

* * * *

Craig Starke, pleased that the kid wasn't going to carry on the family's hidebound Army tradition, had financed that medical education. Four times a year, for the past eleven years, Dick had written him, had spoken eagerly of his medical training. But instead, he had gone to War College—and was now assigned to Space Base 10 under his elder brother's command.

Burning rage replaced all other of Craig Starke's emotions, and his big brown hands squeezed hard on the edge of his desk. Dick, the kid he'd been so blastedly proud of, had betrayed him!

Several moments must have passed before Flight Commander Starke heard the knocking on his door. Setting his jaw grimly, he forced himself to make his voice steady.

"Come in," he barked.

And Lieutenant Dick Starke stepped into the room.

"Craig!" There was joy as well as embarrassment in the younger officer's voice. "Dammit, it's grand to see you, Craig!"

Craig Starke stared frostily at his brother, unconsciously noting the changes in the kid. He was a little taller now, still shorter than Craig though, and was even wider, more muscular than before. His hair hadn't darkened. In fact it was almost a white-blond now. The grin that had jumped so eagerly to his face was now sliding sickly away as Dick noted the expression in his brother's eyes.

"You're sore, Craig. Sore as hell. But I can expl—"

"Lieutenant Starke?" His brother's voice broke in sharply, giving the other no time to finish. "Lieutenant Starke," he repeated, letting the icy formality of the tone sink in, "you are with the new replacement officers, I believe."

"Look, Craig," his younger brother started again, a sort of desperation in his voice.

"It is customary, Lieutenant Starke," the other went on, "to address your superior officers by title." His voice became heavy with sarcasm. "I suppose your instructors at War College taught you as much."

Lieutenant Dick Starke snapped rigidly to attention, his eyes the only remaining indication of the emotion that filled him.

"As I was saying," Craig Starke grated, "you are with the new replacement officers. All of you are new to the front, new to war of any sort other than the bosh they hand you in school. This is space war, Lieutenant. In case you're not aware of it—it's sheer unadulterated hell up here. The invaders play for keeps, and kill to stay killed."

He paused, seemingly calmer, but his big hands still gripped the edges of his desk fiercely.

"You are also a bit worn out by your journey from Earth, I presume. Go to the quarters I have assigned the others. That's all!"

Lieutenant Dick Starke seemed to hesitate for a moment, debating against the rage of his brother and the futility of his own explanations. Then he did a smart about-face, after saluting, and was gone.

For endless seconds after his brother had left him, Craig Starke sat leaning back in his swivel-chair, staring blankly at the paneled pattern of the ceiling. At last, aloud, he said:

"So he wants to play soldier, eh? Wants to kill rather than heal. Well, dammit, he won't play soldier under my command! I'll get him out of here faster than a rocket charge!"

* * * *

Once more in his role of flight commander, Starke leaned forward, flicking the switch on the televisor box that sat on his desk. There was a static spluttering, then the white screen glowed orange, finally pale gray, rugged features taking form on it.

Craig Starke looked at the face of the Base senior officer, old "Iron" Walters. The venerable Army officer's profile was seamed with the brown ruts that only space war can sear into a man, and his thick white drooping mustache bobbed as he spoke.

"Well, Starke?"

"Wanted to talk to you, sir," Starke replied. "It's about my brother, just arrived with the new replacements. I want him transferred out of here, immediately!"

"Why?" there was amazement in the senior officer's voice, on his stony features.

"He doesn't belong here," Craig Starke insisted. "It's not right that he should serve under me. The other officers will think—"

"To hell with what the other officers think! They shan't have a chance to think of anything. I was the one who had your brother Richard assigned here. Thought it would surprise and please you, don't y'know."

The older officer's face beamed pontifically out of the televisor box.

"Didn't suspect he was at War College, eh?" Senior Officer Walters winked slyly. "Knew it would please you, however. Both my daughter and I were sure that it would be stupid for a Starke to become a sawbones. Not in the breed. Too many Starkes have been damned fine soldiers, to have one go to pot as a medico. Knew he belonged in the Army. We convinced him, daughter and I. See you at mess."

The box spluttered once again, then paled, the vision of the venerable officer's face fading away.

Flight Commander Craig Starke rose to his feet, cursing. So that was the way the wind blew! The damned meddling old fossil had been the cause of Dick's deserting the medical profession. Commander Walters was so filled with the Army he couldn't see anything else. And his daught—

Starke stopped short. That was it. She was the cause of it! Old Iron Walters would never have lured Dick away from medicine, but his pretty daughter, Bea, could wrap Dick around her little finger.

Craig Starke suddenly remembered at least ten mentions of the girl's name in his brother's letters to him. So Dick had fallen for Bea, and she had talked him into the change. And Bea Walters, daughter of the Base commander, was here with her father. It all added up perfectly!

Flight Commander Craig Starke seized his uniform cap, slammed it on the back of his head, and stalked out to his office. He knew, as he strode angrily past the space ship hangars and on through the officers' dining room, toward Officers' Row, that he was going to have it out with Miss Bea Walters.

CHAPTER II

Catastrophe

When Lieutenant Dick Starke arrived at Officers' Quarters, he found that his room had already been arranged for by young Chanes. The two of them were to share the same place. Chanes was sprawled comfortably out on the cot by the window, smoking a cigarette and turning his head occasionally to watch the mechanics working over the space combat ships at the far end of the hangars.

Wordlessly, Dick threw his luggage beneath his own cot and proceeded to remove his military dress tunic. Then he sat down on the cot occupied by Chanes, letting his head rest in his hands.

"Didn't work out so well, eh, Dick?" Chanes observed sympathetically. "Five will get you ten that he wouldn't even let you explain."

"No," the younger Starke said dismally. "He wouldn't give me the chance to say a word."

Chanes was thoughtful, rubbing his jaw in mute contemplation.

"If you don't mind my saying so, he's a helluva tough baby—even for a flight commander."

Dick shrugged. "He's been up here ten years, don't forget."

"Yeah," Chanes replied. "I guess ten years at the front can process any given material into steel." He proffered a pack of smokes to Dick. "Have one."

There was a minute of silence, as young Starke lighted his cigarette, broken at length by Chanes' next remark.

"Seen Bea Walters yet?"

At the mention of the name, Dick Starke seemed to brighten perceptively.

"No," he answered. "But I'll get a chance to see her after mess this evening."

Chanes smiled. "I envy you, fella. Not only have you got one of the swellest-looking *jemmes* in the cosmos, but you're lucky enough to have her as the daughter of an Army commander, living with her daddy at the same Base you're stationed at."

Dick Starke disregarded the levity in his companion's tones, frowning as he answered,

"I don't know, Chanes. Bea's being up here at the front with her dad worries me. I don't like it. Supposing the invaders get wind of the Base location and come over to sprinkle their radium bombs on us. This isn't exactly a safe place for a woman."

"Old Iron Walters isn't going to let his daughter stay around, if there's even the remotest chance that such a thing might happen," Chanes assured him. "No, I imagine we're pretty damned safe from the invaders. It'll be a long time before they locate this base. We're so well hidden that—"

Chanes broke off abruptly. His gesturing hand paused in mid-air, and he looked sharply, quizzically at his new roommate.

"What's that?" he demanded.

Dick Starke stared at him. "What's that?"

Chanes' forehead was wrinkled, and excitement tinged his face.

"Listen," he repeated. "Can't you hear it? Atomic motors overhead! Lots of them, from the sound. I think—"

The rest of his sentence was drowned in the wail of raid sirens, dismally screeching out their warnings of death and danger above. Chanes and Dick Starke were on their feet instantly, grabbing tunics and dashing for the door.

"An attack!" Dick shouted. "The invaders are above the Base!"

"Wow!" shouted Chanes. "Action at last!"

* * * *

The two young officers were already dashing down the long barracks corridor. Other doors along the hall were flying open, and more figures emerged in hurried excitement. There was an increasing babble of voices, and through the same amplifier that had sounded the siren warnings, there came the staccato piping of a bugle.

"Assembly, before the hangars," Chanes gasped into Dick's ear. "Hot damn, we're going up after 'em!"

Most of the flight officers were already lined up before the space ship hangars when Dick and Chanes arrived. Dick saw that his brother was already on the scene, moving quietly up and down the line, issuing orders to men and mechanics. Hangar turrets were rolling up, and bullet-nosed, sleek-lined space combat ships were being rolled forth.

As Flight Commander Craig Starke went down the line of officers, speaking to all in turn, each man fell out of line and made for the combat rackets assigned to him; Dick and Chanes had joined the line at the far end. Finally, however, Starke was before them. He was calm, cool, and might have been lecturing a student group for all his manner.

"Chanes," he said softly. "You'll report to the commandant's office with Starke and the other replacements who arrived today. I'm not sending any of you up on this flight. You haven't had time to adjust yourselves to our conditions yet."

Enthusiasm drained from the faces of the two younger officers like water from a leaky bucket. Disappointment was clearly written in their every expression. Dully then the pair fell out of line and began trotting in the direction of the commandant's office. Neither spoke, each was too full of his own bitterness. They were lost to the furor around them.

Then the first radium bomb fell.

It came with a singing, screaming, tearing impact, landing far to the left of the hangars. The detonation was terrific, hurling both Dick and Chanes to the ground, spreading orange flame in every direction.

Dick's ears rang deafeningly, and blood trickled slowly from the corners of his nose and mouth. Somewhere, the scream of a man in horrible agony drifted past. The raid siren was wailing once more. An Emergency

Squad Unit passed by, ten men bearing stretchers and apparatus. Chanes was on his feet again, and Dick regained his.

Now the atomic motors of the Base's own combat ships were sputtering angrily, and the reverberations of their engines smashed the sir as they climbed spaceward. One after another, the sleek combat space ships left the ground; streaks that zipped, became dwarfed, then vanished into the fog of the tipper strata.

Dick and Chanes were running again, heedless of the confusion and terror surrounding them. By now four more radium bombs had scored hits somewhere on the Base. Most of the combat ships, however, were off the ground by now. Not many more bombs would land before the huge space battleships of the invaders would be driven off.

At last the two young officers were before the quarters of old Iron Walters. Dick was up the steps in a bound, through the door, with Chanes at his heels. The room they entered was half-filled with wives and children of other officers. In charge were the other three replacement officers who had arrived that day. Wildly Dick's eyes searched the roam for a sign of Bea Walters.

* * * *

Then he saw her. She was in the far corner of the spacious room, her back turned to him. Several of the officers' wives were grouped around her, and Dick saw that she was crying, for her slim shoulders shook with sobs and her lovely blond head was bent.

He was across the room in an instant and at her side.

"Bea," he found his voice sounding strange in his ears, husky. "Bea, darling. What's wrong?"

A short plump woman, one of the officers' wives, turned to him soberly.

"Her father," she said. "Commander Walters was killed by one of the first bombs."

Dick's features hardened as he mentally cursed the terror of the invaders, then softened as he looked at Bea.

"Brace up, honey," he half whispered. "The old fellow was a soldier. No tears. He wouldn't have wanted to go any other way than in battle."

Bea Wallers' sobbing quieted, and she wiped away the tears from her large brown eyes.

"Sorry, Dick, I didn't think of it that way. I suppose you're right. I shouldn't carry on like this."

Dick gripped her arm warmly. "That's the way," he encouraged.

Then he looked about the large room. There were others, from the sound of things, who had lost much in the fury of the invaders' attack.

"Maybe we can be of some use to the rest," he added.

And at that moment Dick realized that the sound of steady bomb explosions had ceased as abruptly as the raid had begun. But for the faint, far-off whine of the ships in space above them, all was now deathly quiet.

Chanes had followed on Dick's heels.

"The invaders," he said, "They've been driven oft."

A uniformed dispatch carrier worked his way through the throng. His eyes searched the group, looking for an officer. He spied Dick and was beside him in a moment.

"A message," he blurted. "The strata-telegrapher picked it up on his space band three minutes ago. He said to relay it to an officer immediately, sir."

Dick nodded automatically, taking the message. The dispatch carrier saluted and was gone. While Bea and Chanes crowded dose, Dick unfolded the communication. Simultaneously, an exclamation of startled horror broke from their lips. For the message read:

NEW YORK HAS FALLEN BENEATH A CONCERTED MONGOL DRIVE. KAMA KHAN'S HORDES SWEEPING WESTWARD ACROSS U. S., MEETING SLIGHT RESISTANCE. BATTLE WAGING FURIOUSLY ALONG ROCKY MOUNTAIN FRONT. PREPARE TO ABANDON SPACE BASE 10, OBJECT OF INVADERS' NEXT DRIVE.—GENERAL S. K. BLAINE, COMMANDER-IN-CHIEF OF U. S. ARMY FORCES ON EARTH.

"Good God," Dick muttered. "It looks like the end of things, if Blaine and his forces can't stop the Mongols at the Rockies."

"New York must have been attacked less than a week after we left War College to come up here," Chanes muttered incredulously.

Bea was white, lips tensed, saying nothing. Her lovely face portrayed mixed emotions of fear and rage. She was trembling slightly, from the shock of the past minutes.

"Abandon Space Base 10," Dick said bitterly. "For what? If Khan's forces sweep the United States, the last territory on Earth to hold out against the Mongols, where can we go? Space Base 10 is the only refuge we have here in the cosmos. Khan and his Mongol hordes have already conquered the other planets."

His jaw tightened, and he faced Bea and Chanes.

"Don't let word of this get out," he commanded. "It can't do any good, and might do irreparable harm. I'll give the message to Craig as soon as the combat squadron comes back."

CHAPTER III

New Orders

Flight Commander Craig Starke sat at his desk, one hand wrapped around a pony of brandy, the other absent-mindedly loosening the collar of his military tunic A cigarette hung almost forgotten from the corner of his handsome, somewhat cynical mouth. Starke was trying, as he had tried many times during the past ten years, to forget the memory of another afternoon's combat in space.

"Six more gone," he thought bitterly. "All of them pals. Burned to cinders in space. One of them might have been my brother."

And then, to drown the rage and futility that swelled in his throat, he gulped the remainder of his brandy in a swift gesture.

A moment later. Lieutenant Dick Starke stepped into the room.

"Well," Flight Commander Starke spoke angrily. "You might knock, Lieutenant."

He glared at his brother, watching the youngster's eyes flick quickly, accusingly, to the glass he held in his hand.

"A message," Dick said quickly, "came in over the stratagraph less than fifteen minutes ago."

He held out a paper in his hand. And while his brother unfolded the white sheet, Dick added:

"I also wanted to tell you that one of the invaders' bombs got Commander Walters, He's dead."

Starke looked up sharply, for an instant fighting against emotion. Then he was calm, apparently.

"I—I'm sorry." He ran a hand across his brow. "He was a great soldier, a gallant commander." Then his voice hardened. "But that's war. Lieutenant, the 'glamorous', 'glorious' adventure you've found for yourself." Then he turned his attention to the message.

As his brother read the message from General Blaine, Dick saw his face pale beneath its tan. Then the muscles of the lean jaw went tight, into hard small knots. At length he looked up.

"You've read this?" he asked. Dick merely nodded. Starke went on, "With Walters dead, that means that I'm shouldered with command of the entire Base. There was one thing Blaine didn't know when he sent this message—the Mongol invaders have already drawn a steel ring around Space Base 10. We found that out this afternoon, when we went up to drive their bombers away from the strata-lines. We've no chance of breaking through them. Not now—inasmuch as we're unable to get help from Earth any longer."

"But, New York—I never thought they'd take New York," Dick blurted.

"No. None of us imagined they would. But they have. And now we're ringed in up here. II looks like the end."

There was an awkward silence. "Isn't there a chance of breaking through?" Dick flushed at his brother's hard stare. "I mean, can't some of us—volunteers, for example—take a crack at breaking through the ring around Base 10?"

"Your ideas," Craig Starke observed acidly, "are as foolish as they are melodramatic, Lieutenant. Tactical plans lie in my authority, not the authority of a junior officer. Please remember that. Good day, Lieutenant!"

Crimson, Dick wheeled and stamped out of the room. There was a strange light in his brother's eyes as he watched him leave, a light that betrayed something of grudging admiration.

* * * *

In orderly entered a moment later.

"This letter, sir," he said, "was addressed to you by Commander Walters. He ordered it delivered to you—in case anything happened to him."

He saluted and closed the door. Starke opened the letter.

Dear Starke:

If you receive this message, it will be because I am no longer with you. As my second in command, you will have taken over responsibility for the Base. There were certain letters from the War Department, which you will find in my wall safe, that you never knew about. They concern emergency orders issued to me less than six months ago—vital information that I was not permitted to pass on even to you. If it becomes necessary to rely on these emergency instructions, for God's sake do so.

It was signed simply "Walters."

Starke rose, buttoning the throat of his tunic. He'd have to get those instructions.

Bea Walters met him at the door of the late commander's quarters. She was dressed in a dark dress that accentuated the lovely blondness of her hair, the delicate lines of her oval features. Her eyes showed she had been crying.

"Come in, Craig."

For a moment he stood awkwardly in the hallway, twisting his uniform cap in his hands, wishing that he could properly phrase the words that he felt inside him. The best he could do was,

"Sorry, Bea. Sorry as the devil. We all are. You know that."

"Yes, Craig," she said simply. "I I understand."

Then he told her of her father's message, of the papers he was supposed to take from the safe. She nodded in acquiescence and he followed her through the living room.

In the study where her father had kept most of his effects, Bea closed the door and walked to a picture on the wall. She pushed this back, revealing a safe. After a moment she had opened it.

"Take whatever is necessary, Craig," she said.

He found the envelopes, big and bulky, with the official stamp of the War Department on them.

"These are all I'll be needing Bea."

She closed the safe then, and the two of them walked in silence back to the living room.

"Wait, Craig." Bea spoke the words softly, yet quickly. He turned to face her.

"I wanted to talk to you," Bea went on, "about Dick." Her eyes indicated that she was aware of the sudden mask that slipped over his features. "Please, Craig," she said. "You must listen to me."

"Well?" Starke spoke brusquely, huskily.

"I asked him to quit his medical studies, Craig. I had father get him signed to this Base."

"I'd figured as much," Starke told her.

"I'm sorry now, Craig," Bea said softly. "I never knew what I was getting him into until today."

* * * *

Starke said sharply, "It doesn't really matter any longer. Good day."

Then he was trotting briskly down the steps of the house, and out onto the hangar field. Darkness was closing in on Base 10 by the time he reached his office once more. Entering, he snapped on the light, slid the catch to the door, and walked over to his desk.

Methodically, he slit open the envelopes he'd taken from the wall safe, arranging them on his desk. He moved across to his cabinet, returned with a decanter of brandy, cigarettes and a small glass. Then he loosened the collar on his tunic and got down to intensive study. These were Craig Starke's emergency instructions. And the emergency was now at hand.

CHAPTER IV

Suicide Squadron

Five hours later, Starke was still in his office. The papers from the War Department had long since been digested, and were now reposing once more in the breast pocket of his tunic.

The decanter of brandy was half empty, and the cigarette tray on his desk was heaped with stubs.

He pondered Commander Walters' instructions about the shipment that had come from Earth six weeks before—a War Department consignment, the labels on the boxes had said.

They were still in the old arsenal, those crates, guarded day and night—though Walters had been the only man who knew what they contained. And now it was Starke's job to bring those crates forth and order their contents assembled. For those crates contained space ships.

Moving in sudden decision, Starke strode over to his desk, snapped on the televisor box. In a moment the face of the communications orderly focused on the screen.

"Yes, sir?" said the orderly, hastily turning his head to face his superior, stuffing a news bulletin out of sight.

"Tell all flight officers, junior and senior, to report here in my office immediately," Starke directed.

Half an hour later, facing the assembled flight officers of Base 10, Craig Starke said:

"I called you men to my office to inform you officially that I have taken over the command vacated by the death of Commander Walters."

Someone coughed nervously in the silence that followed.

"Also," Starke continued, fingers restlessly toying with the letter opener on his desk, "I have several important matters to discuss with you gentlemen. The first being," he reached into his drawer to produce the message his brother had given him earlier in the day, "a stratagraph message from General Blaine, ordering the immediate evacuation of Space Base 10."

Starke paused to light a cigarette.

"You men who went up with me this afternoon, to drive off the bombing attack of our enemy, are all aware that Base 10 has been thoroughly surrounded by enemy squadrons." There was a murmur among the officers.

"I sent scout patrols out into space immediately after we drove off the bombers. These patrols returned with information concerning the strength and position of the enemy."

Starke nodded at a stocky, red-haired little officer.

"Captain Shay, here, has the report of the scouting patrol. Please read it, Captain."

Shay cleared his throat self-consciously, unfolding a chart which he'd been holding in his hand.

"Base 10, as far as can be ascertained," he began, "is completely surrounded by four enemy space squadrons. These squadrons comprise four flotillas totaling eight space battleships, which are patrolling our first Base defense line. In addition, the enemy has a roving squadron of ten cruiser-type space boats, three space ship carriers, and an aggregate of twenty of the smaller combat type space ships.

"This is a total unit strength of forty-one ships capable of independent battle action. The range patrolled by the enemy is the equivalent of our entire border area."

* * * *

There was a moment of suspended silence.

"That," Craig Starke remarked dryly, "is the situation which we face, gentlemen. Briefly, it amounts to this: With our fighting strength at present status, the odds of our combat ships breaking through the ring are roughly—five hundred to one."

He stared for a moment at the tensed faces of his men. Then he went on.

"We have enough supplies on Base to last us for several months. As it stands, the invaders haven't enough strength to take the Base from us. We can hold them off until our supplies run out. But after that—" He broke off, spreading his hands in an expressive gesture.

Looking speculatively across the faces of his officers, Starke debated swiftly the best manner of approaching the reason for this meeting. He caught his brother, in the rear of the group, whispering excitedly to the rosy-cheeked Chanes, who stood beside him. That gave Starke his cue. He said:

"One of our recently arrived replacement officers made a suggestion this afternoon—a suggestion that carried more weight than he imagined. He made mention of a volunteer squadron. That, gentlemen, is precisely what we shall have to count on to break the ring that encircles us."

"But at five hundred to one!" Captain Shay had stepped forward again. "It's madness to think of such a venture, Commander!"

Starke smiled, but without humor. "Five hundred to one, yes. But those are odds based on our present combat fighting equipment. I am speaking of equipment which you men know nothing about. Equipment which arrived at the Base here secretly less than six weeks ago, and which is now stored in the old arsenal."

There was a gasp of surprise from the officers assembled. Starke held up his hand for silence.

"Yes, that's correct. The War Department, expecting some such emergency, sent a special shipment of five hundred large crates—supposedly extra parts for our present space ships—which contain forty unassembled 'mystery' space ships. They are a type that have never been used in this war before. In the Government's files they are referred to as 'suicide ships.' They are single-seater space fighters."

The first gasp of astonishment was nothing compared to the comment aroused by Commander Starke's last sentence. Chanes spoke the amazement of all when he repeated incredulously,

"*Single*-seaters?"

Starke nodded briskly. "That's right. Forty-five of them, to repeat myself. All of them are equipped for one single purpose—to wreak havoc among enemy squadrons. And—*they weren't constructed to return after their work was completed!*"

An officer, at least twenty years Starke's senior in service, stepped forward. His rugged features were perplexed.

"Commander Starke, might I remind you that you haven't given any reason, as yet, for such an attempt? What is to prevent us from asking aid from Earth? Surely, the most sensible strategy would be to wait for help!"

* * * *

Starke answered him calmly enough.

"You're quite within your rights in asking that question. Major Casey. But here is your answer. I was forced to hold this information back until now. New York has fallen before the forces of Kama Khan, and our armies have been driven back to the Rocky Mountains front!"

Above the excited bedlam of voices, Starke pounded his fist on the desk. For fully four minutes, however, the turmoil went on unabated. At length the room quieted, and he could be heard again.

"There gentlemen, is the situation we must face. I needn't add that I'm counting on each one of you to stand by. If we play our hand closely, there's a chance that the majority of us will come out with whole skins. Report at the hangars directly after assembly tomorrow morning. I'll have had the mechanics working on the new ships by then, and all of you will have to become thoroughly acquainted with them. That's all. Dismissed!"

As he watched the last of his subalterns file out of his office and into the darkness of the parade ground, Craig Starke felt suddenly, sickeningly weary. The responsibility of leadership, carried for ten years of ceaseless effort at the front, had been doubled within the past twenty-four hours. And he felt this responsibility pressing down upon him mercilessly, relentlessly.

"I hope," he muttered with eyes half shut, "that I won't let old Walters down. I can't let any of them down. Whatever happens from now on is directly up to me!"

He walked dejectedly back to his desk, slumping down in his worn leather chair. Then he picked up a pen, scratched rapidly for a few moments, signed his name, and leaned back. In the morning, assembling of the suicide ships would get under way.

CHAPTER V

The Roll Call

Excitement ran high on Base 10 the next morning. The news of their plight was received by both Army and civilian residents of the Base with an attitude of quiet determination. Walking from Officers' Mess, Chanes commented on this to Dick Starke.

"Their chins are still up, thank God," Chanes said. "That's half the battle."

"If it weren't for the circumstances, you'd think that a holiday spirit had taken hold of the Base, eh?" Dick answered.

Chanes nodded. "They're all hanging around the arsenal, evidently waiting for the first of the new ships to be carted out."

"Single-seaters," Dick observed, half to himself. "I still don't get it. What chance in hell will such ships have against the enormous battlecraft of Kama Khan?"

"That," Chanes replied, is what we have to find out. Let's get over there." The pair turned their steps toward the hangars.

Mechanics were assembling the new fighters before an interested audience of officers, privates and civilians when they arrived on the field. The first of the new ships was almost assembled, and Dick and Chanes had to elbow their way through the crowd before they could study the craft.

"Well, I'll be damned," Chanes gasped. "Look at that baby!"

Dick's jaw, too, had dropped open in surprise. The single-seater rocket fighter was incredibly small, approximately twelve feet in length, shaped almost like a space torpedo. The pilot's cockpit was just barely large enough to permit movement. Mounted at the nose of the craft were twin atomic mortar guns. On the sleek, steel stomach of the space fighter, there were releases for as many as six space bomb discharges.

The nose of the single-seater was what held Dick Starke's attention. It had been constructed to hold something inside its metal turret, but whatever that something was, it hadn't been installed as yet. Dick commented on this to Chanes.

"What do you suppose is going into the nose?"

Chanes looked at him sharply.

"Didn't you know?" Then, smiling wryly, "Nitroglycerin compression fluid!"

"Huh!" Dick was jolted. "The damned thing not only carries every conceivable type of space weapon—it's a veritable bomb in itself!"

"Exactly."

They fell silent then, watching mechanics rapidly assemble the bomb carriages on the stomach of the tiny space fighter.

"It's funny," Chanes said softly. "Here we are, standing around watching the construction of our own coffins."

"Not necessarily," Dick said. "We don't know who's going to be assigned to them."

"Why," Chanes spread his hands, "it will be a question of volunteers, of course. What else?"

There was a strange sensation in the pit of Dick Starke's stomach. His hands felt moist, his throat dry. He wasn't afraid of death. And he knew, beyond all certainty, that he would be one of the first to volunteer. He knew, in other words, that his remaining hours of life were numbered. And, being young, he didn't want to die.

* * * *

He looked instinctively at Chanes.

From the expression in the other's eyes, Dick saw that Chanes, too, was thinking along much the same lines. Dick grinned. Chanes smiled and squeezed his roommate's arm in mutual sympathy. They turned then, these two young officers, and sauntered away from the hangars. Both of them were silent, each with his own thoughts. They didn't hear the first shout.

"Dick!" It was a girl's voice. "Dick!" They turned, to see Bea Walters running up behind them. She was still dressed in her somber black costume, but she was smiling now, and the blond loveliness of her hair crowned the perfection of her features.

"I heard," she said, "that there's going to be an attempt made to break through Kama Khan's squadron blockade."

The two young officers nodded mutely.

"This might be the turning point in the war," Bea went on. "Ok, I do hope that this new plan is successful. I understand that the invaders have the most important sections of their space squadrons waiting in the first strata. I—" She broke off abruptly at the expression in Dick's eyes, the expression he couldn't hide. "Why, Dick, what's wrong?"

"Nothing, honey," Dick said quickly, slipping an arm about her waist. Then he saw the look on Chanes' face. It said, plainly, "Better tell her, fella. She'll know sooner or later."

Dick bit his underlip. "I have to talk to you alone, Bea. There's something you ought to know." Then, to Chanes: "Do you mind?"

"Not a bit," his companion nodded. "I'll run on along; some things to attend to, anyway."

Wordlessly, Dick led Bea over to the deserted side of an old hangar.

"Dick," Bea said anxiously. "What is it? What's wrong? What's happened?"

"I might as well tell you, honey. It's about the flight, the attack that's planned to break the invaders' blockade around Base 10."

Pain came suddenly into the girl's eyes. "I know, Dick," she said. "It's going to be terribly dangerous. Space war always is. I ought to know. After all, father—"

She stopped, then went on quickly. "I know, at any rate, that the situation is more than most of us realize. I was only trying to be cheerful for your sake—to make you think that I was able to keep my chin up."

Suddenly hot little tears were running down the girl's cheeks. "Oh, Dick, Dick, I can't bear it any longer! It's all my fault. I brought you up here, through father, and now—" She buried her face against his chest.

Dick fought for control of himself, iron control that would enable him to tell her the truth. In a strained, husky voice, he heard himself saying,

"It isn't just war, this time. It's more than that, honey. I've got to tell you. You've got to know."

Bea had raised her head, and was looking at him from tear-stained eyes. Dick hated himself for what he must say next.

"This is going to be a suicide attack, darling. No one has been chosen. Volunteers will be called for. Naturally, I'll have to be one of those volunteers. None of us is expected to return."

He continued grimly, explaining in detail the nature of the new fighter craft that was to be used in the attack. Suddenly he stopped, his voice catching in his throat.

* * * *

Bea had gone limp in his arms, fainted…Dick carried her home, grim-faced.

Back in his quarters, he walked slowly into his room, found Chanes already there, characteristically stretched out on his cot, smoking a cigarette.

Dick didn't speak, and Chanes merely said, "You told her?"

Dick nodded, slumping down on his bunk, head in hands.

Chanes' voice came to him. "What the hell, Dick, I understand…." There was embarrassment, tempered with unspoken comradeship. Then Chanes was going on, haltingly.

"I had a girl like Bea, once. She was—she died—four years ago, when the Mongols took Berlin." His voice suddenly hardened. "So it's easier for me. There's no one left to give a damn."

Dick jumped up and grabbed his roommate by the shoulder. He shook Chanes until the other's teeth chattered.

"Don't say that!" he rasped between set teeth. "Don't ever say that again. You've been like a brother to me, and you know it."

And then Dick Starke blushed like a schoolboy, and Chanes punched him softly in the jaw.

* * * *

They met that evening in the old arsenal. Sixty flight officers and some twenty mechanics, and no one was smiling. Flight Commander Craig Starke, looking more worn and haggard then before, faced them silently for several moments.

"Gentlemen," Starke began, his voice husky, "we are all aware of the reason for this assembly. All of you have had an opportunity to acquaint yourselves with the nature of our new combat ships this afternoon. Last night, I informed you as to the nature of the attack that we had planned. I told you frankly that the officers who man these space fighters are not expected to return."

Standing beside Dick, somewhere in the rear of the assembly, Chanes nudged him sharply.

"Here's the pitch," he whispered.

"There are forty-five of these ships," Starke went on. "We shall need the same number of men for our patrol." He looked meaningly at the ranks of men before him. "I've checked the roster of our squadrons, eliminating ten of the senior officers. They will not be permitted to sacrifice themselves, for obvious reasons stated in War Department instructions." He paused. "That leaves fifty men from whom I must draw my volunteers."

The silence was intense.

"I want all of you to understand that no one is obliged to offer himself for duty in this attack…. That's about all, gentlemen. Now I must ask for all who would volunteer to step forward."

The ranks of flight officers moved forward to a man.

Craig Starke smiled, rubbing his hand across his eyes.

"I expected as much," he said quietly. "But I can't use you all. We'll need men to remain at the Base. I'll check our roster, select those of you I need."

His eyes picked out his younger brother's face from the ranks.

"Dismissed, men," he said. But he was still looking at his kid brother.

CHAPTER VI

Off to Battle

Shortly before midnight an orderly knocked on the door of the room occupied by Dick Starke and Chanes. Dick, who had been sitting sleeplessly on the edge of his bunk, crossed the room in a stride and threw the door open.

"Lieutenants Starke and Chanes?" the orderly inquired.

"That's right." Dick's heart was pounding.

"Commander's compliments, sir," the orderly went on, handing two envelopes to Dick. "Instructions for the morning, sir."

Chanes hadn't been asleep, and now was up beside Dick, reaching for the envelope addressed to him.

"This is it!" he said excitedly. Then they were reading the instructions entailed in each message. The orderly's heels could be heard clicking off down the hall.

"At six a.m.," Dick was reading aloud, "report at the hangar line for attack duty. Additional instructions will be issued there."

"Mine," said Chanes, "reads exactly the same. Well, fella, it looks as though we've been elected...."

Before the sun rose on the following morning, Chanes was out of his bunk, quietly slipping on his clothes. When he had finished dressing he tiptoed cautiously across to where Dick lay sleeping, listened for a moment beside him. Then, satisfied that the other still slept, he crossed to the door. He opened it cautiously, listening again for a moment. Carefully he shut the door and moved off down the corridor.

Once outside Officers' Hall, Chanes turned toward the Strata Communications Building, some three hundred yards across the parade ground. Still moving carefully, he made his way across the field, climbed the steps to the Communications Building.

At the top of the steps he stood for a moment beside the door. Then he rapped softly, three short knocks followed by one heavy rap. After what seemed an eternity, the door opened and Chanes faced a rotund little man dressed in the uniform of a dispatch officer.

Chanes Stepped into the lighted room, and the rotund little dispatch officer closed the door quickly behind him. The fat little fellow turned angrily.

"Are you a fool," he snarled, "coming here at this hour?"

"Take it easy," Chanes hissed. "I just wanted to check with you. The attack is planned, as you know by now, for sometime after six this morning. That gives you two hours in which to warn the ships lying outside the strata line of defense. They can spread the word to the others."

"Yes, yes," the little man snapped. "I'll take care of those details. You handle your end of it, and I'll carry out mine."

"Don't worry about me," Chanes scoffed. "When I get finished with the regular combat ships, there won't be one of them that can reach the strata line."

The other's eyes widened. "The regular combat ships are to convoy the new suicide rockets to the strata line?"

Chanes smiled. "That's the idea. Then the combat ships are to aid the suicide squadron in the attack. You did your work well. The High Command will be pleased, if you don't muff the last of it. These fools here are certain that New York has been taken. That phony message from General Blaine did exactly what Intelligence expected it to do. Now they've revealed their suicide fleet, and it can be destroyed with the utmost simplicity. Then, possibly, our commandant, the Great Khan, will actually take New York—once he has Base 10 under control."

* * * *

The rotund little dispatch officer smiled hastily.

"Fine. Excellent. I'll warn the Red Fleet, then, as soon as you leave."

Chanes was at the door. "Good enough. And I'll handle those combat convoys. Don't forget, tell the Red Fleet commanders that each of the new craft is equipped with high explosive in the nose. Careful marksmanship, with guns trained on that explosive, will eliminate the suicide fleet before they can do any damage."

Then Chanes was outside once more, slipping softly along in the shadows, moving toward the hangar line....

Sharply, the bugler's blasts woke the garrison of Base 10, two hours later. Lights flickered on in Officers' Hall, and men began to pour across the field. Mechanics threw open hangar doors, rolling out the space fighter ships. Moments passed. Mingled voices, hushed with excitement, rose and fell as men moved about.

Then the sudden ear-splitting din of the rockets, splatting to a crescendo, as mechanics warmed the ships. Orange spurts, a long line of them, flashed through the half darkness of the morning. Flight Commander Craig Starke stood in the center of the parade ground, before him a row of flight officers.

He was peering upward, studying the sky, which was a quilting of clouds scattered across gray splotches that would turn into blue with the coming of the sun. The cloud strata behind those splotches was thick, yet ragged enough to give Starke some idea of the conditions in the world behind the gray cotton—a world wherein the invaders' flotilla lay in wait, like a tiger about to pounce.

Dick Starke, standing beside Chanes, shivered slightly in the cold of the morning, shivered too from the excitement that held the field in an electric static.

An officer was moving along the line in which they stood, handing out paper disks, upon which numbers were stamped. He gave the disks to Dick and Chanes.

"What are these for?" Dick muttered to his companion.

"The number on the disk designates the single-seater to which you're assigned," Chanes replied, his eyes following the progress of the rotund little dispatch officer who moved along handing out more disks.

The banging of the rockets had been subdued. Subdued enough for Craig Starke's voice to carry to the men who stood before him.

"Gentlemen, you will be escorted by regular combat ships. There have been only thirty-five of you assigned to the suicide fleet. In the nose of each suicide ship is enough explosive to blow a full-sized space dreadnought to smithereens. This explosive is the last measure which you will be called upon to employ."

"The use is obvious. But don't forget, dive for the enemy only after all your other ammunition has been exhausted. There are radio control panels in each of the new single-seaters. Through means of this, I shall keep in touch with the suicide fleet. Good luck, gentlemen!"

Then Dick was gripping Chanes' hand, hard. His voice was husky.

"Good luck, fellow."

Chanes looked at him for a moment, wordlessly. A look as of pain crossed his face. His voice, when he replied, it was unsteady.

"So long, youngster. Tough it had to turn out like this...."

* * * *

Dick had been assigned single-seater 8. Chanes was slated for number 7. They walked together silently for perhaps thirty yards before arriving at their crafts.

Looking down the line, Dick saw that his brother was climbing into one of the combat space fighters, with two other officers and a gunner. Something came into his throat then.

He, Dick Starke, was going to die. He a soldier, and death was a soldier's lot. But Craig—Craig hadn't even spoken to him—

"Dick!"

The young officer wheeled, to face Bea Walters. She was standing misty-eyed before him, but her chin was firm, her head upraised.

"Bea!" The name came brokenly from him, and he stepped forward, folding the girl in his arms. "Bea," darling," he murmured. "I wish you hadn't come. It makes it harder for me to leave you."

"I'm not here to stop you, Dick," Bea said, her voice quivering. "It's just to say"—her voice broke—"good-by!"

"Good-by, darling." Somehow Dick had managed to say it. And then he was pushing her from him, climbing into the tiny single-seater space ship. It was easier that way, quicker.

A mechanic was rolling the glass turret across the cockpit, a turret that permitted almost complete visibility on all sides. But the gauges in front of Dick Starke were a blur, and he wiped a hand fiercely across his eyes.

Then, from the radiophone panel, he heard the voice of his brother, issuing the first command.

"Combat ships are to go up first. They will wait for the regular combat squadron to follow, just inside the strata line."

The noise that had been deafening a moment before increased to incredible proportions now as the full blast of the combat rockets was turned on. A series of swishing, silver streaks, disappearing beyond the gray of the sky, marked the take-off of the first space fighters.

Then Dick was gunning the rockets of his own tiny ship, ears ringing to the clamor of the other suicide fighters on the line as they too prepared to scream upward.

In the moments before he released full throttle force, Dick inspected the bomb releases, and the forward gun mechanisms. All was in order. Then his hand sought the throttle, pulled back. A moment later, and the tiny ship was hurtling upward into space.

CHAPTER VII

In Crucial Combat

Dick Starke was through the first overlayer, making for the strata line, when he took his first look about him. On all sides, flying combat formation, were the other single-seaters. Dick wondered vaguely where Chanes had taken position. Then, for a sickening instant, he remembered the nitroglycerin that was stored in the nose of the craft. He would never land again.

Last flight! The words beat over and over again in his brain until at last, by sheer power of will, he drove them out. He felt better then. He was a space fighter out on patrol. Nothing more. Forget the rest. Didn't help to think of it, anyway....

Minutes later the mystery ship attackers sighted their combat convoy.

Ten ships, motors idling, rockets silent, waited their arrival, Dick managed to pick out the ship in which his brother was riding. Craig Starke hadn't said "so long," hadn't made the slightest gesture in his direction. To hell with it, Dick thought bitterly. I'm a space fighter, that's all. A human bomb.

The combat ships, on sighting the single-seaters, came to life, rocket splashes spitting orange from their tails, and moved up to meet the convoyed suicide squadron.

Dick cut the throttle, and the light on his radiophone panel glowed. Then Craig Starke's voice came in.

"Follow closely on the tails of your convoy. According to estimates, we encounter the enemy inside of fifteen minutes." Then: "To Lieutenant Dick Starke. Good luck, kid!"

A lump came swiftly to Dick's throat. That had been Craig! Craig! He'd not forgotten him. Dick swallowed hard, grinned a funny half grin. Hell—it wasn't so bad, now. Not nearly so bad!

Five minutes later the panel light glowed again. Flight Commander Starke's voice came in this time with calmness, steel written in every inflection.

"Single-seater 7," he said. "Single-seater 7. You have been under observation ever since arrival at Base 10. You were closely watched several hours ago."

Dick frowned in perplexity. "What the devil— Why, that's Chanes' number!"

His brother's voice went on harshly.

"The messages sent to the enemy were permitted to go through, Lieutenant Chanes, because we wanted it that way. The ships you tampered with this morning were repaired before flight—even the ship in which you now are, the single-seater from which you removed the explosives—hoping to save your own hide.

"The nose of your ship is loaded, Chanes, loaded with explosives! Your scheme boomeranged a hundred percent, Chanes. Now you've got to pay the penalty."

Dick was thunderstruck. Explosives? Chanes had removed the nitro from his own ship? Impossible! Absolutely insane....

"Yes, Chanes," Dick, heard his brother's relentless voice. "You didn't get away with it. We're safely in apace now, Chanes. You can't reach the enemy. And you're cooked. Through. Washed up!"

There was a static interruption, then Starke's voice flooded through, clearly.

"To all men in the suicide squadron! It is only now that I am able to announce that *there is no explosive in the nose of any single-seater!* It was a necessary ruse, gentlemen, to thwart spies within our ranks. Yon are not a suicide group, men. You're a fighting unit—and I'll expect some hell-for-leather combat from the bunch of you! Stay clear of ship 7, piloted by Chanes. His ship carries high explosives!"

Dick's head was swimming with a thousand unanswered questions. Chanes a *spy?* Had this all been a trick to delude the enemy into acting on false information? The realization came with considerable of a shock, the more so because he had grown fond of his erstwhile roommate.

* * * *

Then, swiftly, Dick saw a silver streak shoot out in front of their formation, throttle wide open, fast disappearing.

It was Chanes! Chanes, heading for his Mongol comrades, trying to arrive before the Earth fleet engaged the hordes of Kama Khan. Craig Starke barked through the radiophone:

"There's our spy! After him! He'll take us straight to the enemy!"

Dick gunned forward full throttle.

But the formation, bound by military flight lines, couldn't hope to catch Chanes. Ten minutes passed without a sight of him. Then they saw his ship—and the huge space dreadnoughts of the Red Fleet. They had contacted the enemy!

A thrill raced down Dick's spine as he saw his brother's combat space ship kick over in a wheeling arc, signal for the attack.

Chanes had been trying to signal, warn the Mongol fleet; but Dick, as he drew closer, saw instantly what had happened. The invaders, mistaking him for an enemy, had driven him off with a vicious burst of fire!

For a lit second Dick felt a surge of pity for the young spy. Then his brother's voice, barking combat commands, came through.

"Single-seaters bear down on the largest of the space battleships! Combat craft, engage the dreadnought group. All spacecraft, stay clear of Chanes. He's still dangerous, with that explosive. If you get the chance, fire on him from long range—and aim for the nose of his fighter! He's the only 'suicide fighter' in this man's outfit!"

Dick barely heard the last. Dick didn't hear anything for the next few minutes, because he suddenly found himself in a fight that he'd never forget if he lived to be a hundred.

For as he dived, in formation with three single-seaters, the huge sides of the Mongol space battleships came whipping up at him through the gunsights of his forward detonon mortar. He pulled the trips savagely, releasing shell after shell at the red side of the nearest enemy craft.

He could see men running pell-mell along the decks of the vessel in crazy panic. The guns of the huge dreadnought swiveled helplessly, trying to line on the Earth ship. Then he was past the craft with a final burst of shellfire.

Wheeling in a fast arc, Dick was about to return to attack when the last shell his detonon gun had projected burrowed into the dreadnought's vitals.

There was a mushroom of white flame followed by a terrific explosion. Dick held on for dear life as his little pursuit fighter was tossed about like a cork in a gale.

When he had regained control, he peered out through the glass turret over the cockpit. He ducked his head instinctively, as a rain of fragments showered down. Score Number 1 for the Earth fleet!

Then Dick found himself midst of a milling, spitting vortex in which Earth pilot and Mongol killer fought viciously for supremacy. He felt his ship she, jerked his head around and found a Mongol fighter hard on his tail.

Shouting his defiance, Dick made his century's version of an Immelmann turn and was blasting away at his opponent's rear in a matter of seconds. There was a sudden *puff!* and the Mongol simply disintegrated.

* * * *

Dick pulled up and took a hurried inventory. All over the sky Mongol dreadnoughts were being engaged by the speedy little hornets which Craig Starke had unleashed upon them. The protective guard of Mongol pursuit ships circled helplessly about, unable to compete in such swift maneuvering. Every few seconds there was another explosion as a Mongol battlecraft blew up.

Suddenly Dick found himself on the outskirts of the battle, about to circle back into the fray. He scanned the skies for any lurking Mongol fighter—and caught a lone scout streaking heavenward in an Earth ship.

Chanes! Teeth grimly locked, Dick screamed in pursuit. In three minutes he was within range. Bat Chanes' ship was just as fast. Like two angry wasps, Mongol and Earthman buzzed about each other.

Dick never knew whether he or Chanes was the better pilot. He only knew that his ex-roommate was loaded up with nitroglycerin and was in much the more dangerous position. He only knew that suddenly he was streaking broadside at Chanes, and that all at once the spy's frantic face loomed behind the closed-in glass turret.

Chanes made frantic gestures, and abruptly Dick understood. If he fired at the spy, the resulting detonation from the nitroglycerin would blow both to kingdom come. He could afford only to shoot at the ship from long range.

And that, Dick couldn't force himself to do. "I'm a space pilot, not a butcher," he told himself fiercely. "That—that smells too much of boxing a rat in a trap."

Further strain on his conscience was relieved when Chanes suddenly unholstered a revolver-like ray gun he'd evidently concealed on his person. Chanes gestured then, motioned for Dick to make tracks. And Dick understood.

The spy was going to shoot through the fuselage of his ship, toward the nose. He, Chanes, had failed in his mission. He was disgraced. For an Oriental, there was no other way out.

Tears came to Dick's eyes, angry tears. So Chanes was giving him a chance to escape—because the resulting concussion at such a short range would mean double annihilation. Chanes—spy, Mongol, deadly enemy to his race—was a man after all!

Dick edged closer to the spy. "Go back!" he shouted over the interspace radiophone whose mouthpiece was set in place in his helmet. "I'll take you prisoner! Land!"

And through his headphones came back, "Sorry, fella. But they shoot spies, you know. And even your influence couldn't get me off. It's better this way, Dick. After all, I'm a disgraced man. I failed in my mission. Turn off your headphones, son...."

There was a whistling streak through the sky, and Chanes screamed away in a widening arc. For a moment Dick sat rigid, holding his breath. Then quickly he switched off his headphones, in the nick of time. With a tremendous detonation Chanes blew himself into oblivion. The explosion was so great that even at this distance, thousands of feet away, Dick's pursuit craft tossed about madly. If he had left the headphones on, that last blast through Chanes' radiophone would have torn his eardrums right out of his head.

Shaking the tears from his eyes, Dick barged back into the battle. But there was no more battle. Every single Mongol dreadnought had been blown asunder. Off toward the horizon were flashing streaks, remnants of the Mongols' pursuit ship convoy, streaking for home for their very lives.

An hour later, the victorious youngsters of Space Base 10 gathered in the office of Flight Commander Craig Starke. Each instinctively counted noses. Ten men were missing. Others among them showed the grueling strain of the battle, in bruised heads knocked against cockpit coamings, stiff limbs, eyes still narrow with the horror that had raged.

"Gentlemen!" Craig Starke rose from his chair. "Gentlemen, my congratulations. You have done well today—very well indeed. As a result of your successful flight, the Mongol hordes have been dangerously weakened. They have lost some of their most powerful space battlecraft. Gentlemen, I believe this flight today marks the turning point in the war."

The pilots of Space Base 10 looked at one another, and there were fervent murmurs of approval.

* * * *

A girl stood up then, as Starke beckoned to her. A girl with glorious blond hair, who had been sitting next to the commander's desk. A girl whom everyone knew as Bea Walters, daughter of their late senior officer.

"Gentlemen," Starke said vibrantly, "we have this young lady to thank for the lives of all of us. It was she who discovered that Chanes was a Mongol spy."

"How?" came the chorus from a score of husky, amazed voices. Starke smiled at their eagerness.

"Miss Walters is—ah—a woman," he said. "And being a true member of her sex, she was struck intuitively with the fact that when the invaders bombed us in that vicious raid, Chanes seemed to be less shocked, less indignant than any of us.

"The more she thought about it, the stranger it loomed in her mind. So one evening at mess, when all the officers were out, she slipped into Officers' Hall and went through Chanes' outfit with a fine-tooth comb. And she found—this."

Dramatically he took a small object from his desk and held it up to view. It was a gold circlet attached to a linked gold chain. The circlet pictured a rising sun, with little diamond satellites on the horizon.

"Chanes wore that next to his heart," Starke explained. "He'd been up for a physical examination that afternoon, so he'd left it tucked away in his suitcase. After Miss Walters turned it up, we had him watched every second."

Dick Starke flushed and blurted out, "And you knew that all the time—when he was right in the same room with me!"

Flight Commander Starke smiled tolerantly. "You never would have believed me," he said softly. "You might have—er—spilled the beans to Chanes, and then we would have lost that much ground. After all, he was like a second brother to you—wasn't he, Starke?"

Craig Starke's nearest of kin blushed furiously. The rest of the pilots took the cue and trooped quietly out of the room, grinning broadly. Bea walked over to Dick's side and put her arm through his.

"It's just one of those things, Dick," she murmured.

Flight Commander Starke rubbed his chin. "I'm afraid the little lady's right, Dick," he said, in a smile that was anything but official.

The youngster's head jerked up. He saw that smile.

"Oh! So you weren't sore at me! You—"

"Sure I was sore at you—still am. I want you to be a doctor, not a space gunner. Hell, Dick, you ought to know that a fellow can't show favoritism in this man's airforce. Bad for morale, discipline—"

Dick strode forward and made a pass at his brother. Starke ducked, caught him about the middle and dragged him to a bench, kicking furiously.

He laid him out over his knee, flexed his big hard palm and brought it down hard and often. Dick howled:

"Craig, I'll bust every bone in your body! I'll—I'll—Ouch! Hey, cut it out! That hurts!"

"Give the password, son," Starke barked, whaling away, "or murder it gives!"

"Uncle!" Dick shouted desperately. "Uncle!"

Starke gave him one more whack that raised dust and blisters, and then let up. Dick stumbled to his feet, very red in the face and very sheepish.

Craig Starke got up and caught him by the ear. He led the protesting young space pilot over to where Bea Walters was standing, enjoying every minute of it.

"If you think war is hell," Starke grinned, "try marriage!" And he gave the youngster a shove which sent him straight into the girl's arms. Then he slammed out the door....

"I suppose this is romance," Dick said ruefully as he wrapped one arm around the girl and rubbed his breeches tenderly with the other hand.

"Well," said Bea Walters coyly, looking into his eyes, "you've got to learn the ropes sometime!"

THE STRANGE VOYAGE
OF HECTOR SQUINCH

"Sirs: Remember, I said that the June issue was nearly the best one you put out? Well, the August issue is way ahead of it. This really is the best one. The stories were all so good that I hate to place them, but here goes. 'The Strange Voyage of Hector Squinch' takes first by a mile. This was the only story I had no trouble rating...."
—Wallace Buchholz, Ripon, Wisconsin
Letter to the Editor,
Fantastic Adventures, October 1940.

* * * *

"I don't know why I ever married you, Hector Squinch!" For a moment the shrewish voice ceased while a pair of exasperated eyes swept their gaze scornfully up and down Hector's quaking form. Then the voice went on:

"Go and see your silly science exhibits," it stormed. "Here's sixty cents for your dinner. I'm going to see things for myself. And mind you, meet me here at six o'clock. If you don't...."

"Yes, Cynthia," Hector said meekly, properly awed by the unvoiced threat in her voice. He well knew what the "if" meant; he'd gone through two-week sessions of reenacting the life of a worm many times before. "I'll be here, I promise I will."

"You'd better!" Cynthia snapped and swept majestically away into the crowd.

When she had vanished, Hector leaned against a statue just inside the Hall of Science, and tried to assume an air of nonchalance he didn't feel.

Short and sly-shouldered, Hector was not the jaunty type. And as he peered rather wistfully at the happy throngs milling through the, turnstiles for the opening day of the 1940 World's Fair, he looked even more like what he actually was—one of Life's pipsqueaks.

Hector began to make plans for his two hours of freedom.

There was a bubble dancer at the Parisian Inn—Hector closed his eyes and sighed—whom he was sure Cynthia would not approve of. And then there was his hobby. He fancied himself as something of an Edison, or maybe a Newton. At any rate he liked science. Cynthia didn't approve of science either. So Hector planned to kill two birds with one stone. He was going to drink in all the science he could, for an hour, and then he would seek out the bubble dancer. He felt almost devilish.

Joining the sluggishly moving line of spectators; Hector Squinch, pale eyes beginning to glint enthusiastically behind his horn rimmed spectacles, drank in the glories he beheld. Whirling gadgets, bubbling tubes of multi-colored liquids, fascinating charts and wires—all these received his excited study. He didn't have much, idea of what any of them were about. But they were all quite scientific. That was all that mattered.

He was leaving the "Woman of the Future" exhibit when he saw it.

For a moment the little man almost fainted from sheer excitement. It was incredible. It was magnificent. It was glorious. It was a rocket ship, part of the "Transportation of the Future" exhibit. The mere implications of the huge, bullet-like vessel sent Hector's imagination scurrying feverishly to Elysian fields. A rocket ship!

Crowds jostled by him, pushing, elbowing, but Hector was totally un-aware of anything save the ravishing beauty of the metal monster. A space ship, a real life-size, space ship!

It left Hector Squinch very breathless, and for more than half an hour he stood with skeptical audiences listening to a uniformed attendant's lec-tures on the craft. After the conclusion of each lecture, the guide conducted a brief tour of inspection through the huge ship. Hector followed dazedly along on each of these inspections.

The inside of the rocket ship was very similar—except for gadgets—to the inside of a giant transport plane. There were rows of seats, separated by a tiny aisle, which faced the nose of the ship where there was a sort of pilot's seat. On each inspection, when the audience was invited to sit down. Hector edged timidly further forward—wishing that he had the courage to try the pilot's seat, to sit in it, to pretend he was—in fact—the pilot.

Instead, however, he contented himself with the regular seats where, unnoticed, he could close his eyes and conjure visions of exciting inter-planetary voyages and furious battles with Martians. In each of these day dreams Hector Squinch was the hero, and a sharp voiced woman named Cynthia was noticeably absent.

Hector was bidding adieu to a beautiful Martian woman, whom he had just rescued from peril by means of blazing rocket pistols. Then, in spite of the bravado of his dream, the danger of his position frightened him into wakefulness. He opened his eyes abruptly. Looking wildly about, he be-came aware that he had dozed, that the inspection party had left the ship. He was alone.

* * * *

For an awful instant his stomach had the uneasy sensation that follows a swift drop in an elevator. He glanced quickly at his watch. It was 6:30. He had been napping for over a half hour! Looking out the window beside him, he could see that the attendant was gone, more than likely to dinner, and that the crowds around the exhibit had vanished. Hector was grateful. He would have no embarrassing explanations to make to the guide or spectators. Standing up, he moved down the aisle to the door.

Tugging at the knob, Hector pulled inward, then out. It seemed to be stuck. Putting all his strength into the effort, he tried again. It *was* stuck!

Feverishly Hector threw his shoulder against the door, wincing as he was rewarded with only a sharp pain for his trouble. Quite suddenly it came to Hector that he was locked in. Beads of sweat trickled down his brow. He gazed owlishly through the thick window. He wished now that there was someone outside, remembering as he did, that it was dinner time. He banged futilely on the window.

Hector sat down and thought of suffocation. He thought, too, of Cynthia. The thought of suffocation was more pleasant, so he returned to it, remembering the stories he'd read in newspapers about such things.

"I must not lose my head," Hector told himself firmly.

Somewhere he had read something about doors that opened from the inside as well as the outside. You pushed a button and they opened. Hector began to search for buttons. He found all sorts of them.

With every button he pushed, Hector rushed to the door and tried it. After the tenth unsuccessful button. Hector was growing frankly terrified.

"I must be calm," he said aloud.

But supposing he ran out of buttons? The thought was terrifying. He shuddered and began a search for more buttons, working up toward the nose of the ship.

It happened very suddenly. He had pressed a large red button to the right of the pilot's seat, and was running back to try the door, when hell broke loose.

He felt the floor rising violently to meet his face, and heard a shattering, splattering roar at the same instant. The Hall of Science was still reverberating to the crescendo of rockets exploding when a blazing streak of silver screamed skyward, leaving a ragged gap in the roof of the exhibition hall. Hector was riding in the blazing streak. He'd pressed the wrong button!

* * * *

Minutes later, still dazed and with a bloody nose. Hector pulled himself painfully to his feet, vaguely aware that something had happened. Supporting himself with one hand on the back of a seat, he leaned over to the window, momentarily afraid that people would be descending on him from all corners of the hall. He had a feeling that he might have blown a fuse—or something.

Hector looked blankly out the window for perhaps three full seconds before he grew conscious of what he was gazing at. Instead of the familiar surroundings of the Hall of Science, he was staring out at a frighteningly dark emptiness.

Far back in the distance a ball, very much like the tiny globe of the earth which he kept in his bedroom at home, was fading into nothingness. The realization of his plight didn't descend on his consciousness gradually. It hit with the speed and force of a mule kick. He was speeding through space—that was the only possible explanation!

Hector didn't waste time. He fainted promptly.

* * * *

Hector didn't know how long he'd been lying on the floor of the rocket ship, but as consciousness came flooding back to him he recalled instantly what had happened.

For a moment he crouched trembling on the floor, not daring to rise to a level that would enable him to look out the windows. At last, steeling himself against another swoon, he rose to his feet and made his way unsteadily forward to the nose of the rocket. Uneasily, he took a seat in the pilot's compartment, his eyes fixed determinedly on the floor. Hector recalled that workers on tall buildings never looked down. He wished he knew what the gadgets on the instrument panel before him meant.

Suddenly, and for no apparent reason, Hector thought again of Cynthia. He shuddered at the picture of his wife's face. She would be terribly angry with him when he returned.

When he returned. He almost choked on the thought. Would he return?

Hector wished fervently that be knew where he was going. Then he'd be able to tell if there would be any returning. Hysterically, it occurred to him that he might be headed for Mars. He shuddered violently, remembering the famous Welles broadcast.

After a while—how long he couldn't tell—time had become a vague blur to Hector Squinch. His watch had been broken as he fell to the floor when the ship shot from the exhibition hall. After what seemed to be an eternity. Hector felt his eyelids growing heavy. Then he was asleep.

* * * *

It was daylight when the dipping of the ship threw the fast slumbering Mr. Squinch to the floor. Waking instantly. Hector perceived what was happening. The ship, which had been climbing before, was now pointing downward. There was no doubt of this in his mind as he worked his way forward to the front porthole of the rocket and peered out through the thick paned glass.

A ball, still very much like the globe on his desk at home, was rushing head-long at the ship—or vice versa!

Nearer and nearer came the globe, growing larger with every passing second. There didn't seem to be any way of avoiding a collision. Frantically, Hector realized that the ship and the object were due to collide within a very few minutes. In desperation the little man fought his way to the rear of the ship, There he clutched in a frenzy of hysteria to one of the cushioned seats, bracing himself for the shock he knew was coming. Hector closed his eyes and prayed.

* * * *

"What's he muttering?" asked the bland, plump little man in the ridiculous looking nightshirt.

"Now I lay me down to sleep," replied the bronzed young man kneeling next to the body.

"Funny thing to be muttering," mused the plump little man. "They usually say 'where am I' or something equally unoriginal." He looked across the field at the huge steel bullet-like ship, which had landed like an arrow, nose in the mud.

At that instant Hector Squinch regained consciousness. He sat bolt upright, looking about in amazement.

"Where am I?" he asked.

A series of groans came from the crowd.

"You shouldn't have said that," said a handsome young face bending over him.

Hector looked at the face, then at the body under the face. The fellow was dressed in something resembling a Grecian toga. To his amazement everyone else in the group standing around him was similarly garbed. Everyone, that is, with the exception of the rotund little bald man in the nightshirt, who advanced toward him and spoke.

"Welcome to Olympus," said the night-shirted gentleman.

"Olympus?" Hector was baffled.

"Olympus," repeated the nightshirt firmly, "welcome to it."

"Who are you?" Hector managed to gasp.

"The Civic Betterment Bureau and Chamber of Commerce Greeting Committee for the Planet Olympus," said the little man, with no apparent loss of breath.

"We, the citizens of Olympus, welcome you to our fair planet," the night-shirted chap continued. "Consider each and every one of us at your service during your stay here."

He reached into his nightshirt which, Hector noted, was equipped with pockets, and drew forth a large key.

"Allow me," he murmured pleasantly, "to present the key to the planet."

Bewildered, Hector took the key and stood up. Suddenly it was snatched from his grasp. To his astonishment he saw that the plump little fellow had taken it back.

"Thank you," said the man in the nightshirt coldly. "You aren't supposed to *keep* it, y'know. It's merely a gesture. It's the only key we have. Besides, it doesn't open anything."

The plump little man put one hand behind his back, one foot forward, and cleared his throat. He opened his mouth to speak.

"Come on!" The bronzed young man seized Hector by the arm. "This is where we came in. He's starting his welcome speech."

Swiftly he propelled Hector across the field to a nearby road. The rest of the group also took flight, leaving the little man in the nightshirt quite to himself. But apparently the rotund little nut didn't mind, for he kept right on speaking.

"And we can point with pride," were the last of his words which Hector heard before they were out of hearing.

* * * *

"Please," said Hector as he sat in the back of a sleek limousine whipping swiftly along a country road, "what's all this about? Who are you people? Where am I? Who was the man in the nightshirt? What's all that talk about Olympus?"

The bronzed young man, now sitting on his right, smiled disarmingly.

"Whoa! One question at a time. To begin with, you're on the Planet Olympus. We are, as we said before, citizens of Olympus."

Hector Squinch felt that he might be going insane. He took a grip on himself.

"Olympus," he said as evenly as he could, "is inhabited by the gods."

"That's right!" The bronzed young man was beaming.

"Then you, you people, are gods?" Hector bleated.

"Sure. Why not?"

Hector could think of no answer to that.

The young man continued. "My name, incidentally, is Bacchus. I'm the god of wine and rioting, y'know. You'll like it here, I think," he went on. "That pudgy fellow in the nightshirt was Morpheus, god of sleep. He's the local bore. Makes all the speeches at banquets, commencements, etc."

"Is he the chief greeter?" ventured Hector.

"Self-appointed," explained Bacchus. "Never misses a chance to run off at the mouth."

Hector looked at the assorted personalities draped in and around the limousine in which they rode.

"Are all these other people with us gods?" he whispered timidly.

"For the most part," Bacchus replied. "You'll get to meet more of them later. First of all, however, we have to take you down to the city hall to meet the mayor."

"The mayor?" Hector was startled.

"Sure," Bacchus declared. "The Big Shot, Jove. Chief of the planet."

The reception at the city hall was in keeping with the tenor of everything else that had occurred to Hector, during the previous half hour. There was a drive through the city, motorcycle escort, cheering crowds lining the streets, and finally old Jove, himself, standing genially at the steps to greet him. He reminded Hector of pictures he had seen of General Grant.

With Bacchus to guide him, Hector posed for photographers. He shook hands with Jove, shook hands with Bacchus, shook hands with everybody and anybody while the flash bulbs popped. It was all very confusing.

* * * *

Somehow, he was finally seated across a mahogany desk in the mayor's office, facing Jove. The old man was speaking cheerfully about the weather, horse racing, and topics of a general nature, when he suddenly stroked his long black beard reflectively, stood up, and walked quickly over to the door;, He paused there for a moment, listening with his finger to his lips.

"Good," he said finally, crossing the room and resuming his seat. "I was afraid someone was listening."

"No one is?" said Hector.

"Of course! Scads of people are outside eavesdropping on us," Jove declared happily. "Spies. All sorts of them."

Hector was completely bewildered. "You like that?"

"Why not?" Jove answered. "Shows I'm still important. When I get to the point where people don't even bother spying on me, I'll certainly have become unimportant. I'd hate to be unimportant."

Jove then reached behind his desk and pulled forth a box of cigars.

"Have one," he offered.

"I'm afraid I don't smoke," Hector confessed.

"Damned fine thing," Jove said cheerfully. "There was only one left in the box, anyway." His voice took on a confidential note. "How are you fixed for insurance?"

"Insurance?" Hector fairly bleated in astonishment.

"Sure. Life insurance. Good thing. I've a double-indemnity job here that'll be just the thing for the wife and kids. Got any kids?"

"No," said Hector. "I'm afraid I can't afford any now. That is, I'm afraid I can't afford any insurance."

"Oh," said Jove dismally, "if that's the way you feel about it." He pushed the sheaf of papers back in his drawer. "No harm in asking."

"But why do you sell insurance?" persisted Hector.

Jove waved a hand at the ornate furnishings of his office. "Don't let all these trappings fool you. Sure, I know, I'm mayor of Olympus. But times are tough. My salary isn't what it used to be. Been cut four times in the last six centuries. A chap just has to have a side racket to keep going."

"But life insurance on Olympus," stammered Hector. "I always thought the gods were immortal!"

Jove hushed his voice confidentially. "That's the hell of this racket," he admitted sadly.

With a flourish, Jove rose to his full six feet ten inches, pressed a buzzer on his desk, and smiled warmly at Hector.

"You're more than likely worn out from that trip. Want to get some rest. I've taken the liberty of arranging rooms for you at the Acropolis Hotel. One of our best."

Bacchus stepped into the room in response, apparently, to the buzzer.

Jove turned to the, handsome, slightly dissipated young man.

"Bacchus, I want you to take care of Mr.—" he paused, turning to Hector. "What name are you using?"

"Squinch, Hector Squinch."

"Fine," boomed Jove heartily. "Take care of Mr. Pinch, then, Bacchus. See that he gets around, sees the sights."

He paused to wink knowingly at Hector. "Bacchus," he explained, "is almost as fast as I used to be when I was younger."

Hector was being led dazedly from Jove's chambers when he and Bacchus almost, ran into a beautiful blond woman, who was headed in the opposite direction.

"Hello, toots," Bacchus winked.

"Howzit, Big Boy," the blond answered.

Then she was moving on, and they were walking down the hall.

"That blond girl," Hector stammered bewilderedly.

"Oh, her." Bacchus grinned. "That's Venus. She's private secretary to Jove." He nudged Hector slyly. "Some looker, eh?"

"Yes, yes she is, indeed," Hector agreed slightly hysterically, "but how can she be a secretary, how can she type, without any arms?"

Bacchus smiled. "She doesn't have to. Jove just likes her to sit in his lap and keep him company."

Hector walked on in shocked silence.

* * * *

The Acropolis Hotel was like nothing Hector had ever seen outside of the movies. It looked like a producer's dream of the Grand Hotel and the Ritz thrown together, with an annex built on. There was pride in the glance Bacchus gave him as they walked into the lobby.

"Nice joint, eh?"

"Nice," gasped Hector, "it's magnificent!"

They walked for what seemed to Hector to be several miles over deep, rich rugs to the registration desk. The clerk, a young toga-clad chap wearing severe spectacles, gazed frostily at Hector and his guide.

"Well?" He gave Hector a look that turned his knees to water.

Bacchus, however, was quite in stride.

"What sort of accommodations do you have in this flea-trap?" he demanded.

Taken aback, it was the clerk's turn to gasp.

Bacchus pinched Hector's arm.

"This gentleman would like your finest suite." He looked at Hector. "How many rooms, ten or twenty?"

"T-t-t-t-t-t-," Hector began.

"Twenty," said Bacchus to the clerk. "And make it snappy."

The clerk disappeared and Hector, now thoroughly awed, turned to Bacchus.

"How will I ever pay for such rooms?"

Bacchus frowned.

"Pay? Pay? Why, you don't, of course. All one has to do around this planet is sign an I.O.U."

"An I.O.U.?"

"Naturally. We did away with money years ago. It seemed as though no one ever had enough of it to suit them. So Jove got a brainstorm and established the I.O.U. system. Whenever anyone wants anything, he just has to sign an I.O.U. Now everyone who cares to be, is rich as hell."

Hector was dazed. Dazed but determined. He tried one last query.

"But what about the financial structure of Olympus? How can it hold up?"

"It doesn't hold up," Bacchus replied patiently. "It collapses once every week. But what difference does it make? No one has any money to lose. Jove calls in all the I.O.U.'s every Saturday, tears 'em up, and Monday we start all over again."

Hector didn't understand. It was too simple. There was no sense in arguing in the face of such stupendous simplicity.

* * * *

For more than an hour Hector wandered about his twenty room suite. Bacchus had left him, saying he'd be back around supper time. And now Hector was finding his sanity in definite need of strengthening.

Hector bathed and Hector ate. Then Hector bathed again and ate again. The bathroom was the size of a gymnasium, the tub the proportions of a pool. The breakfast nook, in which Hector dined, must have been planned for a banquet hall.

In one of the rooms Hector found a radio. He turned it on and, much to his surprise, heard dance music flooding from it. He didn't recognize the tunes but they seemed nice enough. At the end of the dance program there was a fifteen minute news broadcast, which turned out to be that of a gossip columnist.

"What local belle," the columnist asked, "was very put out at a local night spot when a jealous girl friend turned her hair into snakes?"

Hector's jaw hung aghast as the Olympian Winchell continued his banter. He was even more amazed at the tune-off lines.

"You have just heard fifteen minutes of red hot news brought to you through the courtesy of the Morpheus Mattress Company," the announcer stated. "Tune in again tomorrow night for the showdown and the lowdown from the lips of the Oracle of Delphi."

Hector staggered to a chair and collapsed gratefully into its depths.

As if delayed until this moment, the tremendous wallop carried in what had happened to him during the past twenty-four hours descended on Hector Squinch. He began to realize things. And, as he did so, he began to think.

In the little man's mind, wheels were spinning, making necessary adjustments. There was no question now of either accepting or rejecting his fate. The situation was as it was. Nothing could change it. It existed. He was on Olympus, God knows how far from earth, and there was nothing he could do about it. He had to resign himself to circumstances. And resigning himself to circumstances was the easiest thing in the world for Hector. He couldn't have been married to Cynthia for fifteen years without learning how to do so.

Suddenly another thought struck, him. For a moment its stunning implications left him breathless. Did he really want to return to earth? Was there anything on earth which was worth returning to?

Picking at the back of his mind was a sharp insistent devil. What about his duty to Cynthia?

Yes, that was true. He did have a certain duty to Cynthia. He couldn't forget her completely. No one who had ever lived fifteen years in the same house with Cynthia could ever completely forget her.

But she could get along. Trust Cynthia to get along. Was there anything else on earth he wanted? People on earth didn't know he existed. They had never paid the slightest attention to Hector Squinch. He was a nonentity. But here on Olympus he was important. Why, he couldn't tell. But he was. That was what mattered.

Hector faced the facts, met the summing up. There was nothing on earth to which he cared to return!

Wondering hazily if he had found Paradise, Hector Squinch fell peacefully asleep.

* * * *

Two hours later, Bacchus shook him out of his slumber. The handsome young god had returned clad in a beautiful dark red toga, evidently Olympian evening wear. He was grinning broadly, as usual, and holding a newspaper in his hand.

"Hello," said Hector pleasantly. "I must have dozed off. What time is it?"

"Time to start the evening," Bacchus replied. Then he threw the newspaper into Hector's lap. "They certainly gave you a lot of ink."

Puzzled, Hector glanced over the front page. There was his picture plastered beneath the top headline. Then his eyes popped wide at the screaming black type on the streamer, reading, "CHAMP FROM MARS ARRIVES FOR TILT WITH ACHILLES!"

For a moment Hector was stupefied. He read the headline over again. Then he reread it. His lips moved silently over it a third time, his veins rapidly filling with ice as a premonition of what it all meant crept up his spine.

He, Hector Squinch, was labeled as the "Champ From Mars!"

Bacchus was still grinning. "Sorry your identity had to get out so soon. But one of the newshounds pumped Jove. Your arrival was expected, more or less, for the past two weeks anyhow."

Hector didn't know what to say. He turned back to the paper, reading the news story with mingled amazement and horror.

In accordance with the time honored policy of settling interplanetary disputes in the prize ring, Olympus today welcomed a gladiator from Mars who has come to battle the local champion, Achilles, in the centuries-old rivalry between Mars and Olympus.

The representative chosen by Mars, traveling incognito under the absurd pseudonym of Hector Squinch, arrived at noon and was rushed immediately to the city hall, where he was formally greeted by Jove and other local dignitaries.

Slugger Squinch, "The Martian Mauler" as he has already been dubbed by advance notices, will take quarters immediately in the Acropolis Hotel, where a twenty room suite has been engaged for him.

Achilles, when asked for a statement concerning his first impression of "The Martian Mauler," was terse but serene.

"Too bad he has to be immortal," said Achilles, "The Axe," "he looks like a cinch to murder."

"Although Slugger Squinch is far from formidable in appearance, local sports authorities are not in the least deceived. They are certain that he must have something on the ball, else he would never have been selected by Mars to represent that planet in the interplanetary championship bout."

Hector finished the article, letting the paper slide from his nerveless grasp. His brain was whirling madly. So that was why he had been received with such fanfare! Hector "Slugger" Squinch!

The little man shuddered violently. This was awful. This was incredible. This was terrible. It had to be set right, set right immediately!

He opened his mouth to speak to Bacchus, but it was almost a minute before the words would come. They were cracked, shaky, when they did.

"Look," said Hector in a half-bleat, "we have to get this straightened out immediately. I am not 'The Martian Mauler.' There has been a mistake. A grave mistake. I might say there has been a horrible mistake. I have never been to Mars in my life. I am Hector Squinch, formerly of the U.S.A.!"

Bacchus grinned tolerantly. "I can never understand you Martians. You always insist on going around under assumed names, hiding every movement in deepest secrecy. That's what your fighter said three years ago. Told us he was from Juno, can you imagine that?

"I can see the psychology of it, however. Mars knows that if his fighter gets licked incognito, he can always swear he never sent a fighter. But the first time one of his incognito battlers wins, just watch him claim victory!"

Bacchus laughed pleasantly, as though sharing a good joke. "Okay, Martian Mauler. Have it any way you want. If it makes you feel any better I'll tell people to pretend that they don't see through your disguise."

Something in the tone of his voice, something in the way he stood there grinning, convinced Hector that he would never be able to make Bacchus believe he was anyone but the Martian Mauler. Hector sighed. His breath trembled with despair.

"Come on," said Bacchus. "Let's get going."

"Where?" Hector inquired resignedly.

"Out and around the town," Bacchus declared with a vague wave of his hand. "You want to see the sights while you're still in one piece."

There was a queasy feeling in Hector's knees, cotton in his mouth, as he replied.

"I…I'd rather not, if you don't mind. I don't feel very good. No. I don't feel very good at all. In fact I feel sick."

"Tush," admonished Bacchus. "I know just the thing to fix you up."

So saying, he seized Hector Squinch by the arm, propelling him easily from the room. Pushing the elevator button, Bacchus turned to wink knowingly at his charge.

"We'll hit the high spots," he promised.

* * * *

When Bacchus declared they'd hit the high spots he was guilty only of understatement. Hector Squinch knew of night clubs, knew of them from the picture weeklies back in the U.S. But he wasn't ready for the Olympian brand.

The Centaur Club, their first stop, was all the famous night spots of the world rolled into one. It was colossal, packed to the ceiling with wildly celebrating Olympian socialites. They were led to a table near the dance floor, near the excellent rhumba band.

Suddenly a voice spoke from behind their table. It was a high, nasal, querulous voice, and Hector turned to face the speaker.

"Hello, Bach," the voice repeated. "Introduce me to the new celebrity."

Bacchus was on his feet instantly, his face wreathed in a wide grin.

"Mercury!" he exclaimed. "You old son-of-a-gun." His hand slapped the startled Hector on the back.

"Meet Hector Squinch. Hector, meet Mercury!"

The nasal voiced young man removed his winged hat and stretched out a paw in cheerful greeting. He had a wide, cherubic face, spotted by a milky way of freckles and stopped by a tawny thatch of uncombed hair.

Glancing swiftly at his shoes. Hector was both surprised and relieved to see that, sure enough. Mercury was wearing winged sandals. Noticing his glance, Mercury grinned.

"Yeah," he said, "just the type of shoes I'm supposed to wear. Can't disappoint the public, y'know. But they're hellish when it comes to dancing."

With that, the young god took a seat next to Bacchus, waving an impatient hand at the waiter. He didn't give Bacchus, or Hector, a chance to say a word before he started chattering again.

"Here's luck, all right," he began.

"All night, ever since I heard that you dropped in on Olympus, I've been worrying what sort of odds I can get on your scrap with Achilles. Now I'll have a chance to size you up personally. Never make a bet unless you know the dope, that's what I always say."

Bacchus broke in momentarily.

"Mercury is quite a gambler," he explained to Hector. "The races are his specialty, but he puts his notes down on any fairly sure prospect."

"Oh?" said Hector noncommittally, "oh?"

"Yeah," Mercury went on. "Just like Bacchus says, I know the dope before I place my bets. That's what I'm getting at now." He paused to wink confidentially at Hector. "Tell me frankly, old man, what do you think your chances with Achilles will be?"

Hector paled. Momentarily he had been able to forget Achilles, and now the mention of the name was enough to give him another queasy feeling in the pit of his stomach.

"Please," he began, "don't wager anything on my…ah…er…battle with Achilles. That is, I mean, don't bet on me."

Bacchus winked broadly at Mercury.

"He's modest," he said by way of explanation.

"Oh! Heh —heh —heh." Mercury laughed metallically. "Why, of course. That's right. I forgot. Like the papers say, he's modest." He lapsed into a disappointed silence.

* * * *

Something inside Hector's mind was insisting that he scream out to these odd young men. Scream out the truth. Tell them that he wasn't planning to fight anyone, let alone the most powerful god on Olympus. Something else wouldn't let him speak. He held his tongue, and a moment later the waiter came up to their table bearing a tray of slim stemmed cocktails.

"What," asked Hector when one of the glasses had been set before him, "is this?"

"A drink, of course," Bacchus frowned. "What does it look like?"

Hector remembered that Cynthia had never approved of him drinking, even if he had ever had the chance. He felt embarrassed, uneasy, and a little frightened. Hector had never tasted anything alcoholic before.

"Is, is it alcoholic?" Hector stammered.

He saw Mercury look sharply at Bacchus, and Bacchus returned the glance with one to equal it. They both turned to Hector.

"That's good," Bacchus chortled. "Capital. Very funny. Of course riot. Ha—ha—ha. Drink it, pal."

Hector did as he was commanded, hurrying himself because of the imperative glances that the two young gods fixed upon him. Although he almost choked on the too great quantity of liquid trying to pass down his throat in one swallow, the stuff tasted like nothing he had ever experienced before in his life.

It tasted heavenly. That was the only word he could think of. Sweet, cool, fresh, splendid. And heavenly. He said so.

"That, that was heavenly!" Hector declared in amazement. "What was it?"

"Nectar," Mercury replied. "It's all we serve up here."

"Actual, honest-to-goodness nectar of the gods?" breathed Hector, who was already beginning to feel a strange glow about him.

"That's right," said Bacchus. "Made in my very own distillery. I control the liquor rackets up here."

The waiter reappeared, placed more glasses before the trio. "Try another," ordered Bacchus with pride in his voice. "Each tastes better than the last."

Bacchus, Hector, and Mercury raised their glasses as one, draining them in a gulp.

Hector noted, with pride, that he didn't choke on the second. He also was beginning to realize the truth of Bacchus' boast. The second drink did taste better than the first—an apparently impossible feat.

Five drinks later, the seventh in all, Hector was vaguely aware that life seemed incredibly merry. Bacchus was laughing. Mercury was laughing. And Hector was laughing louder than either of them, and talking more, too. It was all very rosy, very splendid.

"Lesh ha' 'nother," Hector cried gaily.

The waiter brought the eighth.

Five minutes later the ninth had vanished down three eager throats.

At the fifteenth drink somebody was teaching somebody how to yodel. Hector, after peering owlishly around to see who was guilty of singing in public, realized that he himself was the yodeler.

Bacchus and Mercury were his pupils.

"Yodelllleeeoooo," sang Hector.

"Yodelllllayyyyyyhheeee," echoed Bacchus.

"YodeleoleoleOoooo," Mercury finished.

* * * *

They moved on, then, to another and even more pretentious night spot. How they arrived there. Hector wasn't exactly sure. But they found themselves at another table, in another club, in something less than fifteen minutes.

People were coming over to the table, and Hector was exceedingly busy—what with rising to say hello, sitting to gulp a nectar, and rising to say hello. He thought fuzzily that this was good. Exercise was just what Cynthia had always wanted him to have. He was getting plenty.

Some of the people who stopped at their table stayed to drink with them, and the waiter kept adding more and more chairs and tables to the group until finally it was comparable to a small banquet.

Hector was supremely happy. Mercury was his pal. Bacchus was his pal. People all listened while he sang. They seemed interested while he expounded thoroughly, if thickly, on third term ideas, tariff questions, and the rising price of corn.

Hector was happy. Happy as he had never been before in all his life. People liked him.

It was while he recited the "Shooting of Dan McGrew"—between glasses of nectar—that the sudden death-like silence fell over the table. Hector had gone on into the third verse before he realized anything was wrong. Then he stopped abruptly, reading something in the eyes of those at the table.

He turned. Looked in the direction in which the others gazed. A large, superbly muscled, animalish looking man was crossing the dance floor toward their table. Even loose toga lines failed to hide the lithe, incredible strength of the man. Hector heard a goddess whisper in hushed awe to her companion.

"Achilles," the goddess whispered.

And then Achilles was at the table, smiling crookedly down at the assembled revelers, looking at last at Hector, who stood, glass in hand, staring open mouthed at him.

"Hello, folks," Achilles purred.

"Who's the lily standing there with the glass in his hand?"

"He's looking for trouble," Bacchus whispered hoarsely into Mercury's ear.

Hector felt the eyes of all assembled searching his face, as if waiting for him to handle the situation. He took a deep breath.

"Who," he inquired of Bacchus, while pointing disdainfully at Achilles, "is this ugly ape?"

"Achilles," Bacchus muttered, "meet Hector. Hector, meet Achilles."

"Thug," said Hector weaving slightly and reaching for another drink. "He's as stupid a thug as it has ever been my acute displeasure to gaze upon."

Then, smirking happily at all present, Hector pointed a none too steady finger at Achilles again.

"I can hardly wait," he said loudly and fuzzily, "to get him into the ring with me."

* * * *

Achilles, apparently possessed of even less intelligence than Hector gave him credit for, stood shocked and spluttering before them. He obviously didn't know quite what to make of it.

Hector wasn't quailing. Yet he looked like a man born to quail.

The attention of the entire night club was now focused on their table. Even the orchestra had stopped playing. A dropping feather would have sounded like falling timber at that moment.

Then Bacchus was on his feet, grinning widely, applauding wildly.

"Atta boy, Hector. You'll mow him down." Turning to those at the table: "Three cheers for Hector!"

The group at the table responded with drunken enthusiasm, while the bewildered Achilles stood gaping stupidly at the scene. Hector, between effusive bows to the cheerers, gulped another glass of nectar and moved out from the table toward Achilles.

Hector held up his hands to silence the cheers, and when they had subsided he weaved tipsily for a moment before the mammoth, mighty-muscled god. He peered at Achilles intently, speaking at last.

"Correction," he said to Bacchus. "I'm not going to mow this gargantuan goon down—I'm going to murder him!"

More cheers rang in Hector's happy head, and he bowed so low, so enthusiastically, that he tipped over flat on his face. Bacchus helped him to his feet, pulled him back to the table while the cheering went on unabated.

Infuriated, bewildered, and thoroughly maddened, Achilles' stamped away from the table, in cadence to the crying catcalls of all present.

"And furthermore," Hector screamed after him, "you're nothing but a no-good bum!"

Mercury was slapping him on the back, while the wild confusion continued.

"It's a cinch. Now I know who to put my notes on. It's a cinch. You're the guy who's gonna pin that big baboon's ears back for him. You'd never have had the nerve to tell him off, if you didn't have plenty on the ball!"

Bacchus banged loudly on the table with his palm. And when a half-silence was attained, he spoke loudly to all within hearing.

"Gods and goddesses," he began. "Olympus has at last found its savior. Our friend, Hector Squinch, will lead us from the wilderness into the golden era of pugilism we have so long desired. He will give Achilles the fight of his life!"

Hector, reaching for another drink, was pleased. But he was also puzzled. He spoke. "Whash thish?" he demanded.

"At last we will have the sort of sport we of Olympus have tried to get. We are betting on you. Hector Squinch, to win!"

Hector frowned. "Don't get it. Achilles is an Olympian. Supposed to fight for Olympus, supposed to lick me." He reached for another drink.

Bacchus was grinning. *"We* don't care who is champ, just so he is a *real* champ. If you win, it will give the fight world a new life. Achilles can always come back in a return match—if he's good enough to do it!"

Even through his fuzzy skull Hector began to see the light. He nodded.

"You mean the game's been kinda off-color lately; fighters taking 'dives' and things like that?"

"That's it. Not that you could blame them. Mars has been sending a lot of palookas, and Achilles is quite a mountain. Nobody had the courage to stand up to him and slug. Why I remember one guy who pedaled around the ring for eleven rounds before Achilles managed to catch up with him.

"But we know you'll put up a fight. It'll bring public interest right back to the fight game with a bang!"

Hector rose unsteadily to his feet. "I am for you fine people here on Olympus. I'll lick Achilles if it's the last thing I do!" Then, quietly, with dignity and amid wild cheering. Hector passed out—utterly.

Bacchus was on his feet. "Three cheers for Hector Squinch," he cried loudly. "He's here to put the fight game back on its feet."

"Hip-hip, hooray!" the crowd responded.

"Hip-hip, hooray!" Mercury added.

"Hip-hip, hooooray!" Hector concluded, coming out of his coma for but an instant and passing out again a moment later.

* * * *

When Hector woke the following morning the sun already had climbed above his window ledge, revealing the fact that Mercury slept on one side of him and Bacchus on the other.

Hector felt his swollen head, running a thick tongue over his cottonish lips.

"Oooooh," Hector moaned.

It was enough to wake his sleeping companions.

"What's up?" said Mercury, waking with a start.

"Hector," Bacchus answered, sitting up also.

"How do you feel, pal?" they both inquired of the suffering Hector.

"Oooooh," Hector repeated. "Oooooh!"

"Gotta feel in shape," Mercury stated.

"Yeah, gotta fight tonight," Bacchus added. "Must be in shape to meet Achilles."

Sitting there in bed, head pillowed in his hands. Hector let the room stop spinning around. And as its giddy whirl subsided, he began to recall, with horrible remorse, the events of the previous evening. They were all there, in terrible clarity.

"I'm not going to fight anyone," Hector moaned.

"Don't be silly," Bacchus snapped. "Merc and I have put down wads on you. You can't fail us."

"No," Mercury agreed. "We're your friends. Can't fail your friends."

"Haven't enough time to train for it," Hector said in a desperate attempt to lie his way out.

"Train?" said Mercury.

"Train?" repeated Bacchus.

"Uh-huh," Hector replied, suspecting the worst.

"You don't train for fights up here. Nobody trains," Bacchus was explaining. "Besides, even if you wanted to train, wanted to break a sacred tradition among our dissipated pugilists, you wouldn't have time for it. You fight tonight."

"Tonight?" Hector's voice was a horrified squeak.

"Tonight," Mercury repeated firmly.

"Ohhhhhhh," said Hector Squinch, collapsing in a heap on his pillow.

"Don't let it worry you, pal," Bacchus reminded him. "It's gonna be a cinch, after the way you told Achilles off last night!"

"Ohhhhh," said Hector, who had been trying very hard to forget that incident. "And I was just beginning to enjoy it so up here!"

"Get some sleep," Mercury advised, "and you'll feel a lot better about the whole thing."

"Yes," agreed Bacchus, climbing out of bed. "Get some shut-eye. You'll be needing it when Achilles is chopping at you."

Then Mercury and Bacchus were gone.

* * * *

After an anguished half hour of tossing about in his bed, Hector forced himself to rise. He forced himself to dress, and forced himself to face himself in the mirror.

His head wasn't nearly as large as it felt at the moment. His tongue, when he extended it, didn't have nearly the thick covering of moss he suspected it had.

He noticed, however, the trembling in his hands as he tied his cravat. Noticed, and wondered if the trembling could be blamed on the night before or the night vat hand.

"There won't be any night at hand," he told himself aloud. But even as his quavering voice split the silence, he knew that he lied to himself. There wasn't any way out of his predicament.

"I could run away," he thought desperately.

"But where?" the face in the mirror answered. "Where could you run to? Besides, Bacchus and Mercury are your pals. You've never had pals before. Pals don't let pals down. It just isn't done."

"But I'll be murdered," Hector told his reflection.

The reflection wiped away the start of a tear from a rheumy eye and answered, "You just can't let them down. They believe in you. No one has ever believed in you before. It's too late."

"Yes," Hector agreed with himself. "It's too late. There's nothing I can do."

Suddenly, from out of the gloom and dejection which hung about him like a shroud, there came a ray of hope. A faint, wan ray, but hope, nevertheless.

"The real Martian Mauler might appear in time to save me!" Both Hector and his reflection spoke as one.

Hector repeated the wish all day long. But as night came, he knew it was a futile thing. Bacchus called for him at seven.

They took a cab to the Colosseum, where the bout was to be held. Mercury, it seemed, had been delayed at the last minute. Something had come up. But he would get to the arena before the battle, Bacchus assured Hector cheerfully.

Several times during the journey Hector was on the verge of breaking down, of making a more or less hysterical confession to Bacchus, a plea that would save him from Achilles. But something held the little man back.

He was scared. Scared as hell, and jittery. Bacchus saw it in his every gesture. He commented on it, bewilderedly.

"What's up?" he asked. "Haven't got the jitters?"

Hector couldn't admit shame before Bacchus. Bacchus was a friend. Bacchus was a pal. They all were. He couldn't let them down. Somehow, he couldn't do it.

This was Hector's first opportunity in life to come through. And he was determined, with a fierce burning emotion, that he'd not fail them. Even if it killed him.

"Don't mind me," he said in a trembling falsetto, "I always seem frightened before a fight. It's just a nervous reaction. Makes me all the more like a killer when I climb into the ring."

"Oh," Bacchus said, his voice heavy with relief.

They lapsed into silence for the rest of the journey.

In the dressing room of the Colosseum, Hector was herded over to a locker by three stalwart bald-headed attendants. There his clothes were swiftly removed from him, and a loincloth substituted instead. It was a gaudy affair, made of some silky substance, and striped with horrible orange and purple lines.

Bacchus, Hector was relieved to note, had gone to take care of the details of the match.

Then, when his feet had been shod in the many-thonged Grecian sandals that were thrust upon him. Hector stood up. The attendants, who hadn't been particularly noticing his physical dimensions previously, stepped back aghast.

"Wow," ejaculated one of the three bald-heads, "look at th' phizzick on the punk!"

* * * *

Hector blushed, painfully conscious of his washboard ribs, toothpick arms, pale, hairless body, and thin, knock-kneed legs. He was acutely aware that he was not at his best in such attire. The loin cloth had been tailored for a chap twice as large as himself, and hung dejectedly from his scrawny body—as though ashamed of the wearer.

By now the bald-heads were bent in gales of laughter. Loud uncontrollable, painfully embarrassing derision rent the dressing room. Head bowed, crimson cheeked beneath the scorn of the attendants, Hector thought bitterly that execution was bad enough, but such a shameful execution was almost past bearing.

Bacchus entered the room, and the bald-heads fled in rapid confusion before his icy glare.

"Well," said Bacchus, looking long and thoughtfully at Hector. "Well, well!"

"Hello," said Hector Squinch. Bacchus, not being the dullest of gods, perceived the shame that poured forth from the little man's eyes. He decided to take a stab at cheering him up.

"Well, anyway, no one can accuse us of having fattened you for the kill."

The words had the opposite effect on Hector from that which Bacchus had intended. He shuddered violently, remembering the gigantic, bone-crushing stature of Achilles. Nevertheless, he bit his lip. He was determined Bacchus should think him nervous rather than afraid.

"Remember," chattered Hector, "I'm always this way just before a fight."

"Buck up," pleaded Bacchus.

"What's it matter? Brains are what count, little fellow, not brawn."

Hector said nothing, but the expression on his face indicated that he refused to be consoled. He put his hands behind his back and began to pace back and forth very dramatically—a gesture that lost its drama when he tripped himself up on his oversized sandals.

Bacchus helped him to his feet.

"Come oil. You're to go on in five minutes. We might as well get started. The preliminary matches are just about over."

The roar of the mob gathered in the Colosseum drifted down to the dressing room corridors, loud to their ears. Yes, the last bout before Hector's was apparently ending in wild excitement.

Bacchus found a cloak which he draped over Hector's thin shoulders, giving the little man some respite from the embarrassment he felt.

"There now," Bacchus said. "The cloak will keep you warm. Don't let all this get you down. It won't last long."

"Which," said Hector starting out of the dressing room, "is about as pretty an exit line as I've ever heard."

* * * *

As they walked down the long tunnel-like corridor leading to the arena, Hector paled, the noise of the crowd becoming bedlam, growing louder and louder while they approached.

Then, suddenly, the noise subsided. All was quiet for an instant, then a hoarse, frenzied screaming broke from thousands of throats. Hector stopped dead in his tracks.

"What," he muttered thickly, "has happened?"

Bacchus shrugged amiably. "Just the end of the last preliminary fight, I guess."

Less than two minutes later, when they were nearing the opening that led into the arena, Hector observed a panorama that proved the accuracy of Bacchus' guess.

Four trainers, carrying a body awkwardly down the aisle of the arena, were approaching. As they entered the tunnel, Hector and Bacchus were forced to step to one side. The two caught a glimpse of the fighter being carted back to the dressing room.

One look at the bloody, twisted, pulverized features of the gladiator was enough for Hector. He grabbed tightly to Bacchus' arm. Grabbed tightly to keep from fainting.

Emerging from the tunnel opening into the brightly lighted arena. Hector and Bacchus were met with a swift and spontaneous burst of cheering. Somehow, as they walked down the aisle to the ring. Hector felt less lonely, a little warmer.

Bacchus, grinning, clapped him on the back. "That's for you. The crowd likes you, Hector."

"Like me in the all-concealing raiment," Hector corrected him. "Wait until I have to remove it for the battle."

Then they were at the ringside, climbing the steps. There were many men there, officials, reporters, photographers, guards, but Hector was too dazed to notice any of them.

Someone was pushing him into a corner. He looked up wildly to see that it was Bacchus, still wearing his perpetual grin, saying words that Hector couldn't catch above the roar of the crowd and the pounding of his heart. He knew it didn't make any difference. Nothing that anyone said would make any difference now.

His vision focused more clearly as he calmed somewhat, and he looked swiftly across the ring, to the opposite corner, to see if Achilles had arrived yet. The Killer Giant of Olympus was not yet in the ring. But Hector's relief was momentary, for he knew Achilles could be depended upon to arrive at any instant.

Not less than ten seconds later, bedlam let loose over the packed Colosseum. Achilles was making his triumphal entry into the arena. Somewhere in the gallery, a band struck up Entrance of The Gladiators and the tune brought nostalgic pangs to Hector. It was the air they had played when he, as a kid in Iowa, watched the circus entertainers parade into the Big Tent.

But this was no chorus. This was Achilles.

* * * *

Hector glimpsed his shaved skull gleaming under the huge lights, bobbing down the aisle toward the ring. There were rows and rows of handlers following the massive giant, reaching out to pat him on the back, shouting loud encouragement.

Achilles grinned cockily at all this, waving clasped hands above his head, nodding, bowing, flexing his tremendous muscles for the adulation of the multitude.

Hector winced, trying to draw his eyes from the fascinating animal grace of his opponent.

Then Achilles was climbing into the ring, moving panther-like around it, waving to his backers, smiling with his big yellow dog teeth. Men were clearing the ring until at last Achilles took his position in the corner opposite Hector, and there was no one left in the squared canvas except the gladiators, the referee, and an announcer.

Bacchus stopped grinning. A frown creased his forehead.

"Can't understand what's happened to Mercury," he muttered.

A hush fell over the arena while the referee stepped to the center of the ring and held his hands aloft for silence.

"Lajryyyyydeeeze and Gemp'men," he roared. "We are here tonight to see the interplanetary rough-and-tumble champeenship!" He looked at Hector. "We hope," he added, dubiously.

The outburst that followed took a full ten minutes to quell. Men shouted, women, screamed, children yelped, and the Colosseum went mad.

At last the referee was moving toward Hector, who was still clutching frantically to his cloak. The referee pointed a finger at him, then grabbed one of his hands.

"In dis corner we got the representatiff from Mars." Cheers. "One Slugger Squinch, de Martian Mauler!" Good natured laughter and more enthusiastic cheers.

Bursts of additional cheering carried on for several minutes, indicating that there are always people willing to champion the underdog.

"Squinch weighs," the referee began, then looked quizzically at Hector. "Squinch weighs," he began again. Then, disgusted, "Oh, well, folks. It don't make no difference wot his weight is." He looked curiously at Hector, shook his head again, as if troubled by grave doubts.

Then he strode across the ring to the corner occupied by Achilles. Stopping within three feet of the muscular giant, he pointed his finger dramatically.

"An' in dis corner," he paused for emphasis, "in dis corner we got the champeen of da woild, universe, an' incidental solar systems, Achilles—da Axe!"

* * * *

The volume of sound that split the silence was deafening, pouring down on the I ring from every corner of the arena.

Achilles danced nimbly to the center of the ring, holding his hands clasped aloft and grinning—like a wolf before the kill.

Hector made for the ropes and tried to crawl through them to the safety of the aisle. He wanted to leave, rapidly.

Bacchus, however, seized him gently but firmly by the collar of his oversized cloak, forcing him back on his stool.

"Be calm," ordered Bacchus. "This could be worse."

"How?" Hector, inquired logically enough.

A hush that was as terrifying as it was sudden, fell over the arena. Hector, heart hammering furiously against his thin chest, knew that the battle was, about to start. Bacchus was tugging at the cloak around his shoulders, and before he could prevent it, Hector felt it slide free—leaving him in his much-too-big loin cloth and absurdly large sandals.

"I don't have to give you any advice," Bacchus was speaking rapidly into into Hector's ear. "You ought to be able to size him up in a round. Then you can get to work on him. Don't forget, it's rough-and-tumble. No holds are barred. Good luck, pal!"

The bell clanged simultaneously with the movement of Hector's stool being jerked from under him. He was forced to hang to the ropes until strength returned to his knees.

Achilles, the man-eating, giant-killing Achilles, was advancing across the ring toward him. The fight was on! The fight was on. Achilles was moving down on him. And Hector was as yet unable to move a muscle. The little man was paralyzed by fear!

The screams of the crowd had settled to a dull unnoticed din in his ears, had become merely a background. Achilles was less than five feet away, but advancing cautiously toward him—a little bit wary of the man who had nerve enough to tell him off just the night before.

Achilles, three feet from Hector, gathered himself for the spring. The screams of the crowd were ear-splitting. And still the little man in the absurdly oversized toga didn't move.

It happened as one motion. Achilles leaped, launching his gargantuan hulk through the air, covering the remaining distance to Hector. It happened at the same instant that Hector's knees gave out completely and he sagged to the floor.

The crowd went mad. Hector could hear them going mad as he lay there on the canvas wondering why he was still unharmed.

Opening his eyes he saw the reason.

* * * *

His swoon had been as perfectly timed as a swift ducking under the leap might have been—and Achilles had hurtled past him. Hurtled past him and out through the ropes of the ring, into the press row!

The referee was counting, for Achilles, who was still trying to clamber back into the ring. Hector, somehow, had risen weakly to his feet, was backing toward the other end of the ring, staring at his gigantic opponent with unconcealed amazement.

Then, for but a second, the din of the crowd registered on Hector's consciousness once again. They were cheering. They were cheering for him. They were cheering for Hector Squinch. Slugger Squinch!

Hector's eyes were misty, and his knees grew strong again. But his soul was stronger. The cheers of the crowd had given strength to the absurd little gladiator.

Hector spit on his hands.

The crowd roared.

Hector beckoned to Achilles, laughed at him, beckoned once more. The crowd went crazy.

In the back of Hector's mind there was a thought. A small but terribly important thought. It concerned a legend—about Achilles' heel. He wondered why he had never remembered it until this moment. Achilles was tough. But he was a sucker for a tap, on the heel!

His plan was straight in his mind as he saw Achilles climb back into the ring, bellowing with rage, and advance upon him. Hector knew he wouldn't have the strength to go after the heel tooth and nail. He remembered the Japanese. Win by yielding.

He would yield. He would let Achilles bounce him around a bit, working to get his hands on that heel!

Achilles rushed. Hector, like the first of the ancient martyrs, stepped forth to meet him.

The next few minutes were impossible agony. Three times Achilles lifted Hector's frail body into the air. Three times he sent it smashing to the canvas. At last he fell full length on the little man—the little man who was bleeding from ears and nose, but whose battered mouth was smiling.

Achilles reached for a leg-lock on Hector, which put Achilles' legs in position before Hector's face. This was it!

The pain was unbearable, but somehow Hector fought off the swimming nausea that seemed to cloud his brain. He had to get that heel. Had to get it before he passed out.

His small hands clutched around the giant's ankle, drew the foot toward him. Brought the foot to his face. Hector bared his teeth. He was going to bite that heel as it had never been bitten before.

But even as he saw the foot. Hector paled. Both of Achilles' sandals were made with thick copper plates to protect his heels!

Blackness descended on Hector. Somewhere in the distance he heard a gong ringing, loudly.

* * * *

Bacchus was talking, and Hector was back on his stool.

"Good work," Bacchus said. "You almost had him, if you hadn't gone unconscious. Wear him out. Dodge the brute. Like you did at the start. You're a master at that technique. Capitalize on it. Don't tussle with him."

"What about his heel?" Hector said, pushing the ammonia bottle away from his nose. "I have to get his heel."

"Forget his heels," Bacchus advised. "He's kept them well protected for centuries, ever since he lost a decision on one of them. That's an old gag. He's wise to it."

Hector was silent. But he knew that, somehow, he had to get Achilles' heel plate off. It was his only chance. He wasn't a master dodger. He'd been lucky when he swooned. Bacchus didn't know that.

Then the gong rang again, and the comforting stool was jerked from beneath Hector. Another round. The bell had saved him in the last one. If he didn't get that heel plate off, nothing would save him in this one.

Never in his life had Hector been so spent, so utterly weary. He wasn't a strong man to begin with. And Achilles had put him through every conceivable torture. He couldn't stand much more, Hector knew. This would be his last effort.

But first he would need a few seconds more of rest. He watched Achilles moving confidently in on him. Then he darted to the other side of the lumbering giant.

With a bellow of rage, Achilles turned, making for him again. Hector artfully skipped around him once more.

The crowd screamed.

Hector ran, and continued to run, in spite of the rage that Achilles thundered after him, in spite of the fact that the noise from the crowd was beginning to be sprinkled with boos.

He faced Achilles at last. Savagely, the huge Olympian rushed in on him, lifted him shoulder high. Hector winced, as he felt the canvas smashing up at him. But it was going to be worth it. It had to be.

They were down again, and through the maze of pain that racked his brain and body. Hector knew that Achilles was atop him once more, in the same position as before.

Hector grabbed the foot. But he didn't bother with the heel. It was the sandal he was after. The heel plates were attached to the sandal. Remove the sandal and you had the heel.

Hector worked feverishly on the sandal lacings. Achilles, busily engaged in bending Hector's own legs into pretzels, apparently didn't notice him.

The crowd had evidently sensed Hector's objective, for they were screaming frenziedly. He couldn't distinguish what the crowd was saying, for blackness was slipping over him once more. He fought it off. He had to keep conscious. The sandal was almost off.

At last, the sandal came loose in his hand!

Hector wasted no time. He brought the bare heel of Achilles up to his face. Furiously, he sunk his teeth into that heel. Achilles, if the legend was true, would collapse!

But Achilles didn't. He kept right on tying Hector's legs into pretzels. And as Hector glanced at Achilles other sandal, the one he hadn't removed, he saw a tiny lock at the top of the lacings.

Despair flooded the very soul of Hector Squinch. He knew now what the crowd had been trying to tell him. He'd been working on the wrong heel!

A cloud of blackness rushed over Hector again.

* * * *

He was on his stool. Two people were talking. One was Mercury, the other, of course, Bacchus. Mercury must have arrived.

"Is it all over?" Hector murmured through bloody lips.

"No. You were in luck, pal," Mercury was saying. "Saved by the bell again."

"Saved," Hector said bitterly.

"Saved!"

"Don't talk," Bacchus advised him. Then Mercury placed something to his lips. It was nectar. Hector swallowed great gulps of the refreshing stuff. He drank the whole bottleful. He reeled in his seat.

The bell rang again. The stool was gone. Somehow he was on his feet once more. But he was through. Hector knew he was through. He'd never have a chance to get that other sandal off, even if he were able to open the lock. But he laughed happily. He felt like bouncing. He felt like flying. He spread his arms like wings.

Hector saw Achilles lunging at him. Hector grinned and waited. Best to get it over with quickly while he was happy.

Achilles seized him about the waist, lifted him high, slammed him down to the canvas.

Hector bounced up like a streak! He got dizzy when he stayed down! Hector was "out on his feet" in any man's language. But an inner exhilaration was still forcing him up from the canvas every time Achilles downed him. He felt no pain, and he rather liked the bouncing.

Hector lost track of the number of times in the past seven rounds that Achilles had bounced him to the canvas. Maybe a hundred. Maybe two hundred. What did it matter, he couldn't feel it.

The crowd was hysterical. Never had they seen such courage, never had they suspected that the beaten, bloody, tortured little absurdity in the ring had such guts. It was incredible. He refused to be downed!

Achilles was wearying. Smashing a man to the canvas can become terribly monotonous. Especially if he keeps getting up, when by all the laws of God and man he should stay down.

But Achilles, weary as he was, was not to be daunted. He resolved to try again.

Disinterestedly Hector watched the big fellow moving across the ring toward him, felt again those massive hands lifting his bruised and battered body high into the air.

He crashed to the canvas. The jarring almost ripped him apart. Something tinkled beside him.

Hector's outstretched hand closed around a metal plate.

And then Hector sobered. He felt wracked with pain. He was being killed! The nectar Mercury had given him had dulled his senses. But now, he could feel again. Once more would kill him—he knew it!

Achilles dropped to his knees beside the prostrate Hector, grinning wolfishly to see that the little man was apparently down for good this time.

And something clicked in Hector's brain. In his hand was a copper plate! Achilles' heel plate!

Hector turned himself over painfully, reached desperately with his closed hand for Achilles' sandal. The big man laughed at his absurd efforts to reach the heel. Even extended it mockingly.

Hector, grabbed it and bit—deep—with all his last remaining strength.

And Achilles, the Axe, the Killer, the Great, howled with pain!

The crowd which had become hushed in an awed tribute to the last stand of Hector Squinch, heard that bellow. Heard that bellow of pain and rose to its feet shouting madly.

Hector had Achilles on the run!

The gigantic battler was on his feet, or one foot, for he was hopping along holding his heel, screaming. Hector dragged himself up from the canvas by sheer will power, setting out after his massive opponent.

Achilles wasn't used to hopping about on one foot. And when he fell sprawling to the canvas a moment later, Hector threw himself upon the giant, sank his teeth once more into the heel.

Achilles passed out cold!

Hector teetered to his feet, smiling foggily at the screaming, maddened crowd. The referee was holding his hand aloft. People were swarming into the ring, lifting him to their shoulders.

Then Hector, too, passed out completely.

* * * *

The long tables were crowded with brilliantly attired people. Hector had lost the first self-consciousness he felt with the opening speeches in his honor. Jove was talking now.

"And we wish to welcome dear Hector Squinch a second time. Not, as a visitor, but as a brother and permanent resident of Olympus. As Mayor of this planet I can heartily say that all of ushered are honored to have such a chap in our midst."

Loud cheers, clacking of knives on table tops.

Tears ran unashamed down the cheeks of Hector Squinch. He smiled warmly at Mercury who sat on his right, and Bacchus who occupied the seat to the left of him. He, Hector Squinch, had found his place in the world. Well, maybe not in the world, exactly, but in the cosmos, anyway.

Jove, was about to continue when there was a sudden interruption at the far end of the banquet hall. A voice was heard, ringing stridently.

"I'm sorry, I have to get in," said the voice.

Jove looked up.

"Who is it?" he bellowed.

There was a flurry, and a tall, thin old man with a wrinkled face and kindly eyes, dressed in a toga and carrying a staff, entered.

"Charon," the name exploded from Jove's lips.

"What brings you here, Charon?" someone shouted.

The old man advanced to the side of Jove.

"There is an alien in our midst," he announced.

"Charon is the immigration boss on the river Styx," Mercury whispered into Hector's ear.

Then Charon was pointing a gnarled finger at Hector.

"You, sir. Are you Hector Squinch?"

Hector rose, an awful premonition clutching at his heart.

"Yes," he gulped. "Yes, I am."

"I'm sorry," said Charon, and Hector felt sure the old man was sincere. "But you'll have to come with me. Achilles insisted that I look you up. I had to do it. Found out you aren't from Mars. Found out you're from Earth, from the United States. I found out you aren't even immortal!"

There was a gasp from the assemblage, a gasp of shock, sorrow, and surprise.

Jove looked at Hector.

"Is this true, Heck?"

"Yes," Hector admitted, voice choking. "I'm afraid it is."

* * * *

Charon reached into his toga and was holding a sheaf of papers.

"I'm sorry," he said fumbling apologetically with his papers, "but the law says you'll have to leave, now, with me. Only immortals have a place on Olympus. Can't do anything about the law. You haven't died yet, y'know, so you can't be immortal."

"This is outrageous!" Jove bellowed. "Heck is an all right guy. I'll vouch for him!"

Charon shook his aged head.

"Sorry, Jove, but you know the law as well as I do."

Jove fell silent, a huge tear trickling down his face onto his black beard. The bottom had fallen out for Hector.

In the space of twenty-four hours he had held utter happiness in his hands. And now it was gone. He had to leave. Had to return to Earth, to Cynthia, to a mad, stupid, heartless world—where people hated, and thieved, and fought among themselves. A world that had no place for Hector Squinches.

His eyes were affected with a dimness that made the room seem to swim before him. Faces looked up sympathetically at him from the long banquet tables. Faces of friends, people who liked him for what he was, and loved him for what he wasn't.

His voice, when he turned to Charon, was husky, off-key.

"I guess you're right," he conceded.

"I'm not an immortal. Just a Squinch, a Hector Squinch, at that. I'd better be going with you."

He turned, then, and made his way slowly along the banquet hall, shaking hands with the friends he might never see again.

"I'll save you some nectar," Bacchus said huskily.

"When you come back, I'll give you some sure bets," Mercury promised him, then turned to hide his watery eyes.

"Don't worry," said Jove. "I've got some influence. I'll do all I can."

He was at the door, waving to them all for the last time, when voices broke forth, led by the faltering basso of Jove.

"For he's a jolly good fellow, for he's a jolly good fellow. For he's a jolly good felloooooooow, which nobody can deny!"

* * * *

Hector Squinch blinked back the tears and walked slowly from the room. Charon, staff in hand, followed mournfully behind him.

They were at the Styx, pausing on the bank, for one last look at Olympus. Hector turned to Charon.

"It's been fine," he said softly. "More than fine." A moment of silence, then, "I don't suppose I'll ever see it again."

"When you die," Charon reminded him, "they'll get you back here. Jove has influence."

"Jove. Good old pompous blustering well-meaning Jove." Hector smiled in remembrance.

"He is a bit of an ass, isn't he?" Charon agreed clumsily.

"But you couldn't want a better Mayor." They both spoke the words at the same instant, stopped short, then smiled. Charon extended his hand.

"Don't usually fraternize with my passengers but I want to say goodbye to you. I couldn't help what happened. Forgive it."

"I know," Hector nodded in understanding. Then he stepped into the little boat at the bank.

"Think you can make it alone?" Charon asked.

"Yes, I think I can make it alone."

Then the boat was drifting out on the current, toward a whirlpool in the center of the stream. Charon, standing on the bank, waved once in final farewell. Hector replied. A moment later the craft was sucked into the whirlpool, Everything was enveloped in darkness...roaring filled his ears...sparks and dancing visions...hands reaching out...more noise and confusion...falling...falling through space...endlessly...then a brilliant flashing searching light.

Hector was standing. He could feel the ground beneath his feet. It was solid, cement, a sidewalk. Hector opened his eyes against a brilliant sun. Traffic roared past him, trucks, busses, taxies, private limousines. He was on the corner of Times Square. The sign above his head told him as much.

Back on Earth!

Funny. It was so simple. A minute before he'd been on Olympus. And now he was at Times Square. With trucks dashing past, and busses. Hector knew what had to be done. There wasn't any sense in wasting time.

He lighted a cigarette unhurriedly, deliberately. For a moment he dragged deep on it—this little man whose soul had grown out of proportion to his body.

Then he smiled, quite happily.

"Now let's see what sort of influence Jove can muster in my behalf," he said aloud. He stepped out into the traffic. He stood directly in the path of a speeding truck.

It was too late for the driver to apply his brakes. Hector knew it would be too late. But that was the way he wanted it to be.

BILL OF RIGHTS, 5,000 A.D.

Those David Wright O'Brien stories that appeared under the pseudonym John Cabot York were as popular as those published under his own name—and sometimes more. The following power- ful short story from the June 1941 issue of Fantastic Adventures proved to be very popular indeed—not bad for a story that is only 1,362 words long.

"John York Cabot's 'Bill of Rights, 5,000 A.D.' was marvelous for a mere thousand words or so. This Cabot fellow seems to be getting the knack of short-shorts down pat. More please!"
—Joe J. Fortier, Oakland, California,
Letter to the Editor,
Fantastic Adventures, August 1941.

* * * *

Shar had never seen the sky. Like the thousands and thousands of his fel- low toilers who were born and lived and died in the vast, underground labyrinthine cities of Earth, Shar didn't know of the sky. Shar knew little of anything except the Supreme State—and his Task.

There was a world above him, Shar knew that. Now and then—perhaps twice a year—visitors from that world came down to inspect the mines and factories in which Shar and his fellows labored.

Shar toiled in the mines, and sometimes in the middle of his digging he had looked up furtively as these visitors passed. Then after they had gone he would make up fanciful stories about them in his mind—even though he knew it was dangerous to wonder and that only work was right.

Shar's flights of imagination concerning that upper world were never wistful, and only were ignited by a tiny spark of curiosity in the back of his mind. However, he kept this spark of curiosity strictly to himself, for he had been taught that anything not concerning his Task and its relation to the Supreme State was bad.

The punishment of those who would sabotage the State was swift, and just, and somewhat terrible. Shar shuddered when he remembered some of the whispered rumors of that punishment, and how it had been adminis- tered to those who had been ungrateful to the Supreme State.

So Shar kept to his Task, and remained grateful to the Supreme State. For did not the State give him his work? And did not the State supply him with clothes, and food pills, and a compartment in the general compound for him to use for sleep?

The State gave much, Shar knew this, and asked in return only complete concentration on his Task. The State had let Shar marry, and bring his wife to his compartment for a month each year. And the State provided for the children of that union, seeing that they were raised and educated to their Task. Shar had never seen his children, for, of course, the State had assumed immediate responsibility for them. But he was grateful in the knowledge that they would always have compartments, and clothing, and food pills, and Tasks.

So Shar labored diligently at his digging and remained useful and grateful, as the words in the State pamphlets told him to, and tried to keep his curiosity in check. Until The Day.

* * * *

On the morning of The Day, Shar had been digging alone at the end of a faintly illuminated tunnel. Digging stolidly and concentrating on his Task—until his shovel encountered an oddly hard substance. When he bent over, probing his calloused fingers into the damp clay beneath his feet, he felt something smooth and cold and hard.

Shar frowned, and squinted in the faint light, as he bent down to pick this strange object up in his hands.

It was small, the object, and as he chipped away the clay that covered it, he began to recognize it as a box. For an instant he wondered if he should summon one of the Watchers and turn it over to him. But in the next instant he decided against this, for that spark of curiosity burned in the back of his mind.

"See what it means, Shar," a tiny voice inside him was insisting. "See what it means, first."

Unaccountably, Shar's heart began to thump quickly and sweat broke out on his brow. Furtively, he looked down the long tunnel. There were no Watchers in sight. Then—even though he knew it to be wrong—Shar turned back to the box.

His first efforts to open it were fruitless. But by finally putting the box on the ground and prying it open with his shovel tip, Shar managed to snap the catch that held the lid. His hammering heart told him that he was taking a great chance, as he bent to pick up the open box, but his curiosity was now a flame over which he no longer had control.

Shar's hands shook as he lifted the box and breathlessly peered into it. And then he was filled with a sudden anger and sharp disappointment as his eyes took in the contents. He was about to hurl the box back to the ground thinking of covering it over again with clay so that his crime would not be discovered. That was when his eyes suddenly narrowed, peering closer at the contents, puzzled.

He didn't hurl the box to the ground. He sat down, unconscious of the risk he ran if a Watcher found him that way, and leaned against the wall. He held the contents of the box in his gnarled paws, regarding them intently, utterly absorbed.

* * * *

And so it was that Shar was apprehended by the Watchers some four hours later. But he was not caught in the tunnel assigned to him. He was not caught sitting alongside his shovel with the contents of the box in his hands. He was caught several miles away from there, shouting wildly to other tunnel toilers in other shafts. He was tracked down only after his words had been carried to many others of his fellows—who in turn breathed them through the underground labyrinths, echoing them endlessly onward.

And thus it was that Shar—shackled and beaten—was taken by Guards into the World Above, and for the first time saw the sky. Saw the sky, and other things which he had never dreamed existed—huge buildings, tubes shooting through the air, and many people whose faces did not bear the pallor of the underworld. Until at last he was led into a gigantic hall, and pushed stumbling before a great dais on which ten men sat.

"The traitorous prisoner!" Shar's guards announced, their words ringing loudly in the vast hall.

Then one of the men on the dais was speaking, and Shar noted that he was like the others in this Above World—like the visitors who had sometimes inspected the mines.

"This is the undercreature accused of treason to the Supreme State?" The man on the dais asked. "This is the man who carried words of lies to his fellows?" And Shar heard the guards answer affirmatively.

Then, to Shar, the man on the dais said:

"You have sabotaged the State, and are here to be sentenced for your crime!"

But Shar, even to his own surprise, did not cringe, did not tremble. He held his head high, and his words were strong as he answered. "I have a right—" he began.

But Shar never completed those words.

His last impression was one of terrible pain, and he slumped to the floor seconds after his guards crushed his skull with their merciless blows. And then, while they stood breathing heavily over the lifeless body of the creature from the underworld, the man on the dais addressed the guards.

"You acted wisely, justly, and swiftly in silencing those treasonable words," the man on the great dais said. Then, as in afterthought: "This is the first breath of treason in three thousand years. Have you the evidence that you were to present?"

And then the guard closest to the dais stepped forward. In his hands, he held papers, yellowed and dry. The man on the dais took them wordlessly, glancing at the ancient lettering upon them.

"We hold these rights," the script on the yellowed sheets read, "to be self-evident: that all men are created equal—" the man on the dais paused, his face whitening. Then he read on: "That they are endowed by their Creator with certain inalienable rights, among which are Life, Liberty, and the Pursuit of Happiness."

Purpling with rage, the man on the great dais rose, tearing the yellowed sheets again and again, while the guards trembled at his wrath....

But deep in the bowels of the underworld, creatures like Shar were echoing those words along the dim, labyrinthine cities. And the murmur was swelling...swelling.

BEYOND THE TIME DOOR

* * * *

"I killed him! Yes, I did it, all I right. But he was a rat. He deserved killing. I ain't never killed anyone but a rat."

The words were whispered by the man who sat in the death cell in the big prison. They weren't bitter words of protest, just simple statements of fact. No rancor.

"Rats oughta be killed," repeated the doomed man. "And I guess that's what they think about me, too. They're gonna kill me."

Mike Cardoni, condemned killer, rose from the hard little cot in his bleak gray cell as he heard them coming down the corridor for him. He moved to the bars and stood there with his thick paws on them, waiting. In the cell block, he could hear the other prisoners stirring, moving to the front of their cells to watch the procession that was to come.

Cardoni grinned crookedly. He'd heard it was this way just before the Last Mile. Funny—he was the newest guy in the block, and yet he was going to be the first to take the walk down to the little green door. Most of the others had been able to get stays, or their time was a couple of weeks off. But even twenty-five grand in the paw of the sharpest shyster in the business hadn't been able to get him a stay of execution.

And so here he was, head shaved and trouser legs slit, waiting for them to come and get him. Cardoni felt no resentment, no fear, just a queer sort of curiosity.…

"I'd be a fine mug to squawk," Cardoni had told old Father Perillo, just that afternoon. "The guy I bumped off had it coming to him. A lousy skunk if I ever seen one."

Father Perillo had been somewhat shocked, his kindly old eyes registering a swift instant of pain. Then Cardoni had tried to explain it as he saw it.

"I wouldn't be here now, Father," Cardoni had said, "if I'd let that copper have it. Could'a' filled the guy with lead and got away clean. But mebbe he's got a wife an' kids, see? Mebbe it'd break them up pretty bad if I bumped him. So the copper nabs me. Mebbe he'll get a promotion outta it, huh?"

But Father Perillo had shaken his head sadly, and Cardoni had seen that the old priest was praying. Cardoni felt rather bad, not being able to put his angle across to the old man. But what the hell. It was something inside of him. Something that got all mixed up when he tried to put it into words. He'd bumped mebbe fifteen guys in his years in the rackets. But they were rats and so what. So Cardoni had sighed, and let the white-haired old priest continue his prayers....

Cardoni smiled crookedly again, as the procession stopped in front of his cell and the turnkey opened the door. The warden was there, and Father Perillo, and some other guys whose faces were vaguely familiar to Cardoni. Cardoni stepped out of the cell and in between the guards.

"Courage, Mike," Father Perillo said, touching him on the arm. Somehow, Cardoni felt a surge of gratitude at the old priest's words, at his being there. It wasn't because he was scared. He hadn't been scared since he was a kid in Hell's Kitchen and had pulled his first heist. But it was kind of good to have somebody sticking by you—even if you weren't going to be around for much longer. Cardoni was still grinning as they began the solemn march down toward the little green door. The other guys in the cell block were quiet for the most part, and most of their faces were strained and white like something was pulling their insides to shreds. Funny, Cardoni thought, why did they have to come to the bars and look out if it made them so damned jittery?

Suddenly, Cardoni wished someone would say something, anything. He turned his head, catching the warden's eye, and winked. The warden was an all right gee; he winked back and that broke the tension. Cardoni suddenly sensed that these men walking beside him, these men taking him down the Last Mile, kind of understood. Kind of knew he wasn't all rat. Maybe it was because he'd given the copper a break. Maybe it was because he never bumped no one but hoods.

It made Cardoni feel better inside. And he threw back his swarthy head and laughed.

"Relax, boys," he chortled, "I'm the only mug whose gonna play cinder!"

But they didn't laugh, and from the cold clammy corridor, the echo of his laughter was the only answer. Then they were at the door, and sweat beaded Cardoni's thick brow for the first time.

The sweat beads were still there, but Cardoni hadn't lost his crooked grin as they strapped him in the chair. Father Perillo was right beside him now, and asking him something he didn't hear.

Cardoni nodded, and the old priest bent his white head, his lips moving soundlessly.

After that, they all stepped back, and Cardoni was left quite alone. The black hood that now covered his face prevented his seeing anything else. But he could hear muttering, and something about time. Then, suddenly, Cardoni felt a swimming sensation. Everything wheeled wildly around beneath the blackness of his hood, roaring, roaring—a million miles away.

* * * *

Someone was helping Cardoni to his feet. The roaring in his ears and mind had subsided, and all that remained was a sensation of giddy instability. He found it difficult to keep his knees from giving way beneath his weight. There were lights all around him, bright lights that burned his eyes and made him shut them tightly in an effort to regain focus. Then a voice was speaking.

"Take all the time you need to adjust yourself, Cardoni," the voice said quietly. "It will take a little time."

Then Cardoni was blinking his eyes against the brightness of the lights and the whiteness of the bare room in which he stood.

"Who in the hell are you?" Cardoni demanded. He was gazing open-mouthed at a ball-headed man about his own age. A bald-headed man whose stature and physical characteristics were similar to his own, short, stocky, and with a swarthy complexion.

The bald-headed man drew his lips tight against his teeth, as if essaying a smile. "My name, although it will mean nothing to you, is Tojar," he said.

But Cardoni's eyes, even as the other spoke, were appraising Tojar's dress. A blue tunic of some material that had the sheen of metal, and shoes of the same composition and color were what he wore. And then Cardoni's attention was drawn to the fellow's eyes. They were blue-gray, cold, and with an intentness that somehow made Cardoni shiver.

As Cardoni looked dazedly around the strange bright bare room, he remembered his last sensations, remembered where he had been before the blackness of the death hood had blotted out consciousness.

"What the hell is this?" Cardoni rasped. "Where am I? How did I get here? I was—"

Tojar broke in: "You were in your own world, Cardoni, less than five minutes ago according to your standards of time." He drew his lips flat against his teeth again and his cold eyes seemed to glitter. "But now you're in my world."

"This is a gag, and a pretty rotten one," Cardoni snarled. "Damn you, I—"

"Gag?" Tojar interjected. "Gag? Oh, I see, you mean jest. You think this is some mad hoax, eh?" He paused. "I've saved you from death, Cardoni. I think you should be grateful for that much."

Cardoni could only stand there, his mouth open foolishly in an effort to utter words he couldn't find. He had always scoffed at superstition. But minutes ago he had been prepared to die, and now.... Was this some afterworld? Cardoni looked again at the other's eyes—clearly, it wasn't Heaven.

"You aren't stupid, Cardoni," Tojar said, his voice still on the same quiet pitch. "Criminal, yes, but not stupid. I am going to explain all this to you. And after a little bit, you will understand." He paused, to try that same icy smile again. "You see, Cardoni, you are no longer in your own world—your world of 1940—you are in another era of time. This is the year 3000, the thirty-first century!"

Cardoni stepped back, as though struck by a blow. His face was a mask of incredulity and then of growing rage. At last he found voice. "I told you," he began, "if this is a gag—"

"Look, if you must be convinced," Tojar said. And as he spoke, his hand went to a button on the wall beside him.

* * * *

The floor beneath Cardoni suddenly glowed. Orange, then amber, then pale gray—becoming a transparent sheet of glass. And as Cardoni gazed in stupefied astonishment he found himself looking down on a vast, towering, incredible metropolis of spires and strange labyrinthine roads, layered one upon another and twisting among huge domed buildings!

Tojar touched the button again, and the scene faded away, the floor once more seeming solid beneath them.

Cardoni was breathing hard, his voice was flat as he spoke. "Okay, buddy. You got all the openers. Talk on!"

"Good," Tojar said softly. "I was certain that you weren't stupid. You are beginning to believe me, Cardoni, from that glimpse of the world in which I live. What you saw beneath you was New York. Not New York as your mind conceives it, but New York as it is today, in the thirty-first century. I've brought you into this century, out of your own, and away from the certain death you faced."

Cardoni's voice was still flat. "Why?"

Tojar registered his chrome-steel smile again. "I can use you. Or, I might say, we can use one another. You can do me a favor, and I can return the favor for you."

"The talk is still double," Cardoni said. "Get on to the pitch. If this is all level, what's the play?"

"You've killed fifteen men, Cardoni. To you, and to your world, murder is not unknown. But here, in my century, things are vastly different. No one kills here. No one is able to kill."

Cardoni frowned, and Tojar's icy eyes caught his bewilderment. "This is a different civilization. It is what might be called a perfected civilization. There is no murder, no slaughter in war, no hatred or greed. For a thousand years our scientists have been conditioning the world, until now, as it is here in the thirty-first century, it has reached an emotionally perfect balance."

Tojar shrugged. "Even I am physically unable to kill."

Cardoni's brows knotted in concentration. "So we'll say this is on the level; that you can't, that no guy can. I still ain't got the answer. Where do I come in?"

"I said I was physically unable to kill," Tojar's steely smile was once more prominent. "But I didn't say that I wouldn't wish to kill. I didn't say that there is no one whom I would like to kill. There is a person whose death would fit in perfectly with a plan of mine. I want you to kill this person for me."

"You want to bump a guy?" Cardoni said perplexedly. "But you said that no guy can hate or play the graft in this setup. How come you do?"

Tojar's voice was still quite calm, but the expression in his eyes gave Cardoni a sensation of chill. "In this emotionally stabilized world I am, fortunately, a throwback. And fortunately no one knows this but me. My body is so conditioned that I cannot actually commit murder. But my mind has been unaffected by those around me. I have kept this from everyone, waiting my time. And now it is necessary that I kill." Tojar reached into the pocket of his tunic, and his hand came forth holding a gun. Cardoni recognized it instantly as an automatic.

"A rod," Cardoni gasped. "Do you still have those?"

Tojar shook his head. "This weapon is a museum piece. I have others like it in a perfectly preserved collection. Unfortunately, they do me no good. We have no weapons in this civilization. It has been centuries since we have had."

"Will it work?" Cardoni blurted.

"I said it was perfectly preserved, and with bullets to fit its chamber," Tojar replied softly. He still held the gun in his hand. "It is loaded now."

"And you want me to bump a guy with it," Cardoni broke in. "You want me to use it because no one else in this set-up can?" He paused. "So supposing I do, what then?"

"I will repay the favor," Tojar said, his voice silken steel, "by sending you back to your world in the manner in which I brought you here." His eyes caught Cardoni's uncomprehending frown. "I brought you here by a time device—a machine which took you from your era to mine," he explained.

Cardoni's voice was suddenly harsh. "And you'll send me back that way, huh? Back to the chair!"

* * * *

Tojar shook his head. "No, Cardoni, not to the chair. If you do me this favor, I'll send you back *one year before the time you were caught and sentenced to death.* Do you see what that means, Cardoni? You can return to your century a free man. You can see to it then that you don't take the step that led you to the chair! You can see to it that the circumstances which led to your being sentenced to death will *never happen*!"

Cardoni put his thick hand to his face, shaking his head as if to clear it. "This is screwy. Screwy as hell. But I see your pitch, buddy." Suddenly he looked up at Tojar. "How in the hell didja pick me for this job?"

Tojar shrugged. "Chance. When I knew what I wanted, I knew that I would have to take someone capable of murder, used to killing, into this century from the past. A study of case records of ancient civilization revealed your record. Such records are kept as oddities now. Your case was recorded, even to the time and date of your death in the electric chair. Through that, I knew I could bring you here—by setting my time device to several seconds before your death—and have something to offer you as inducement to serve me."

Cardoni was shaking his head almost dazedly. "And if you send me back, I won't die?"

"You won't die. You can prevent it."

Cardoni laughed harshly, humorlessly. "And all I was hoping for was a reprieve. Okay, buddy, it's a deal!"

Tojar smiled, those icy eyes boring into Cardoni, and held out the gun. "I knew you'd be the man."

Cardoni took the gun, and the feel of it was familiar in his paw. Then he looked down at his slit trouser legs, prison shoes, and denim shirt. He rubbed his shaved head reflectively.

"I can't go running around in this get-up. It ain't how you people dress," he said. "The only thing you and me got in common is our bald domes." Suddenly he laughed, thinking of the warden and old Father Perillo. Rich, that's what it was—rich! Bump a rat to save yourself from frying for bump-ing a rat!

Cardoni was still smiling grimly as Tojar brought him a change of dress and gave him his instructions. And when he had gotten everything straight, and Tojar's instructions were set in his mind, Cardoni laughed once more. As he laughed, Tojar said: "And then you can return here—swiftly."

The laughter died in Cardoni as Tojar spoke. For once again those eyes bored into him, making him chill inside. As Cardoni stepped from the room, he thought for an instant of those eyes. Then he realized, they were like a snake's. Cardoni shivered, then shrugged, closing the door behind him. Ahead lay this strange new world. But the gun in his tunic pocket re-called to him that his mission was neither strange nor new. It would just be the sixteenth time he'd killed a man....

* * * *

It was two hours later when Cardoni returned to the bright, bare, white room where Tojar awaited him. Cardoni slammed the door behind him and leaned hard against it. His breath came in sobbing gasps as he stared word-lessly at Tojar.

Tojar had been standing next to a small cabinet in the far corner of the room. Now he turned from it, facing Cardoni, his eyes regarding him care-fully, coldly. "You did it?" Tojar asked.

Then Cardoni was talking, as though the words inside him had sud-denly broken free of a dam. "You got it across that no guy could bump another. You got across a lotta other stuff about civ'lizashun, stabluzashun, and all like that. I thought I got whatcha meant. But I didn't. I hadn't seen it. I hadn't felt it."

Cardoni seemed to choke for a moment, then he stumbled on. "There was an old guy you wanted me to bump. Well, I found him, like you said I would. But I found something else—something I wasn't looking for. I seen it in the old guy's eyes, just as I let him have it —just as I pumped a slug in his skull, God!"

Cardoni was sobbing now, and his breath tore in his lungs. "Those eyes—the old guy's eyes, they wasn't like yours, or like mine. They was like a kid's—a kid who's been slapped hard across the mouth and hurt bad inside! Damn you," Cardoni's voice trembled with harsh rage now, "damn you, he was a right gee! Good, like everyone else in this set-up. I seen a lot'a' them. They was all good gees. The whole damn set-up is right! It's like—" and Cordoni choked off, unable to find the words he sought.

Tojar's eyes were flat and half-lidded, and the corners of his mouth twitched in satanic amusement. He seemed to be waiting until certain that the outburst was over. Then he spoke.

"You've fulfilled your end of the bargain, I take it. Good. That's all that concerns me. Now, if you can harness your puerile emotions long enough, I'll carry out my part of the agreement. This device here," Tojar pointed to the cabinet in the corner, "is the machine by which I'll send you back to your own time era." And as Tojar spoke, he threw a lever on the side of the cabinet. There was a sudden soft humming, and a light tube across the top of the cabinet glowed to a luminous orange.

The humming from the cabinet was growing in volume. Tojar stepped back a few feet from it, watching, while a faint shadow began to form directly beside it. The shadow appeared dimensional, and was darkening. Darkening until at last it was an eerie void of ebon blackness.

Tojar smiled. "There is your door," he said. "There is—" and suddenly his face went hard. For Cardoni had pulled the automatic from his tunic pocket and was levelling it at Tojar.

"Damn you," Cardoni swore softly. "Damn you."

* * * *

Tojar found voice. "Don't be a fool," he hissed. "It won't help you to kill me. You'll never get back if you do. The time device is still set to return you straight to the chair, two seconds before the juice was to be thrown. I'm the only one who can regulate it so that you'll return to a year before that time. Put down that gun!" His voice had risen as he spoke, and his last words were shrill, almost hysterical.

Cardoni held the gun unwaveringly. Hate filled his eyes and there was loathing in his voice. "This whole damned world of yours is right," he said. "But you ain't. I never killed no one but rats until a little while ago. Now I think I'll get back to rats."

Tojar's face was white, and instinctively he backed away as Cardoni moved forward. His lips trembled as he tried uselessly to form words. His face was suddenly bathed in sweat. Cardoni took another step forward. Tojar backed once more. Backed once more, and screamed wildly. For even as an infinite expression of horror froze in his cold eyes—Tojar was disappearing into the inky void of the Time Door!

And then Cardoni's big body was torn by wild, sobbing laughter. Tojar was gone, and only the black shadow and the cabinet remained. Tojar was gone—and Cardoni knew that that unwitting backward step had sent him hurtling down through time—to the certain death that waited in the chair!

Cardoni raised his gun. Raised his gun and sent one shot blasting into the glowing orange light tube on the top of the cabinet. The tube burst in a blast of flame and tinkle of glass, and the shadow beside the cabinet disappeared.

Now Cardoni stood there dazedly, the gun still in his hand, while everything turned crazily around in his brain. For here in this strange world into which he had been unwillingly thrust, he had found his answer. The answer—materializing all the emotions that Cardoni would never be able to phrase. The emotions that were deep inside him, mixed, and never to be voiced.

He realized this even as he knew he would never fit into this pattern of time. The gun in his hand, the blood on his soul, had forever alienated him from this paradise of peace and harmony. The gulf that separated him from this, was more than one of time.

Quite suddenly, he was sobbing no longer. He stared at the wreckage of the cabinet, a curious smile twisting the corners of his mouth. Then he muttered: "If the warden and old Father Perillo could see me now. Jeeze it's rich—rich!" Cardoni threw back his head, laughing wildly. At last he stopped, whispering one sentence.

"Except for one right gee, I killed nobody but rats—and this last won't be no exception."

There was a swift, aching second in which something wrenched unbearably at Cardoni's heart. Then, deliberately, he raised the automatic to his temple and fired....

SHARBEAU'S STARTLING STATUE

"Sharbeau's Startling Statue" marks the first time that a David Wright O'Brien story appeared under Ziff-Davis Publication's house pseudonym of Clee Garson. Over the next decade eleven O'Brien stories would be published under this name.

"Clee Garson, a newcomer to our pages, rather tickled us with his little short in this issue. 'Sharbeau's Startling Statue' might make you think this is just another one of those 'living statue' stories until you get to the last few paragraphs. Then you're going to find out you were wrong. This story has what we need in these war-tortured times. A little chuckle, and a little reality."

—Raymond A. Palmer,
The Editor's Notebook,
Fantastic Adventures, November 1942.

* * * *

Monsieur Paul Sharbeau is a friendly, amusing, easygoing little man with the emotional temperament of a poodle. He has small, dark, dancing little eyes, the expected little black moustache—waxed at the tips of course—and an utterly blasé disdain for the mysteries of life.

I was not surprised, therefore, to hear his voice coming excitedly over the telephone that night pleading shrilly that I come to his modest residence immediately for "some wine and ze convairsation." Not surprised even though it was after midnight and most normal people were in bed, Sharbeau had often, merely on impulse, called me at ungodly hours when he felt in the need for wine and companionship.

I was very much surprised, however, at his closing remark over the telephone when I had finally assured him I would be over as quickly as I could.

"Clee," he had concluded, you know vairee much about ze occult, no?"

And before I had been able to frame a suitable reply to this, he had signed off.

"Zat is good. Zat is vairee good!"

I sat there looking at the telephone in my hand, the *click* still rever-berating in my ears. Sat there frowning in perplexity over the fire-cracker conclusion of my little French friend.

Sharbeau's impression that I was an authority on matters of the occult had undoubtedly been born of several conversations we'd had in which I'd confessed that I had a cursory interest in things supernatural which amount-ed to nothing really more than a hobby. Been born of that, no doubt, plus the fact that I'd mentioned Poe to be my favorite author, and had myself turned out an occasional yarn of fantasy-horror.

I sighed, wondering irritably what on earth had been the cause of Shar-beau's sudden concern with a subject toward which he had previously ex-pressed indifference.

Then I remembered that Sharbeau possessed an excellent wine stock which he had managed to smuggle out of France shortly after the Vichy sell-out convinced him his life would no longer be safe under German dom-ination. Remembered, and forgot my irritation.

For excellent wine was excellent wine. Even at a quarter past midnight. And Sharbeau was an interesting enough chap conversationally, and might, after all, have unearthed some occult evidence which I might regret miss-ing.

I thumbed my nose at the typewriter, put away the chapter I'd been polishing, and got my coat....

Monsieur Sharbeau lived in an old brownstone residence on the near North Side. One of those buildings remodeled into spacious, four room, kitchenette apartments. Sharbeau had converted one of the rooms, the one with the wood-burning fireplace, into a sort of library-study. We engaged in most of our conversational and wine bouts there.

He met me at the door, obviously in a state of great agitation about something, and before I'd scarcely had time to remove my coat, he led me immediately into his study.

There was the ever ready bottle of rare vintage waiting on a thick, ma-hogany table between two glasses, and as I found an easy chair Sharbeau immediately placed a filled glass in my hand and poured himself a drink. His face was flushed, his dark eyes button bright.

"You will nevair believe what it is I 'ave to tell you," he said, downing his drink in jerky haste.

"Sit down and tell me about it," I suggested. I raised the wine to my lips, savoring the delicious bouquet before taking a sip. Rare stuff, and potent.

Sharbeau ignored my suggestion. He strode over to the mantel above the fireplace.

"Regard!" he said dramatically.

I followed his pointing finger. There was nothing atop the mantel but a stone statue—one that had been there on every occasion I could remember—some fourteen inches high. It was the statue of a Greek warrior in an attitude suggesting he was running.

I made my voice tactfully polite.

"It's a very nice statue. A very nice statue indeed. I've noticed it every time I've been here. Often intended to comment on it. What about it?"

Sharbeau closed his eyes for an instant, drawing in a shuddery breath.

"You notice nozzing unusual about it?"

I shook my head. "I don't know exactly what you mean."

"I mean since you are regarding it ze last time you are here."

Again I shook my head. "No, Sharbeau. I'm sorry. I never noticed it very carefully before. If something's happened to it, if it's broken, I'm terribly sorry."

Sharbeau seemed suddenly to realize his glass was empty. He stepped over to the table and filled it to the brim again. Once more he downed the liquid in a quick gulp. A strange procedure for one as fond of fine wines as my little friend.

He stepped back to the mantel, pointing a finger again at the statue. And again there was the same throbbing drama in his voice.

"Regard!"

I was getting badly confused.

"Perhaps you'd better be explicit," I said. "I told you be—"

"Ze limb of ze statue," Sharbeau said, "ze right limb, is forward!"

I saw what he meant. In the running attitude of the figure, its right leg was stretched out ahead of the left. But so what?

Sharbeau interpreted my expression. "Allllways," he said, "it was ze left limb forward!"

I perked up a little.

"Are you certain of that?" I demanded. Are you positive that the left leg of that thing was always stretched out in front of the right?"

Sharbeau nodded. "But of course. I 'ave ze statue ten years. It is one of my favorites. I know every contour of it. Every line!"

His finger suddenly shot up to point to the face the running figure.

"Regard!" he exclaimed again.

"All right' I told him instantly. I see what you're driving at. What changes do you think have occurred in the facial expression of the statue?"

Sharbeau stared at me somberly.

"Allllways," he said, "ze face smiles. Now it frowns ever so slightly!"

I smiled suddenly.

"And you want me to explain it?" I asked.

Sharbeau nodded.

"Someone, maybe a prankster, has switched statues on you," I told him. "That's the only explanation there could be."

Sharbeau gave me a clearly disappointed glance. He sighed. "I am sure you, ze great student of ze occult, would 'ave somezing sensible for to explain it." He paused to sigh deeply again. "And you give me stupid answers!"

I got a little impatient. Obviously my friend Sharbeau was a trifle drunk.

"Don't be so damned silly," I told him. "When there's a perfectly logical explanation for something it's stupid to try to pin it on an occult theory."

* * * *

Sharbeau seemed suddenly on the verge of tears. He moved over to my chair and gripped my arm with fierce intensity. Perspiration broke out on his brow. His button eyes were pleading.

"But, Clee, it is not anothair statue!" he said with hoarse frenzy. "I am sure it is anothair statue, jus' like you are, until I check everywhere and find that there is no such stone as what this is made from anywhere in ze United State!"

Sharbeau was a trifle tipsy, but he wasn't in the babbling stage. He was sincere, I could tell. And if he had checked, if he *had* found out beyond a shadow of a doubt that this was the only statue of similar stone in the United States—then it seemed highly unlikely that such a prank as I had suggested would have been possible.

"You're dead *certain?*" I demanded.

Sharbeau released his grasp on my arm and stepped back, throwing his arms wide in a melodramatic gesture.

"Regard!" he demanded. "Do I, Paul Jacques Sharbeau, look like ze deceitful man? 'Ave I not allllways been on ze hup-and-hup wiz you?"

I admitted that he was the soul of integrity.

"Then I will tell you more," he said. Tonight, shortly before I am call you, I find ze statue by ze table in ze study here, on ze floor, in ze completely changed attitudes I 'ave describe!"

"But—" I began.

Sharbeau cut me off, holding up his hand.

"I look on ze mantel, knowing it must be anothair statue put in ze place of my favorite statue which must be stolen! Voila—there is no statue on ze mantel. Ze statue on ze floor is ze only one!"

"Still—" I started.

Sharbeau once again cut me off.

"So I am convinced as first you were. I am know ze statue on ze floor is imitation of ze real statue. A prank. And yet," Sharbeau paused dramatically, when I am pick up ze changed statue, I am see that, but for the vairee strange changes in left limb and right limb and facial expression, it is just like my own."

Even so—" I started again. I got no further.

"I am remembaire," Sharbeau continued, "a vairee good friend, a de-laire in antique art and curios who 'ave once see my statue and tell me it is ze only kind of zat stone in ze United State."

"You made sure the stone in the statue was the same?" I asked.

"But of course," said Sharbeau. "I know ze texture, ze grain of it. Even wiz ze change in limbs and expression, ze texture and grain of ze stone is like alllways." He paused. "But rapidly I am calling ze art and curio dealer, am asking him is he certain what he tell me before about ze statue. He says yes."

"No chance, then, of this statue being a clever substitute," I concluded.

"None whatsoevaire!" Sharbeau said emphatically. "Now you believe me, no?"

I shook my head grudgingly. "Now I believe you," I admitted. "But, what you have proven is that that statue *somehow moved*, got down from the mantel, and started across the floor. The change in leg position most certainly points to the fact that it moved on its own legs and forgot to assume its former attitude when you walked in on it." Suddenly I stopped. Hand to my head.

Sharbeau looked at me in alarm.

"What is ze trouble?"

"My God!" I exclaimed. "I've been talking about that statue as if, as if it were *animated, alive,* and, and—" I faltered.

Little Paul Jacques Sharbeau spread his hands expressively in an elaborate gesture.

"But of course," he exclaimed. "Zat is what I am trying so vairee hard to tell you!"

* * * *

For the rest of the evening we discussed that damned statue until we were blue in the face and more than a little blotto from the wine. And from Sharbeau I gained every atom of information that I could about its history.

He had picked it up while in Greece. Bought it from a dealer who had claimed it to be centuries old and especially rare. No, there had never been anything strange about it during the ten years in which it had been in Sharbeau's possession. Never until this very night.

For my contribution to the discussion I vocally sorted through all the available information in the back of my mind dealing with the occult as related to statues or images. There was a surprising hodge-podge of stuff I'd gathered and long forgotten, but none of it seemed specifically to fit the purposes. Not a whit about living statues. It was pretty discouraging, especially to Sharbeau, who still had the fixed notion that I was "ze great authority" on anything supernatural.

The best I could do was a promise to barrage the Public Library and several private informational sources I had on such matters the first thing the following morning. Maybe there would be a clue.

Sharbeau, on the other hand, vowed to keep a closer watch on the statue and let me know the instant anything else inexplicable occurred to it.

When I finally rose to leave, I teetered a little drunkenly over to the mantel and stared broodingly at the stone image of the runner. There was something about it, something in the facial expression, which Sharbeau swore had once been smiling, that was defiantly determined.

It made me shudder, and I turned away.

My head was fuzzy, and I figured a cold towel on my face might be a good idea before leaving.

"Where's your bathroom?" I asked Sharbeau.

"Ze vairee first door on ze right," he told me.

* * * *

Morning found me, in spite of a slight hangover, right on the Library steps the moment the doors were opened. For the affair of the startling statue was the first thing to enter my consciousness on wakening.

And even as I ate breakfast and read the paper, my mind strayed constantly from my bacon and eggs and latest headlines, always ending up in a wrestling match with the eerie enigma to which Sharbeau had introduced me the night before.

I telephoned Sharbeau before heading for the Library, and his sleepy voice told me that he'd remained awake the rest of the night just on the chance that the statue might begin to prowl again.

Even though I told him to go to bed and get some sleep, I had a hunch that the little Frenchman would remain on watch before that stone statue until he'd one bottle of wine too many and passed into merciful slumber in spite of himself.

By noon I was finally positive that there would be nothing gained by any further canvassing of the Library. The files there didn't present a source that seemed to give the least hint of what I was looking for. I even took a longshot chance and poured through a thick, dull tome on ancient Grecian sculpture. Sharbeau's statue was evidently not quite important enough to be listed in it, for it wasn't mentioned.

I couldn't get in touch with two of my private sources, and the other one proved to be utterly unenlightening. It took me the entire afternoon to accomplish exactly nothing.

Gulping a hasty dinner, I walked down Michigan Boulevard to Sharbeau's place. I had to ring the doorbell at least a dozen times before it was answered. An then a sleep-fogged Sharbeau, clad in the wrinkled remains of the suit he'd been wearing the night before, opened the door.

"*Mon Dieu!*" he exclaimed in horror, peering out past my shoulder. "It is night-time again, no?"

"It is night-time again, yes," I told him, stepping past him into the apartment.

"I was asleep, on ze floor of ze study," said Sharbeau, confirming what I'd already figured. "Ze wine, it must 'ave hit me shortly before noon. Ze bell ring and waken me."

"What about the statue?" I demanded. "Did it move again?"

Sharbeau blinked, then clapped his hand to his brow. "*Mon Dieu*—I do not know! I 'ave been asleep!"

He turned and hurried back into the study, and I was right on his heels. The place reeked of wine, and there were no less than eight quart bottles of the stuff, all empty, sitting around. Sharbeau had had quite a watch of it.

He came to an abrupt halt, emitting a gurgling cry, and staring down at the floor in horror.

Perhaps five feet from the door, in still a different posture from the one of the night before, was the figure of the stone statue!

"Well," I choked feebly, very feebly, "well!"

"Again it happen!" Sharbeau gasped.

"While you were asleep at the switch," I managed at last, "it went on the prowl again."

I felt a creepy chill along my spine. But I forced myself to bend down and examine this new posture of the stone statue.

The left leg of the statue was thrust forward this time. And just the night before, with my own eyes, I had seen the right one forward!

And the expression on the features of the image was changed also. Where it had been defiantly, scowlingly, determined the night before—in contrast to its former smile it was now much more markedly grim, much more resolute and fiercely, savagely determined!

Sharbeau had seen all this too.

"*Mon Dieu!*" he moaned softly.

* * * *

I couldn't think of anything to add to that. I stared wordlessly at the stone figure, my brain wheeling madly but none of the cogs meshing any too well.

And then something that might or might not have been significant occurred to me. I put my hand on Sharbeau's arm.

"Listen," I said, "was this, this runner facing in the same direction last night when you discovered him down from the mantel?"

Sharbeau nodded, uncomprehending.

"Toward the door?" I insisted.

"But of course."

"Is he any nearer to the door in this attempt than the first time?" I asked.

Sharbeau thought a moment. "But of course. It is so. Vairee much nearer."

"Then," I declared, "we have at least something to work on. The statue is not just prowling. On each occasion it made for the door. It is trying to get out of here!"

Sharbeau reflected on this. "Oui, it seems so. But why?"

He had me there. And even though it was a reasonable question I was nettled.

"I don't know," I snapped. "Anyway, we've got a little more information than we started with."

Sharbeau nodded.

"Look," I said suddenly, "put your statue back up on the mantel where it belongs and go to bed and get some decent rest. I'll watch the thing until you relieve me. Then I catch a few hours sleep, here. You can wake me up when you're tired and I'll relieve you. That way we'll keep a constant watch. What do you say?"

Sharbeau nodded. "A vairee good idea, Clee." He picked up the statue and took it back to the fireplace, where he put it atop the mantel. He looked at it haggardly for a moment, sighed troubledly and turned back to me.

"What did you learn from ze Librairee?" he asked.

I told him the disgusting truth, which seemed to slump his weary shoulders even more than before. I realized, then, that if this thing wasn't cleared up within a damned short time, Monsieur

Sharbeau was going to be a psychopathic wreck.

"Think I'll wash up," I told him, as he was shuffling out of his study to get his much-needed shut-eye.

"Ze first door on ze right," he said automatically....

The hours I spent on guard in Sharbeau's study passed slowly, and the ash tray at my side was heaped with cigarette butts when midnight finally rolled around.

I sighed and stretched, suddenly aware that my eyes had been fixed in what amounted almost to a fuzzy sort of hypnosis on the statue atop the mantel.

I sat suddenly erect, straining my eyes into focus on the figure. No. Of course it had been my imagination. It hadn't moved. It was in precisely the same posture as when I'd taken post before it.

Only then was I really aware that Sharbeau's life wasn't the only one that was going to be messed up badly if this thing weren't figured out pretty damned quickly.

It was driving me quite a little bit batty. And I was finally getting wise to the fact. Cursing myself for ever having gotten involved in the weird mess, I rose, yawning, and went out to rouse Sharbeau and take over his bed.

He woke easily, for he'd had plenty of sleep by now. And after promising not to wake me until nine the next morning, he shuffled back into his study to take up the watch before the stone statue.

I was dead tired, and fell asleep to a whirling half-dream in which I did a stately gavotte on the White House Lawn with a stone statue that always wanted to run away. Sharbeau played the accompaniment for the dance on a bottle of rare wine which had been fashioned into a sweet potato whistle....

* * * *

Someone was rocking the boat quite ungently, and when I opened my eyes I blinked into the visibly excited and tremendously elated face of my little chum Sharbeau.

"I 'ave solved him. I 'ave solved him!" he was shouting. "Ze problem of ze statue is ovaire!"

I sat up, startled.

"Huh?" I gasped. "You mean—"

"I mean it is ovaire, forevaire!" Sharbeau cried, pulling at my arm excitedly.

I bounced out of bed, rubbing my eyes. My watch told me I'd been asleep three hours.

"Come to ze study!" Sharbeau insisted.

I followed him into his book-lined library, looking quickly around to see evidences of a struggle, of a broken statue. I don't know why, but these were the first things that came to mind. I didn't see either. I just saw the statue, back on the mantel top where it belonged.

"It moved again," Sharbeau said, grabbing my arm and forcing me into a chair. "It moved again, and I, Sharbeau, am see it move!"

"But I thought—" I began.

But Sharbeau was bound and determined to tell this thing through to the bitter end. He wouldn't allow interruptions.

"It is get down from ze mantle!" Sharbeau said. "Right before my vai ree eyes!" He sucked in his breath to emphasize this. "I am watch wiz horror. My throat she is filled wiz ashes. I cannot speak. My 'eart is pound pound pound. *Ze stone statue climbs down from ze mantle like a living thing!*" Sharbeau paused to roll his eyes.

"Go on," I demanded. "Good God, man. Don't stop now!"

"It is on ze floor, now," Sharbeau recounted. "I am still watch in choked horror. It moves toward ze door, in slow, difficult steps."

I closed my eyes, shuddering, getting a mental picture of that small stone creature moving laboriously across the floor while Sharbeau watched on, bug-eyed.

"I cannot stand it," Sharbeau exclaimed. "I am afraid, but I cannot stand ze suspense. I force myself to step toward ze moving statue. Force myself alzo my soul cries out against it. I am bending down, reaching for ze moving statue, *when it speaks!*"

The words almost knocked me out of my chair.

"Speaks?" I bleated. "Good God, you don't mean s—"

"I mean speaks," said Sharbeau. And suddenly his face was wreathed in a reflectively happy smile. "And I am so glad ze statue speaks, once I am hearing what it has to say."

I was on the edge of the chair.

"What DID it say?" I almost screamed.

Sharbeau cocked his head reflectively, as if making sure he was quoting the precise words of the stone statue. "It say, 'Only once in fifty years am I forced to do ziz. I had to speak. I could not be thwarted again.'"

I blinked, repeating the words. "Only once in fifty years was it forced to do this? It had to speak? It couldn't be thwarted again? It said that to you?"

Sharbeau nodded.

"But what was the meaning behind those words, behind the very moving statue itself?" I demanded.

Sharbeau held up his hand. He beamed. "Vairee simple, vairee simple indeed, mon ami. It is a wondaire we do not think of it before. The statue then ask me a question."

"A question?" I bleated.

* * * *

Sharbeau nodded. "Oui. It is ask me this question. It is breathe it in my ear." He paused, his face coloring reminiscently. "I am blush wiz embarrassment, and it is all I can do to answer. But I am giving ze satisfactory answer, ze statue completes its mission, and now it is back on ze mantle like always before."

My glance shot up to the mantle. The statue was there, all right. There and exactly as it had been before any mysterious transformations had started on it. The left leg was thrust forward in the running position, just as it should be.

And the facial expression, just as it should be, was positively beaming with joy and serenity. Gone was the scowling frown.

I turned to Sharbeau.

"But the answer to his question," I demanded, "what was it?"

Sharbeau beamed.

"It was simple, as I say," he told me. "I am answer by saying to ze statue: *'It is ze vairee first door on the right'!*"

I didn't say anything. I couldn't. I just looked at Sharbeau and up at the mantle where the statue now postured serenely. The very first door to the right, eh? Once in fifty years, eh? I glared at Sharbeau, and the glare slid into a squint of doubt.

Hell, the statue never moved an inch after that. And Monsieur Paul Jacques Sharbeau is an honest man, a person of integrity. And once again he has assumed his utterly blasé disdain for the mysteries of life.

THE SOFTLY SILKEN WALLET

David Wright O'Brien's next posthumously-published story appeared in the July 1946 issue of *Fantastic Adventures*. "The Softly Silken Wallet" is a departure from the typical O'Brien tale, a horror-driven short story where you know that something really awful is looming ahead, but you never know just exactly what.

"The Softly Silken Wallet" was recently included in the 2014 short story anthology *Horror Gems*, Volume Eight.

* * * *

The thin, sharp-featured little man standing at the rear of the elevated platform in the swirling snow that chilling March afternoon, was pleased. His pleasure was evident in the smirk on his thin lips and the glitter in his gimlet eyes as they moved restlessly, appraisingly over the crowds that jammed the station.

Marty Merkin was thinking that, despite the cold and the snow and the crushing jam of passengers waiting on the platform for trains, this was a hell, of a good day for business.

On a day like this, he reflected, people were conscious only of their own weariness, discomfort and the immediate problem of forcing their ways through the elevated doors to find seats for the homeward trip.

On days like this, consequently, sharp-eyed pickpockets like little Marty Merkin were in clover.

An Evanston Special rolled up to a stop, and Marty grinned as he watched the people on the platform surge forward, fighting each other to be first inside the opening doors.

But he didn't move forward to mingle with them and press closely against them. Instead he stood there watching and smiling and taking his time. There was plenty of time, just like there was plenty of fish, he told himself. It was just a matter of standing back and casing the crowd until a really ripe customer happened along.

That big fat guy, Merkin observed, arms full of bundles, was well dressed and obviously in the chips. Yet Marty's long practiced analysis told him unfailingly that the fat guy wouldn't be the sort to carry his dough around in big wads. There'd be maybe ten, maybe fifteen, in the fat guy's wallet. Not enough to bother with on a day like this.

"Day like this," Marty told himself, "I don't settle fer no small stuff."

So he continued to watch the crowd, smirking happily at the prospects he knew to be ahead, taking his time and watching for the right one.

The right one came along less than ten minutes later. He was a tall guy and thin as a beanpole. Marty watched him come out onto the platform, noting that he had musician-length gray hair that came almost to the collar of his thin gabardine topcoat. This right one was middle-aged, Marty saw, with a long, lean, horse-like face and deep, sunken gray eyes.

He was carrying a large instrument case, which Marty judged to contain a cello or some stringed instrument similar in size and shape. That was, of course, the absolute confirmation of. Marty's judgment that the guy was a musician.

The thin, beanpole-ish guy stood there on the platform, the wind and swirling snow flapping his topcoat grotesquely against his thin shanks and gaunt frame.

Marty couldn't restrain a grin, as a gust of wind caught the man from the rear and outlined, momentarily, the bulky block of a wallet in his right hip pocket.

That was double confirmation for Marty. Confirmation that these musician guys were the type to carry most of their wad with them, and to be very careless about it. He wet his thin lips in anticipation, and moved forward until he was less than four feet behind the musician.

* * * *

A Ravenswood Express rolled into the station at that moment, and the tall, gaunt, horse-faced musician began to move forward to push with the crowds toward the door.

Marty stepped up directly behind the fellow, pressing hard against him, as if he too were trying to push for a seat on the Ravenswood Express. Several other passengers pushed in behind Marty, which increased the surging pressure and pleased Marty additionally.

The beanpole-ish musician was having a time of it with his big cello case. He had to hang onto it with both hands, and turn it from side to side to keep the crowds from damaging it. This was an additional boon to Marty, though he scarcely needed it.

It was really almost too simple to take. Marty felt what almost amounted to a twinge of guilt as he flipped open the razor sharp blade of his pocket knife.

In the half dozen steps remaining to the door of the elevated train, Marty expertly slit through the topcoat, slipped his hand inside the rent, and removed the fat wallet from the musician's hip pocket.

In half a minute more, Marty had eased out through the crowds until he was on the back of the platform. He slipped the wallet into his own pocket and hid the knife in his sleeve in these brief seconds. And now he turned to glance at the train door, where the big scarecrow with the cello case was just moving through the door.

He was the last one on the car as the doors slid shut. And Marty saw the sudden, startled expression on the gaunt guy's face as he turned to face the window. The scarecrow had taken one hand from his cello, and was groping with the other at the rent in the back of his topcoat.

Marty saw all this in a glance, and smirked as the, train began to roll.

The last glimpse he had of the musician guy was his expression of surprise and stricken dismay as he became aware of his loss.

Marty moved nimbly through the crowd to the regular exit, lost himself in the comforting numbers, and was down on Wabash Avenue a few moments later.

He walked briskly along for several blocks, moving south toward the section of cheap bars and restaurants, flophouses and salvation missions that comprised the district on that border of the Loop.

After three blocks he stopped casually before the large plate window of an antique shop. He looked easily to his left, the direction from which any possible pursuit might come. He knew he had cleared himself neatly, but habit made him careful. As he had figured, there was no pursuit.

He snapped the razor keen pocket knife shut, dropped it from his sleeve into his pocket. Then, putting his other hand into the pocket of his overcoat, he felt the fat, promising bulk of the smooth leather wallet.

He had to laugh. It had been a breeze.

* * * *

Marty moved on, then turned a corner after several blocks more and abruptly entered a small, beer-reeking tavern with dirty windows and dirtier customers inside.

He nodded casually to several of his acquaintances as he moved along the bar. Then he found an untenanted booth in the rear, and sat down to see what his profits were.

He made no secretive pretense about examining the wallet after he had placed it on the table before him. Such hypocrisy was quite unnecessary in this particular den of thieves.

A barkeep came up to the table, just as Marty was opening the wallet.

"What'll it be, kid?" he demanded, his oily eyes flashing to the wallet in Marty's hands.

"Wait'll I see," Marty smirked. He glanced inside the wallet. He whistled appreciatively. "Make it Scotch. The real. Double. I drink like a gent after this kinda haul," he said.

The barkeep grinned, exposing yellowed crags of broken enamel. His oily eyes flicked again to the wallet, and then he moved off without any further comment.

Before the barkeep returned with the drink, Marty tabulated the results of the day's work. Two hundred bucks. In tens and twenties. Plus, of course, some chicken feed of three wrinkled singles. The other bills, being fresh and crisp, Marty suspected of having come recently from a pay envelope.

Marty removed the cards and identification from the wallet, not bothering to read any of them. It was a matter of complete indifference to him who or what his victims happened to be.

He tore the cards across several times, dropped them into the spittoon. He was about to look about for a disposal place for the billfold when he suddenly changed his mind.

It was a damned nice wallet, smooth and slick to the touch. Marty was an expert on wallets. He'd seen plenty of them, and knew that this one was considerably better than run-of-the-mill.

He shrugged, glanced again at it, and put it in his pocket.

Hell, maybe he could sell it to some stiff at a bar.

The barkeep came back with the Scotch.

"Stand 'em up for the house, once't," Marty said expansively. "This is gonna be my night fer a little celebrating."

The barkeep grinned.

"Even better than yuh thought, huh, Marty?"

Marty shrugged his shoulders noncommittally, but his leer was proudly boastful.

"Oh, I dunno," he said....

* * * *

When Marty Merkin woke, the following morning, the elevated trains jarring past the window of his dingy room almost tore his head off with their racket.

He was conscious of an extremely thick tongue, a faint nausea in the pit of his stomach, and the fact that he had a grandfather of hangovers.

He sat lip in bed, his skinny fingers digging deep into his balding scalp as he tried to massage himself into complete wakefulness.

It was then that he noticed the hairpin on the pillow beside his own— and the faint reek of cheap perfume that hung heavily in the room.

He looked quickly around, saw that he was alone, cursed, and climbed shivering from his bed. The lipstick wounds on the tips of the crushed cigarettes in the dresser atop the ash tray were further evidence that he had not been alone earlier that morning.

He squinted, trying to remember where he'd been, what he'd done. But it was tough sledding. There were plenty of parts in the evening, particularly the latter ones, that he drew blanks on. He could recall buying drinks for the house in a number of joints, of singing and boasting, and ordering more, and of laughing, red-mouthed girls who clung to his neck.

Suddenly he thought of the wallet, his own wallet, in which he had carried the profits of his day.

He cursed and lurched for the dresser. It was not there.

He found his pants, still cursing, turned them upside down and shook them. Some change, matches, a key fell from them. But no wallet. His coat proved to be equally barren.

"Damn her, that little—" Marty cursed his anonymous visitor.

He felt suddenly considerably more sick than he had on rising. The thought that everything but a few pennies had gone, was hard to bear.

And then, in a corner of the room, he saw the slick, expensive wallet which he had heisted the afternoon before. The sight of it was not pleasant. It reminded Marty that he had had two hundred bucks less than twenty-four hours ago. Two hundred bucks which he didn't have now.

"The dirty little so-and-so," Marty snarled. "The cheap little—"

* * * *

His sentence died abruptly. There was something about the wallet lying in the corner of the room that was peculiar. Something plump and sleek and inviting.

Instinct prompted Marty to go over to the wallet and pick it up. Instinct told him, the moment he touched it, that something was screwy as hell—but wonderfully screwy.

He flipped it open quickly, gasping involuntarily as the contents were revealed. Bills, a number of them! Bills of big denominations!

Marty's hands shook as he held the wallet and flip-counted the money inside it.

There was almost three hundred bucks there!

He stared hard at the money, gimlet eyes almost popping. It was all old dough, greasy and wrinkled and well-used. Obviously unlike the crisp two hundred he'd had a little while back. But, just as obviously, real dough.

He was suddenly shaken by laughter, wild, relieved laughter that choked him finally and started him coughing hackingly.

He went back to his bed and sat down on the edge, coughing and laughing and holding the plump, money-stuffed wallet in his hands.

This was a scream, this was a riot. It was funny as hell. As drunk as he'd been, as cockeyed, roaring tight, he'd carried on his business with his pleasure and managed to filch another billfold, netting a haul even greater than the one from the musician.

It occurred to Marty that he'd been a smart operator indeed to place the take from this unremembered heist in the wallet he had filched from the musician guy. When the dame had gone through his own wallet, she'd probably taken every cent and been too dumb to look for this second wallet.

Marty frowned. He must have tossed away the wallet in which he'd swiped this last haul. Probably it hadn't compared to this sleek, expensive job that had been the musician's. As drunk as he'd been, he'd probably remembered that he had the fine wallet and put the money into it, rather than into his own, when he tossed the other wallet away.

He touched the wallet fondly. It was lucky. That's what it was. Lucky. The musician guy had not only given Marty a wad big enough for an evening's entertainment, he'd also given him a wallet that was good to hang onto.

Much of Marty's hangover was disappearing with his new, fine spirits.

He found a bottle in the bathroom that had a couple of drinks left over in it, and he downed these quickly, splashed some cold water over his face, rubbed the moss from his teeth with a Turkish towel, and began to dress.

Marty breakfasted at a fairly ornate and expensive restaurant. He had the works, paid for it with a flourish, and decided to take in a show. There was a war picture playing at one of the edge of the Loop theaters, and Marty decided to drop in and have a look at it. He was just in time for the first matinee, which was rather discouraging, because customers at a first afternoon show were never as well heeled as those at the evening performances.

However, Marty was able to push professional thoughts aside and to concentrate on the screen performance instead of business. After all, he was exceedingly well-heeled and he wouldn't have to work again for another two or three weeks if he didn't feel like it.

Marty walked out on the war picture in the middle of the first reel. He couldn't stomach all that guff about the suckers running out to get their heads shot off. They was just saps, plain saps, and the lingo they sprouted about liberty and justice and all like that was just straight cornoroo. He knew.

* * * *

At a billiard parlor, half an hour later, Marty found a few chums to play a little balk-line with. Marty was very good at billiards, and very proud of his ability. His eye was sure, his hands nimble and unerring. His cue work was of the best. But he lost twenty dollars to a sharper he'd never seen before, and walked out knowing he'd been taken. He knew he'd been built up to his loss, and that he'd played sucker, but he'd lost on the square and there wasn't any kick he could make about that.

He casually took a paper from a newsstand while the newsboy's back was turned, strolled into a drugstore, ordered a coke, and sat there pondering the race, results. After a bit, he ordered a, complete luncheon, which he topped off with several extra pieces of pie.

On his way out of the drugstore, past the cashier, Marty paid the nickel check he received for his coke, pocketed the eighty-cent check he'd gotten for the luncheon. This small profit pleased him.

Marty stopped at Gibby's Cigar and Magazine Store to place a few racing bets and pass the time of day. There he encountered Leo the Louse, a swarthy, heavy-set operator whose specialty was fleecing visiting schoolmarms on blackmail charges.

"How's business, kid?" Leo asked.

Marty told him business was good. He asked how Leo fared.

"I dunno, kid. Seen the papers today?"

Marty was puzzled. "Yeah, I seen them."

"Read the front page?"

Marty was pained. "You know I don't read that pap. I read the jokes and the races, that's all."

Leo took the paper out from under Marty's arm. He flipped it open so that the front page was visible.

"Looka that," he said.

Marty blinked at the headline. POLICE SWEAR DEATH DUEL ON UNDERWORLD.

"Heat's on, huh?" Marty deduced.

"You said it."

"Why?" Marty demanded indignantly.

"You dope, don't you read no further than your nose?" Leo demanded disgustedly. He opened the paper again, pointed a stubby finger at the smaller heads on the front page.

Marty stared, SLAYINGS HAVE OFFICIALS AROUSED. Another: DRAGNET FOR ALL CRIMINALS SEEN AS POLICE SEEK SOLUTION OF FOURTH RIPPER MURDER IN WEEK.

"Well, I'm damned;" Marty confessed. "The net, huh?"

"That means they might be bothering us," Leo said. "That means that maybe we'd be smart to lay low for awhile and knock off work until it all blows over."

"Ahhhhh," said Marty, "g'wan. That don't mean nothing."

Leo shook his head. "Maybe you think it don't. Maybe I think it does. Anyway, I'm taking it easy. That's always the way, this so-called Jack the

Ripper who's committed them four murders this last week, he's an amatoor if I ever seen one. Them nut killers is all amatoors. But what happens, we professional heist operators has gotta suffer onaccounta an amatoor's blunders."

Marty picked up the contagion of Leo's indignation.

"Yeah," he said. "The rat!"

* * * *

Marty placed his bets, bid the time of day to Leo, and left the cigar store. His recent conversation, however, left him no peace of mind as he strolled slowly down State Street in the direction of his favorite tavern.

That dragnet business was no good. Even if they didn't nab you for what they wanted, they always found something else. Marty had been the victim of general dragnets several times before. They weren't pleasant. Maybe Leo had something. Maybe it would be smart to stop operating for a few days, maybe a week, until this thing blew over. Hell, he had enough dough.

Almost three hundred bucks—well, about two-fifty anyway. That was enough to see him through a couple of weeks, provided that he didn't go on any benders.

Marty stroked his weasel chin. "Yeah," he muttered. "Maybe Leo ain't so dumb. Maybe it's smart I should take myself a vacation of a coupla weeks."

It was a source of annoyance to Marty that he felt ill at ease passing the uniformed copper on the corner a moment later. Hell, his nerves were getting bad, he told himself.

"A little layoff," he decided, "don't hurt nobody."

Marty hurried onward, suddenly anxious to get to his hotel room. The nervousness the sight of the copper had brought on was now increasing.

He stopped at a liquor store several blocks from his hotel, and ten minutes later was safely closeted with a bottle in his room.

After a snort or two, Marty pulled forth his lucky wallet and examined once again its smooth, fine leather texture. It was almost as soft as satin, almost as smooth as human skin. He moved from his pleasurable examination to the even more satisfying examination of the billfold's contents.

Flick-counting the bills with his thumb, Marty stopped short, stared popeyed at the roll, then counted again, carefully and slowly.

His voice was hoarse as he spoke aloud.

"Geeeeze, four hundred and twenty smackers!"

There should, of course, have been something less than two hundred and fifty dollars. There should not, under any circumstances, have been such an appreciable increase.

Marty counted the money again, this time swiftly. There was no doubt about it. Absolutely no doubt. Somewhere, somehow, the contents of his wallet had increased.

Marty tore the bills from the billfold, spread them out on his bed, counted them feverishly. He licked his lips, swallowed uncertainly. He felt a feverishly greedy elation at his discovery but was somehow uncertain in his joy.

"But how?" he muttered. "How did I pick up this extra moola?"

It occurred to him that he might have miscounted earlier in the day when he had first discovered the billfold. But he knew that such an error would have been in direct contradiction to his habits of a double dozen years. No, that could not possibly serve as an explanation.

Marty put the money carefully back into the sleek wallet, put the wallet in his shirt pocket, and had a drink on his discovery. Then he had another. The succession that followed was inevitable.

* * * *

In the room adjoining his own, someone had turned on his radio more loudly than necessary. A newscast was in progress, and Marty found himself unwillingly listening to the announcer's voice.

"Police Commissioner Eaker has promised that the general criminal dragnet he forecast earlier today will be started without further delay," the announcer was saying. "This declaration comes as a result of two more 'Jack the Ripper' killings which were discovered today. The badly mutilated body of an unidentified man, discovered early this morning in an alley in the Ravenswood district, and the similarly mutilated body found late this afternoon on a south side beach, brings the number of such murders to six, all perpetrated within the last ten days."

Marty had no way of shutting off his neighbor's radio. But he was able to walk into his bathroom and turn both washbowl spigots on full. Their noise drowned out the announcer's voice.

His hand was not too steady as he poured himself a long hooker a moment later. The announcer had reminded him all too forcefully of the dragnet he feared, and had added positive prediction to his fear, by stating that the dragnet was no longer in the planned stages, but was starting immediately.

"Hell," Marty said, disgusted with himself. "Supposing they pinch me. I kin get sprang inna hour. Besides, I got this dough. I ain't no vag. I kin stand my own bail."

He had succeeded only in half reassuring himself, however. In the back of his mind was the memory of more than one occasion when—picked up in a dragnet—he had been unable to spring himself with any such ease. On those occasions, however, he told himself, it had been different. He had not had the money he now possessed. Nor had he had the cockiness his present affluence gave him.

He had another drink, while considering this. He was now reaching a condition of bolstered ego. A devil-may-care sort of recklessness was taking hold of him, pushing aside the inborn caution of criminal experience.

He took the wallet from his pocket again, opened it, removed the money, rifled it speculatively, put it back in the wallet.

"Hell," he muttered a trifle thickly, "they ain't got nothing on me."

He put the wallet back in his pocket, looked about for his coat, donned it, struggled into his topcoat, found his hat and started for the door.

Once outside his hotel, Marty hesitated a moment, then decided to find a saloon which was not so likely to be subject to a police raid.

A taxi was passing, and Marty hailed it. He gave the driver the address of a downtown bistro which, to Marty's mind, was a most respectable place.

Hell, he thought, settling back against the cushions, if he was going to have a time of it, he might as well enjoy himself among the elite, and in surroundings which were the best.

Marty magnanimously told the driver to keep the change when he paid him off with a dollar bill in front of the semi-swank bar he'd selected.

Marty was already going through the doors of the place when the driver, staring at the bill, called out:

"Hey! What the—"

The driver's jaws suddenly clamped shut, he folded the bill neatly, put it in his pocket, stared hard at the door through which Marty had vanished, then, grim-faced, threw the cab into gear and roared away from the curb.

* * * *

Inside the plush surroundings of the bistro, Marty found a place at the bar, ordered a double Scotch and soda, and sat back on his stool to drink in the higher-priced atmosphere which was the hallmark of the place.

This wasn't the sort of joint to be raided. He'd be perfectly safe here from any dragnet stuff. It occurred to him that he might even be smart to register at the hotel of which this bar was a part. He'd be safer in its confines than he would in his own cheap dollar-a-day hideout.

The bartender returned with Marty's double Scotch. Marty found the sleek-soft wallet, removed a twenty-dollar bill from it casually and flipped it across the bar.

The bartender picked it up, to Marty's disgust, without a second glance or any indication that he was impressed by the bulging wallet from which it came.

Marty watched him carry it to the cash register, ring up the sale and begin to shove it in the drawer of the till. The bartender's back was to Marty, so he didn't see the sudden whitening of the man's face, the swift horrified alarm that came into his eyes.

But Marty did see the man swing around toward him, twenty-dollar bill in his hand, and fix him with a shocked stare.

The bartender's reaction was not at all what the little pickpocket had expected. It caught Marty quite by surprise and nettled him considerably.

Suddenly the bartender had returned to where Marty sat, the bill still in his hand, and was standing there before him, white-faced and distraught.

"Say, mister—" the barkeep began.

Marty cut him off.

"Whatsa matta? What's eating you?"

"This," the bartender said, shoving the bill toward him. "How did you come by this bill?"

Marty stared down at the bill, bewildered.

"Whatsa matter with it?" he demanded.

"Good God, man, didn't you notice?"

Marty squinted at the bill through eyes clouded by alcohol. And then he saw the inch-wide smudge in the corner of the twenty. It was a red smudge, a sticky smudge. A red, sticky smudge to which a strand of unmistakably human hair was stuck.

Marty almost broke his glass in the sudden horrified impulse that made his fists squeeze together hard. He felt suddenly out of breath, panic-stricken. His gimlet eyes bugged.

"Blood and hair," the bartender whispered huskily. "How do you explain it, mister?"

Marty's mental gears were grinding furiously in an effort to set his nimble wits into motion. They took hold, but his effort to keep a straight face, didn't match the quick alibi that popped from his lips.

"I—I hadda accident," Marty heard himself saying. "Cut myself a little while back onna window."

Marty glanced at the mirror behind the bar, then, and his reflection told him all too clearly that his effort to keep a poker face to match the alibi had failed. And, from the expression on the bartender's face, so had the alibi itself.

"Where," he demanded suspiciously, "did you cut yourself?"

"Gimme the bill if you don't want it," Marty croaked hoarsely. He pulled out his wallet, dug desperately in it until he found a dollar bill. He shoved this across the counter, grabbed for the twenty.

"Just a minute!" the bartender exclaimed, grabbing the twenty just as Marty's fingers touched it.

They both pulled at the bill simultaneously. It ripped apart.

* * * *

Marty was badly frightened now, He looked around, saw that the scene was beinjg watched by the other customers in the place. His panic increased. He could think only of flight.

He pushed himself back from the stool. It tipped sideways, crashing to the floor. He turned, bolted for the door.

"Hey!" the bartender shouted. "Stop that—"

The rest of the cry was lost to Marty's ears. He was in the street, running, moving south along Wabash Avenue as though pursued by a million demons.

His breath was coming hard now, searing his lungs, and the blurred vision he had of pedestrians' faces as he passed them on the run told him that he was drawing too much attention to himself. He turned down the first alley he came to, slowed to a gasping walk. He had to walk, his legs could run no further.

Wildly, Marty looked back over his shoulder. He could see no signs of pursuit. His gasping sob was one of relief. He stopped, leaning against the fusty lower braces of a fire-escape foundation.

Though it was cold, perspiration ran in rivulets down Marty's forehead, soaked his shirt to his back, the ache was leaving his lungs, strength was returning to his legs, and his dazed brain was trying to comprehend what had happened.

* * * *

That bill…bloody money. What the hell? Why? Marty found the wallet, opened it with trembling fingers. It was fatter than it had been before, considerably fatter.

He forced himself to count it. Five, twenty, a hundred, a hundred and fifty, two hundred, three hundred, four hundred, four-fifty, sixty, five hundred dollars! More had been added!

It was while he counted them dazedly the second time that he realized that many of the bills were sticky, bloodstained. Marty's sob was terrified. It was not the money, not the bloodstains, that made him sickly frightened. It was the implication, overwhelmingly, horribly insinuating, that filled his soul with terror.

Suddenly he became aware of the soft, silken texture of the wallet in his hand. Not as he had been aware of it before, however, not with the pleasure of knowing that it was fine and expensive. This new awareness was different, frightening. There was something, hideously familiar in the softness of the leather, something he could not bring himself to name, something that stuck in the passages of his mind and sent all other thoughts tumbling one upon the other in a jumble of panic.

He became once more aware of where he was, of the sounds of traffic, the noise of the Loop everywhere about him. It crashed in on his ears thunderously as if the gates of his hearing had suddenly been opened to its flood.

In a daze that was half-terror, half-drunkenness, he crouched there, shrinking up against the side of the building, staring down in horror at the wallet in his hands.

He shrieked, trying to throw the thing from him. But it seemed adhesively a part of his hands. He shook his hands wildly, wringing them together hysterically in' an effort to wash the wallet from them. He could not rid himself of it.

* * * *

Across the alley there was a door. It was the fear of pursuit that moved him toward it, made him hurl himself against it. The door was unlocked, and Marty tumbled through it as it gave before his slight weight.

He landed on his shoulder and side, jarringly. And as he climbed wildly to his feet, he saw that he was in some kind of a storage room, musty and dimly lighted by a single bulb hanging from a cobwebbed cord above a pile of packing cases in a corner.

The door through which he'd hurled himself had closed as it rebounded from his impact.

He stood there, staring wildly at the emptiness of the room, his body shaking in convulsions of terror. He didn't dare look down at his hands. The wallet was still in them, his fingers closed tightly around the silken smooth leather, powerless to release their grasp on it.

And it was then that he realized, there was someone else in the room. Even though he could neither see nor hear the other person, Marty knew he was not alone. He could feel the presence of the other, and he knew, without having to look, that his companion in the room lurked behind those packing cases in the corner.

He found himself moving toward that corner of the room in spite of the screaming fear that told him not to. His face was bathed in sweat, his balding hair plastered flat against his rat-like skull. His steps were slow, deliberate, like the mechanical motions of a powerless puppet.

They drew him irresistibly toward the corner of the room.

Saliva drooled from the corners of the pickpocket's mouth, his stare was idiotic, his mechanical steps grew shuffling.

And then the other person stepped out from behind the packing cases.

Marty had known instinctively who that other person was. But his appearance brought a dull moan from Marty's sweat-caked lips.

He was tall, cadaverously thin. His face was long, horse-like, and his eyes were dark, sunken sockets from which a pair of yellow-gray sparks flickered mockingly. His hair was long, its bristly gray strands coming to his collar. He wore a gabardine coat which hung shroud-like over his bony frame.

It was the musician from whom Marty had stolen the wallet on the elevated platform.

"No," Marty gurgled. "No. Damn you—" His throat constricted and he could say nothing more.

The tall, cadaverous, sunken-eyed man in the flapping gabardine coat spoke expressionlessly.

"You have brought it back to me."

His eyes didn't move from Marty's face, but the pickpocket knew what he meant.

The sunken-eyed man stepped back as Marty shuffled forward. He matched his steps to the pickpocket's, retreating as Marty advanced, until they were behind the packing cases.

Then the cadaverous fellow spoke again.

"Hand it to me," he said tonelessly.

He had stopped, his back against the packing cases, his thin, claw-like right hand extended toward the pickpocket. But Marty didn't notice the outstretched hand. He was staring in awful fascination at the open cello case which lay beside the other's feet. The inside edges of the case were stained a brownish red, a freshly sticky red.

And the contents of the case sent Marty reeling backward as screaming insanity shred the remaining fibers of his reason.

The gaunt, gray-coated figure grinned ghoulishly.

"Yes, human skin. I will make a wallet even softer than the one you have brought back to me."

Something burst inside Marty Merkin's brain then, and he began to giggle. Then his laughter rose shrilly to a higher, louder pitch. He screamed harshly, insanely, and laughed again, saliva sliding down the corners of his mouth, tears pouring from his eyes. He was screaming and laughing and sobbing all at once, and the wallet was clutched in his hands...the soft, satin-like wallet...the wallet as smooth as silk...smooth as human skin, which it was....

* * * *

They found Marty Merkins beside the ghastly cello case some hours later. The wallet was still in his hands, and he was crumpled inertly over it, laughing and sobbing and gibbering idiotically.

There was no one in that storage room, of course, save the utterly insane little pickpocket, the gruesome evidence in the bloodstained case, and the horribly damning wallet of human flesh.

Perhaps the judgment of the court might have been more fair had Marty been committed to a mad house, as the attorney for his defense pleaded. But public indignation toward the ripper-killer—and the evidence that he was the killer was undeniable—insisted on the supreme penalty.

He was babbling idiotically about the man in the gabardine coat even to the moment they turned on the current of the electric chair. Which was ridiculous, of course. For had there been a man such as the one he droolingly insisted existed, the ripper-killings would not have ceased with Marty Merkins' death.

Yet they did cease then. At least around that section of the world. There might have been others. Somewhere else....

THE PLACE IS FAMILIAR

"Sadly we present the last story in our files by David Wright O'Brien, who is now a gunner in Uncle Sam's biggest plane, the B-29, which, by the time this sees print, ought to be making history slapping down the Nazis and the Japs from distances that make our head swim to contemplate. Yes, that B-29 is a ship such as even science fiction never dreamed about! The story is 'The Place Is Familiar' and that might be applicable to Tokio later on, insofar as O'Brien and the B-29 are concerned!

"By the way, both William P. McGivern and David Wright O'Brien dropped in on us for coffee, while enroute to their war duties, having finished training—and we never saw two lads who looked better. Our secretary fairly swooned with adulation and we felt nothing but sheer admiration. Losing forty pounds certainly did things to them! O'Brien is doing a local radio show as part of his duties for the air force!"

—Raymond A. Palmer, "The Editor's Notebook,"
Fantastic Adventures, February 1944.

* * * *

"After a succession of several dull issues, which were inadequate to say the least, the February *Fantastic Adventures* stands out like an orchid in a patch of skunkweed. Top yarn this trip was David Wright O'Brien's 'The Place Is Familiar'—one of the best of the rather vast DWG output. Mr. O'Brien has written some splendid stuff, along with a number of distinct flops, and I'm glad to see that you chose one of his more notable efforts for his farewell appearance."

—Chad Oliver, Cincinnati, Ohio,
Letter to the Editor,
Fantastic Adventures, April 1944.

Editor's Response: Your editor, as is his wont when enthused, made a remark to his staff that "The Place Is Familiar" would rank first in the issue, and better, rank as one of the best, if not the best, of David Wright O'Brien's stories. Thus, in view of the letters we have received, saying just what you said, we are pleased, but definitely! We predict now that it will rank as a minor classic...."

—Editor.

O'BRIEN HIT THE JACKPOT HERE

"Sirs: 'The Place is Familiar' by D. W. O'Brien was very good. More!!!!...Wishing you a good year in '44."

—An Old Reader, Letter to the Editor,
Fantastic Adventures, June 1944.

Editor's Response: "Our prediction regarding O'Brien's yarn came true. It was easily one of the best stories of the year...."

—Editor.

* * * *

"...The other issue that I have read is the February [1944] issue. The one story which fascinated me most was 'The Place Is Familiar'—the humor in that story had me howling with laughter—MORE!!"

—James L. Cribelar, Indianapolis, Indiana,
Letter to the Editor,
Amazing Stories, January 1945.

Editor's Response: "We are pleased to know that you feel we are hitting the field of fantasy and imagination so squarely. We believe fantasy is the highest type of literature yet devised by man; being the highest expression of the mysterious quality that makes him more than a mere animal. As for (David Wright) O'Brien, we feel that in 'The Place Is Familiar' he has done something unique—he has created a delightful fantasy, and yet his people are so real and down to earth that we cannot possibly question their reality. Combine this with the unequaled sense of humor he displays in the uproarious situations in the plot, and you have a masterpiece. In that last word we sum up the composite opinion of our readers as they have expressed it to us m numerous letters. Speaking of Mr. O'Brien, he phoned us from Rapid City, South Dakota this very day (September 13, 1944) and informed us that he had finished his last training mission and was on his way overseas to join his buddy. Bill McGivern, who is already in the fray. Bill is on the ground and Dave in the air—which is the first time they have ever been parted."

* * * *

It was one of those balmy late New England spring days and everything along the country-side was fresh and verdant and pretty wonderful. We had been about four hours on the road from New York—four hours so away from the stink of carbon monoxide, the scream of traffic and the hundred million other nerve-shattering nuisances that people call life in the big city.

I filled my lungs with fresh New England air. "What a couple of fools we were," I told Lynn.

She didn't answer. She was looking somewhat stonily at the crouching chrome nymph atop the hood of our low slung convertible.

This didn't faze me. Lynn was going to take a lot of selling on this idea, and the battles we had had over it in the past month were unrivalled on any list in the War Atlas.

I turned my attention back to the road.

It had been almost a month to the day when I told Lynn that I was through with the job I'd been holding down in her father's brokerage house—was through with the stupid, smug, money-counting monotony of the life I had been leading.

Naturally she thought I was kidding. "That's very funny, Tommy," Lynn had smiled, "and I suppose it's prompted by a chance encounter with one of your friends from your Bohemian and collegiate periods."

"I'll ignore that remark," I told her pleasantly enough, "and try to make my point more clear. I'm through, finished, washed-up with this washed-out parody of a life I've been living. When we married two years ago you persuaded me to step into your father's firm just long enough to pile up a nest egg to tide me over for a year working on that book in my system."

A knowing look had come into Lynn's eyes. Her voice suddenly took on a too sweetly humoring tone.

"Now, Tommy," she began, "haven't we gone over this ground before?"

"Yes indeed," I agreed.

"Then it is really very silly, isn't it, to go into the matter again when we've both agreed—"

I cut her off. "We've never agreed on anything concerning this issue, Lynn, and you know it. The last time I brought it up was over six months ago. You pointed out, at the time, that it was ridiculous to consider the matter since we hadn't nearly enough put away to tide us over the year of my big effort."

"And the situation isn't altered a bit since that time, Tommy," Lynn said. "You've still got to face the same cold facts. We're quite able to live comfortably and with a reasonable metropolitan decency on your salary. But it just happens that we can never get a cent put aside in the bank. What do you expect us to live on while you're off in some deep forest for a year banging away at a typewriter?"

I smiled.

"I'll ignore the forest remark, since you know damned well that all I had in mind was a place in New England—something with peace and quiet and serenity."

Lynn cut me off.

"Well, forest, farm, or houseboat, we still just wouldn't be able to manage it."

I held up my hand, grinning like a cat picking canary feathers from its front teeth.

"But that, my pet, is precisely where you are in error. We have just enough to take care of the matter comfortably."

* * * *

Lynn almost lost her lovely white teeth in surprise. And while she was doing a double take, I continued to smirk.

"Wha—what on earth are you talking about?" she spluttered.

"I am merely announcing the fact that I have at present in a private bank account some four thousand dollars, gained within the last three months on modest stock speculations of my own. And that takes care of that."

It had.

Not as simply as that of course. My announcement had been merely the opening gun in a month-long siege. Lynn used every device known to the wiles of women in an effort to shake me from my purpose. She sulked, she cajoled, she pleaded, she shrilled, and, of course, wept profusely. But I went right along my merry way visiting real estate brokers, renting agents and resort proprietors in my search for a suitable Shang-ri-la.

When, at the end of three weeks, I'd picked the site of my great adventure, I announced the fact to Lynn. That was the signal for her to rush the reserves into the fray—said reserves being her father—also my employer—her mother, and her somewhat neurotic sister, Katherine.

I had expected this. I was all set to trump her ace in the hole. All it took was dogged, solid refusal all around. Old Oliver Jerem, my dear father-in-law, acted about as could be expected. He warned me against my folly from each of his dual roles.

"This is quite preposterous, Thomas," he boomed. "Absolutely unheard of. The thought of Lynn becoming some—some farmhand is absolutely ridiculous. She would be utterly miserable under any such circumstances. She has been raised for something quite a lot better than what you are planning to force her into."

"Undoubtedly you raised her," I agreed amiably enough. "And undoubtedly it must have been some job. But whether or not you raised her, I married her. She is my wife. I think that establishes my viewpoint clearly enough."

Then, of course, the old boy had taken another tack. He brought in, but heavily, his second role—that of my employer.

"Is it that you are dissatisfied with your position in our firm, Thomas? If that's the case, young man, let me assure you that the board of directors and I have been giving considerable attention to your progress of late. We feel that you're just ready for a big step upward. There isn't a young man on Wall Street who wouldn't give a million dollars for a chance such as yours. Any idiocy on your point in your career would be disastrous. I'd never be able to explain it to the board, and this great chance would undoubtedly be lost you forever."

"If you must explain it to the board," I told him, "you might say that I have never enjoyed working with or for them in their marts of money, nor had ever any intention of making a lifetime job of wearing their harness. I am a writer. Or at least I think I am, enough to take a whack at trying to prove it. If it turns out that I'm a dud, well, perhaps I'll slide meekly back into whatever niche they can make for me. But I don't think it's going to turn out that way. Now, do you think that would be sufficient explanation?"

* * * *

Lynn's mother tried her hand at that point.

"But, Tommy, it is so utterly insane. If you really want to write I am sure Oliver could make some connections with some solid, sensible, financial journals that would be only too glad to have you contribute articles to them now and then."

I didn't have any trouble at all squelching her brief, futile, and somewhat hysterical two-cents worth.

"In which case," I smiled sweetly, "I'd undoubtedly wind up turning out all my copy on an adding machine instead of a typewriter. I'm afraid you didn't get the idea at all. I want to write; not bore a lot of bumble-headed business big-shots into a stupor."

Lynn's neurotic sister, Katherine, had strangely enough kept out of it. And I looked expectantly to her for a few well-chosen words on my future. She didn't have any, but the snide glances she and her tailor's dummy husband, Walter, exchanged, seemed just a little too secretive to suit me.

I looked around the family circle then to Lynn.

"It's been so nice to have had this little talk, and even better still to clear the air. Now I think we'd better be going. There is so much to be done in tying up the loose ends of our past life, that we'll have to do a lot of rushing if we are going to be able to move into the little New England place I have picked out on the day I've arranged for!"

That had been the climax—but not entirely the end of the matter. Lynn had with a great deal of martyrdom helped a bit in tying up some of the loose ends. There was our little too-expensive apartment in Manhattan to be gotten rid of, a matter of storage for much of our gilt-edged furnishings, and my solemnly worded resignation from Jerem and Jeffers, Investment Brokers, Inc., and the usual last minute extrania which crop up to plague any such departure.

But at last we were on our way—and this was it.

Lynn still was carrying a shield of martyrdom and a considerable amount of hostility. But she was with me, beside me in fact, and we were now approximately two miles from Chatam, the sleepy, pleasant little New England village beyond which lay our new home.

Waiting for us in Chatham would be a short, thin-featured, nasal-voiced realty dealer named, appropriately enough, Abner Land. He was a representative of the New York firm through which I had located the comfortable, cleverly modernized New England farmhouse in which we would make our stay. Land had the lease ready to be signed sealed and turned over. In his possession too, were the keys and information concerning the handywoman and cook I had engaged to make Lynn's martyred lot somewhat less vulnerable to squawks.

* * * *

It was Friday and scarcely noon. Lynn and I had managed to get an early start, and I had figured this to be a particularly bright idea inasmuch as it would be better for Lynn's first sight of the place to occur in the bright sunshine of such an ultra-pleasant sunny afternoon.

The place I had rented was really quite a find and, frankly, I was damned well pleased with myself. It was a two-story, eight-roomed affair that had only last summer been done over completely on the specifications of a well-known architect who had taken a fancy to the place, bought it, done the remodeling, and for some zany and temperamental reason stayed there only a couple of weeks. It hadn't been occupied since, but was—thanks to the directions of the New York realty firm—now awaiting us in perfectly ship-shape condition.

I had no delusions that Lynn's first glimpse of the house was going to be all that would be necessary to change her from blackness and rebellion to sweetness and light. But certainly she'd be forced into a grudging sort of liking for the place, and some of the ice at present encrusting her attitude would be thawed. The additional melting—which would of course take a little bit more time—would be up to me. And I was determined to carry through a concerted softening and selling campaign that would eventually have her chirping with a robin-like delight at our new life in our new surroundings.

Lynn suddenly said: "How much farther on is Chatam?"

"A few minutes more, baby," I told her. "You'll really get a kick out of the little village. It's hard to find anything there that's changed since the days of Ichabod Crane. Characters are strictly Yankee, strictly rustic, strictly nice people. It'll take a little time for us to get on really friendly terms with them, since they aren't the sort to accept strangers—particularly big city strangers—with pop-eyed joy."

"I'm sure I'll love it," Lynn said icily. "Perhaps I'll be able to go to tatting circles with the women of the vesper society, and you'll be making speeches in the town hall, in no time at all. I can scarcely wait."

I sighed, turned my attention back to the road. We were coming to the top of a high hill now, and in the little valley below and beyond it lay the village of Chatam....

* * * *

It wasn't hard to find the office of Abner Land. It was smack in the center of the village, right on the main street. He was locking the front door of his place as we pulled up in front of it.

"Hello, there!" I yelled.

He turned, saw the roadster, turned back and opened his office door again.

"How'j'do?" he yelled back nasally. "Was jest going out fer some lunch."

"Come on, baby," I told Lynn, climbing out of the car. "I'd like to have you meet Mr. Land."

"I'd rather wait here in the car," Lynn said frigidly.

"Sure," I grinned. "Sop up some sunshine. I'll only be a minute."

"Made good time," Abner Land observed, as I followed him into his musty little office. "Didn't expect you'd be here till a few hours later."

"We got an early start. Lease all ready to sign?"

Abner Land got out the lease.

"Sure is," he said. "Year's payment in advance, special rate of nine hundred and thirty-two dollars, in full."

I handed him the certified check I'd had made out for that amount, signed the necessary papers including the lease, and he turned over the keys to me.

"How about the cook and handywoman?" I asked. "Been able to find one for us?"

"She'll be out there sometime this afternoon," Land said.

"That's fine," I told him. "Then there's nothing else to take care of."

"Good woman, too," said Abner Land. "Her name's Marthy, Marthy Spingler."

"Huh? I mean, oh—yes, I see. You mean the cook and handywoman," I said. "Of course. Martha Spingler. Fine. We'll be expecting her in time to prepare the dinner."

"Place been all cleaned up, shiny new," Abner Land said. "Everything you'll need, excepting fodder, will be on hand."

"That's fine, Mr. Land," I said, taking his skinny hand and pumping it enthusiastically. "I'm sure everything is going to be just dandy."

Abner Land gave me a grin that I didn't remember as being somewhat peculiar until later. "Might be at that," he conceded.

* * * *

Outside, I started up the car again and turned to grin at Lynn.

"We're all set, honey," I told her. "Lease and keys are in my pocket and the world is in our arms. The future is bright and shining, and our cook will be out in time to prepare dinner tonight."

Lynn permitted herself to enter the conversation slightly.

"Let me see the lease," she said. "It might be a good thing if it were looked over carefully. After all, if we should decide that we didn't want to stay on, we wouldn't want to be committed to some ghastly bargain. I understand these Yankee traders are sharp."

I decided to pass over her crack about *our* deciding that we didn't want to stay on. I took the lease out of my pocket and gave it to her.

We drove along in silence, leaving the little village of Chatam and starting westward in the direction of our new place. Lynn maintained the silent status quo, and from the corner of my eye I could see her frowningly trying to make something from the whereofs and whereases in the fine print.

After a little while, Lynn looked up.

"Tom," she said puzzledly, "it says here that, quote, 'the party of the first part is'…Never mind, skip it."

"Sure," I said, grinning inwardly. Lynn knew as much about such matters as a child, but she wasn't going to pass up an opportunity to pretend differently.

I found the turn fork I was looking for, and we went off along a gravel road way which—if it proved to be the right one—would bring us to our destination in another fifteen minutes.

"Tom!" Lynn said suddenly and very sharply.

I turned. "What now?"

"It says something here that I don't quite understand," she said. "It says something about nine hundred and thirty-two dollars for the year, paid in *advance*, as per agreement. What does that mean?"

"Exactly what it says," I told her. "I got the place for a song, merely by paying up one year in advance, rather than a month at a time. Isn't that clear?"

The expression on Lynn's face was peculiar.

"But a year," she wailed, "in advance. If we should decide to leave, to go back to New York. I mean—if we should find something wrong and decide to get out."

I stopped the car abruptly and turned to face my wife.

"Now look, Lynn," I said quietly. "You know that I decided on a year's fling at the typewriter. Not six months or eight months or ten, put a year. This is the place I picked out. This is where we've planned to spend that year. You knew all that, so what reason can you possibly have for objecting to my picking up a bargain price by paying a year in advance?"

Lynn didn't answer immediately. She pursed her pretty lips and frowned darkly. Then she said:

"But a year seems so final, so positive."

"The decision I made *is* final, *is* positive," I reminded her. "I'm not embarking on some gay twenty-day lark, baby. I've quit my job with your dad's firm, we've stored our furniture, given up the apartment, and all in all made a clean, definite break."

* * * *

Lynn didn't answer. She just turned and stared out the window. I put the car into gear and we started off again. Fifteen minutes later, on the other side of a sharp, tree-banked bend in the road, we came upon our new house.

"This, my love, is it," I told Lynn. "Look once and look again. Isn't it a beauty?"

The place did look swell. It had a fresh paint job, and some clever new landscaping, and was bright and spic and welcoming. I felt enormously pleased with myself, and glanced at Lynn to catch her reaction.

She was obviously surprised. Undoubtedly she had expected to be brought out to some gaunt, gray barn in a dismal forest, and this was a million miles in the opposite direction for any such gloomy forebodings.

Yes, indeed, surprise was certainly all over her face. But she was determined not to admit it vocally.

"It looks nice enough," Lynn said without any particular display of cheerleading enthusiasm.

I got a good firm grip on my temper, remembering my plans to soothe and sell her into an adjustment to it all. There was no sense in having our very entrance into the place marred by a wrangling battle.

"That's good," I said as cheerfully as a realty agent. "That's just fine. I'm awfully glad you like it, Lynn. You don't know how hard I tried to pick a place that would appeal to you."

Which was the truth. I knew Lynn's tastes backward and forward, and I had done my level best to find something which would please her eventually, if not immediately.

Lynn got out as we pulled to a stop in the drive in front of the place. I removed the luggage, got back in, and wheeled the convertible around into the garage at the east side of the house.

When I got back from the garage, Lynn was standing beside the luggage on the flagstone walk, staring meditatively at the house. I grabbed up the luggage, and took a deep, gymnasium instructor's breath.

"Ahhhh!" I exhaled. "This is the life—and this is the place to live it! Right, baby?"

Lynn didn't answer that one. She just walked along beside me in silence as we went up the walk....

* * * *

Most of our luggage had been unpacked, and clothes placed in order, and the eight rooms of the place inspected one by one inside of the first two hours. Then Lynn and I settled down in the big, roomy cheerfulness of the remodeled parlor, and I tried to get a blaze going in the fireplace.

Lynn was deep in a book she'd started back in town, and didn't look up from it until the first traces of smoke began to seep grayishly back into the living room.

"What on earth are you doing?" she demanded.

I told her that I thought I was making a fire. She told me why didn't I go ahead and make one, then, instead of filling the place with smoke that was enough to choke a person.

I managed to keep my temper, and continued at my fire-making chores, gathering more and more wood from the basket beside the hearth and stuffing loose newspaper pages and innumerable matches into the smoking disorder.

The fumes from my efforts began to get a little worse.

Lynn started to cough. I gave her a quick glance and saw that I was being glared at—but good. The smoke was beginning to fill my eyes and ears and nose, and none of it seemed to want to go up the chimney the way well-trained smoke does.

"Good heavens!" Lynn cried exasperatedly. "Let me fix that thing."

She got up and stamped angrily over beside me. She bent over, leaned forward, and reached up and into the fireplace. There was a sharp noise of something iron being pulled open, and when Lynn sat back on her heels, the smoke was suddenly well-behaved and coursing upward through the chimney.

"You might have had sense enough to open the vent," she told me. "Oddly enough, it's often a great help to a fireplace."

I didn't say anything to that. After all, there wasn't anything that could be said. I left the fireplace and the living room and went back intq the kitchen to prowl through the larders and see what would be needed in the way of supplies and foodstuffs.

I had almost completed my list when Lynn came out. She asked me what I was doing and I told her.

"I can drive into town and buy the stuff," I said. "I don't imagine we can expect our cook to bring tonight's dinner along with her."

Lynn nodded abstractedly.

"You might try to pick up a nice-sized turkey, Tom," she said suddenly, "for tomorrow night's dinner."

I nodded happily, glad that she was beginning to pitch in with suggestions.

"How many pounds?"

"I think fifteen would be fine," Lynn said.

"Fifteen? That's a lot of bird for two people, baby."

Lynn's eyebrows raised in innocent—too innocent—surprise.

"Oh, didn't I tell you, Tom? I asked Mother and Father and Katherine and Walter out for sort of a housewarming. They'll arrive late tomorrow and leave early sometime Sunday morning."

Of course she hadn't told me. And of course she had deliberately waited until now to do so. It was suspicious, damned suspicious, and I didn't like the sound of it a bit. But I was trying to smooth Lynn's feathers and there was no reasonable objection I could make against their coming.

So I said: "No, Lynn. You didn't tell me about it. But that's fine. That's just fine. I'd like to have them see the place."

"So," said Lynn ambiguously, "would I."

* * * *

On the way into the village for groceries, I did a considerable amount of thinking about the guest deluge that would descend on us the following afternoon. Obviously, it was an inspection trip of sorts, and, just as obviously, there was more behind it than immediately met my eye. My adversaries had not retired in complete confusion, apparently, and the victory I thought I had scored seemed now to have been something less than a rout.

Maybe old Oliver Jerem, Lynn's papa and my ex-boss, was going to bring along a few cards he had forgotten to play in our original argument. Maybe he was going to do something idiotic like refusing to accept my resignation. It was hard to say what the shrewd-minded old financial bandit had under his handsome white head.

I wondered if the idea for the visit had been Lynn's or her family's, and decided it had probably been the latter's. While she was near them, Lynn's family managed to hoodwink her into anything they wanted. They always did so cleverly, playing on her love for them and their deep affection for her. This fact, of course, had been one of the flies in our marital ointment ever since we'd walked out of the church into a shower of rice.

It had been the clever manipulations of Lynn's family that had forced me into taking that job with her father's firm immediately on our return from our honeymoon. I hadn't intended to do anything of the sort, of course. It had been my plan to use the several thousand I had in the bank at the time to purchase a cabin in the Catskills and get to work on my novel.

But Lynn's family had persuaded her that they were thinking only in terms of our mutual good when they suggested that a nice job awaited me in Jerem and Jeffers brokerage house.

"Just for a bit, dear," they'd told Lynn, "until Tommy has saved enough to carry out his plans handsomely."

I had been trapped into taking the job.

The salary had been good enough, and normal living would have enabled us to save enough in a year-combined with the two grand I had in the bank to enable me to go through with my delayed plans in super style. But somehow we weren't able to save a damned nickel; and in less than six months, I had gone through the two thousand as well. Lynn's family had been instrumental in this removal of my claws. The merry-go-round of night life and parties and week-ends at swank country clubs on which we rode kept us broke, and was forced upon us by the shrewd Papa Oliver Jerem, *et al.* They knew, of course, that dough would make me independent, and that with such independence I might do any crazy thing that came into my head-like quitting my much-loathed job and starting my chosen career. So it was seen to that we always had just enough dough to keep up the pace imposed upon us, and never enough to put any away.

It took me almost a year and a half to discover their system, and at the end of that time I started getting a little smart for myself. I watched and waited until a chance came along, and put five hundred bucks on the nose of some stock shares. They came across the line winners, and I had outfoxed the entire Jerem family for good.

* * * *

A truck, rolling heavily along the highway and holding close to the centerline, made me drop my mental rehashing and concentrate on getting out of its way.

Three minutes later I was in Chatam.

The characters lolling around the local grocery store, which was actually a general store, looked like something out of Floyd Davis illustrations. Yessiree.

The grocer, or storekeeper, to be more exact, was a lean, long, hawk-nosed New Englander with a Yankee twang that sounded like piano strings breaking.

"Yessiree," he said. "What can I do fer you."

I got out the grocery list and handed it to him.

"I'd like everything you have that's on this list," I said.

He scanned the list and looked up at me interestedly.

"Heap of grub," he said.

I agreed that it was.

"You must be the feller moving in tuh the remodeled place off Kingston Road, eh?"

"That's right," I said. "It's certainly a lovely house."

"Oh, I wun't deny that it's attractive tuh look at," he admitted, turning away to get the first of the stuff on the list. There was something grudging, something odd in the way the storekeeper had said that. He came back with a dozen bars of soap, and I asked him:

"What did you mean when you emphasized the *to look at?*"

The Yankee looked up, putting a stub of pencil behind his ear.

"Did I emphasize that that way?" he asked innocently.

"That's the way I heard it," I told him.

"Wal, now," he twanged. "Mebbe I was a mite careless in my speech. Ferget it." He turned back to the list, scanned it, and walked off to get more supplies.

I was getting impatient. When he came back again, I asked:

"Listen, is there something wrong with the house I rented? Does it have leaks or landslides or earthquakes or something? After all, if there's something out of the way about it, I ought to find out now. I've paid up a year's rental in advance on it, you know."

The storekeeper looked at me sharply. "Did Abner Land sign you up tub a year's lease, rent paid in advance?" he demanded.

"That's right," I said. "I paid him just a few hours ago."

My Yankee friend broke into cackling laughter.

"Wal, I never!" he exclaimed. "That's a hot'un, all right. That's rich." He cackled some more. He's a sharp'un, that Abner Land. Slick dealing, all right!"

I was getting a little alarmed and a little frantic.

"Listen," I broke in on my storekeeping informer's happy cackling. "Will you tell me why you think my signing a lease on that place and signing for it in advance is so hilarious?"

The Yankee storekeeper stopped laughing.

"Why, stranger," he said "I don't see why not. The place is a plumb white eleefant. It's jinxed, that's what. That there architect feller who remodeled it from an old broken down deserted farmhouse only stayed there ten days afore he left and never come back."

"But what's wrong with it?" I demanded.

The storekeeper went back to my shopping list, taking his stub pencil from behnd his ear. He looked up long enough to remark casually:

"Everything."

I was getting sore. I leaned across the counter and tapped him on the chest.

"Look, friend," I said. "You started this. Will you please conclude it coherently? What in the hell is the matter with the place I've rented-specifically?"

* * * *

The storekeeper gave me a glance, turned away to grab a paper bag, snap it open, and bend over the egg case behind the counter. He didn't answer until he'd filled the bag with two dozen eggs. Then he straightened up and said:

"Hants."

I blinked.

"Hants? What do you mean by—oh, I get it. You mean haunts?"

"That's right. Hants. That's what's wrong."

The wave of relief that swept over me was wonderful I looked at the lean, dour-faced Yankee storekeeper tolerantly. He was considerably more rustic that I had imagined.

"Well, well," I grinned. "So the place is haunted."

"Yup."

"That's very funny," I laughed.

"That all depends," said the Yankee.

"Depends on what?"

"Your sense of humor," he said.

I gave him an amused smile. He shrugged, picked up the grocery list and walked to the back of the store to complete the rest of it. When he finally returned, arms full of packages, he put them on the counter with the rest, and said:

"That'll be eight dollars and twenty-two cents."

I got out my wallet.

"I suppose there's a legend that goes with the so-called haunted house I've rented?" I asked dryly.

He took the ten dollar bill I handed him and went over to an early vintage cash register to ring up the sale. He returned with a dollar and seventy-eight cents.

"Eight twenty-two, eight twenty-five, eight seventy-five, nine dollars, ten dollars," he said putting the change in my hand. "Thank you, mister. You need some help carrying these out tuh yer car?"

I looked at the packages.

"No, thanks," I said. "I think I can manage okay."

He helped by piling the stuff into my arms.

"Careful of them eggs," he said. "They're pretty close tub the top."

He came around the counter and stepped ahead of me to hold the door open. I took the packages out to the convertible and dumped them in the front seat beside me.

I was starting the car before I realized that my rustic Yankee store keeper hadn't answered my last question. He hadn't told me if there was a legend to go with the ridiculous local opinion that the house was "hanted."

I put the car in gear, and mentally decided to make a note to check into the quaint superstition on my next trip to town. It would be interesting to hear, even though undoubtedly pretty much standardized according to the usual legends of its sort.

It occurred to me while driving back to the village that the grocery-general store anecdote would be an amusing thing to relate in detail to Lynn, a humorous touch to help unfreeze her icy attitude.

And it occurred to me less than a split second later that it would be the last thing on earth to tell her, for the very thought that there was something off-key about our new home would be all she'd need. Lynn was a modern, somewhat intelligent girl, and definitely not given to superstitions. But, of course, she was a woman. Reason is not the prime motivating factor in any action of a member of that sex.

So I decided to forget the incident as far as Lynn was concerned, and I thanked my private gods that she hadn't heard it first.

There was considerably more to think of, anyway. Things such as the matter of the new cook, the settling down, the starting of my novel and, most important at the moment, the week-end visit by Lynn's relatives. I'd have plenty to keep me busy for a bit, without beginning to steep myself in local native folklore.

* * * *

I turned off Kingston Road and onto the gravel roadway leading to our place some fifteen minutes later, and by that time I was dep in the realization that I had forgotten to get in a supply of liquor, and also forgotten to get the turkey Lynn wanted for the following night's meal. Shrugging them off as best I could, I decided to let both problems ride over until the following day.

Lynn met me at the door after I'd parked the car in the garage.

"The cook has come," she announced.

"Fine," I beamed. "That's great. Like her?"

Lynn followed me into the front room.

"She hasn't cooked anything yet. How can I tell?" she said.

I felt properly rebuffed. I encountered the cook when I marched into the kitchen to dump the load of groceries in my arms. She was a big-boned, tall and angular woman, not especially easy on the most unparticular eyes, and she was busy at the moment polishing the sink.

She looked up at me challengingly. "Hello," she said. Then, indicating the kitchen table with the end of the small scrub brush in her hand, she said: "Put them there."

I put them there, while the cook's eyes watched the depositing critically. When I had unburdened myself I turned to face her somewhat uneasily.

"I'm Mr. Kelvin," I began. "I'm—"

She cut me off.

"I got eyes," she reminded me. "You sure don't look like no grocery boy." The sentence might have had some flattering salvation if she hadn't made it sound as though grocery boys were number one on her hit parade.

"And you are Martha Spingler, is that correct?" I asked, wincing at the rebuff.

"Mrs. Spingler," she corrected me. "My first name is Marthy, all right. But people don't use it less'n they know me a spell longer than you have."

"I'm glad to know you Mrs. Spingler," I murmured, backing a hasty retreat from the kitchen. "There are some—uh—groceries. See if you can whip up an evening meal from them. Anything that might be missing on that list—uh—just order on your own hook."

I went back into the living room. Lynn had taken an armchair close to the fireplace and had her nose buried in that book. I didn't feel particularly like an icebreaker at the moment, so I said:

"Did Martha take the bags upstairs, baby?"

Lynn raised one eye from the page. "I took them up."

"Oh. Oh. That's swell. Thanks, baby. You shouldn't have done it. I—ah—was going to when I got back from the village."

Lynn didn't say anything to that. Her attention went back to the book. I went into the front hallway and removed my coat, hat and gloves.

* * * *

Then I decided to go upstairs and unpack the several small suitcases which Lynn had taken up to our room. The bigger part of the luggage had, of course, been moved up there by yours truly on our arrival that afternoon. The stuff Lynn had taken up amounted to four or five bags of overnight size. However, I knew that in her mind she had now firmly established the notion that she'd done all the baggage work unaided.

My week-end grip and overnight case were on the big four-poster bed in our room when I got up there. They lay open, and much of my stuff had been strewn this way and that across the bed cover.

I was a little bit surprised. If Lynn had started to unpack for me there would have been some pattern of order to the scene. You didn't unpack a bag by ransacking it as thoroughly as my bags had been.

"She's getting nice and spiteful, also," I reasoned. "It's a wonder my shirts and ties and stockings haven't been knotted into granite-like lumps."

It struck me at that moment that—had Lynn been spiteful, or trying to be—she would most certainly have done more than muss up the contents of my luggage, and probably would have done some knotting of neckwear and shirt arms.

I frowned, stepped out of the room and walked over to the staircase. I leaned over the bannister and yelled down:

"Lynn, oh Lynn!"

"Yes?" her voice came faintly and in annoyance from the living room.

"Did you open my luggage?"

"Of course I didn't," her voice snapped, considerably more loud this time.

"I just wondered," I muttered. Then: "I just wondered," I yelled.

I went back into the bedroom and stared at the messily opened bags on the bed. Suddenly I thought of Mrs. Spingler, the cook. Her room was down at the end of the hallway.

Stepping out of the bedroom again, I moved somewhat stealthily down to the door at the far end where Mrs. Spingler was to be quartered. In the back of my mind was the idea that suspicion would be pointed at the dour cook if her luggage had already arrived and was in her room—inasmuch as that would point to the fact that she had already been prowling about upstairs with sufficient opportunity to get into our bedroom and mess up my luggage.

I'd soft-shoed less that three yards when I realized what an asinine idea that was.

If Mrs. Spingler were the malicious sort, she wouldn't take spite out on a total stranger. And if she were dishonest, a professional servant-crook, for example, she would work for us a week or more until she had thoroughly cased the place and decided on what she wanted to run off with. I straightened up out of my crouch and walked back into the bedroom, feeling like a foolish Sherlock Holmes.

Back in the bedroom I sat down and stared gloomily at the opened luggage atop the bed.

Lynn had said that she hadn't opened the luggage. I *knew* I hadn't opened it. And it was silly to suppose the cook, Mrs. Spingler, could have had anything to do with it.

All right. That was fine. That left only one thing to figure out. Who in the hell did do it?

I fished around for a cigarette, found one in my vest pocket, badly crumpled, smoothed it out and lighted it.

* * * *

I turned my attention to the bed again, and in another minute I was overcome once more by a Sherlock complex. I got up and went over to the bed and looked more closely at the disordered mess of shirts, socks, ties, handkerchiefs, and so forth.

If any clues as to the culprit who had put the stuff into that condition were in evidence, I missed them completely. I went over to the window, tested it, found it locked.

Then I thought to look in the closet.

It was disappointingly barren of culprits, fairly well stocked with Lynn's dresses and my suits. I slammed the closet door shut disgustedly and went back to the chair by the window and sat down.

I told myself that I was making a mountain out of a molehill and an unholy ass out of Thomas Kelvin.

"This is ridiculous," I muttered suddenly, getting up. "The locks on both bags undoubtedly snapped open suddenly as Lynn tossed them on the bed. They probably spilled most of my stuff out on the bed as they sprang open. That's the only reasonable explanation—even if they were both locked the last time I saw them."

I was turning away from the window when I saw the small Ford truck coming up the drive. Lettered on its side was:

"Chatam Electrical Company. Uriah Epply."

The truck stopped in front of the walk, and a small, bald-headed, leather-jacketed, roly-poly chap climbed out. He had a coil of electrical wire in one hand and a tool bag in the other.

I watched him start up the walk, stop, turn around and go back to get something else.

I left the window and went downstairs. Lynn was still in the living room, reading in the armchair near the fireplace. She looked up as I entered.

"What were you doing thumping around up in the attic?" she demanded.

I blinked at her.

"Thumping around up in the attic?" I echoed puzzledly.

"Not thumping, perhaps," Lynn said, "but dragging things around up there, anyway." She glanced at the fireplace. "The sound from the attic carries down through the fireplace here. It was very plain."

I opened my mouth to answer, then thought a minute. The bedroom I had just left was in the south end of the house, not near the attic. The living room was in the north end, and above it two guest bedrooms, and above those, the small attic. What Lynn had said was possible. That is, sounds from the attic, through which the chimney ran, might conceivably come down into the living room.

But I hadn't been in the attic.

"What were you doing up there?" Lynn repeated.

I gagged a moment.

"Oh, nothing much," I gulped. "Nothing at all, really."

The front doorbell rang, at that moment, cutting off the next question that undoubtedly would have followed Lynn's sharply puzzled look.

"I'll answer it," I said hastily.

* * * *

When I opened the door the little bald fat man from the electrical truck stood there grinning amicably. He had his coil of wire still in one hand, and his tool bag and a small hacksaw in the other.

"Hello," he said. "I'm Uriah Epply, Chatam Electrical Company. Abner Land sent me out here to connect your telephone and all that."

"Oh," I said. "The telephone. I see. Sure. The telephone and all what?"

The little man brushed by me into the hallway.

"And all that," he said.

I followed him through the hallway and into the living room. Lynn looked up again from her reading.

"The man from the electrical company," I explained. "He's going to connect the telephone and—uh—all that."

Lynn went back to her book without comment.

I followed rotund little Uriah Epply through the living room, the dining room, and into the kitchen. Mrs. Spingler glanced up sharply at our entrance, looked curiously at Epply, and went back to peeling potatoes.

Epply crossed the kitchen to the door at the far end opening down into the cellar. He turned, at the door, and said:

"Main switch down in the cellar."

I nodded, and he opened the door, found a light-switch on the side of the staircase, snapped it on, and started down the stairs. I followed along behind him.

In the cellar proper, Epply found another light-switch and snapped that on, flooding the place with a sudden glaring illumination.

"You seem to know your way around here," I observed. "You put in all the electrical systems?"

He shook his head, laying down his tool bag and wire coil

"Nope. Connected the system, though, for the architect fella who had this old place remodeled last year. His contractors come out from New York to lay out the system. Guess he didn't trust us local idjits to get it right. We were only good enough for turning it on when the time came."

"Oh," I said. "I see."

Uriah Epply bent over his bag of tools, opened it, and selected several. Then, whistling sourly through a missing front tooth, he marched over to a wall fuse-and-connection box and opened it.

I went over into a corner and took a seat on a dusty barrel.

"What made the architect move out in such a hurry?" I asked. "Didn't he like the place after he changed it to suit him."

Epply turned from his work long enough to grin.

"He liked it fine. That is, at first." He went back to work.

Mentally I cursed the laconic strain in all New Englanders. I phrased my next question ·with a little thought, hoping to put it so I'd get a little more than the usual eyedropper full of information.

"What do you mean by that? I mean, what happened? I'm interested in hearing what you know about it."

Uriah Epply tinkered for a moment while he considered the question. Then he turned around and thoughtfully jabbed his round chin with a wire snippers.

"Seems like he—this architect fella didn't realize that this here house was jinxed. Anyways, if he did know it, he seemed to think he could change the jinx by changing the house. Course he couldn't. House looked mighty different when he got through. But underneath, I guess, it was the same old house. Just a different face, if you see what I mean."

"I see what you mean," I said.

* * * *

Uriah Epply *tsked* reflectively, and turned back to work. Again I did some mental cursing and again phrased another question that would bring forth another droplet of information.

"What was it all about?" I asked.

Uriah Epply looked up from his work. "All what about?"

I felt like screaming. Instead I said:

"The jinx on the house. How did it start? I mean, how did the story about it start? What makes people around here think it's haunted or jinxed, or whatever they think? There must be a local legend about it."

Uriah Epply carefully put his tools on the floor, found a pack of cigarettes in his leather jacket pocket, took one out and lighted it. Then he turned to face me.

"You never heard?" he asked.

I wanted to kick him in the mouth and stamp him into insensibility. What in the hell did he suppose I as asking for, if I'd heard?

"No," I said with amazing calm. "No. I've never heard."

"That so?" Uriah Epply marvelled, his round little face wrinkled in mild astonishment. "That's really funny. The architect fella knew. I mean, he knew before he even bought the place and started remodeling it. He called it all a lot of guff and nonsense, though."

Uriah Epply's pause prompted me to ask despairingly:

"He called what a lot of guff and nonsense?"

"The story about the house," said Epply.

"Oh," I said chokingly. "Oh, I see. Well what is the story about the house?"

If my voice rose on the last three words Epply didn't show any sign of noticing it. He took a reflective drag from his cigarette and smiled.

"I guess you never heard of the Baggat boys, eh?" he said.

"No," I told him. "I never heard of the Baggat boys. What do they have to do with the story?"

Pulling teeth was like picking posies compared to the job of getting information out of this New England electrician. He shook his head wonderingly.

"Most folks around these parts know the history of the Baggat boys from Ebenezer to Zekial," he observed. "Sure seems funny you don't know it."

"Maybe," I said carefully, "I haven't been around these parts long enough. And maybe you'll oblige by telling me who in the name of blazes the Baggat boys are."

"Was," corrected Uriah Epply mildly.

"All right," I conceded, "who was they—I mean, were?"

"Ever hear of the James boys?" Epply asked by way of an answer.

"Frank and Jesse?" I asked.

"That's right," said Uriah Epply. "They was a little better known, though than the Baggat boys was."

"Oh," I said, considerably less irritated now that we seemed to be making a *little* sense. "The Baggat boys were notorious bandits around these parts, eh?"

"Wasn't hardly a bank in all New England they didn't knock over," said Uriah Epply with a touch of local pride in his voice.

"I see. How long ago was that era?"

"Same era as when the James boys was gunning up the wild and woolly west," Epply said. "Come to think, could be why the Baggat boys didn't become better known. Come to think, the James boys probably took all the publicity themselves."

"I see," I told him. "Sounds reasonable. Now tell me how the Baggat boys fit into the legend around this remodeled old New England farmhouse."

* * * *

Of course, Uriah Epply didn't answer my question directly.

"There was two of the Baggat boys," he said. "They was blood brothers. One was Bob Baggat; the other was Hiram Baggat. Bob was the smartest of the two, Hi was the quickest with a gun."

Epply paused and half closed his eyes, as though visualizing Bob Baggat being bright and Hiram Baggat being bloodthirsty. He sighed, opened his eyes again, dropped his cigarette to the floor and crushed it out methodically with his foot.

"How," I said thinly, "do the Baggat boys figure into the superstition around this house?"

Uriah Epply gave me a look of mild surprise.

"Superstition, you say?"

I was beginning to show my irritation and impatience.

"Of course," I snapped. "What else?"

Uriah Epply shrugged his shoulders, raised his eyebrows.

"Don't tightly know what else," he said. "Always looked on it as fact, myself. After all, that's what it is—fact."

"What's fact?"

"The story," said Epply imperturbably. "The whole thing is fact. In history books, old newspapers, right in the Chatam Library you can see the newspaper clippings about the Baggat boys, Bob and Hi. Can't call historic fact like that superstition."

"Please," I begged quietly, "tell me the story. Tell me how they fit into the superst—ah—attitude locally taken about this house."

Uriah Epply grinned.

"Glad to," he said. "Didn't know you'd be interested. Funny thing no one else ain't told you by now. Abner Land, of course, now he wouldn't be likely to tell you. Not and being the real estate man who was trying to rent this house ever since the architect last summer took out and run—"

I cut him off.

"The story," I said hoarsely. "Remember?"

"Sure," acknowledged Epply. "These Baggat boys, like I was telling you, or trying to tell you, was desperadoes—just like Frank and Jesse James was. They lived wild and high and handsome and kept the whole darned countryside in these parts terrorized. Night after night they stuck up bank after bank. High flying, hell-riding devils they was. Trains, too; stuck up many a train and robbed the mail of the U. S. government no less. Oh, my yes. They was plenty poisonous."

I didn't bother to interrupt again in an effort to get him to the point of the story. There was no sense in that. All I could do was let him ramble. I knew that he'd reach it eventually.

"Well, these Baggat boys, brothers, like I told you," Epply continued, "got away with murder and robbery and Lord knows what all for darned near three, four years. And the more they robbed and shot and the likes the more people around these parts got madder and madder. But trouble was, as the people got madder and madder, the Baggats got more and more cocky, understand? See how it was?"

I said that I could understand how that would be logical.

"Finally the people round these parts has had just too much from them Baggat boys. They appeal to the governor. Yes sir, right to the governor of this fair state himself. They tell him they want the state militia called out and put on the trail of these here Baggat boys."

* * * *

Epply paused to search through his leather jacket for another cigarette. He found one after a minute, put it in his mouth, and lighted it. He had to wait until the end was burning to suit him before he went on.

"Well, the Baggat boys heard that the governor was sending out the state militia against them, and they sent out a bunch of cocksure challenges to all the villages, defying the troops to get 'em. The Baggat boys was like that, you understand, cocky as hell and proud as twin devils. They was up in the hills a few miles from here, right at the foot of the Henner Mountain, in fact, hiding out. And to show the state troops what they thought of them, they planned to stage a bang-bang bank robbery right under their noses. You see, there was a troop of state militia sent to Chatam, first off."

I was less impatient now, and beginning to be actually concerned with the details of the Baggat boys and their escapades. I nodded eagerly for Epply to get on with his narration.

But now that the rotund little electrician had been winding me around his little finger, he surprisingly enough didn't take advantage of the situation. He got right on with it.

"The entire town of Chatam was up in arms to think that the Baggat boys picked out their little village to insult that way," Uriah Epply said. "And don't think that the state militia on guard in the village wasn't burned up, either."

"The Baggat boys sent out notice that they were going to pull a hold-up of the village bank in Chatam?" I asked in astonishment.

"Nothing less," Uriah Epply said. "Sent the notice to the mayor of Chatam himself. Happened that the mayor was also president of the little bank and a colonel in the state militia."

"Good lord," I marveled. "What happened then?"

"The mayor and the entire village, as well as the militia, went plumb crazy mad. They sat up night and day in shifts, all carrying guns and vowing to fill the first sign of anybody looking like a Baggat boy with lead. You see, the Baggat brothers even told the mayor that they was gonna rob the bank within a certain two-week period, starting that very day."

I whistled my admiration at the audacity.

"And when did they try it?" I asked. "Or did they?"

"Try it?" Uriah Epply seemed surprised and a little indignant. "Try it? They did it! And they walked off with thirty thousand dollars right out of town."

"But—" I began.

"Course the entire town and all the state militia was right on their heels," Epply said. "Shooting and hollering and chasing the Baggat boys to beat hell. Understand there wasn't more than couple hundred yards between the Baggat boys's horses' heels and the guns of the pursuing citizenry."

"A few hundred yards?" I gasped.

"Well, maybe half a mile, maybe a mile. No more than that," Uriah Epply amended.

"Did they shake loose from their pursuers?" I asked.

"Nope. Couldn't quite. They had to change their plans when Bob Baggat's horse was hit. They had to take to hiding quick, and they picked out this here old farmhouse."

* * * *

I looked wordlessly around the cellar, thrilling at the thought that the Baggat boys might possibly have held whispered conferences in the very corner in which I sat.

"Did the townspeople and the militia trace them to here?" I asked.

"Course," said Epply. "Trail was easy to follow. The posse after 'em tracked 'em here in less than three hours after they robbed the bank."

"What about the people who were living in the farmhouse here at the time?" I demanded.

"Baggat boys let 'em loose without killing any," Epply said, "when they saw that the posse had caught up with 'em and was surrounding this here house."

"Gallant gesture," I said.

"Maybe. Maybe they didn't want 'em in the way when the shooting started, interfering with their aim."

"Then the Baggat brothers decided to hold the fort and shoot it out with the posse?" I demanded.

"'Course. They was proud. The posse was ringed ten men deep all around the farmhouse. Mouse couldn't sneak thorough in the black of night, without brushing a human's shoe. The Baggats knew all this, but they was damned if they'd face the humiliation of getting captured alive."

"Oooff!" I grunted. "What customers they must have been."

Uriah Epply nodded proudly.

"Sure was. When the posse had the place completely encircled, ten deep like I said, the mayor—who was also a militia colonel—snaked forward on his belly into the clearing edge near the house and hollered for them to surrender. Bob Baggat shot his hat clean off his head, by way of answering."

I nodded in pop-eyed wonder.

"Mayor went back to his posse line and told the boys to open fire at will," Epply continued. "My grandpappy—he died when I was just a youngster—used to tell me about it. He was one of the villagers in the posse. Well, when the mayor gave his order, you never heard the like of noise that started."

"Bang, bang, bang, bang—it was terrible. Most likely three hundred bullets a minute pouring into that farmhouse on the Baggat boys."

"And that did them in very shortly, I suppose," I said.

Uriah Epply looked indignant.

"Did not," he snorted. "Baggat boys killed eleven men in the posse in less'n forty minutes of that one-sided exchange. The posse kept the house just as completely encircled, but had to fall back out of range."

"It's almost incredible," I said.

"'Tis," said Epply, "but you'll find it in the library down to Chatam any time yeu want to look. State history has it, too."

"Go ahead," I begged him. "How did it wind up?"

Uriah Epply smiled curiously.

"Hard to say that, completely. I'll explain. The siege lasted six days."

"Six days?" I broke in.

"And one night," added Epply. "Yessiree. That's how long it lasted. Posse tried to rush the farmhouse ten times in all. Lost two dozen men in killed and wounded trying. They knew the Baggat boys was out of food and water and wasn't sleeping scarce a wink, so they just waited them out after the last try at rushing the place. Safer that way."

"How'd they know when the Baggat boys would be broken?" I asked.

"Every so often they'd let loose with a few hundred bullets into the house and the Baggat boys allus answered fire. They figgered that when they finally let loose with a volley and didn't get any answer, the Baggat boys would be half a day away from dead."

"How did the Baggat brothers hold out on ammunition supply?" I asked.

* * * *

"They'd picked up some they'd had buried away in a cache nearby. Picked it up in running from the bank, before they made this here farmhouse. They had plenty to stand off a siege."

"And so they Baggat boys didn't answer fire on the sixth day, eh?" I asked.

"The afternoon of the sixth day," Epply specified. "The posse was hopeful, then, and volleyed again around nightfall. The Baggat boys still didn't return the fire. Well, then they rushed the farmhouse, the first line of the posse did, that is. The rest, nine deep, then, kept the ring and waited, just in case. They saw to it that it would be impossible for the Baggat boys to get through the ring, even though they might slip through the front ring rushing the house. Mouse couldn't get through without being seen."

"And the posse found the Baggat boys dead of starvation or bullets, eh?"

Uriah Epply paused to take a deep, contemplative drag from his cigarette. He looked at me and grinned strangely.

"You're wrong," he said. "They didn't find the Baggat boys at all. Not a trace of them."

"Is that right?" I began. Then, as the realization of what Epply had said suddenly dawned on me, I blurted:

"What?"

"That's right. They didn't find a trace," said the rotund little narrator. "They found empty food larders, empty water jugs, empty shells, and a house that was in ribbons with bullet holes everywhere. You couldn't put a quarter on the floors or walls or even the ceiling without touching a bullet hole. But the Baggat boys just wasn't present."

"But that's impossible!" I bleated.

Epply nodded agreeably.

"Sure it was impossible. They couldn't have skipped out at any time during the siege. Like I said, an ant would have been noticed if he tried to get through the ten deep ring around this here farmhouse. Was just impossible, that's all. Impossible."

"Then they must have been here in the farmhouse," I protested. "In the attic, or down here in the cellar."

"Weren't nowhere in the farmhouse. Every place and nook and board and cranny remaining of this here farmhouse was searched up and down and high and wide. One militia trooper even looked under the rugs on the floor. But the Baggat boys just wasn't to be found."

"But where did they go?" I demanded.

"From the facts of the case, real history, mind you, seems like they didn't go anywhere," Uriah Epply said. "They musta stayed right in this here old farmhouse."

"But that's ridiculous," I protested. "If they'd been in this farmhouse, they'd have been found. Or, at any rate, their bodies would have. It's preposterous to suppose otherwise. Undoubtedly they escaped, through some miracle, and took to the hills. That's the only explanation."

"There's another," said Epply, "that's been considered seriously by folks in Chatam ever since."

"And what's that?"

"That they're still here," said Epply, "even now."

"Absurd," I snorted. But in spite of my opinion and the strength with which I held it, a tiny sliver of a chill jabbed into my spine.

"If you can believe they walked right through a wall of human flesh to freedom," Uriah Epply said calmly, "it isn't a great deal more silly to believe that they're still here in this house, and that they was in this house when the posse searched it, only wasn't seen."

My rotund little New Englander turned around then and began tinkering once more with the electric unit box. It was obviously a sign that the discussion, as far as he was concerned, was ended.

I got up from my barrel and walked over to the stairs.

"It's ridiculous," I said.

Uriah Epply didn't bother answering. I clumped disgustedly up the stairs and into the kitchen....

* * * *

The dinner served by Mrs. Spingler that evening was a culinary heaven. It was amazing to think that such a sour old witch could be such an incredibly good cook, and I mentally noted this variance in her outward and utilitarian selves for discussion sometime with a psychiatrist.

The dinner was so delicious that it even worked noticeable improvement on Lynn's disposition.

For that feat alone I would have happily trebled Martha Spingler's wages, had I been able to afford to.

Lynn used much of her improved attitude in discussion of the following day's visit from her family. I chimed in as amiably as I could, keeping away from any angles that might become sparks for an argument, and the meal was finished with a remarkable degree of good feeling.

We sat in the living room, smoking and talking and laughing over reminiscences for several hours after dinner, and Lynn went upstairs and came down again with a fifth of Scotch she had tucked away in one of the steamer trunks.

We opened the bottle and had a few drinks, and a couple of hours after that I almost slipped and told Lynn the silly legend around the history of our new home. But I managed to cover up all right, and kept clear of anything that might trip me into it again.

About ten o'clock Mrs. Spingler—who had been busy at some damned self-made chore in the kitchen—came into the living room to announce that she was going upstairs to her room for some sleep, and inquired about the time we wanted our breakfast.

Lynn told her that we'd probably sleep a little late, and to have our morning meal on the griddle about ten thirty or a quarter to eleven. Mrs. Spingler showed obvious disapproval of such a wastrel's breakfast hour, and went upstairs muttering things about city people.

I turned on the radio and got some news, and about fifteen minutes later Lynn yawned and announced that she was all in.

"It's been a long day for both of us," I agreed. "I'll turn in now, too."

Lynn started upstairs and told me to turn out the lights in the living room. I did so, happily, realizing that although our battle was not yet done, nor won, Lynn was at least willing to carry along for a bit in the status of a friendly enough truce.

I heard Lynn's sharp exclamation of alarm when I was halfway up the stairs. She had reached the bedroom a minute ahead of me.

"Tom!" she cried, then. "Tom!"

I ran up the rest of the stairs and burst into the bedroom to find her staring in horror at the bed. My heart was in my mouth, and I didn't dare think of what I was going to see.

"What's wrong, baby? What's the matter?" I gasped.

"Look at the bed, Tom," she gasped strickenly. "The fools forgot to get sheets. It's made up without sheets and we'll have to sleep between blankets!"

The water left my knees and my heart came back to its normal position in my chest.

"Whew!" I gasped. "You had me worried for a minute, baby."

Lynn looked at me with dismay.

"But this is terrible, Tom," she wailed.

"We'll just have to make the best of it," I told her. "I can drive into the village first thing in the morning and get enough bedsheets to supply all of India for a thousand years."

Which was all we could do—make the best of it. And Lynn although she admitted as much, was right back into her stony mood of that afternoon. The spell of Mrs. Spingler's cooking, the pleasant evening of chatter we'd had, everything that had been thawing her out, was a thing of the past again. The truce was off.

I was awake long after Lynn's even breathing told me she was off in dreamland. Awake and staring at the ceiling, thinking about the big bad Baggat boys and a number of other things.

Of course, I knew that the double-time beat on my imagination was due merely to the darkened room and the wind sighing through the trees in the moonless night outside. But even so, I gave much consideration to the mysterious rummaging that had been done on my suitcases, and the attic noises that Lynn had heard coming down through the chimney and out the fireplace. Noises that she thought had been made by me. Noises that were made in a room which was, or should have been, deserted.

I went to sleep determining to have a look in the attic the following morning, first thing. Went to sleep as the rain started to patter down against the window pane, and the thunder crackled in the distant hills....

* * * *

Lynn woke me up. I heard the rain beating monotonously against the window pane and the guttural growling of thunder as I blinked away the sleep and stared around the gloomy grayness of the room.

"What time is it?" I demanded.

"Nine o'clock," Lynn said.

"Morning or noon?" I gagged quite unfunnily.

"Look at that storm outside," Lynn groaned.

"I can hear it and imagine what it's like by now," I said. "it was starting off about the time I fell asleep last night. Evidently it's been hard at it ever since."

"The driveway to Kingston Road is a swamp if it's all like the stretch outside the house," Lynn said. "What on earth will Father and Mother and Katherine and Walter do?"

"Get a little wet, I suppose," I said, which turned out to be the very thing I shouldn't have said. Lynn glared at me.

"You wouldn't *care*," she snapped.

"Of course I would," I said soothingly, hastily. "Only there doesn't seem to be anything I could do about it, does there?"

"Wake up Mrs. Spingler," said Lynn by way of answer to that. "And tell her to make us some breakfast. I'm starved."

A jagged bolt of lightning split the sky at that instant, as thunder crashed. It made me think of Mrs. Spingler's probable reaction toward anyone with gall enough to rouse her.

"No, thanks," I said. "You wake her. I'll munch soda crackers rather than face that old girl."

Lynn gave me a look that was half vicious lion and half angry wife.

"You craven coward!" she said. She climbed out of bed and struggled into a quilted housecoat. "I could starve to death in this Godforsaken forest, for all you care."

"It's not a forest," I began.

A brisk rapping on the door interrupted my protestations.

Before I could yell, "Come in," the door was pushed open and the cause for our quarrel stuck her unlovely face into the room.

"I heard your voices," said Mrs. Spingler, "and I wanted to know if you'd like me to fix breakfast now."

Lynn told her to do so by all means, and that we'd be right down to it. Mrs. Spingler took her head out of the door and closed it. Lynn gave a wordless, contemptuous look that told me exactly what she thought of the craven cowardice that had made me flinch at the thought of asking such an obviously willing cook to make breakfast.

I ignored the glance, but I couldn't help ruminating on the fact that Mrs. Spingler had, indeed, seemed considerably less dour this morning than she had last night. In fact, she'd practically had a merry gleam in her rheumy eye when she'd asked if we wanted breakfast.

I decided the only explanation for her cheerfulness was the storm. It was probably all deeply psychological, and prompted by the fact that storms made normal, happy people miserable and therefore brought cheery good will into the hearts of Salem witches and Mrs. Spinglers.

* * * *

Lynn and I arrived at the breakfast table in gloomy, mutually appreciated silence.

The breakfast was superb, positively royal. If you can imagine a banquet being held for a breakfast rather than dinner, you'll have some idea of the repast Mrs. Spingler set for us.

Lynn ate ravenously, and I didn't exactly ignore the fare myself. Mrs. Spingler, cheery as a lark, buzzed back and forth from kitchen to dining-room like a May Queen dashing around the pole.

What few words Lynn and I exchanged were sadistically savage.

"You'll have to make several trips into town, today," Lynn reminded me.

"Through the storm."

"Why several?" I asked innocently enough. "I can pick up everything in one trip."

"There'll probably be something I'll forget," Lynn said. And from the way she said it, I knew that the statement was a promise and a threat.

"I'll wait until you remember what you're planning to forget," I said, trying to ease the strain.

"Bedsheets," said Lynn, "will be necessary for each of the bedrooms. Four pairs of sheets for each. Sleeping beneath those scratchy blankets last night was one of the most loathsome experiences I have ever had."

"Mrs. Spingler's room was also minus sheets," I said. "She doesn't seem to have minded it a bit."

"She'd undoubtedly prefer a good stiff haircloth sleeping bag," Lynn said, "placed on a plank."

Lynn was in a lovely mood. She was hating everybody. I tried to change the topic to someone she couldn't hate.

"The storm might delay your family a few hours," I said. "Particularly if the roads flood over."

"You'd like that, wouldn't you?" Lynn snapped.

"Now, listen…" I began.

Lynn cut me off, her voice growing more angry with each word.

"Oh, yes you would. You'd relish that, Thomas Kelvin. You'd sit there warm and dry in front of the, fire and rub your hands over it. I know you would. I can tell just the way you made that crack!"

"My God!" I protested, forgetting my placating role momentarily. "I didn't' make anything like a crack. All I said was—"

"I heard what you said," Lynn cried, rising indignantly from the table. "Don't try to turn the words around to get out of it. And the smirk you had on your face when you made that crack was worse than the crack itself!"

I sighed, and picked at some sausage with my fork.

"It couldn't have been," I told her. "It just couldn't have been worse than my saying that I hoped your entire family was caught in a road flood and drowned like pack rats."

Lynn reached for the left-over pancakes on the platter before I had wind of her intention. They caught me flush on the side of my unshaven chin, and a thin trickle of syrup rolled down my neck as she stamped out of the dining-room and upstairs.

Mrs. Spingler appeared at the door between kitchen and dining-room a split second later. She was beaming.

"It's quite a storm we're having, Mr. Kelvin, isn't it?"

I picked the remains of Lynn's missile from my face and stood up with as much dignity as I could muster.

"Mrs. Spingler," I said with acid politeness, "may I call you Martha?"

* * * *

Lynn kept to her room for an hour or so, while I panthered around the living room and listened to the storm play hell with the radio reception.

It was almost eleven o'clock when Lynn came downstairs. The expression she wore was the one, she'd use on a ticket-taker in a depot—cold, impersonal, and utterly emotionless.

"Isn't it about time you started for the village?" she asked. "I would prefer to have everything in order when my family arrives."

The tone she used implied that she'd like to have everything in order as much as it could, possibly be so in such a hole and under such exceedingly trying circumstances:

I sighed inwardly, and pushed a few remarks I'd been rehearsing off any tongue. It was going to be more important to placate Lynn while her family was present than at any other time in the battle. To get her too sore while they were around would just be playing into their hands, and I was determined not to do that.

Swallowing my pride wasn't too hard, when I made a mental check to pay Lynn back later for those pancakes.

"Okay, baby," I said. "I'll run upstairs and shave and get into an unpressed suit. I'll be into the village and back in plenty of time before they arrive. You got a list of what you want?"

Lynn handed me a list, and I stuffed it into the pocket of my bathrobe, essayed a forgiving we'll-be-friends smile, and started upstairs.

I was in the process of changing clothes when I remembered my resolve of the previous night to have a look in the attic. In the gloomy light of morning it didn't seem nearly so important.

"What the devil," I told myself, "I'll let it go until later in the afternoon. The attic might be a good place to be while Lynn's family is here."

I slipped into a gabardine topcoat and stuck my hand into the pocket wondering if I'd left the keys to the car then. The keys were there, plus a folded sheet of coarse paper. Examination of the folded paper showed it to be the sort that butchers use, or used to use, to wrap up meats. Brown and, as I said before, thick and coarse.

Thinking it might be a receipt I picked up unthinkingly in Chatam's general store, I unfolded it casually.

It wasn't a receipt. It was a note.

The note was written in a loose, scrawling, childish hand, with a thick, smeary black substance that seemed to be charcoal. It was brief and to the point:

This is noe plase fer a stranger. This is yewre ferst warning. Take heed uv it.

It was unsigned.

I reread the note several times, jaw foolishly agape. And then I thought of the messed-up luggage and the noises in the attic and realized I had now another incident to ponder.

I stuffed the note back into my pocket and went downstairs. Lynn wasn't in the living room, and I heard her talking to Mrs. Spingler out in the kitchen.

When I went out there, Mrs. Spingler smiled in what she probably believed to be bright domestic cheeriness and handed me a small piece of paper.

"The missus says she wants turkey at dinner tonight," said the cook. "And I made out a list of some of the things I've planned to have with it."

I took the list and glanced at it with more than idle curiosity. Mrs. Spingler had written it in a fine, precise, schoolmarmish hand. There was nothing loose or scrawly or illiterate about it, and the amateur Sherlock in me was convinced that she hadn't written the message I'd found in my pocket.

"Don't forget anything," Lynn said. I promised I wouldn't, and wondered if she had. Then I left by the back way, through the kitchen, and went around to the garage, slogging through mud and merciless rain.

After five minutes spent in cursing the awkward mechanism necessary to endure in order to put the top of the convertible up, I was under way.

* * * *

The gravel roadway leading to Kingston Road was heavily flooded, but I managed to get through it without portaging the roadster across the streams on my back.

The Kingston Road proved equally damp but considerably less difficult, and I was able to make Chatam in the somewhat snailish time of forty minutes.

I picked up the stuff on the lists given me by Lynn and Mrs. Spingler without too much difficulty, and, thoroughly soaked, climbed back behind the wheel almost an hour later and started back for the place.

The rain had now settled down to a sloshing monotony minus the previous thunder and lightning, and there didn't seem to be any indication that it would clear up for some time.

There was more water going back than coming, of course, and the driving was even a little tougher than before. It was a matter of forty-five minutes before I finally turned off onto the flooded gravel roadway leading to our place.

I managed to cover several hundred yards before I ran into trouble at the first turn. The trouble was in the form of a washout which had turned the roadway at that point into a three-foot-deep stream.

Maybe I made my mistake in gunning the motor and trying to smash straight through it. At any rate, the points in the motor must have gotten a thorough soaking as I splashed head-on into it, for the motor coughed and stopped right in the middle of the washout.

I sat there motionless, throwing together a dictionary of improper names as I stared through the windshield into the downpour and wondered what in the hell I was going to do.

Futilely, a few moments later, I tried to start the motor again. It wasn't having any, thank you, and didn't even bother to cough apologetically.

I looked through the side windows and ascertained that I was squarely in the middle of a miniature lake. Getting out would be like stepping into a children's wading pool.

Then I thought of the stuff I had piled up in the back. It wasn't so much that I couldn't carry it the additional mile up to the house in one load, but at the same time, it wasn't the sort of stuff, for the most part, that could be safely lugged one mile through a deluge of rain and mud.

I looked at the clock on the dashboard.

It was twenty minutes after one.

"Lynn's family is probably already entrenched in the living room," I muttered, "warming themselves in the snug dry comfort of the fireplace."

I pushed that pleasant probability from my mind, since it served only to make me more dismal than warranted even by my present plight.

I found a slightly dampened cigarette and lighted it th the third soggy match from a pack in my pocket. I was smoking resignedly and staring dourly at nothing when I suddenly remembered the big tarpaulin in the rumble seat.

That was a solution.

I could get out the tarp, bring it around to the front and pile practically all the packages into it, using it like a huge knapsack. Carrying it that way, like a grotesque Santa with an enormous sack, I could get the stuff up to the house without any of it suffering from the elements.

I was especially pleased with my resourcefulness, even when I opened the door and stepped out of the car into three feet of cold rain water.

* * * *

The scheme proved practicable, and inside of another ten minutes I drenched to the skin, but had managed to collect all the packages into th tarpaulin and sling the load over tny shoulder. I left the car in the center of the washed-out roadway and started for the house. The rain was still pouring buckets, and the footing underneath made me think of swampland and quicksand, but it really didn't matter. I was as soaked as any human being could be before I'd even started.

It took me about fifteen minutes to get to the house, and when Lynn opened the front door to see my bedraggled, bemudded and besoaked condition she almost fainted.

"Tom," she gasped. "What's happened, Tom? Did you have an accident? Have you been hurt?"

I shoved the big tarpaulin knapsack through the door ahead of me, and the packages spilled across the hallway as it came open. Then I stepped inside and Lynn closed the door behind me.

I told her briefly what had happened, and added:

"Your folks safe and dry in our midst?"

Lynn shook her head.

"No. I'm terribly worried. They haven't arrived yet. You'd think they'd telephone if anything had happened to delay them."

"They're all right, Lynn," I assured her. "It's just very slow going on the roads today, even the smoothest highways."

Lynn went into the living room, and I clumped puddles up the stairs to the bedroom. I changed completely, getting in a hot shower between costumes. I came downstairs, then, feeling very hardy and very virtuous for having braved the storm and rain—and extremely happy that I was no longer doing so. Lynn was smoking a cigarette nervously d pacing back and forth between the fireplace and the big front window that looked out on the rain-swept roadway.

"Don't worry yourself into a state, baby," I said. "They'll be all right. Maybe they stopped off to pick up some water wings."

Lynn glared at me, but didn't say anything. I went into the hallway and saw that Mrs. Spingler, or Lynn, had removed the packages I'd left there.

"Where's the liquor I brought?" I yelled out to Lynn.

She didn't answer and I went back into the kitchen and saw Mrs. Spingler putting away a lot of the stuff I'd gotten. The half case of Scotch was in the corner under the sink.

"I'll pack this way in the cabinet in the living room," I told the cook.

Lynn was sitting in a chair by the big window when I brought the bottles into the living room and began to store them in the cabinet bar there.

"Like a drink, baby?"

She shook her head. I opened the bottle that we had left from the previous night, found a glass, and poured myself a stiff, warming hooker.

I sighed as I sank into an easy chair near the fire, tumbler full of Scotch in my hand.

Lynn got up again, lighted a cigarette, and began pacing restlessly back and forth. I was tempted to bring up the old saw about a watched kettle never boiling, then thought better of it.

By the time I'd poured myself a second drink, Lynn was out in the kitchen occupying her mind in overseeing Mrs. Spingler's preparations for dinner.

I got up and turned on the radio, searching for a news broadcast. I had found one, and was starting back to my chair, when I glanced casually out the big front window and saw Lynn's family.

* * * *

They were slogging up the gravel roadway in the deluging rain, on foot, and I have never seen four more miserable spectacles than the four of them presented.

Oliver Jerem, Lynn's dad, led the procession. He was a short, paunchy, red-faced white-haired man who looked like a cartoon of a successful business tycoon. At the moment he carried a pair of enormous suitcases, one in either hand, and was swathed Indian-fashion in an automobile robe. His once jaunty Homburg was a sodden droop of fine felt over his ears, and his pin-striped trousers were caked to the knees with mud.

Second in the line of approaching guests was Lynn's mother. She was a small, thin woman who looked at the moment like a thoroughly irate wet hen. For shelter from the deluge she held some soaked, pulpy newspapers over the drooping feather of a once jaunty hat.

Katherine—Lynn's tall, thin, pseudo-blasé and extremely neurotic sister—brought up the rear with her husband, Walter Lurgar.

Walter was—generally—the perfect model of a tailor's dummy. The impeccable suit he inevitably wore was invariably "gentleman's attire" with the one exception that they were a little too sharply tailored, a trifle too keenly pressed. The suit, topcoat and natty fedora he now wore might once have suited his tastes. Now they'd be sneered at by a scarecrow.

I stood there a moment at the window, grinning from ear to ear, and then I dashed into the kitchen and announced their approach to Lynn.

She looked at me in glee that swiftly faded into horror.

"Did you say they're afoot?" she demanded aghast.

I nodded. "Car must have broken down on them, or had the same thing happen to it that happened to mine."

Lynn went into action then.

"What are you standing around uselessly for, Thomas Kelvin?" she demanded. "You said yourself that they've their baggage with them, and in that terrible downpour I don't see how they can—"

I cut her off.

"Your father is carrying both suitcases," I said. "And he seems to be getting along just fine with them. If he needs extra help, there's always Walter, who isn't carrying anything but a miserable scowl at the moment."

Lynn glared at me and flashed into the living room and ever to the window. She stared out at her family's procession for half a minute, then turned and bolted for the hallway. I went over to the window and looked out. The Jerems and the Lurgars had made it to the walk, by now, and were slogging up to the door.

I took a deep breath and hid my grin under an anxious, sympathetic expression. Then I followed Lynn into the hallway.

* * * *

She had the door open, and rain spray was sifting in through the opening. I stood behind her and watched the party advance grimly up to the front step.

"Daddy!" Lynn cried. "Mother!"

And then, before I could stop her, she made a dash out across the stoop and threw her arms around Oliver Jerem.

"Oh, you poor, poor dears!" she exclaimed. "You're all drenched to the skin!"

Oliver Jerem muttered something that sounded like a growling agreement and enlargement on that statement. Mrs. Jerem broke into a shrill cry of anguished greeting, and I could see Walter Lurgar exchanging under-the-breath curses with Katherine, his wife and Lynn's sister.

Then I stepped back from the door and the inundated little caravan puddle into the hallway.

"Hello, folks," I greeted them, "glad to have you with us."

"Thomas," grunted Oliver Jerem, giving me a frosty glare, "is that your triple damned thirty blanked jib-jab convertible down on that washed-out stretch of the road?"

I nodded.

"Same thing must have happened to both of us, eh, Mr. Jerem?"

The head of the Jerem household gave me a withering and piercing stare.

"What do you mean by that?" he demanded.

"Motors konking out, thanks to the splash of the miniature rivers that thwarted us," I amplified.

"*We* were forced to walk a mile to this place because your machine is still blocking the road and it is quite impossible, what with the flood and the storm, to pass by it. Nothing happened to the motor of my limousine. It is still in excellent condition and would have delivered us to the door if it hadn't been for that—that—blasted convertible collegian's car of yours!" he thundered.

Lynn swung on me then.

"You deliberately left our car in the middle of a flooded road, blocking the way to our house a mile off?" she gasped angrily.

"I didn't do anything of the sort," I said protestingly, "not deliberately, at any rate. My car stalled in the middle of that minor river out there. How in the blazes was I to move it? Besides, I thought your family had already arrived. After all, they were supposed to be here around noon. How was I to know that they'd be blocked off in a stor—"

Lynn's mother cut me off.

"Thomas," she said with mild, martyred reproof, "you don't stop to think. That's the only trouble with you."

I shut my eyes tightly and counted half-way to ten. Then I sighed, opening them.

"You people are drenched," I said. "The best thing to do is get right upstairs to the guest rooms and change. I'll mix some drinks and have them ready when you come down."

There was much muttering, much stamping around, much solicitous murmuring from Lynn about the general condition of the little party. But eventually, they started upstairs and I was left alone in the living room.

Grimly, tight-lipped, I set about mixing some hot toddies. This involved going out into the kitchen and ordering Mrs. Spingler to cease her turkey plucking long enough to put a pot of hot water on to boil.

Then I went back into the living room and measured out good stiff portions for all of them, and an even stiffer dose for myself.

I looked at the toddy mix I had started off for yours truly, then decided to fix another one, and downed that one straight. I needed it. Things had started off with just the sort of a bang I'd been trying to avoid.

* * * *

Lynn came down a little later. She was strictly grim and tight-lipped. She stood in the archway of the living room a moment, watching me pour out another measure of whiskey for myself.

"Well," she said at last, "you most certainly made things hideously difficult from the very beginning."

I remembered, with difficulty, that this would be no time to return Lynn's hostile attitude. There was, unfortunately, a bond of mutual animosity already existing between Lynn and her folks. Anything I did to further it would be contributing to the downfall of Thomas Kelvin Inc. So I looked a little hurt, and a trifle on the apologetic side, and said:

"It wasn't intentional, Lynn, I thought they were already here. And in addition to that, I had no idea that the convertible breaking down in the place it did would block off the road. I guess I just forgot about the fact that the flooded road made it impossible to bypass the car. Under ordinary conditions there would have been plenty of room for another car to use for passage. At any rate. I'm awfully sorry that your family was put to such an inconvenience."

One thing about Lynn, soft talk such as that was generally fairly well received. That is, she knew that she couldn't carry on a strictly knock-down-and-drag-out quarrel alone, especially when the party of the second part is as unwilling as I was at the moment, and as apparently willing to be friends.

Lynn sighed.

"Oh, Tom, everything out here has been so terribly messed up. It's not at all like Manhattan. Everything was so much more simple then."

I counted half-way to ten, realizing that the very presence of her family in the place had started it all out again.

"Now, Lynn," I argued amiably, "it's not fair to say that so soon. We've scarcely been here twenty-four hours."

"But everything—" Lynn began.

"Not everything," I protested calmly. "We have a wonderful cook. The food has been excellent. The climate isn't always like it is today. I understand, from conversations I had with a few of the villagers, that this sort of storm comes once or twice a year at the most."

Lynn didn't say anything to this. She lighted a cigarette and flopped wearily down on the couch. I figured her silence was—at least in this instance—better than an answer. I went on rapidly, using these last available minutes alone to counteract the seeds that her family would undoubtedly begin sowing in another few minutes.

"It was fun last night, wasn't it, Lynn?" I asked. "Just sitting around the living room, talking and having a few drinks and keeping warm by the fireplace."

I paused, letting the nostalgic note sink in. Lynn still didn't say anything, but she looked considerably less antagonistic about it all.

"There's a lot to this country life, baby," I went on. "We have even started to draw the dividends on it. And besides, it's not as if we were completely away from everything. There'll be weekends we can spend now and then in Manhattan. And, with a cook and maid, all modern conveniences, a beautifully modernized little place like this—it's not as if we're out here roughing it. What did we have in New York that we won't have here?"

Lynn took a thoughtful drag from her cigarette, looked up with a faint smile, and said:

"Subways."

Which wasn't a bad reaction. At least she was able to kid about it. I felt a slight glow of pride, and the situation seemed not nearly so dark as it had been a few minutes ago.

"That water ought to be boiling by now," I said. 'And your folks'll be down wanting a nice hot, bracing drink."

* * * *

I started out for the kitchen, and Lynn, much to my surprise, rose, following me.

She whipped up the rest of the toddy mix in the kitchen while I turned off the gas under the boiling water and managed that department.

We brought the proper ingredients back into the living room, just like a husband arid wife who had nothing in the world to be at odds about. And I put the toddy mugs on a tray while Lynn added the final touches to the servings.

I got the idea, at that point, of squirting an extra little bang of booze into each toddy. And that was when I opened the bottom doors of the liquor cabinet bar and saw that three bottles of whisky—there had been seven but ten minutes before—were all that remained in view.

I started to give cry to the discovery and suddenly shut up.

Four bottles out of seven lifted right out from under our very noses! What in the hell went?

I grabbed one of the bottles and snapped the doors shut.

"I don't think I put quite enough in each of those for a starter," I said to Lynn, making automatic conversation while my mind tore frantically at the edges of the new mystery. "Here I'll add a little to those glasses."

Lynn looked at me frowningly.

"Is something wrong, Tom?" she asked. "You have the most peculiar expression on your face."

"Have I?" I smiled as best I could. "That's odd. What could possibly be wrong?"

We heard the voices of Lynn's father and mother and her sister and husband coming along the second floor landing, then, and realized that they were on the way down.

I was glad, for a change, to have them barge in. Lynn might have gotten more inquisitive about my peculiar reaction to the disappearance of the four bottles of booze—about which she knew nothing at present.

By the time our guests had each had a drink and were ready for another, the toddies had warmed up both the atmosphere and the conversation.

Oliver Jerem, Lynn's dad and my ex-boss, had stopped growling long enough to discuss the international situation and the stock markets with the young psychophant husband of Katherine, Walter Lurgar.

The discussion was cheerful enough, and subtly excluded me from the talk of men-and-high-finance. I knew that old Jerem was trying to bring out a nostalgic rash on me which would set me to reminiscing—enviously, wistfully, he hoped—about the days when I'd been a stockbrokerage slave under him and *had* to chime in on such boring discussions. But of course it didn't go.

Katherine, in the meantime, wandered around the house with Lynn, inspecting the rooms and the furniture and—from what I caught of it every so often—calling things "quaint" more or less indiscriminately.

I was, of course, by process of elimination, stuck with the job of making small talk with my mother-in-law, Mrs. Jerem.

* * * *

I told her I liked everything out here fine, and that Lynn seemed to be taking to the place, too. At which point she countered with several remarks to indicate that she doubted very much the veracity of my last statement.

The time passed somehow, and I mixed more drinks, and pretty soon it was around three o'clock and I was getting just a trifle high on the toddies and old man Jerem wasn't doing so badly either.

Lynn and Katherine had ended the tour of the house, and Katherine was trying to get her rat-faced husband's attention away from his father-in-law long enough to indicate to him by subtle remarks that she thought the place was a hideously rustic mess.

It was all very much messed up with undercurrents as yet unspoken, and yet I knew that it wouldn't be smart strategy for me to be the one who brought the troubles to the surface. They were out here for one purpose—to try to make Lynn change her mind, abandon this fiendishly grim existence to which I was chaining her, and come back to New York with them.

Dinner was slated for five o'clock or thereabouts, and by three-thirty the odors of roasting turkey in the kitchen oven had pretty well attached themselves to everyone's nostrils. If my sense of smell was any criterion, Mrs. Spingler's cooking job on the turkey was going to turn into a triumph.

Around four o'clock Lynn went out into the kitchen to get another kettle of boiling water from the stove, and when she came back into the room a little later with the toddy mix, Mrs. Spingler moved unobtrusively behind her. When the cook and handywoman started upstairs, I knew that Lynn had told her to get up and see to it that bedsheets adorned the mattresses in all the rooms—a matter which, to my knowledge, had not yet been taken care of. Along about four-ten, I asked old Jerem:

"Well, what do you think of our humble abode?"

The expression on his face was in direct and obvious contradiction to his words. But he replied:

"It's a nice job of remodeling, I must say, Very cozy, Thomas. Extremely cozy." And then he added. "If one goes for this sort of life."

Oliver Jerem shot a pointed, pitying glance at his daughter as he said that, and the hair on the back of each neck in the room bristled electrically with the sudden tension.

"I certainly go for it," I said, giving him the only answer that came readily to my mind, and trying not to be defensive about it. "Yes, indeed. I certainly do, and I'm sure Lynn will feel just as I do very shortly."

The rain outside was gradually subsiding and I felt pretty certain that evening would find the stars out and the countryside at its early spring New England best. I mentioned this fact to break the silence that followed my challenging retort to old Jerem.

Tailor's dummy Walter Lurgar, Katherine's husband, came in with both feet and a black-jack on that conversational opening.

"That will be good," he said. "In fact, Tom, it'll be a bit of a blessed relief to me. I'm not too sophisticated to be superstition-proof, you know. And the legend I heard in the village about the history of this old place was certainly chilling."

* * * *

Of course, every eye in the room was fixed on the louse. I took a deep breath and tried my damndest, my futile damndest, to turn the conversation into another channel.

"Who'd like another drink?" I said cheerfully.

But no one was paying the least bit of attention to me; every eye was on Walter. And he continued as if I hadn't said a word to jar him from the track.

"Why, after what I'd heard in the village, the sight of this place, bleak and forbidding, outlined momentarily against the sky as the lightning crackled through the storm, was enough to—"

I cut in again. Loudly, this time.

"You ought to write terror fiction, Walter," I laughed. "You must have a swell imagination to picture a remodeled, hundred percent modernized New England farmhouse as a bleak and forbidding ogre's castle."

Walter waited me out, a grin on his face.

"I apologize, old man," he cut in when he found a split second. "I didn't mean bleak and forbidding, exactly, except as a sort of figure of speech. I mean, I was thinking of the house at the time when the notorious brigands were slain here. I was thinking of it during the period it stayed unoccupied and became to be known around the village as haunted."

And so there it was. Out of the bag. Quite deliberately brought forth, as a matter of fact. I didn't have to glance at Lynn to know that she was staring at me in wide-eyed horror, and I didn't need a mirror to tell me that my own expression couldn't possibly conceal from her the fact that I'd known about the legend of the house being haunted and had deliberately kept it from her.

There was one of those silences that you could have measured with a voltmeter. Then I heard Lynn ask:

"What is all this about, Tom? What is Walter talking about?" Her voice was colder than the heart of an ice cube.

I did my best to don an amused grin. "Oh, just some silly local superstition," I said. "I'd heard it, but hadn't even given it enough thought to mention it."

"Is that so?" Lynn asked with a rising inflection that foreshadowed no good. "Is that so? You heard that this place was supposed to be haunted; and you didn't think it worth mentioning?"

"That's right," I grinned sickly. "After all, the whole thing was ridiculous. Modern, intelligent minds have no room for such silly myths as haunted houses and all that sort of nonsense. Why should I have thought any more about it?"

The Jerem family, pop, mom, sis, and brother-in-law, were sitting back smugly and keeping out of this. They knew how to play it smart. Walter had started the ball rolling, and now all they had to do was sit back and watch it bounce wildly back and forth between Lynn and me until we were in the middle of a bloodthirsty battle.

The situation called for all I could give it. And I prayed that what I could give it would be enough, determining that since Lynn's family wanted a fight, that was just what they were not going to be privileged to witness.

My smile was still frozen on my face, and I was still waiting for Lynn's answer. The I-won't-make-a-fight-out-of-this attitude on my part had her slightly stalled, but not completely. At last she snorted:

"Really, Tom. Even though the superstition is positively ridiculous, to any one of intelligence, the very thought that this house is so considered by the townspeople of Chatam should have made you have sense enough not to rent it. Imagine—a house where desperadoes were slain at one time. It's revolting. Why, their blood might stain the earth all around this house."

I was beginning to perspire. I found a handkerchief and mopped my brow, stalling for time. Although Lynn hadn't put her last statement in the form of a question, I knew that she and the rest in the room were waiting for an answer, or some weak sort of rebuttal.

"Good lord," I said, "who knows how many Indians died on the spot where Times Square is now located? Who knows how much of the early Dutch settler's blood now stains the site of Rockefeller Plaza? Why, countless bleached bones may lie in the mud of the river bottom under any foot of the Triborough Bridge. Yet does that keep people away from Times Square? Does it make them shudder and shun Rockefeller Plaza? Does it make them refuse to use the Triborough Bridge? Of course not—it would be ridiculous."

Old man Jerem came in with his two coppers' worth.

"What you say has some truth, Thomas. But you must remember that the cases you cited and the instance under discussion vary a great deal psychologically. No one thinks in terms of Times Square as a burial ground for scalped Indians. No one enters Rockefeller Plaza thinking that Dutch settlers' may have bled and died on the ground now covered by it. People think of the Triborough Bridge as strictly a means of transportation. This is quite a different matter. Apparently everyone in this locality had attached an unpleasant, though admittedly stupid, connotation to this place. They do not consider it as merely a remodeled farmhouse; they think of it in terms of brigands who were slain here and left some taint, some sort of a—uh—" he faltered momentarily.

"Curse," Walter put in obligingly.

"Curse," old Jerem nodded gratefully. "That's it. Left some sort of a curse on the place."

Lynn's mother, who'd managed to keep her mouth shut until now, couldn't stay out of it any longer.

She shuddered dramatically.

"It's—it's positively frightful! I mean, it's like living in Madame Tussaud's Wax Museum and having a room in its famous Chamber of Horrors."

Katherine followed through for the last kick in my face.

"I don't think so," she said eagerly, face flushed in rapt excitement. "I think it would be thrilling to spend a night here." She half closed her eyes and squeezed her hands together in delight. "Just think, the ghosts of the brigands are undoubtedly supposed to be walking the house at midnight, or something. Why, the prospect of meeting them in one of the halls is a positively thrilling challenge!"

I mustered in as firm a tone as I could:

"I think the entire topic is silly. And I think that if none of you have any objections, it could be just as well dropped right now. Frankly, it annoys me extremely."

The swift gambit of glances that were exchanged told me that each of Lynn's family was congratulating the other on having won an important round easily.

I glanced at Lynn, and her expression was unfathomable, although it wouldn't be difficult for me to guess what was going on in her mind.

Walter rose, smirking at me.

"Certainly, old man. If you want the topic dropped, dropped it will be It's your place, you know, even though it is rumored to be haunted." He turned to Lynn. "I'll pop out in the kitchen a moment and get a drink of water, if you don't mind."

* * * *

Lynn said she didn't and Katherine's husband left the room. It was at that instant that old Oliver Jerem coughed and asked if we'd excuse him a moment, since he had—in other words—to go to the gents' room.

That left Katherine, Lynn, their mother, yours truly, and a great big bundle of tension.

I lighted a cigarette and tried to look as nonchalant as the tobacco ads.

Katherine, devilishly, said: "Murad."

"And how have you been, Katherine?" I asked, rising and stepping over to the liquor cabinet to pour myself a big hooker of straight stuff.

The sounds started coming out of the fireplace in the next instant. Sounds coming from the attic, and suggesting something being dragged around up there. I froze stock-still, icicles forming on my spine.

"What on earth is that noise?" Lynn's mother demanded.

"It comes from the attic," I said. "Chimney runs through there."

Katherine said: "Oh."

Mrs. Jerem asked: "Who's up in the attic?"

I said: "The cook, I suppose."

Lynn stepped in.

"I didn't tell Mrs. Spingler to go up to the attic," she said. "I just sent her upstairs to fix the beds. What on earth can she be doing up there?"

The sounds stopped. I relaxed.

Walter waltzed back into the room, munching an olive he had evidently filched from one of the dishes Mrs. Spingler had been preparing in the kitchen.

"I'm starved," he said, tossing the olive pit at the fireplace and landing it on the rug.

"It's this rustic weather," Katherine said. "It would certainly play hell with a girl's figure if she stayed up here too long. My, she'd be stuffing herself ravenously all day long until she got as fat as a pig."

I took a deep swig of the scotch. There wasn't an angle Lynn's tribe were ignoring.

Mrs. Spingler came down the stairs, then. Lynn looked up as the cook started across the living room on her way to the kitchen, and asked:

"What were you doing in the attic, Mrs. Spingler?"

Martha Spingler's unlovely face wrinkled in bewilderment.

"Attic? I don't rightly understand what you mean, Missus Kelvin. I wasn't in the attic."

The expression that came suddenly into Lynn's eyes was not good—from my point of view. She said:

"Oh, nothing. Disregard it, Mrs. Spingler. We thought we heard sounds coming down the chimney from the attic, that's all."

"Wind, more'n likely," said the cook, taking leave.

"It didn't sound like wind to me," Mrs. Jerem said helpfully. "It sounded like something being dragged over a floor."

"What're you people talking about?" demanded Walter.

Katherine obligingly brought him up to date on the matter, explaining about the sounds from the attic.

"Well," said Walter, "well, well. If Tom hadn't outlawed the topic, I'd say that—But," and he grinned good-humoredly, "we can't talk about ghosts and houses that are supposed to have them."

Mrs. Spingler's cry was loud and stricken.

For a moment we all gaped toward the kitchen in frozen horror. The cook's scream had been blood-curdling enough to make your hair stand up strand by strand.

I was the first one out there. The others followed.

Mrs. Spingler was standing in the kitchen staring at the open door of the oven, apparently stricken into statue-like frigidity by what she saw.

"What's wrong?" I cried, taking her arm and shaking her gently. "Tell us, what's wrong?"

Mrs. Spingler pointed a dramatic finger at the oven door and the compartment beyond it.

"It's gone!" she said. "It's vanished. The turkey is gone!"

* * * *

In the moment of silence that followed, we all tried to digest that bit of information as quickly as possible, by staring into the empty oven.

"Broiler tin and all," wailed Mrs. Spingler. "Gone—plain vanished into thin air!"

Then, of course, someone—maybe it was me—made the remarks that that was impossible. Someone else added that it must have been stolen. And I turned to see how Walter Lurgar was taking it. He was, it seemed, as astonished as the rest of us.

But I had a hunch that the lull in the excitement wouldn't last long, and took immediate advantage of it by moving quietly over to the cellar door, which was in the right corner of the kitchen, then to the back door—in the opposite corner.

A quick glance at the first showed me that it was locked, and that the key was protruding on the kitchen side. The back door was also locked, key on kitchen side. But I turned the key quite casually, mentally praying that it wouldn't be noticed.

I wasn't. When I joined the circle around the oven again I had at least the satisfaction of having twisted evidence to make a plausible explanation of the turkey's disappearance.

Walter went into action, a moment later. He went to the cellar door, as I had done, and with his hand on the knob, asked in Sherlockian tones:

"Where does this door lead to?"

Lynn told him the cellar. Walter saw, then, that the door was locked and that the key was on his side of it. He stepped across the room to the back door.

"That leads out into the back lawn and garage beyond that," I told him. Walter glanced down at the key, as he turned the knob. The door opened immediately.

"There's the answer," I broke in quickly. "Some sneak thief crept in here when Mrs. Spingler was upstairs working, filched the entire bird right out of the oven, broiler pan and all, and hit for the woods."

"I didn't leave that back door open," Mrs. Spingler wailed suddenly. "I left it locked."

All eyebrows instantly elevated a notch.

"And I certainly didn't touch the door or the lock while I was back here in your cook's temporary absence," broke in Walter. "Who else left the living room?"

"Your father-in-law," I said maliciously.

"Really!" Mrs. Jerem gave me a shocked stare.

"But he didn't come back here," I said. The only way into this kitchen is through the back door—which is now unlocked—and through the dining-room door. Anyone entering the dining-room would have to pass through the living room, and we know no one did that. Q.E.D. A sneak thief came in the back door and made off with the turkey."

* * * *

Oliver Jerem walked in on the tail of my summation.

"What goes on here?" he demanded.

Everyone, save yours truly, told him at once. When he had finally gotten the matter straight, he turned on me.

"Good heavens, Thomas, what sort of country is this out here? Thieves running rampant, doors miraculously opened, turkeys stolen, footpads terrorizing decent citizens."

"You're a little bit ahead of yourself," I said. "No one is terrorizing anyone as yet, as far as I can see."

Old Jerem frowned disapprovingly.

"That's the next step, Thomas, my boy. You mark my words. I don't like this, any of this. Frankly, I knew this entire idea of yours, taking Lynn from decent surroundings into dangerous, savage forests and untold hardship, would turn out something like this."

I began to get hot under the collar.

"Don't talk such nonsense," I snapped. "This isn't far-off Tibet. It's civilization of the New England variety, located less than a day's drive from New York City. The forests around here all are full of peacefully grazing cows. The dangerous Indian trails carry Burma Shave signs. I'm getting fed up with the general impression you people are trying to create!"

Old Jerem was staring at me foolishly.

"You arrived in a storm that could happen anywhere. Your disposition was ruined because you happened to be forced to walk through rain and mud for a mile because of a washed-out roadway that was an act of God. Now a turkey is stolen by some petty sneak thief, and you try to make it sound like we're being stalked down slowly but inevitably by Jack the Ripper." I took a deep breath. "Nuts!" I declared as an anti-climax.

I turned my back on them all and stalked into the living room, realizing that I'd probably pulled a tactical boner as far as Lynn's reaction was concerned, but glad to have gotten some of my feelings on the matter off my chest. I stepped up to the liquor cabinet to pour myself a Big Joe.

All the liquor was gone. Not a single bottle was left!

There had been two full bottles, unopened, and one about finished. But now there weren't any. I stepped back from the cabinet as though it were alive and capable of biting.

And at that instant, while I was staring aghast at the cabinet, Lynn, her father, mother, sister and brother-in-law, trooped into the living room.

"What now?" Jerem thundered, before I could wipe the expression of amazement from my features.

Walter helped out by rushing to my side to gape at the empty cabinet.

"The liquor," he blurted. "Tom had two or three bottles there just a moment ago when we went into the kitchen. Now there isn't one of them left!"

I could gladly have throttled my brother-in-law by marriage right then and there. In an instant a circle just like the one that had formed incredulously before the empty oven had gathered before the empty liquor cabinet.

And then, of course, I saw the note.

It wasn't folded this time, but it was written on the same coarse brown butcher's paper that the other one had been scrawled on.

* * * *

I beat Walter in the grab for it by a split second. One glance at the crude, scrawling, charcoaled script was enough to tell me that it was—save for the message—identical to the one I'd had left in my topcoat pocket just that afternoon.

"Now will yew git while the gitting is good?" it read.

I was crumpling it into a ball to toss it into the fireplace when Oliver Jerem, cleverly anticipating my move, snatched it from my hand.

"Let me see that, Thomas!" he grunted.

I stood there helplessly, while Lynn's father smoothed out the coarse paper and read the message on it. He read it once, frowned, then read it again. Then he looked up and fixed me with a glare.

"What is this all about?" he demanded.

I colored, and began to splutter around for an answer. I knew that Lynn and the others had all seen my effort at disposing of the note in the fireplace, and it didn't place me in any light other than that of suspicion.

"How should I know?" was the best that I was finally able to get out of me. And from the instant reaction of the others, I knew it wasn't especially convincing.

Mrs. Spingler's hysterical outburst didn't exactly save the situation, but at least it created a diversion.

The cook had come up behind the rest of us silently, had heard enough to figure out what this second riot was all about, and then let out a shriek.

"I am not a-staying here another minute!" she wailed shrilly. "I'm a-packing bag and baggage right this instant."

And with that our unlovely but wonderfully capable cook turned and made for the stairs and her bedroom.

"Ohhhhh!" Lynn wailed. "What are we going to do? Whatever are we going to do?"

I tried to step into the breach.

"Now there's no sense in our losing our heads over two trivial incidents such as those," I said. "We can persuade Martha to stay long enough to prepare dinner, and—"

"What dinner?" Katherine cut in acidly.

"Why—ah—uh—we can throw something together, surely," I stammered, glaring at her.

Oliver Jerem cleared his throat angrily. "I presume your telephone is in working order," he said.

"Yes," I said. "Sure it is. That's an idea. We can call the village and get the restaurant there to send up something already cooked to take the place of the turkey, and—"

Jerem cut me off.

"I will call the village to get the town garage to send a limousine and a towing truck out here. The first to carry us to the local train station, the second to remove my limousine from the mud your stupidity caused it to bog down in," he said. "As soon as they arrive we will say good-bye, Thomas. We have had quite enough of this weekend not to want any more."

* * * *

I started to protest that it was raining outside, and then saw that the downpour was over. I looked at Lynn, and became sickly aware of which side she was on.

"If you care to explain what that note means, and why you tried to destroy it," old man Jerem said, "it would be of interest to me, although it wouldn't alter my plans one iota."

I shrugged dejectedly.

"I wrote it myself," I said, "as a big gag. I ingeniously managed to steal the turkey out of the oven while sitting in the front room with Mrs. Jerem, Lynn, and the rest of you. I am a Master Criminal and on cold, moonless nights I grow claws and howl weirdly at the sky, blood running down the corners of my—"

"Tom!" Lynn blazed, cutting me off and glaring at me disgustedly. "That isn't funny!"

"You're telling me," I said.

Walter Lurga piped up then.

"Quite possibly you are behind all this, old boy. That convertible cutting us off on the road a mile from the place—when you knew we'd be forced to walk fully a mile in the filthy storm—could have been a premeditated welcome note on your part. You might well have slipped the village idiot five dollars to make noises in your attic upstairs that would come out of the fireplace and frighten us. Perhaps you planned to recount the haunted house legend about the place later in the evening, when such sound effects, cleverly built toward that end, would frighten us out of our wits."

I didn't bother to keep the hostility out of my voice and eyes as I stared at Walter.

"Is that right?" I said. "You seem to be full of ideas as to how I play host. Go ahead, how would I arrange to have the hooch snitched out of the liquor cabinet? How would I plant the warning note in the childish scrawl?"

Walter was glad to give out with ideas on those angles.

"Simple, enough. The village idiot, after stealing the turkey from a door you left open for him, and getting up into the attic to make noises, just waited until the commotion about the turkey started, slipped downstairs, took the liquor, and left by the front door. You planted the note yourself, then pretended to find it when we came out here."

I smiled.

"You're certainly full of ideas for a pumpkin head," I told him.

I stepped in quickly and planted a right hook on Walter's pointed chin. He went down to the floor like a tired sock, to the accompaniment of screams from Lynn, Katherine and Mrs. Jerem.

I whirled to face the old man.

"And as for you, you old fossil," I snapped. "I'd beat the living devil out of you if you were twenty years younger. Now make that damned telephone call, and the sooner you leave, the better I'll like it!"

* * * *

And with that for an exit line, I turned my back on them all and left the room. I passed a muttering, white-faced Mrs. Spingler on the staircase. She had all her things, a suitcase, a flock of lurid magazines, and a bird cage, in her arms.

"Climb on your broom and blow out of here," I suggested.

She continued muttering and went down into the living room.

I didn't go to the bedroom. Instead, I turned to the right and started down the hallway to Mrs. Spingler's room. But that wasn't my destination. I stopped at the small door on the left side of the hallway about fifteen feet from the cook's ex-room. It was the door opening onto the small steps leading up into the attic.

I was finally getting around to taking a look up there.

The steps were steep, and the slanted ceiling low, forcing me to keep my head down or crack it hard. My back was aching when I reached the top of the stairs and was finally able to straighten up.

The attic wasn't very large as attics go. It was, for a width of twenty feet, high beamed enough to permit me to stand without stooping. But it was short. There were windows, small ones, at either end, and they permitted enough gloomy gray twilight into the room to make visibility possible, though limited.

I looked around most carefully, and saw exactly nothing.

The place was quite bare.

I walked over to the end where the chimney passed through from the floors below and up out of the roof. There was a small, fireproofed vent in the brick which would carry sound down through the fireplace easily enough.

Slowly, I worked my way around the darkened nooks and corners, not leaving any of them until certain they were barren. After about five minutes more of this careful inspection, I was convinced that the place was absolutely empty.

I sat down on the floor, pulled out a cigarette, and lighted it. For five or six minutes I sat there smoking and reflecting on what a horrible mess everything was in.

Lynn would leave with her relatives, of course. I had seen her intention to do just that in her eyes. I didn't have to be told.

I looked at the slightly skinned spots on the knuckles of my right hand and felt a sour sort of satisfaction in having at last told Walter precisely what I thought of him.

But the sensation couldn't counterbalance the fact that I'd lost the important scrap, and that Papa and Mama and Sis Jerem were walking off with their daughter.

I thought for a while about how nice my marital status might have been had I married an orphan.

And eventually I found myself thinking about the Baggat boys.

"You damned stinkers," I muttered aloud, "you've fixed everything wonderfully, haven't you?"

Of course, I didn't get any answer, and hadn't expected one. I sighed, and took another deep drag on my smoke, then crushed it out carefully on the floor.

"Wise guys, aren't you, Baggat boys?" I muttered. "So damn wise you don't even now that the siege is all over and that the posse has gone home a long time again, and that you can get out now."

It was ridiculous, of course. I was just in the mood for some sour clowning, however, and I went on.

"Sure," I muttered aloud. "They've all gone home, and you've had a perfectly good chance to beat it and come out of hiding after all these years. No posse, no shooting. Just walk out bold as brass. Hell, you couldn't be seen in broad daylight, for that matter. People can't see ghosts."

I got up and started for the steps leading down out of the attic.

"Do as you please, boys," I said.

* * * *

I heard the noise behind me just as I started down the stairs. It almost scared me into a headlong forward sprawl. Righting my balance, I turned and saw the coarse sheet of butcher's paper lying on the attic floor less than ten feet away from me.

Of course I almost broke my neck, swiveling my head around frantically to locate the person or persons who'd dropped that note there and made a noise to attract my attention to it.

But the attic was still as barren as before. It contained nothing but the note and Thomas Kelvin, who promptly picked it up and stared at it in wonder.

"Why dint sumone tell us this afore? Thanx fer the tipoff, pardner. Yew arr awl rite."

It was written in the same loose, childish scrawl that the other notes had displayed, and, like the other notes, done with charcoal.

I felt a tiny shiver move up from the base of my spine until it buzzed the hair on the nape of my neck. I stuffed the note into my pocket, looked once quickly around the absolutely empty attic, and bolted down the stairs in much haste.

As I closed the attic door behind me, and stood there a moment in the hallway, I heard voices coming up the stairs from the hallway below. Voices and the faint purr of an automobile motor.

One of the voices was Lynn's.

"You're right, I guess, Father," she was saying. "It will be best to leave with you now. There's no telling what he might do if I had to stay here alone with him."

My stomach turned somersaults.

"Well, hurry, Lynn. We can't wait all evening," her father's voice boomed. "Don't try to take everything. Just pack a small bag. He can ship you the rest of the things later."

I heard Lynn's footsteps starting up the stairs, and I waited there sickly, not knowing quite what to do. As she rounded the bannister at the landing she saw me, stared right through me, and went on into our room.

I heard her rummaging around in the closets, dragging out a small weekend bag, opening and closing drawers, clicking coat hangers, and making all the other incidental sound effects necessary to a departure.

Her father's voice trumpeted suddenly from the bottom of the staircase. "Lynn!"

She came to the door of the bedroom, and still ignoring me utterly, answered:

"Yes, Father?"

"I forgot my briefcase. Important papers in it. On the bed in the guest room your mother and I occupied. Would you get it?"

"All right. I will," she said.

Lynn walked past me to the guest room in which her father had stayed. I was still just part of the wallpaper as far as she was concerned.

I heard her call out from the guest room:

"It isn't on the bed, Father."

But the old boy downstairs didn't hear her, and consequently didn't answer.

Then Lynn exclaimed:

"There it is. It fell under the bed. I see the edge sticking out!"

I heard her grunt in exertion as she got down on all fours to get at the briefcase under the bed. And then I heard her horrified cry of dismay.

* * * *

Forgetting that I wasn't wanted around, I made a quick dash into the guest room.

"What's wrong, Lynn?" I began in alarm.

And then I saw the reason for her exclamation of horrified shock. She was still on her hands and knees, holding up the cover of the bed to reveal a briefcase on the floor beneath it and—behind the briefcase—half a dozen empty whisky bottles of the brand I had had in the liquor cabinet before the theft!

"Jeeeeudas!" I exclaimed.

Lynn looked up in red-cheeked confusion and bewilderment. She forgot that she wasn't speaking to me.

"What does this mean?" she asked, pointing to the bottles.

"Those are the bottles filched from the liquor cabinet," I said. "They're empty. The stuff has either been poured out of the window or tippled, or both."

"But under Father's bed—" Lynn stammered in shocked disbelief.

I shrugged elaborately.

"I don't accuse people without evidence, baby," I said. "You draw your own conclusion from what you see."

Lynn picked up the brief case and got to her feet. And the brief case, being unlocked and upside down, spilled its contents out onto the floor.

Letters, legal and financial papers, envelopes and graphs comprised most of the briefcases' contents. Part of same, however, proved to be torn, note-sized sheets of crude butcher's brown paper. A piece of charcoal was also evident among the mess.

"That's—that's the same sort of paper that threatening note was written on," Lynn gasped, "and probably with that very piece of charcoal."

Again I shrugged, unable to trust my voice.

"But then Father must have been planning to break us up, to get me back to New York and—" Lynn paused. "Just a minute," she cried.

I followed her out of the guest room into the one adjoining it which had been occupied by Walter and Lynn's sister Katherine.

Lynn's instinct was unerring. She made for the closet, threw open the door. A double turkey boiler pan lay on the floor of the closet. In it were bones, Turkey bones, nothing else.

Lynn turned to face me, biting deep into her underlip, eyes damp.

"Tommy," she said. "They were trying to get me to leave you. They were conspiring against you. Poor Tommy—you suspected it all along and you were too sporting to say anything!"

I shrugged, able to speak a few words, noncommittal words.

"Well, Lynn, I won't say that, though I won't deny evidence."

"Tommy!" Lynn exclaimed. "It's so perfectly clear now. All of it is. Every bit of it, including the last two years when they've played on my selfishness to keep both of us under their thumbs. How can you ever forgive me, darling?"

* * * *

The thundering voice that boomed up the staircase belonged to Lynn's dad.

"Are you going to hurry?" it demanded.

Lynn smiled grimly at me then walked out to the bannister and leaned over, shouting down to her father. She had the briefcase, and the contents—minus the wrapping paper—had been returned to it.

"Father!" she called sweetly.

I could visualize old Jerem as he frowned and boomed:

"Yes?"

He undoubtedly poked his head upward at the bannister where Lynn waited, for the next thing I knew, Lynn had let fly with the briefcase, and there was the *thump* of the leather object colliding with skull, plus a bellow of pain and outraged dignity from Oliver Jerem.

"Go away, Father," Lynn said. "And take the others with you. You can all come back when you promise to let my life and Tom's alone!"

There was quite a lot of sound then. All of it bewildered and indignant and coming from Oliver Jerem and those who waited outside in the hired limousine.

Eventually, the motor started up, and the car rolled off. By that time Lynn had been in my arms for five minutes. She stroked my arm with her hand, a little later, and said:

"Am I forgiven, Tommy?"

I thought a moment.

"For everything but that pancake layer right in the bean. There was syrup on it."

Lynn sighed.

"I suppose you'll hit me sometime when I'm not looking."

"I suppose," I agreed.

There was a silence. Then Lynn said:

"It wasn't very flattering, their cooking up a haunted house and ghost story to scare me away from here and you. Do you imagine Dad and Walter figured I'd believe it?"

I figured I might as well tell her the truth, or part of it.

"The story Walter told about hearing in the village is actually local legend, baby," I said. "People around these parts have really believed this farmhouse is haunted for a long time. Your Dad and Walter probably planned to enlarge on it a little to make me look like a heel who'd force his wife to live in a place full of bats and cobwebs and secret panels."

Lynn was surprised.

"There's really such a legend?" she said. Then she added: "But of course it's ridiculous. Just as you said, intelligent, modern people aren't frightened by such stupidity."

I nodded sagely.

"Of course not, baby."

I thought of the note I'd found in the attic. The thank you note for the information I'd spilled in my pseudo-clowning oration to the Baggat boys. I thought, too, of the first note, found in my pocket some hours before Lynn's folks had arrived at the place. And, of course, there had been the ransacking of my baggage right after we'd arrived. The Jerem relatives hadn't been around when that had occurred.

I grinned, marveling at the skill with which a pair of ghosts had framed damning evidence and tied it around the necks of Oliver Jerem and Walter Lurgar—just out of thanks for a get-away tipoff that was a considerable number of decades too late.

"What are you thinking of?" Lynn asked.

I snapped out of my reflections.

"Ever hear of the Baggat boys?" I asked.

"No," Lynn said. "Who are they?"

"Couple of tough monkeys," I said vaguely.

"What about them?" Lynn persisted.

"Oh, nothing," I said. "I was just wondering how in the hell they were able to hide out without being seen by the posse line around the house."

"What?" Lynn frowned.

"Nothing important," I said. "I was just thinking, though, that it would sure as hell have been interesting to be inside the bullet-riddled farmhouse when whatever happened to the Baggat boys happened, if you know what I mean."

"I'm afraid," sighed Lynn, "that I don't."